Books Edited by Jeff Gelb and Michael Garrett

Hotter Blood
Hottest Blood
Hot Blood: Deadly After Dark
Hot Blood: Seeds of Fear
Hot Blood: Stranger by Night
Hot Blood: Fear the Fever
Hot Blood: Kiss and Kill
Hot Blood: Crimes of Passion
Hot Blood X

Books Edited by Jeff Gelb

Hot Blood *(with Lonn Friend)*
Shock Rock
Shock Rock II
Fear Itself

HOT BLOOD

EDITED BY
JEFF GELB
AND
MICHAEL GARRETT

POCKET BOOKS
New York   London   Toronto   Sydney   Tokyo   Singapore

This book consists of works of fiction. Names, characters, places and incidents are products of the authors' imaginations or are used fictitiously. Any resemblance to actual events or locales or persons, living or dead, is entirely coincidental.

Some of these titles have been previously published.

An *Original* Publication of POCKET BOOKS

POCKET BOOKS, a division of Simon & Schuster Inc.
1230 Avenue of the Americas, New York, NY 10020

Copyright © 1998 by Jeff Gelb and Michael Garrett

ISBN: 0-671-00950-8

First Pocket Books printing October 1998

10 9 8 7 6 5 4 3 2 1

POCKET and colophon are registered trademarks of Simon & Schuster Inc.

Cover art by Gerber Studio

Printed in the U.S.A.

Copyright Notices

This book is dedicated to the friendship of coeditors Jeff Gelb and Michael Garrett, whose original acquaintance as teenagers over thirty years ago spanned the nation between New York and Alabama, bringing the two of them together through a shared interest in comics and monsters.

May our friendship last forever.

CONTENTS

Contents

INTRODUCTION

Welcome, class, to *Hot Blood X*. We're your instructors, Jeff Gelb and Michael Garrett.

In nine previous, unforgettable lessons, *Hot Blood* has explored experiments in sexual chemistry gone awry. Along the way, you've learned what can happen when you mix two hormone-driven humans: the results are sometimes dangerous, usually explosive, and always erotic!

Today's lesson: Just what constitutes horror anymore? Is it witches and werewolves, vampires and shapeshifters? Or, as the millennium approaches and the wackos come out of the woodwork, are the truly scary stories those we see on TV or in the newspapers daily? The serial killers, mad bombers, suicidal cults, and despots with nuclear bombs?

The answer, as we see it here in *Hot Blood* land, is all of the above. And as the face of horror changes, so too does *Hot Blood*. That's why we've broadened our thematic and author horizons, to encourage the exploration of—if you will—virgin territory.

You'll see what we mean as you tackle your homework assignment: to read the following superb stories by the world's premiere alchemists of high-octane horror and dark, dripping suspense. We don't call it "X" for nothing!

Warning: Be prepared, because this assignment may be followed by a multiple-orgasm test!

HOT
BLOOD

THREE IN THE
SIDE POCKET

Lawrence Block

Lawrence Block has written novels ranging from the urban noir of Matthew Scudder (Even the Wicked) *to the urbane effervescence of Bernie Rhodenbar* (The Burglar in the Library). *His articles and short fiction have appeared in* American Heritage, Redbook, Playboy, GQ, *and* The New York Times. *A Mystery Writers of America Grand Master, a multiple winner of the Edgar, Shamus, and Maltese Falcon awards, he lives in New York's Greenwich Village.*

You'd think they would have a pool table. When you walked into a joint called the Side Pocket, you expected a pool table. Maybe something smaller than regulation, maybe one of those dinky coin-operated Bumper Pool deals. But something, surely, where you poked a ball with a stick and it went into a hole.

Not that he cared. Not that he played the game, or preferred the sound of balls striking one another as background music for his drinking. It was just a matter of unfulfilled expectations, really. You saw the neon, THE SIDE POCKET, and you walked in expecting a pool table, and they didn't have one.

Of course, that was one of the things he liked about his life. You never knew what to expect. Sometimes you saw things coming, but not always. You could never be sure.

He stood for a moment, enjoying the air-conditioning. It was hot out, and humid, and he'd enjoyed the tropical feel of the air as he'd walked here from his hotel, and now he was enjoying the cool dry air inside. Enjoy it all, he thought. That was the trick. Hot or cold, wet or dry. Dig it. If you hate it, then dig hating it. Whatever comes along, get into it and enjoy it.

Right.

He walked over to the bar. There were plenty of empty stools but he stood instead. He gazed at the light glinting off the shoulders of the bottles on the top row of the back bar, listened to the hum of conversation floating on the surface of soft jazz from the jukebox, felt the cool air on his skin. He was a big man, tall and thickly muscled, and the sun had bronzed his skin and bleached blond streaks in his brown hair.

Earlier he'd enjoyed being in the sun. Now he was enjoying being out of it.

Contrasts, he thought. Name of the game.

"Help you?"

He'd been standing, staring, and there was no telling how long the bartender had been right in front of him, waiting for him to order something. A big fellow, the bartender, sort of an overgrown kid, with one of those sleeveless T-shirts cut to show off the delts and biceps. Weight lifter's muscles. Get up around noon, pump some iron, then go lie in the sun. Spend the evening pouring drinks and flexing your muscles, go home with some vacationing schoolteacher or somebody's itchy wife.

He said, "Double Cuervo, neat, water back."

"You got it."

Why did they say that? And they said it all the time. *You got it.* And he didn't have it, that was the whole point, and he'd have it sooner if they didn't waste time assuring him that he did.

He didn't like the bartender. Fine, nothing wrong with that. He examined the feeling of dislike and let himself enjoy it. In his imagination he drove two stiffened fingers into the bartender's solar plexus, heard the pained intake of breath, followed with a chop to the windpipe. He entertained these thoughts and smiled easily, smiled with genuine enjoyment, as the fellow poured the drink.

"Run a tab?"

He shook his head and drew out his wallet. "Pay as you go," he said, riffling through a thick sheaf of bills. "Sound fiscal policy." He plucked one halfway out, saw it was a hundred, tucked it back. He rejected another hundred, then found a fifty and laid it on top of the bar. He drank the tequila while the bartender rang the sale and left his change on the bar in front of him, returning the wallet to his side pocket.

Maybe the bar's name had nothing to do with pool, he thought. Maybe the Side Pocket meant a pocket in a pair of pants, not the hip pocket but the side pocket, which could have made it an *un*hip pocket, but in fact made it a more difficult target for pickpockets.

They had a pool table there once, he decided, and the owner found it didn't pay for itself, took up space where he could seat paying customers. Or the bar changed hands and the first thing the new guy did was get rid of the table. Kept the name, though, because he

3

liked it, or because the joint had a following. That made more sense than pants and pickpockets.

He kept his own wallet in his side pocket, but more for convenience than security. He wasn't much afraid of pickpockets. Draining the drink, he felt the tequila stirring him and imagined a hand slipping artfully into his pocket, groping almost imperceptibly for his fat wallet. Imagined his own hand taking hold of the smaller hand. Squeezing, breaking small bones, doing damage without looking, without even seeing the face of the person he was hurting.

He saw the bartender was down at the end of the bar, talking to somebody on the telephone, grinning a lazy grin. He waited until the kid looked his way, then crooked a finger and pointed at his empty glass. Get it? *You got it.*

A pair of double Cuervos gave you a nice base to work on, got the blood humming in your veins. When the second was gone he switched to India Pale Ale. It had a nice bite to it, a complicated flavor. Sat comfortably on top of tequila, too. Not so comfortably, though, that you didn't know it was there. You definitely knew it was there.

He was halfway through the second IPA when she came in. He didn't exactly sense her presence, but the energy in the place shifted when she walked through the door. Not that everybody turned to look at her. For all he knew, nobody turned to look at her. He certainly didn't. He just stood there, his hand wrapped around the base of the longneck bottle, ready to refill his glass. He felt the shift in energy and turned it over in his mind.

He caught sight of her in the back bar, watched out

of the corner of his eye as she approached. One empty stool separated the two of them, but she showed no awareness of his presence, her attention directed at the bartender.

She said, "Hi, Kevin."

"Lori."

"It's an oven out there. Sweetie, tell me something. Can I run a tab?"

"You always run a tab," Kevin said. "Though I heard someone say Pay As You Go is a sound fiscal policy."

"I don't mean a tab like pay at the end of the evening. I mean like I'll pay you tomorrow."

"Oh," he said. "The thing is I'm not supposed to do that."

"See, the ATM was down," she said.

"Down? Down where?"

"Down as in not working. I stopped on the way here and it wouldn't take my card."

"Is Jerry meeting you here? Because he could—"

"Jerry's in Chicago," she said. "He's not due back until the day after tomorrow." She was wearing a wedding ring, and she fiddled with it. "If you took plastic," she said, "like every other place . . ."

"Yeah, well," Kevin said. "What can I tell you, Lori? If we took plastic the owner couldn't cook the books as much. He hates to pay taxes even more than he hates to bathe."

"A wonderful human being."

"A prince," Kevin agreed. "Look, I'd let you run a tab, the hell, I'd just as soon let you drink free, far as it goes, but he's on my ass so much these days . . ."

"No, I don't want to get you in trouble, Kevvie."

He'd been taking this all in, hanging on every word,

admiring the shape of it even as he'd admired her shape, long and curvy, displayed to great advantage in the pale yellow cotton shift. He liked the way Kevin had quoted his pay-as-you-go remark, a sure way to draw him toward the conversation if not into it.

Now he said, "Kevin, suppose I buy the lady a drink. How will that sit with the owner?"

This brought a big grin from the bartender, a pro forma protest from Lori. Very nice little lady, he thought, but you have done this before. "I insist," he said. "What are you drinking?"

"I'm not," she said. "That's the whole problem, and you, kind sir, are the solution. What am I drinking? Kevin, what was that drink you invented?"

"Hey, I didn't invent it," Kevin said. "Guy was drinking 'em in Key West and described it to me, and I improvised, and he says I got it right. But I never tasted the original, so maybe it's right and maybe it isn't." He shrugged. "I don't know what to call it. I was leaning toward Key Hopper or maybe Florida Sunset but I don't know."

"Well, I want one," Lori said.

He asked what was in it.

"Rum and tequila, mostly. A little OJ." Kevin grinned. "Couple of secret ingredients. Fix you one? Or are you all right with the IPA?"

"I'll try one."

"You got it," Kevin said.

During the first round of Key Hoppers she told him her name was Lori, which he knew, and that her husband's name was Jerry, which he also knew. He told her his name was Hank Dettweiler and that he was in town on business. He'd been married once, he told her, but he was long divorced. Too many business trips.

During the second round she said that she and Jerry weren't getting along too well. Too few business trips, she said. It was when they were together that things were bad. Jerry was too jealous and too possessive. Sometimes he was physically abusive.

"That's terrible," he told her. "You shouldn't have to put up with that."

"I've thought about leaving him," she said, "but I'm afraid of what he might do."

During the third round of Key Hoppers (or Florida Sunsets, or whatever you wanted to call them) he wondered what would happen if he reached down the front of her dress and grabbed hold of one of her breasts. What would she do? It was almost worth doing just to find out.

There was no fourth round, because midway through the third she suggested they might be more comfortable at her place.

They took her car and drove to her house. It was a one-story box built fifty years ago to house vets. No Down Payment to GIs, Why Rent When You Can Own? He figured it was a rental now. Her car was an Olds Brougham a year old and her house was a dump with Salvation Army furniture and nothing on the walls but a calendar from the dry cleaner's. Why rent when you can own? He figured Lori and Jerry had their reasons.

He followed her into the kitchen, watched as she found an oldies station on the radio, then made them both drinks. She'd kissed him once in the car, and now she came into his arms again and rubbed her little body against him like a cat. Then she wriggled free and headed for the living room.

He went after her, drink in hand, caught up with her, and put his arm around her, reaching into the front of her dress and cupping her breast. It was the move he'd imagined earlier, but of course the context was different. It would have been shocking in a public place like the Side Pocket. Here it was still surprisingly abrupt, but not entirely unexpected.

"Oh, Hank," she said.

Not bad. She remembered the name, and acted as if his touch left her weak-kneed with passion. His hand tightened a little on her breast, and he wondered just how hard he could squeeze before fear and pain took the place of passion. They'd be more genuine emotions, certainly, and a lot more interesting.

People always got more interesting when you handed them something they didn't expect. Especially if it wasn't what they wanted. Especially if it was painful or frightening, or both.

He pulled her down onto the couch and began making love to her. His touch and his kisses were gentle, exploratory, but in his mind he hurt her, he forced her. That was interesting, too, a mental exercise he had performed before. She was vibrating to his touch, but she'd be screaming her lungs out if his actions matched the images in his mind.

Just something for his own private amusement, while they waited for Jerry.

But where was good old Jer? That was the question, and he could tell it had occurred to her as well, could tell by the way she worked to slow the pace. It wouldn't do if he got to nail her before the Jealous Husband burst through the door. The game worked best if he was caught on the verge, made doubly vulnerable by guilt and frustration, and awkward, too, with his pants down around his knees.

Happily, their goals were the same. And, when his pants were indeed around his knees and consummation appeared to be right around the corner, they both froze at the sound of a key in the lock.

"Oh my God!" she cried.

Enter Jerry. The door flew open and there he was. You looked at him and you wanted to laugh, because he was hardly the intimidating figure he was supposed to be. Traditionally, the outraged husband was big as a house and meaner than a snake, so that his physical presence alone would scare the crap out of you. Jerry wasn't a shrimp, but he was a middle-aged guy who stood five-ten in his shoes and looked like his main form of exercise was changing channels with the remote control. He wore glasses, he had a bald spot. He looked like a store clerk, night man at the 7-Eleven, maybe.

Which helped explain the gun in his hand. You take a guy five-four, eighty years old, weighs no more than a sack of flour, you put a gun in his hand, you've got a figure that commands respect.

Lori was whimpering, trying to explain. Hank got to his feet, turned from her, turned toward Jerry. He pulled up his pants, fastened them.

"You must be Jerry," he said. "Now look, just because you got a gun don't mean you get to jump the line. You gotta wait your turn, just like everybody else."

It was comical, because Jerry wasn't expecting that. He was expecting a load of begging and pleading, explanations and justifications, and instead he got something that didn't fit any of the slots available for it.

So he didn't know how to react, and while he was figuring it out Hank crossed the room, grabbed the gun in one hand, hit him with the other. His fist went right into the pit of Jerry's soft stomach, just about midway between the nuts and the navel, and that was the end of the war. You hit a person there just right, before he's had a chance to tense his stomach muscles, and if you put enough shoulder into the punch you can deliver a fatal blow.

Not instantly fatal, though. It can take a day or a week, and who has that kind of time?

So he let Jerry double up, clutching his belly with both hands, and he grabbed hold of him by the hair on his head and forced his head down hard, fast, and brought his own knee up hard, fast. He smashed Jerry's face, broke his nose.

Behind him, she was carrying on, going *No, no, no,* clutching at his clothing. He backhanded her without looking, concentrating his attention on Jerry, who was blubbering through the blood that coursed from his nose and mouth.

That was nice, that knee-in-the-face maneuver. His pants were already bloody at the knee, and it was a sure bet there was nothing in Jerry's closet that would fit him. That was the advantage of having the husband be a big bozo, the way the script called for it; after you were done with him, you could pick out something nice from his wardrobe.

But his pants were khakis, replaceable for thirty bucks at the nearest mall. And, since they were already ruined—

This time he cupped Jerry's head with both hands,

brought it down, brought his knee up. The impact brought a great cry from Lori. He gave Jerry a shove and the man wound up sprawled against the wall, jaw slack, eyes glassy. Conscious? Unconscious? Hard to say.

And what did it matter? Eager to get on with it now, he went over to Jerry, put one hand under his chin and the other on the top of his head, and snapped his neck.

Hell of a sound it made. First a grinding noise like something you'd hear in a dentist's office, and then a real sharp crack. Left you in no doubt of what you'd just done.

He turned to Lori, relishing the look on her face. God, the look on her face!

"Honey," he said, "you see what I did? I just saved your life."

It was amusing, watching the play of emotions on her sharp little face. Like her head was transparent, like you could see the different thoughts zooming around in there. She had to come up with something that would leave her with a pulse at the evening's end, and the effort made her thoughts visible.

Thoughts caroming around like balls on a pool table . . .

She said, "He was going to kill me."

"Going to kill us both," he agreed. "Violent fellow, your husband. What do you figure makes a man like that?"

"The gun was pointed right at me," she said, improvising nicely. "I thought I was going to die."

"Did your whole life flash before your eyes?"

"You saved my life."

"You're probably wondering how to thank me," he said. He unfastened his pants, let them drop to the floor, stepped out of them. A shadow of alarm flashed on her face, then disappeared.

He reached for her.

It was interesting, he thought, how rapidly the woman adjusted to new realities. Her husband—well, her partner, anyway, and for all he knew her husband as well—her guy was down for the count, on his way to room temperature. And she wasn't wasting time mourning him. Off with the old, on with the new.

"Oh, baby," she said, and sighed theatrically, as if her passion had been real, her climax authentic. "I knew I was hot for you, Hank. I knew that the minute I saw you. But I didn't know—"

"That it could possibly be this good," he supplied.

"Yes."

"It's Jerry being dead that does it," he told her. "Lovemaking as an affirmation of our own aliveness. He's lunch meat and we're still hot to trot. Get it?"

Her eyes widened. Oh, she was beginning to get it, all right. She was on the edge, the brink, the goddamn verge.

"I liked the bit with the bartender," he said. "Kevin, right?"

"The bartender?"

"You got it," he said, and grinned. "Oh, Kevvie, I haven't got any money, so how am I going to get a little drinkie-poo?"

"I don't—"

"He phoned you," he said, "after he got a peek at my wallet. He probably thought they were all fifties and hundreds, too."

"Honey," she said, "I think all that sweet love scrambled my brains. I can't follow what you're saying. Let me get us a couple of drinks and I'll—"

Where was she going? Jerry's gun was unloaded, he was sure of that, but that didn't mean there wasn't a loaded gun stashed somewhere in the place. Or she might just open the door and take off. She wasn't dressed for it, but he already knew she cared more for survival than propriety.

He grabbed her arm, yanked her back down again. She looked at him and got it. It was interesting, seeing the knowledge come into her eyes. Her mouth opened to say something but she couldn't think of anything that might work.

"The badger game," he said. "The cheating wife, the outraged husband. And the jerk with a lot of cash who buys his way out of a mess. How about you? Got any cash? Want to buy your way out?"

"Anything you want," she said.

"Where's the money?"

"I'll get it for you."

"You know," he said, "I think I'll have more fun looking for it myself. Make a game of it, you know? Like a treasure hunt. I'm pretty good at finding things, anyway. Got a sixth sense for it."

"Please," she said.

"Please?"

Something went out of her eyes. "You son of a bitch," she said. "It's not a game and I'm not a toy. Just do it and get it over with, you son of a bitch."

Interesting. Sooner or later they let you know who they are. The mask drops and you see inside.

His hands went around her throat. "Jerry got a broken neck," he said. "Strangulation's not as quick.

13

How it works, the veins are blocked off but not the arteries, so the blood gets in but it can't get out. Remember those Roach Motel ads? Thing is, you won't be pretty, but here's the good news. You won't have to see it."

Jerry's gun was unloaded. No surprise there.

Jerry's wallet had a couple of hundred in it, and so did Lori's purse, which suggested the ATM wasn't down after all. And a cigar box on a shelf in the closet held more cash, but most of it was foreign. French five-hundred-franc notes, some Canadian dollars and British pounds.

He showered before he left the house, but he was perspiring before he'd walked a block, and he turned around and went back for her car. Risky, maybe, but it beat walking, and the Olds was wonderfully comfortable with its factory air. He'd always liked the sound of that, factory air, like they made all that air in Detroit, stamped it out under sterile conditions.

He parked down the block from the Side Pocket, waited. He didn't move when Kevin let out his last customers and turned off most of the lights, gave him another five minutes to get well into the business of shutting down for the night.

He was a loose end, capable of furnishing a full description. So it was probably worthwhile to tie him off, but that was almost beside the point. Thing is, Kevin was a player. He was in the game, hell, he'd started the game, picking up the phone to kick things off. You knocked down Jerry and Lori, you couldn't walk away and leave him standing, could you?

Besides, he'd be expecting a visitor now, Lori or Jerry or both, showing up with his piece of the action.

What kind of finder's fee would he get? As much as a third? That seemed high, given that he wasn't there when it hit the fan, but on the other hand there was no game if he wasn't there to deal the cards.

Maybe they told Kevin he was getting a third, and then cheated him.

Guy in Kevin's position, he'd probably expect to be cheated. Probably took it for granted, same way as Kevin's boss took it for granted that not all of the money that passed over the bar wound up in the till. Long as the bottom line was high enough, you probably didn't mind getting cheated a little, probably figured it was part of the deal.

Interesting. He got out of the car, headed for the front door. Maybe, if there was time, he'd ask Kevin how they worked the split. Good old Kevvie, with that big grin and all those muscles. While he was at it, why not ask him why they called it the Side Pocket? Just to see what he'd say.

Lawrence Block: *"When I lived on Central Park West and 104th Street, I stopped in one afternoon at a neighborhood bar three blocks away. A big, broad-shouldered guy came up to the bar. 'Beautiful day, isn't it?' he said, hearty as all get-out. The bartender agreed it was a nice day. 'Oh yeah?' the big guy said, 'what's so great about it?' I scooped up my change and got out of there, because this sonofabitch was looking to make something happen, just for the fun of it, and I didn't want to watch. But all that was thirty-five years ago, and he lingered in memory; he was the chap I pictured when this story took shape."*

THE SEDUCTRESS

Ramsey Campbell

Ramsey Campbell's latest novel is Nazareth Hill, *a ghost story. He recently contributed to Stefan Jaworzyn's* Shock: The Guide to Exploitation Cinema, *an essay on the erotic area dealt with in "The Limits of Fantasy."*

*H*e hadn't taken her home before. His mother was out tonight, he told her, smiling a secret smile. "Which is your room, Alastair?" she said eagerly. "Oh, let me see." She heard him call out behind her; he must have been telling her not to go in—but she had already opened the door. After a while she went closer, to be sure of what she was seeing. When she came out she pushed him aside violently, saying "Don't you touch me!"

He followed her through the empty twilit streets, plucking timidly at her sleeve. "It's not what it looks like, Betty. I only did it because I wanted you." She slapped his hand away as if it were an insect, but couldn't stop his voice's bumbling at her. "I'm not interested!" she shouted. "I don't want anything to do with that sort of thing!"

Her voice seemed small between the blank walls. She had never seen the streets so deserted. She hoped someone would come to a door to see what the noise was, but nobody did. "Get away or I'll go to the

16

police!" she shouted. But he followed her to the police station, pleading.

When she emerged, having pretended to a policeman that she'd lost her way home, Alastair had gone. He must have fled as soon as she'd gone in. He wouldn't dare to lie in wait for her; he must be worrying about what she might have told the police.

The streets were darker now, yet they made her feel oddly secure. Her father would never have let her walk through these streets. There were too many things he wouldn't let her do. She was free of him now, and of Alastair. She felt free, ready for anything—for anything she chose.

As she came in sight of her flat, the ground floor of the last house in the Georgian terrace, she smiled. The empty rooms, the spaces between her posters on the walls, were waiting to be filled with new things: as she was.

Next morning she found Alastair's note.

The unstamped envelope lay on the hall floor, on a tray of sunlight. It bore only her name. Should she tear it up unopened? But she was free of him, free enough to be able to read what he'd written. It might give her insights. Insights were what a writer needed.

She walked upstairs, reading. The stairs shook the page in her hands. Halfway up she halted, mouth open. In her flat she read the note again; phrases were already standing out like clichés. Was it a joke? Was he trying to disturb her?

I suppose you told the police everything. It doesn't matter if you didn't. I've never seen anyone look with such contempt as you did at me. I don't want anyone to look at me like that again, ever. When you read this I shall be dead.

What an awful cliché! Betty shook her head, sighing. His note read like an amateur's first story. But did that mean it wasn't true? Could he have killed himself? She wasn't sure. She had realized how little she knew about him when she'd opened the door of his room.

At first, peering into the small dim cluttered room, she had thought she was looking at a mirror on a table beside the bed: she was there, gazing dimly out of the frame. But it wasn't a mirror; it was a photograph of her, taken without her knowledge.

Venturing into the room, she had made out diagrams and symbols, painted on the walls. Magic. The unknown. She'd felt the unknown surrounding her dimly, trapping her as she was trapped in the photograph: the many shadows and ambiguous shapes of the room, Alastair looming in the doorway. But she'd strode to the photograph. Herbs were twisted about it; something had been smeared over it. It stank. She swept it to the floor, where it smashed.

Alastair had cried out like an animal. Turning, she had seen him as though for the first time: long uneven mud-colored hair, a complexion full of holes, a drooping shoulder. All of a sudden he looked ten years older, or more. Had he managed to blind her in some way? When he tried to block the doorway she shoved him aside, unafraid now of him and his furtive room. "Don't you touch me!" She could see him clearly now.

But could she? Could she tell how true his letter was? Of course she could—if she wanted to; but she wasn't interested. She buried the note beneath her notebooks. It was time she worked on her new book.

She couldn't. Her notes gave her no sense now of

the people she'd talked to. The void of her room surrounded her, snatching her ideas before they formed. One strong emotion remained, where she'd pushed it to the back of her mind. She had to admit: she was curious. Had Alastair really killed himself?

To find out she would have to go near his home. That might be what he'd intended. Still, she would be safe in daylight: good Lord, at any time of day—he couldn't harm her. Early that afternoon her curiosity overcame her apprehension.

Alastair's home was one of a terrace of cottages in central Brichester, washed and dried by April sunlight. Betty ventured along the opposite pavement. A cyclist was bumping over cobbles, a van painted with an American flag stood at the end of the terrace. Sunlight glared squarely from the cottage, making Betty start. But in a moment she was smiling. None of the curtains in the cottage was drawn. Alastair had been bluffing. She'd known that all along, really.

She was walking past the cottage—it would be silly to turn, as if fleeing—when the door opened.

She gasped involuntarily. It was as though she'd sprung a trap, snapping the door open, propelling a figure forward into the sunlight. But it wasn't Alastair. It was a tall woman, somewhat past middle age, wearing a flowered flat-chested cotton dress. She gazed across the street and said, "You're Betty, aren't you?"

Betty was still clutching at her poise; she could only nod.

"You must come in and talk to me," Alastair's mother said.

Betty was aware of her own feet, pressed together on the pavement, pointing like the needle of a compass—halfway between Alastair's mother and flight. She could feel the effort she would need in order to turn them to flight. Why should she? The woman seemed friendly; it would be rude to walk away, and Betty couldn't think of an excuse.

"Please," the woman said, smiling bright-eyed; her smile was a gentle plea. "Talk to me."

Perhaps she wanted Betty to help her understand Alastair. "I can't stay very long," Betty said.

The front door opened directly into a large room. Last night the room had been dim; blocks of sunlight lay in it now. Brass utensils hung molten on the walls, jars of herbs on shelves were tubes of light, large containers stood in the corners. There was no sign of Alastair.

Betty sat in a deep armchair; the knees of her jeans tugged at her, as if urging her to rise again. "I'd love to live somewhere like this," she said. Perhaps Alastair's mother meant her to talk without interruption; she nodded, busy with a kettle over the grate.

Betty chattered on, surrounded by silence. Alastair's mother brewed tea and carried the pot to the table between the chairs. She nodded, smiling gently, as Betty drank; her square plump-nosed face seemed homely. Not until Betty had begun her second cup did the woman speak. "Why did you do it?" she said.

Betty had become tense, had been sipping her tea more rapidly because there seemed no other way to respond to the gentle smile. Now her heart felt hectic. "Do what?" she said warily.

The woman's smile became sadder, more gentle. "What you did to my son," she said.

But what was that? Betty felt heavy with undefined guilt; heat was piling on her, though the day was cool.

She was about to demand what she was supposed to have done when the woman said, "Seducing him then turning him away."

Betty had never had sex with him—thank God, she thought, shuddering a little. "Oh really, Mrs.—" (annoyed, she realized that she didn't know the woman's name) "—I didn't seduce him at all."

"Whatever you choose to call it." The woman's mouth smiled gently, but her eyes gleamed. "It didn't take you long to get him into bed with you," she said.

An odd taste had accumulated in Betty's mouth. Her tongue felt gluey; she sipped more tea, to loosen her tongue for a denial, but the woman said, "Perhaps you didn't appreciate how sensitive he was." She smiled sadly, as if that were the best excuse she could find for Betty.

"Perhaps you don't realize what he's been up to," Betty said.

"Oh, I think I know my son."

There was a tic at the root of Betty's tongue. It made her irritable, made her almost shout "Do you know he practices witchcraft?"

"Is that what it was. Is that why you turned him away." The woman gazed sadly at her. "Just because of his beliefs. I thought you young ones weren't supposed to believe in persecution."

"I don't believe in that sort of thing," Betty said furiously. "It's against life. He was trying to trap me with it."

The woman's voice cut through hers. "His body was good enough for you but not his mind, hey? You should like me less, then. I'd only begun to teach him what I know."

She was smiling triumphantly, nodding. "Yes, he'd

just begun to learn his craft. And just for that, you killed him."

Betty felt her eyes and mouth spring wide; the odd insistent taste of the tea filled her mouth. "Oh yes, he's dead," the woman said. "But you haven't seen the last of him."

The teacup clung to Betty; the handle seemed to have twined around her finger like a brittle bony vine. She tugged at it. She must leave hold of it, then she would walk straight out. As the cup rolled in her hands the black mat of tea leaves seemed for a moment to writhe, to grin, to be a man's wet face.

Her hand jerked away from her, the cup smashed against the table. She stood up unsteadily, but the woman was already on her feet. "Come and see him now," the woman said.

She was pulling Betty toward the door to the stairs. The door was ajar on a glimpse of dimness. The dimness was widening, was darkening; it was reaching to pull Betty in. And in the dimness, lying on the bed, or sitting propped on the stairs, or lying ready for her at the bottom—

She dragged herself violently out of the woman's grasp. For a moment fury gleamed in the woman's eyes, as she realized Betty was still stronger. Betty managed to head straight for the front door, although the walls moved like slow waterfalls.

But the door was retreating, moving faster than she could gain on it. She could feel Alastair's mother behind her, strolling easily to catch her, smiling gently again. Suddenly the door surged toward her; she could touch it now. But it was shrinking. The doorknob was enormous in her hand, yet the door was too small for her even if she stooped. It was no larger than the door of a small animal's cage. The door was edging open. Sunlight fell in, over her head. As she staggered into the street, turning to support herself against the door frame, she saw that the woman hadn't moved from the stairway door. "Never mind," she called to Betty, smiling. "You'll see him soon."

Betty squeezed through the shrinking frame. The street dashed sunlight into her face; the frame pressed her shoulders down, toward Alastair. He lay on the pavement, his head twisted up to her over his drooping shoulder, his huge tongue reaching for her through a stiff grin. The frame thrust her down, thrust her face into his.

It wasn't broad daylight, it was only six o'clock. But as she lay blinking in bed, having fled awake, that did little to rid her of her dream. Her room felt deserted, it offered no defense against the memory. After a while she dressed and went out to the park two streets away.

The tea had been drugged. Perhaps she wasn't yet free of its effects; she felt a little unreal, gliding lightly through the gradually brightening streets. Never mind. Once the drug had worn off she would be free of Alastair and his mother.

Mist shortened the streets. It dulled the railings of the park, lay like a ghost of metal on the lake. The colors of the trees were faded, the perennial leaves were glazed; the most distant trees looked like arrested smoke. Betty felt vulnerable. Reality seemed to hold itself aloof, leaving her menaced by her imagination.

On a rise in the ground within the mist, a sapling moved. It was walking toward her: a slim dark form,

23

swaying a little as it descended the path. It was tall
and dim. It was coming leisurely toward her, like
Alastair's mother.

When it stepped from the mist onto the clear path
she saw it was a man. Her gasp of relief was so violent
that the mist snagged her throat; she was coughing as
he neared her. He halted while she spluttered silent,
except for the occasional cough which she could make
sound like an apologetic laugh. "Are you all right?" he
said.

His voice was light, soft with concern; his long slim
face smiled encouragement. "Yes, thank" (cough and
smile) "you."

"Pardon my intrusion. I thought you looked worried."

His tone was friendly without familiarity; it offered
reassurance. Did she look more worried than she
realized she felt? "Just preoccupied," she said, thinking of an acceptable excuse. "I'm working on a
novel." She always enjoyed saying so.

His eyes widened, brightening. "Do you write?
What do you write about?"

"People. That's what interests me." She wrote
about them well, according to the reviews of her first
novel.

"Yes. People interest me too."

In what way? But if she asked, she would be
interviewing. That was how she'd met Alastair; she
had been searching for someone worth interviewing
in a cellar disco, where underground lightning made
everyone stagger jaggedly. He had watched her
searching, had come over to her; he had seemed
fascinating, at the time.

The man—perhaps twenty years older than her,

about forty-five—was smiling at her. "What do you do?" she said neutrally.

"Oh—know about people, mainly."

She deduced he meant that he had no job. Some of the most interesting people were unemployed, she'd found. "I'm in Brichester to talk to people," she said. "For my new book."

"That must be interesting. I know some people who might be worth your talking to," he said. "Not the common kind."

Oh yes? But Alastair and his mother still seemed too close for her to feel quite safe in trusting this man. "Well, thank you," she said. "Perhaps I'll see you again. I must be going now."

She thought she glimpsed the sign of a twinge of rejection. He must be vulnerable too. Then he was smiling and raising his hand in farewell, and she was walking away, forcing herself to walk away.

At the gate she glanced back. He was standing as she'd left him, gazing after her. Nearer her, a movement caught her attention: between the trees, against the muted glitter of misty ripples on the lake—a dark figure watching her? There was nothing when she faced it: it must have been the effect of the light. The man waved briefly again as she left the park; he looked small and rather frail and lonely now, on the thin path. She found herself wishing she'd asked his name.

Brichester was disappointing in the wrong way.

She had shown it to be disappointing in her first novel, *A Year in the Country*. She'd shown its contemptuous openly reluctant pandering to tourists; the way decay and new estates were dissolving the town's identity; the frustrations of the young and the middle-aged, the young settling for violence or hallucinations while they yearned for London, the middle-aged extending their sexual repertoire in glum desperation. She hadn't called the town Brichester, but the local papers had recognized it: their reviews had been peevishly hostile. That had added to her sense of triumph, for most reviews had been enthusiastic.

All she'd written had been partly true; the rest of Brichester she'd imagined, for she had been living in Camside. Perhaps she had underrated her imagination. She had moved to Brichester to write her second book, a portrait of the town in all its moods and aspects, based on observation and interviews. But the reality proved to be less interesting than her version of it; it was full of clichés, of anticlimaxes. No wonder Alastair, with his sense of a secret to be revealed, had seemed interesting.

The more she saw, the more it dulled her. In particular the young people were worse than bored: they were boring. She spent the rest of the day after she'd left the park, and the following day, finding that out. Some trendy phrases she heard a dozen times; if she heard them once more she would scream.

She walked home through the evening. Unpleasantly, she felt less like an observer than an outsider. She knew nobody in the town. But she wasn't going back to Camside, to her father; that would be admitting defeat. She nodded to herself, pressing her lips together, trying to feel strong.

Above the roofs the sky was flat; its luminous unrelieved gray was almost white. Its emptiness was somehow disturbing, as though it were a mirror clear of any reflection. The trees that bowed over the pavement, the bricks of the houses, looked thin, brittle, unreal; their colors seemed feeble. All this fed her alienation. The only real thing she could find in her recent memory was the man in the park, and he was distant now. If only she'd talked to him. Dully preoccupied, she took a shortcut through an alley behind two streets.

The walls paced by, half as tall again as she. Their tops were crowded with shards of glass, dull as ice. Old doors went by amid the brick, bolted tight, no doubt on rusty hinges. She made her way between double-parked bins, their lids tilted rakishly. The whitish sky glowed sullenly in everything. Someone was hurrying behind her.

He wouldn't be able to squeeze past. She could hear his quick footsteps approaching. She began to hurry too, so that she'd be out of the alley before he reached her, so they wouldn't have to squeeze between the bins; that was why she was hurrying. But why couldn't she look back? Wasn't it silly to hurry as if fleeing? The footsteps stopped, leaving abrupt silence at her back.

He had leapt; he was in the air now, coming down at her. The idea was absurd, but she turned hastily. The alley was deserted.

She stared along the blank walls. There was nowhere he could have turned. She would have heard if any of the doors had opened. Had he leapt onto a wall? She glimpsed a figure crouched above her, gazing down—except that he couldn't have leapt onto the glass. The dead light and the brittle world seemed unnaturally still. Suddenly panic rushed through her; she fled.

She ran past her street. The building might be empty, her flat would feel all the more unsafe for being on the ground floor. She ran to the park. The man was there, at the lake's edge. She had never been so glad to see anyone in her life.

He turned as she came near. He was preoccupied; she thought she saw a hint of sorrow. Then he read her face, and frowned. "Is something wrong?" he said.

What could she say? Only "I think someone was following me."

He gazed about. "Are they still there? Show me."

She could feel his calm, the directness of his purpose; they made her feel secure at once. "Oh, they'll have gone," she said. "It's all right now."

"I hope so." He made that sound like a promise of justice and strength. She was reminded of her father's best qualities; she turned her mind away from that, and said, "I'm sorry I interrupted whatever you were thinking."

"Please don't trouble yourself. I've time enough." But for a moment what he had been thinking was present between them, unspoken and vague: a sense of pain, of grief, perhaps of loss. When she'd said goodbye to her father—Perhaps the man wanted to be alone, to return to his thoughts. "Thank you for looking after me," she said.

As she made to walk away she sensed that he felt rebuffed. She had had that sense as she'd left her father: the sense of his mute sorrow, the loss of her like a bond she was stretching between them until it snapped. She thought of tomorrow, of talking to people whom she could hardly distinguish from yesterday's batch, of explaining about her new book over

and over until it sounded like an old stale joke, of
going to her empty room. "You said you could introduce me to some people," she said.

His name was James; she never tried to call him
Jimmy or Jim.

She had no idea where he lived. They always met at
her flat; she suspected he was ashamed of his home.
His job, if he had one, remained a mystery. So did his
unspoken suffering.

She was often aware of his suffering: twinges of pain
or grief deep within him, almost concealed. She tried
to comfort him without betraying her glimpses. Perhaps one day she would write about him, but now she
couldn't stand back far enough to observe him; nor
did she want to.

And the people he knew! There was the folk group
who sang in more languages than Betty could recognize. They sang in a pub, and the barman joined in; in
the intervals he told her the history of the songs, while
his casually skillful hands served drinks. There was
the commune—at least, it was more like a commune
than anything else—trying to live in a seventeenth-
century cottage in a seventeenth-century way: six
young people and an older man, one of what seemed
to be a group of obsessed local historians and conser-
vationists. There was the painter who taught in the
evenings, a terrifying woman whose eyes shone constantly; all her pupils painted landscapes which, when
stared at, began to vibrate and become mystical
symbols.

Betty enjoyed meeting them all, even the unnerv-
ingly intense painter. She felt invulnerable within

James' calm. But she wasn't sure how much use these meetings would be. Sometimes when she thought of her book, she felt irritable, frustrated; it was changing form, she could no longer perceive it clearly, couldn't grasp it. Surely its new form would be clear to her soon; meanwhile she avoided touching it, as if it were a raw wound in her mind. Instead, she enjoyed the calm.

Sex with James was a deeper calm. She learned that the first time he had to calm her down. He'd taken her to a meeting of the British Movement, addressed by a man who looked like a large peevish red-faced schoolboy, and who spoke in generalizations and second-hand anecdotes. A few of the audience asked most of the questions; later these people gathered in someone's front room, where Betty and James had managed to accompany them. They proved to be British Supremacists. Some were young, and shouted at Betty's disagreements; some were old—their old eyes glanced slyly, suspiciously at her notebook, at her. They examined her as if she were a misguided child. Didn't she believe in her country? in tradition? in helping to make things the way they used to be? Just what did she think she was doing? Eventually, mute with fury, she strode out.

James followed her. "I'm sorry," he said. "I thought it would be worth your meeting them." She nodded tight-lipped, not caring whether he realized she didn't blame him. When they reached her flat she still felt coiled tight, wound into a hard lump in her stomach.

She tried to make coffee. She spilled hot drips over her hand, and dropped the cup. "Bloody fucking shit!" she screamed, and kicked the fragments against the skirting-board, ground their fragments smaller with her toes.

James put his arm about her shoulders. He stroked her hair, her back, massaging her. "Don't get yourself into a state," he said. "I don't want you like that." She nestled more snugly against him; her shaking slowed, eased. He stroked the small of her back, her buttocks, her legs; his hand slid upward, lifting her skirt, slowly and gently baring her. She felt enormously safe. She opened moistly.

He switched off the light as she guided him to her bed. Shortly she felt him naked beside her; warm, gentle, surrounding her with calm. In fact he seemed almost too calm, as though he were an observer, detached. Was he doing this simply to soothe her? But his penis felt hard and ready. Her body jerked eagerly.

He held himself back from her. I'm ready, ready now! she pleaded with him, gasping, but he was still fondling more pleasure into her, until it was almost pain. She tried to quicken him: his penis tasted salty, much more so than her first boyfriend's, the only boy (she'd vowed) her father would ever lose her.

Eventually James raised her knees leisurely and slipped into her: thick, heavily knobbed, unyielding yet smooth. The growing ripples of her pleasure were waves at once; they overwhelmed her; all of her gasped uncontrollably. She didn't feel him dwindle. As she lay slack he kissed her forehead. In a minute she was alone.

That was the only thing she disliked: the way he left her as if he were late for an appointment. Once or twice she asked him to stay, but he shook his head sadly. Perhaps he had to return to his home, however poor, so as not to admit he was ashamed of it. She feared to plead, in case that troubled his calm. But alone in her flat at night, she felt uneasy.

She was disturbed by what she had seen looking in at her. A dream, of course: a pale form the size of a head that was never really there in the gap between the curtains when she sat up, frightened by her own cry. She'd seen it several times, at the edge of sleep: an impatient dream, tugging at her while she was awake. But once, when she'd sat up, she had seen it dimly, nodding back from the window. She'd seen something—a bird, a flight of waste paper, the glancing of a headlight. Or a hallucination.

Perhaps it was the last of the drug. She'd thought it had worn off after the footsteps in the alley; surely it had caused them. But it might still be able to touch her near her sleep. She couldn't tell James about the business with Alastair; she didn't know where to start. That helped her to accept that James was entitled to his own unspoken secret, but at the same time her muteness seemed to refuse the reassurance of his calm, to leave her vulnerable there.

Then one day she saw her chance to be reassured. It was evening; they were walking back to her flat. He had introduced her to an antique dealer whose house was his shop, and who lived somewhere among rooms that were mazes of bookcases. James talked about books now as they strolled: for some he'd had to search for years. Did James keep them all in his mysterious home, she wondered? Houses sauntered by. The cottage where Alistair's mother lived was approaching.

Betty tried not to be uneasy. Nothing could happen, she was with James. The sky steamed slowly, white and thick, low above the roofs; it pressed down the quiet, oppressively, until their footsteps sounded like the insistence of relentless hollow clocks. It held down the flat thin light of the streets. The terraces between Betty and the cottage were full of the mouths of alleys. Any of them might propel a figure into her path.

Abruptly the terrace halted. A railing led to open gates; between the bars grass glowed, headstones and a church shone dull white. All at once it occurred to Betty that she still wasn't sure whether Alastair was dead. Wouldn't he be buried here, if anywhere? She was sure any truth would be a relief. "Let's go in here," she said.

The evening had darkened before she found the stone; it was darker still beneath the trees. The new smooth marble gleamed between stains of the shadows of branches. She had to kneel on the grave before she could read anything. At last she made out ALASTAIR, and the date his letter had arrived.

"Who was he?" James said as she rose.

She thought she heard jealousy, a secret pain. "Oh, nobody," she said.

"He must have been somebody to you."

There was no mistaking the sound of hurt now. "Nobody worth bothering about," she said. "I wouldn't have bothered with him if I'd known you."

She held him tight and thrust his lips open. One of his hands clasped her buttocks hard. She was still kissing him when she felt his other hand at work between their bodies. He freed his penis; she could barely see it, a darker shadow, gleaming. "Oh no, James," she gasped. "Somebody might see."

"There's nobody else about. Besides, it's dark." He didn't bother to conceal his pain. He sounded rejected, as though she were refusing him for fear of offending Alastair. She dug her nails into his shoulders, confused. When he began to strip her beneath her skirt and caress her, she protested only silently.

As he entered her, her back thumped against a tree. His glans stretched her again and again, like a fist, as he thrust. Sections of her mind seemed to part, to watch each other. She saw herself proving she was free of Alastair, to herself and to James. It was as though this were a chapter she was writing, an almost absurdly symbolic chapter.

But she could just see James' face, calm, uninvolved. She wanted him to feel something this time, to let go of his calm. Couldn't he feel her giving herself? She strained her body down on his, she wrapped her thighs about his hips, squeezing; the tree trunk rubbed her buttocks raw through her skirt. But when she'd exploded herself into limpness he took himself out of her at once.

She lay on the grass, regaining her breath. The red flashes her lids had pressed into her eyes were fading. Above her something pale nodded forward, peering down from the tree. A bird, only a bird. Before she could make herself look up it had withdrawn into the darkness, rustling.

She must satisfy him. That goal became clearer every time she met him. She loved his calm, but he shouldn't be calm during sex: it made her feel rejected, observed, though she knew that was irrational. Once she seemed almost to reach him, but felt his unspoken pain holding him back. She felt obscurely that he didn't enjoy sex in her flat, that for him there was something missing. If only he would invite her home! Whatever it was like she wouldn't mind. All she wanted was to feel his orgasm.

Ironically—perhaps because she had been too pre-occupied with Alastair to worry about it—her book was taking shape. Now she could see it properly, it excited her: an answer to her first novel, a book about the character of Brichester, about its strangenesses.

She found herself thinking inadvertently of her father. "How can you write such stuff?" he'd demanded. "Oh well, if you *have* to get known that way," he'd greeted the reviews of her novel. They had had a row; she had fled its viciousness, for she'd seen that it could be an excuse to leave him—him and his possessiveness, his cold glum moralizing, his attempts to mold her into a substitute for her dead mother. And now she was contradicting her novel, admitting it was false. She saw her father standing back from his bedroom window where he thought she couldn't see, mouth slack, eyes blindly bright with tears—She didn't need to remember these things. James would be here soon.

He seemed to have run out of people to introduce her to; he was showing her places now. Today's was a church, St. Joseph's in the Wood. They climbed Mercy Hill, which was tiered with terraces. Huge dark stains uncurled sluggishly over the sky. The church stood beyond the top of the slope, deep in trees.

Betty walked around it, taking notes: thirteenth-century; some signs of the Knights Templar had been partially erased; Victorians had slipped stained glass into the windows. The trees surrounded it with quiet. The foliage was almost as dark as the clouds, and moved like them; above her everything shifted darkly, ponderously. In the silence dim vague shadows crawled over the church, merging. She hurried back to the porch, to James. "Shall we go in?" he said.

It was quieter within, and dim. Though small, the church was spacious; their footsteps clattered softly, echoed rattling among the pews. Unstable dark shapes swayed over the windows, plucking at saints' faces. Betty walked slowly, disliking to stay too far ahead of James. But while she stayed close she could feel he was excited, eager. Had he planned a surprise? She turned, but his face was calm.

The stone void rang with their echoes. She stood in the aisle, gazing at the arch before the altar: a pointed arch, veined with cracks but unshaken. On either side of the altar stood a slim window; amber-like, each glass held a saint. She leaned over the altar rail to peer. She felt James' hands about her waist. Then one was pushing the small of her back; the other was lifting her skirt.

At once she knew why he had been excited. Perhaps that was why he had brought her here. "Not here!" she cried.

His hands stopped, resting where they were. She glanced back at his face. For the first time she saw unconcealed pain there. He needed to make love to her here, she realized; he'd admitted it to her, and she'd recoiled from it—the means to his satisfaction.

"Oh, James." She couldn't help sounding sad and bewildered. Part of her was pleading: anywhere but here. But that was how her father would moralize, she thought. His moralizing had turned her against her childhood religion long ago. If James needed it to be here then that was natural, that was life. Nobody would see them, nobody would come here on a day like this. She turned her face away from him, letting her body go loose. She closed her eyes and gripped the rail.

She felt him baring her buttocks; the cool air of the church touched them. Now he was parting them; her sphincter twitched nervously. Why didn't he turn her? What was he— He stretched her buttocks wide and at once was huge and snug within her. That had never been done to her before. Her shocked cry, an explosion of emotions she couldn't grasp, fled echoing around the church, like a trapped bird.

It was all right. She had reached her goal at last. It was experience, she might write about it sometime, write about how she felt. But she suppressed her gasps; the church mustn't hear. God, would he need this every time? She felt him thumping within her, the sounds of her body were strident amid the quiet. Shadows threshed toward her from the altar; the church frowned darkly, hugely. Someone stood at the window on the left of the altar, watching her.

Only the stained glass. But the figure of the saint seemed to fill, to become solid, as if someone were standing within the outline. He pressed against the glass, dim and unstable as the shadows, gazing at her with the saint's face. The glass cleared at once, but with a wordless cry she thrust her hands behind her, throwing James out of her. Her buttocks smacked shut.

She ran down the aisle, sobbing dryly. When she heard James pursuing she ran faster; she didn't know what to say to him. She stumbled out of the church. Which way had they come? The darkness stooped enormously toward her, creaking; shadows splashed over the grass, thick and slow. Was that the avenue, or that one? She heard the church door open, and ran between the trees.

The dimness roared about her, open-throated. The heavy darkness tossed overhead, thickening. She lost the avenue. Dim pillars surrounded her with exits beyond exits, leading deeper into the roaring dark; their tangled archways rocked above her, thrashing loudly. Someone was following her, rapid and vague. She wasn't sure it was James.

The trees moved apart ahead. The wider gap led to little but dimness, but it was an avenue. She ran out from beneath the trees. Foliage hissed wildly on both sides of the avenue, darkness rushed over the grass, but her way was clear ahead. She ran faster, gasping. The avenue led to an edge full of nothing but sky; that must be the top of Mercy Hill. The avenue was wide and empty, except for a long dim sapling in the middle of her path. A crack rolled open briefly between the clouds, spilling gray light. She was running headlong toward the sapling, which was not a sapling at all: it was a dreadfully thin figure, nodding toward her, arms stretched wide. She screamed and threw herself aside, toward the trees; a root caught her foot; she fell.

As soon as they reached her flat, James left her.

When she'd recovered from the shock of her fall she had seen him bending down to her. He had helped her to her feet, had guided her through the hectic darkness, without speaking. There was no sapling on the path. His silence rebuked her for fleeing.

He left her at her gate. "Don't leave me now," she pleaded, but he was striding away into the dark.

He was being childish. Had he no idea why she'd

fled? Most women wouldn't have let him get so far. She'd tried to understand him, yet the first time she needed understanding he refused to try. She slammed her door angrily. Let him be childish if he enjoyed it. But her anger only delayed her fear of being alone. She hurried through the flat, making sure the windows were locked.

Days passed. She tried to work, but the thought of the nights distracted her; she couldn't stand the flat at night, the patient mocking stillness. She drifted toward the young people she'd interviewed. They knew she was a writer, they showed her off to friends or told her stories; they were comfortingly dull. Occasionally boys would invite her home, but she refused them—even though often as she lay in bed something moved at the window. If she drew the curtains tight, they moved as if it had got in.

Each morning she went to the park. Flights of ducks applauded her visits, squawking, before they plunged into their washes on the lake. The trees filled with pink, with white. There was never anyone about: never James.

One night a shadow appeared on her bedroom wall. She lay staring at it. It was taller than the ceiling; its head folded in half at the top of the wall. Its outline trembled and shifted like steam. It was only a man, waiting for someone outside beneath the lamp. It dwindled to a man's size; it ceased to be a menacing giant. Suddenly she realized that the dwindling meant he had come to the window—he was staring in, and his head still seemed oddly dislocated. She buried her face in the pillow, shaking. It seemed hours before she could look to see that the shadow had gone.

The next day James was in the park.

She saw him as she neared the gate. He was standing at the edge of the lake, against the shattering light. She blinked; her eyes were hot with sleeplessness. Then she began to pace stealthily toward him, like a hunter. He mustn't escape again.

No, that was silly. He wouldn't like her playing tricks on him. She strode loudly; her heels squeaked on the gravel. But he gazed at the sunlight scattered on the water, until she wondered if he meant to ignore her. Only when she was close enough to touch did he turn.

His face was full of the unspoken: the memory or anticipation of pain. "I'm sorry," she said, though she hadn't meant to be so direct. "Please come back."

After a while, when his face showed nothing but calm, he nodded. "I'll come to you tonight," he said. "Do you want me to stay?"

"If you like." She didn't want to dismay him by seeming too eager. But at once she saw the shadow in her room. "Please. Please stay," she said.

He gazed; she thought he wasn't sure whether she wanted him. He mustn't wonder about that. She would tell him all about Alastair. "I'll tell you some things I haven't told you," she said. "I'll tell you tonight. Then you'll understand me better."

He smiled slightly. "I've something to tell you, too." He moved away alongside the lake. "Until tonight," he said.

She ran home smiling. At last she dared think they might have more than half of a relationship. She would cook him meals instead of paying discreetly in restaurants. She could work without slowing to wonder whether she would see him today. She would be safe. Her smile carried her across the park.

She tidied her flat. God, what a mess she'd let accumulate! A poster mapping seventeenth-century Brichester, half-read books by Capote and D. H. Lawrence astray from the bookcases, notes for her own book tangled as the contents of a wastebasket: she'd be able to handle those soon. And all these letters she must answer. One from her publisher: the paperback edition was reprinting. One from the GPO about the delay in providing a telephone: it annoyed her not to be able to phone her friends in Camside— to invite them to meet James, she thought. One from a driving school, offering a free introductory lesson. If she learned to drive it would be worth her visiting friends in Camside: she wouldn't be restricted by the absurdly early last bus back.

When she'd finished she felt exhausted. Her loss of sleep was gaining on her. She checked that the door and windows were locked, smiling: she wouldn't need to do that in future. She'd make sure James stayed with her. She lay down on the couch, to rest.

She woke. The room was dark. But the darkness was shrinking. It had limbs and a head; it was walking on the wall, growing smaller yet closer to her. The ceiling thrust the head down at an angle that would have broken a man's neck. The shadow slipped from the ceiling, yet the head stayed impossibly canted. As she realized that, the shadow was extinguished. At once she felt the man lying beside her. She had to struggle to look; her body felt somehow hampered. But he waited for her. When she turned the face rolled toward her above the emaciated body, like a derisive thick-tongued mask that was almost falling loose: Alastair's face.

She woke gasping. The shadow filled the room; it

had pressed against her eyes. She ran blindly to the door and snatched at the light switch. The room was empty, there was nobody outside the window. Night had fallen hours ago; it was past eleven o'clock. James might have come and gone unheard.

Surely he would come back. Wouldn't he? Mightn't he have thought she'd reconsidered, that he'd been right to hear doubt in her voice when she had asked him to come to stay? Might he have taken this as the final rebuff?

She gazed into the mirror, distracted. She must wait outside, then he would know she wanted him. If he came back he mightn't come as far as the door. She tugged at her hair with the brush, viciously. In the reflection of the room, a shadow passed.

She turned violently. There had been a dark movement in the mirror. She felt vulnerable, disoriented by the stealthy fall of night, trapped in unreality. The shadow passed again, dragging its stretched head across the ceiling. Betty ran to the window, but the street was empty. The streetlamp glowed in its lantern.

She couldn't go out there—not until she saw who was casting the shadow. She gazed at the bare pavement, the flat stagnant pool of light. She was still gazing when something dark moved behind her, in the room.

She whipped about, gasping. The shadow was stepping off the edge of the wall, into invisibility. Soon it returned, smaller now, more rapid. Whenever she turned the street was deserted. The shadow repassed, restless, impatient. Each time it was smaller, more intense; its outline hardly vibrated now. Betty kept turning frantically. She heard her body sobbing, felt its dizziness. The shadow was only a little larger than a man; soon he would reach for her. It vanished from the wall, moving purposefully. Her doorbell shrilled, rattling.

Her cry was shrill too. For a moment she couldn't move, then she ran into the hall. It must be James, or someone: not the shadow. The hall rumbled underfoot; the stairs loomed above her, swollen with darkness. She reached the front door and grabbed the light switch. The hall sprang back, bare, isolating her; a shadow stood on the front-door pane, irregular with frosting. She reached for the latch. She wished there were a chain. She opened the door a crack, wedging her toe beneath it, and saw James.

"Oh thank God. Come in, quickly." Behind him the street was empty. She pulled him in and slammed the door.

It wasn't until she had locked them into her flat that she noticed he was carrying no luggage: only a large handbag. "You're going to stay, aren't you?" she pleaded.

Did she sound too eager? His face was calm, expressionless. "I suppose so," he said at last. "For a while."

Not only for a while! she pleaded. She glanced anxiously at the blank wall. Would he see the shadow if it returned, or had it been the drug? "I've got to tell you something," she said. "I want you to know."

"Not now." He had opened the handbag; he took out four lengths of glossy cord. "Get undressed and lie on the bed," he said.

His calm felt cold. She didn't want to be tied up, she would feel like a victim, she wouldn't feel close to him. She was frightened of being tied, when the

43

shadow was so near. But James would protect her
from that. And if she rebuffed him again he might
leave her for good. She stripped unwillingly and lay
down.

At least the cords weren't rough. But he tied her
tightly, spread-eagled. She felt nervous, unsafe. But
she didn't dare protest; if he left the shadow would
come back. She closed her eyes, to try to soothe
herself. He undressed and stooped to her.

His smooth cheeks slid along her thighs. His tongue
probed into her, strong as a finger. It was rough; it
darted deep, opening her. He mounted her; his penis
thrust fiercely. Her hands clutched beyond their
nooses, struggling vainly to reach for his back. She felt
impaled and helpless. Above her his face gazed at the
window, calm, mask-like. Behind his head the blank
wall hung.

Her body twitched with the strain of her bondage,
humiliated, frustrated. His thrusts tugged at her; she
glimpsed herself as he must see her, at the mercy of
his penis. Suddenly, by a translation she couldn't
understand, her genitals began to twitch toward orgasm. It was all right, after all. She could enjoy it too.
She closed her eyes again, beginning to enjoy the
straining of her limbs against their bonds. Outside she
could hear people walking home, from a club or
somewhere; the sound was reassuring, it drove the
shadow away. Her limbs strained. She was nearly
there, nearly—and then he had left her. He was
standing beside the bed, reaching into the handbag.

"Oh, what's wrong?" He was gazing at the darkest
corner of the room, beyond the window. She saw
something move, but not there: on the wall opposite
the window—a shadow dwindling, darkening, advanc-

ing rapidly. Her hands struggled against their leashes to point. "James!" she screamed.

He turned swiftly. His hand emerged from the bag. Before she could react, his other hand raised her head deftly. He thrust the gag into her mouth and tied it behind her head. At once she felt his calm lift; his eagerness struck her like an explosion, leaving her limp and trembling. His voice rose, rose impossibly. "Not James," it said gleefully. "Mrs. James."

When Betty lay trembling, unable to look, the face stooped for her to see. It was Alastair's mother, smiling triumphantly. She passed a hand over her face. As though that reversed each aspect of it she was James again; his long face replaced her square one, her small plump nose was all at once slim and straight. She passed her hand upward and was herself, as if she'd changed a mask. The mask smiled.

Beneath the smile and the flat-chested body the penis was still erect. Mrs. James pulled at it. Betty shuddered back as far as she could, but the woman wasn't masturbating; she'd detached the organ and dropped it on the floor. Betty heard rubber strike wood. "Yes, that was all it was," Mrs. James said brightly. "Now you know how it feels to have your body used. You're beginning to know how my son felt."

Choked screams stuck in Betty's throat like bile. The wall was full of shadows now: the twelfth shrank into place, completing the wall's unbroken frieze of dark blank faces. Betty strained back on the bed; her eyes heaved at their sockets, the gag suffocated her screams.

Mrs. James brought her a mirror to show her who was at the window. Betty saw one of the folk group, and the barman; the oldest man from the commune; the art teacher, two of the British Supremacists, the antique dealer; others to whom she had been introduced. Their eyes were bright and eager. Mrs. James smiled at them. Softly, like an articulate breeze at the window, they began chanting.

"You could get the better of my son," Mrs. James told Betty. "He was a novice. But now you'll see what I can do."

She joined in the chanting. The whispering insinuated itself into the room, slow as insidious fumes. Betty lay shivering, her cheek against the pillow. The nooses held her easily, the gag rested in her mouth. The twelve shadows gazed, whispering. Beyond Mrs. James, in the darkest corner, there was something more than a shadow: the suggestion of a figure, thin and pale as smoke. From the corner came sounds of a crawling among bones.

Mrs. James beckoned. The shape ventured timidly forward, its head dangling. It was surrounded by an inert chill, which fastened on Betty. As Mrs. James turned to the bed, still beckoning, Betty saw her smile. There was more than righteousness in that smile; there was pride.

Ramsey Campbell: *"In retrospect I think 'The Seductress' can be seen as one more trace of the influence of my old and much-missed friend Robert Bloch. After all, what is this except the story of an unhealthily close relationship between a mother and her son, but a story that Bob would have been too much of a gentleman to write?"*

APPETITE

Nancy Holder

*This Californian has sold twenty-three novels and over
a hundred short stories. Her work has been translated
into over two dozen languages. She has also written
computer game fiction, comic books, and television
commercials. She has received four Bram Stoker
awards for fiction from the Horror Writers Association,
and seven of her romance novels appeared on the
Waldenbooks bestseller list.*

*T*abitha stood in her baggy shorts and oversized
T-shirt, trying to program the treadmill to do the
circuit. If she couldn't figure it out within the next ten
seconds, she would simply make it go two point five
miles an hour and start walking. She would die if
someone came over and offered to help her. One of
those hardbodies, all shiny and blond, oozing sexual
desire and wearing next to nothing.

And the men were even worse.

Wasn't anyone else in this gym here because they
needed to be? She stood awash in a sea of crotch-
hugging, boob-uplifting Spandex leotards with all
kinds of cutouts that displayed bronzed acreage, cour-
tesy of Cabo San Lucas, Malibu, and the gym's
tanning beds, which cost more per hour than she
made in a day.

"Can I help you with that?" Oh, yum. The guy was

six feet tall, blond, buff, and his face was a chiseled mask of rough-hewn angles and macho-man planes. His muscles were sculpted and smooth and perfect. What did they call it? Cut. He was cut. Cut to the left was what he was, and in a major way. He had to be an aspiring actor or a model, or both. Or a porn star. They all had to be. No one else in the L.A. basin had endless amounts of time to work on their bodies.

No one else needed to spend endless amounts of time on their bodies.

Her face went hot. "No, that's okay," she said quickly, and punched in two point five. He probably started out at five or six miles an hour and went up to fifty. "Just warming up," she added; then, because she was so warm and nervous, she punched it up to three, as if she had made a mistake.

She would never enter a sweepstakes again.

"Okay." He laid his hand softly—meaningfully?— on her bare forearm. "Just remember, you just have to let me know you want me and I'll be over here in a flash. I'm staff."

"Yeah. Got it," she managed. He glided away, leaving her in a wake of testosterone. She watched his ass as the treadmill started moving. She pretended she was run-walking toward those tight, hard buns. Pretended that if she got close enough to grab them, she would.

And then she would eat them. Ha ha, just kidding. But she was hungry enough to eat a man hung like a horse.

Ha ha ha ha.

She was always hungry. She was five foot five; she didn't know how much she weighed, although they had tried very hard to tell her. It was too much; way, way too much. Her hair was a luxurious brown; and her eyes were green flecked with gold. But no one noticed her hair or eyes, of course. They noticed how fat she was.

As soon as he was out of sight, she slowed the treadmill down to an even two miles an hour because she was afraid she would have a heart attack. Why were the numbers so big and red? So you'd be humiliated if you went too slowly?

Chump, chump, chump, chump. Her feet came down hard. She glanced at them and thought of the man's ass, how his body—his *entire* body—had shown through the Spandex, and began to lose her balance. Gripping hard on the treadmill handles, she found her bearings and set her jaw. *Chump, chump, chump, you*

chump, chump, chump.

Of course she hadn't really won anything. She'd known even at the time she'd filled out the sweepstakes form and stuffed it into the large plastic canister at the donut shop that the purpose of her "prize"—a free month at the Body Palace—was a come-on. They wanted to get her in the door and sign her up for an annual membership at the very least, a lifetime subscription if she was in an especially vulnerable state that day. Which she was. Except the come-on was backfiring. She had already decided she was never coming back.

Not even if that man was waiting for her in the dressing room. *C'mon, porky, sign up for your own private session. I'll flash you if you want.*

"Enjoying your visit?" asked the heavily made-up

brunette who appeared at her side. It was Patti, her "personal trainer" for the day. Patti's job was to show Tabitha how to use the machines and drill into her the need for a *commitment,* as Patti had been saying all morning. A promise to come and use all this great equipment at least three times a week, for Tabitha's health and well-being, for longevity. Oh, and oh, yeah, you'll lose inches and gain muscle, get slim and trim just like the rest of us. We will hone your equipment with our equipment.

Just thought we'd mention that.

"Oh, yeah, I'm terrific," Tabitha said to Patti, huffing. She wanted to wipe her forehead with the edge of her T-shirt, would die if this skinny bitch saw her stomach.

"Gotta go faster, Tabby. Gotta *move.*" With long, red claws, Patti stabbed the buttons below the blazing scarlet numbers until the machine said four miles an hour. "Good." She gave Tabitha a pat and glided away.

Tabitha gritted her teeth. She hated the name Tabby. Hated it.

Had killed over it.

Unlike men's prisons, there were no weight-lifting machines in women's prisons. No treadmills, no barbells. Just the soaps and the talk shows on TV, and makeover classes taught by well-meaning cosmetologists brought in by the equally well-meaning social worker. Who herself was more overweight than Tabitha. In her dresser at the halfway house, Tabitha had stashed more than six hundred dollars' worth of cosmetics samples she'd been given over the duration of her incarceration. She figured Patti the Skinny and

Insincere Bitch was wearing at least two hundred bucks' worth right now.

Tabitha punched the machine back to two and sighed heavily. There was no sense in getting huffy. Losing her temper had been what had gotten her into trouble in the first place.

Chump, chump, chump. She was marching on one of a horseshoe of treadmills, and she noticed now that you could watch TV from the monitors bolted into the ceiling. CNN, some talk show, oh, wow, amazing, a cooking show! It was all new to her. They hadn't gotten cable in prison. Below each one hung a hand-lettered sign with the call numbers of a radio station. The other people on the treadmills—hardbodies all—wore Walkmans. She smiled, nodded to herself. They must be listening to the TV programs.

Tonight she would have to steal a Walkman.

When she had first arrived at the prison, she had considered becoming a dyke. She'd stared at the other women as they undressed for the showers, as they sat in their cells and displayed their wares for the girls who were dykes. They did nothing for her, although she admired the ones who were in good shape.

You could collect a lot of favors if you were young and nice and round and flat and *tight*. At night the halls reeked of sex and vibrated with moaning, *Oooh, baby, oooh, honey*. A lot of the female prisoners had been hookers and they really didn't care if you did it to them with a thingie or a finger or a damn carrot. They should get Academy Awards for their performances. *Ooh, ooh, yessssss.* You'd think other women would know better. Hadn't they been faking it for centuries?

She had, anyway. For what had seemed like centuries.

That feel good, Tabby, Tabby-cat?

Oh, yes, Bobby. It feels just, oh, oh, my God!

She still missed him. It had been stupid to kill him. But a girl had to demand respect.

In prison, she had gotten flabby. Flabby Tabby. They fed you macaroni and cheese and corn dogs and all kinds of cheap, fattening foods. One time a new inmate had thrown her tray on the floor, shouting, "I ain't eating this shit!" They'd hauled her away, stripped her, turned the hose on her, and put her sopping wet in solitary. She had almost died of pneumonia.

Or had that been in a movie they'd seen? One of those weird women-in-prison movies that turned Bobby on so much?

Chump, chump, chump.

Before she'd been arrested, she'd looked better than any woman here. Bobby used to say she could be an exotic dancer if she wanted. He believed it was a damn waste that she was nothing but a packer in the meat department at Hackett's.

Thought that was funny, too. He used to call the store "Hack-It's" and laugh and laugh.

He hadn't laughed too hard when she'd brought home the big cleaver they used to separate the spareribs.

The prison psychologist said she had gained all the weight as a way of performing penance.

Was this thing speeding up? Tabitha glanced from the monitors to the numbers on the treadmill. The blond man with the tight ass was looking at her across the room. Sizing her up. Finding her wanting. Finding her unacceptable. Too much flab; too much to trim away.

At the halfway house, where she currently resided, you couldn't have sharp objects. They didn't even let you use a knife at dinner. They found you humiliating jobs like working for housecleaning services.

For people who had plenty of steak knives.

In prison, they never got decent cuts of meat. Mystery protein; maybe it was hamburger, maybe it was ground turkey, but it was never pork loin or skirt steak or even some top round. She used to lie awake at night while all the moaning and fake orgasms were going on and dream of huge hunks of tender, marbleized meat and touch herself and not fake it, not one bit.

The numbers had been as big and red on the scale at the meat department as the numbers on the treadmill. You thwapped the piece of muscle (they had few customers for entrails, although some people ate beef hearts, more ate liver, and you couldn't pile the intestines high enough for the Hispanics, who made *menudo* out of them) onto the scale and beep, beep, boop! the computer figured out exactly how much to charge.

Yeah, twenty-nine ninety-nine to join, and twenty bucks a month after that.

She could visualize herself inside the casing of her skin, the layers of fat and the sad little muscles beneath. The blond man was short on gristle, that was for sure. He must be lusting after the commission he would get if she went for the lifetime membership. Maybe he was trying to win a trip to Hawaii. Or Skin Cancer Island.

Patti swooped past the blond man with another

mark in tow, giving him a jaunty little wave. He spoke; she stopped. He gestured with his head toward Tabitha. Patti nodded.

Tabitha's face burned. She wanted to die. She wanted to kill them both.

Why had she even come here? What had possessed her?

In prison, she had been certain that they got the women fat as a way to control them. You showed up all wiry and slinky and they changed you into a bowl of pudding. It took the aggression out of you. Took your howl away. Made you depressed; you walked around like they had you on Thorazine, waiting for three o'clock and *Oprah*. How to communicate with your kids. What to give your husband for Valentine's Day.

"Tabitha, she know what to give him," Aleda had said in the TV room, drawing a laugh from the prisoners who had the energy to laugh. Aleda was a nutty Cuban girl who had robbed a bank the same day she'd become a naturalized citizen. She had offered herself to Tabitha in return for protection from the really scary butch-types, but Tabitha preferred to lie alone at night and fantasize about real meat. Aleda hadn't given up, though. She flirted with Tabitha whenever she could, trying to make the others think they were a couple. Tabitha didn't mind. Actually, she didn't care.

Then she began to gain the weight. And she would have fucked anybody in prison for a good, blood-rare steak. She would have let the cafeteria staff sodomize her with their long wooden ladles for a filet. Tie her up and spread her and—

"Hi," the blond man said. "Are you all right? You look flushed."

She stared at him. Then it hit her all at once. What an idiot she was being. Any decent con would have already milked this situation for all it was worth. She thought, *How far will you go for a trip to Hawaii, big guy?*

She touched her forehead and said, "I guess I'm just a little dizzy. I haven't eaten today."

His eyebrows shot up. It was almost five in the afternoon. "Not all day?"

She shrugged. "I got busy at work." It was her day off from the housecleaning biz. "And I was rushing around." She'd been watching Ricki Lake before she caught the bus to come down here, with a bowl of popcorn between her legs. "You know how it is."

He punched STOP on the treadmill. She knew it took half a minute to slow down, so she kept walking. So virtuous. So eager to trim the fat from the muscle.

"That's very bad for you. You should go to our juice bar and get something."

"Oh." She laughed. "I feel so dumb. I didn't bring my wallet. Just my driver's license." *How far? How much? What's the cost of a hamburger against your commission?*

"Tell you what." He smiled at her with unnaturally white teeth. They had to be capped. "If you promise to come back and take our aerobics class tomorrow, I'll treat you to a snack."

"I couldn't let you do that," she said, smiling back at him with her much more natural teeth. In prison you used the bathrooms as infrequently as possible. That's where a lot of the bad stuff went down. As a result, your teeth suffered. "I'll bring you the money tomorrow."

Yeah, right. As soon as she had that burger lolling around in her digestive juices, he'd never see her again.

"Whatever." He smiled back. "It would be my pleasure."

No, baby. Pleasure was thinly sliced roast beef piled high and soaked in gravy. Pleasure was a flank steak seared to perfection. Pleasure was a T-bone, not a boner.

She almost laughed. Instead, she stepped delicately off the treadmill, allowing him to take her hand, and said, "All right. Thanks."

It wasn't called a cafeteria, of course, or a snack bar, but that's what it was.

And there was not an ounce, not one single nibble, of red meat on the menu.

The blond man, whose name was Blaine, looked at her in horror. "No, no, Tabitha," he said, wagging a finger at her. "Red meat is very bad for you. Very, very bad. It can kill you." He sipped from a tiny cup of wheat grass juice. The juice of *grass*. She had to stifle her laughter. Talk about your blood from a turnip.

"There are other excellent sources of iron," he went on. "If that's what you're concerned about."

She sighed and studied the menu. Chicken, fish, veggies. Yuck. She supposed it had been shortsighted of her to assume a place like this would have what she wanted.

"When you introduced yourself, I thought you said your name was Blade," she told him.

His lids flickered. "Maybe I should change it." He

56

was actually serious. She could see him running through a list of potential actor names: Blade Stone. Blade Masterson. Blade Runner.

Blade Sharpener. Run your hand along that, honey.

"You okay?" he said, peering at her. "We have to feed you right away." He rose. "I'll get you a turkey burger, okay?"

"No." It was too much like prison food. "Get me a, a chicken breast sandwich." She'd make do. "Please," she added appealingly.

He gave her a quick wink. "Sure thing. Here." He dodged to a nearby table and snagged a shiny brochure that had been left there. "Read this while I'm ordering."

She looked down. *The Benefits of Exercise.* It was one of the shiny come-ons to get you to join the gym. She smiled to herself. It was going to take a lot more than a fucking chicken sandwich to get that trip to Hawaii, Blade.

But it turned out that he was even more motivated than hauling his big left cut to Hawaii: he was behind in his rent. His phone bill was overdue.

Best of all, he owed money on his car.

In Los Angeles, you might as well walk into oncoming traffic as not have your own wheels.

Without a car, you couldn't make it to auditions (for he was an aspiring actor after all). You couldn't make it to acting classes. You couldn't make it to your day job.

And you could never, ever tell anyone, anywhere, for any reason, that you had sunk so low as to have taken *the bus*.

This all came out slowly during the chicken breast,

hesitantly, with heartbreaking directness. The point being, she supposed, that he had mistaken her for someone who cared. Some poor butterball who would sign up for a lifetime membership to a gym she had no interest in frequenting with money she didn't have for the sake of his freaking acting career.

Never con a con, she wanted to advise him, but instead she said, "You poor guy. Listen, how about I make dinner for you? I'll make a list. You buy the food and I'll cook. Oh. I forgot." She smiled sadly. "You're low on funds."

"No. No, it's okay," he said eagerly. "I, um, I have a little saved."

Liar. She wanted to split him open then and there. But she pretended to brighten. "Oh, *good.*"

Because she didn't have cooking privileges at the halfway house.

They made plans to meet at his place after he got off work, at eight-thirty. She knew they would start looking for her at curfew, which was ten.

She would have to move faster than two point five, that was for certain.

She made up some story about doing errands and he promised to buy every single thing on her list. They waved goodbye at the gym door.

She was warm with anticipation.

Warm and juicy.

How far could she push him?

How far would he go?

Maybe he was telling the truth about his money problems. His apartment wasn't much to look at. The furniture was secondhand. He must think she was rich.

The ring she had stolen from one of her housecleaning assignments might have something to do with that. She let it flash this way, that way, watching the glitter and sparkle hypnotize him.

And then it occurred to her that he was probably thinking way past the commission to getting more out of her. That she was some poor little rich pig, shy and unattractive, blessed with Long Dong here as a dining companion.

She was not a cannibal. That had not been the point with Bobby. That had been a statement.

She had never fantasized about eating people the entire time she had been in prison.

Just about cutting them up.

But now she had a big glass of red wine in her stomach and a huge, sizzling steak in front of her, and he was looking at her expectantly. She whacked off a big bite, watching the blood ooze from the pores, and popped it into her mouth.

"Oh, oh, God," she whispered. It was the most excellent steak she had ever had in her entire life. She closed her eyes and thought she might have a climax then and there. "Oh, that's so *good.*"

"I'm glad," he said in a deep, sexy voice. He watched her eagerly. "Not overdone?"

It was practically uncooked. He had put a pat of butter on it and it melted into the juices on the plate, mingling with salt and pepper and perhaps a pinch of garlic. She shook her head and took another bite. "It's fantastic. It's the best." She couldn't help the way her spine undulated. She was so turned on. She had another bite. She moaned. "Oh, Jesus." She chewed and swallowed, stared at him with utter gratitude.

Prison slid away from her. She had never tasted food so good.

A bite or two of her anger slid away from her.

He stared back at her. Suddenly he rose and took her hand. She blinked; he eased her to her feet and, with as much effort as if she were a mere feather, lifted her into his arms and carried her into the bedroom.

"No," she protested, reaching behind him toward the table.

He lay her gently onto the bed. "Oh, Tabitha," he whispered. "I'm hungry for you."

"My meat," she begged.

"*My* meat," he said, and positioned himself over her face.

She was hungry. Fantastically, wantonly hungry. She said, "If I do, will you let me finish my dinner?"

He laughed and lowered himself.

She did what he wanted. It didn't take long. She was motivated.

Then he untied her and flopped down beside her. He moaned and said, "Wow. You're terrific."

"I'm hungry," she told him.

He laughed and retrieved her plate from the table, went back for her knife and fork. By the time he returned, she had devoured most of the rest of the meat with her fingers. He blinked, said, "Do you have an iron deficiency?"

She cut another piece and watched the blood pool in the center of the plate. "No. I'm a vampire."

He touched his sex. "That I can believe. A sexual vampire. I'm sore."

She was, too. Her throat was sore from swallowing so much so fast. Her taste buds were throbbing.

She said, "Do you want to do it again?" thinking of the leftover bits of steak on his plate.

"Sure." He sounded so young.

So fresh.

After the third time, he gasped and said, "I can hardly breathe. Where did you learn how to do that?"

"I just have a feel for it," she told him. "An appetite." It was eleven-thirty. She was out past curfew.

"I'll say. I've never had such a, well . . ."

"Such a terrific blow job?" she asked boldly.

He colored. "Well, yeah. It was incredible."

She touched his face. "I'm so glad." She meant it. She knew then she was not going to kill him that night.

"I want another one, but I don't think I could take it."

"Kind of like me and steak," she said. They both laughed.

After a time, they dozed. She realized she genuinely liked him. But maybe she was conning herself. Maybe she liked his meat. When she looked at his closed eyes, she tasted the steak.

Her stomach rumbled. She wanted more. And more. And more. Three blow jobs deserved three steaks.

Then she realized he was tossing. He sighed and opened his eyes, stared at the ceiling. Shyer now that she liked him, she pulled the sheets over herself and said, "What's wrong?"

He turned to her and smiled sadly. "Oh, I have an audition tomorrow. I'm in the running for a commercial, but there's this other guy. We always end up competing for the same parts and he always gets them."

She understood that he was telling her something that was true and sharing it with her because he, too, liked her in some way, and she felt an intense rush of warmth toward him. She said, "I've never had better steak."

"I was a chef for a while," he told her. "At Big Wayne's Steakhouse? You know, the one on Figueroa?"

"No. I've been away. I mean, I'm new in town." She touched his cheek, fantastically happy. She said, "This guy. What's his name? Where does he live?"

"Jason Dumas." He rolled his eyes. "If you can believe that. I think he lives somewhere in Tujunga. I see him at this club sometimes. The Hand Me Down." He scratched his chest. "The one on Sunset?"

"Oh," she said.

"Yeah, and he'll get the damn part."

"Parts is parts."

He chuckled. "It's such a meat market up here. I've done everything I could, worked out, had my teeth done. I've been trying for seven years to make it as an actor. There's guys in their twenties who have had face-lifts."

She was quiet for a long time. Then she said, "If you get the part, you'll make me another steak. If you don't, I'll give you a blow job even better than the ones I gave you tonight. Okay?"

He smiled with his eyes closed. Maybe that was the way he could tolerate having such a fat woman in his bed. He said, "That's some bet."

"Do we have a deal?" she pressed.

He laughed. "Sure."

They reunited at the gym the next afternoon. She was on the treadmill at three miles an hour. She figured no one from the halfway house knew about her life here, so she was safe for the time being.

He was beaming. He said, "I got the part!"

She nodded at him, sweat dripping down her face. "What about that other guy?"

"The asshole didn't show." He gave her a high-five and grinned at her. "I owe you dinner."

She said, "I'll make it worth your while."

They never found the body of Jason Dumas.

And she decided then and there that she would never, ever kill Blaine.

Pretty soon, he owed her a lot more than dinner.

Pretty soon, she was his manager, and he was up for an Academy Award in his first starring role, and he was commanding more money than many more seasoned actors.

Pretty soon, she was known as the Meat Eater, all puns intended. With her shocking weight, she was unrecognizable. Her lurid past was buried among the ribs of Bobby, her abusive white-trash husband.

She and Blaine married, and everyone figured that once he made it really big, he would dump her and marry a real tasty chick.

They didn't know about the occasional snotty actress or the clumsy grip or inept gaffer who went missing. Or the boorish casting director who had said Blaine was too "mature" for a fabulous role.

Or about the plastic surgery Blaine had had to have

on his inner thigh. That had been a misstep that both of them survived.

No one could ever figure out why he was so devoted to her. How he had the stomach to put it to her. Something to do with kinky stuff, everyone decided, something to do with the strange hungers of Hollywood and the wild and wanton appetites of the rich and famous.

Which was almost correct.

But not quite.

———————————

Nancy Holder: *"I wrote 'Appetite' after querying the editors about ideas and settings they had not yet seen, and with fond memories of my days as a vegetarian."*

REGENERATION

Max Allan Collins
and Barbara Collins

*She is an acclaimed author of short stories in such top
anthologies as* Murder Most Delicious, Women on the
Edge, *and the bestselling* Cat Crimes *series; and is
coeditor with Bob Randisi of the bestselling anthology*
Lethal Ladies. *He is the Shamus Award–winning
author of the Nathan Heller historical thrillers, a
veteran writer in the comics field* (Dick Tracy, Ms.
Tree), *one of the leading writers of movie tie-in novels*
(In the Line of Fire, Air Force One), *and writer/
director of two cult-favorite suspense films,* Mommy
and Mommy's Day. *The Collinses live in Iowa with
their son, Nathan.*

Joyce Lackey, fifty-five years of age, vice-president
at Ballard, Henke and Hurst Advertising, stood at the
window in her well-appointed office on the sixty-third
floor of the John Hancock Building in downtown
Chicago and looked out over the tops of the other
buildings toward the soothing shoreline of Lake
Michigan. There, joggers and bikers and in-line skat-
ers moved in miniature along a cement path under a
continuous canopy of trees vivid with fall colors. The
late-afternoon sun spread its rays downward like an
endless bolt of gold lamé, while here and there,
sailboats drifted lazily across the turquoise lake.

The view from this window was one Joyce had

worked long and hard to attain. It was a view she relished. It was a view Joyce would never see again.

With a sigh she turned back to the massive mahogany desk where a small leather Vuitton suitcase (no cardboard box for her) lay open, filled with the few office belongings she was allowed to take with her, a sadly austere culmination of thirty years of faithful service. The executive desk set—blotter, appointment book, matching pen and pencil holder with clock, and crystal paperweight—was her own, purchased some years ago in the basement of Neiman Marcus. The numerous awards she had won for the advertising firm during her tenure, however, would have to stay behind on the agency's walls and in the reception-area display case. Which was all right with her. The way she felt now, the plaques would end up in the circular file.

Being forced into early retirement was an eventuality that had never crossed her mind. In fact, retiring at all had never crossed her mind.

Idly she toyed with the Patek Philippe watch on her wrist, a gift the company had given her last week in place of her job. Now she wondered if she should have asked for all those raises over the years . . . though she certainly deserved them. Apparently, she unwittingly priced herself right out of the market, to be replaced by a cheaper, younger—and prettier and sexier—this-year's-model named Heather.

Were the Heathers of this world really old enough, already, to take on executive positions?

Joyce slammed the suitcase shut. Then again, she thought, money might not have had anything to do with it, because she had never seen eye to eye with the company's president, Tyler Brown, a thirty-something male whose Armani suit had apparently been sewn directly onto his body; he had taken over two years ago from the company's founder—a father figure Joyce had adored, both in the boardroom and the bedroom. But neither her mind nor her body (both of which were still in fighting trim) had seemed to appeal to the son.

At their first meeting the client had been an RV manufacturer ready to give Winnebago a run for the market share, and Joyce had worked up the preliminary concept. When she presented it to Tyler in his office, he shook his head.

"The target should be X-generation with money," he'd said flatly.

"But that's crazy," she'd responded. "Retirees have always dominated the RV market."

He looked at her with cool, gray eyes. "Yes. Retirees who lived through the depression and understood the value of a dollar . . . understood the necessity to save in order *to* retire. But they're dying off, replaced by a generation of spoiled brats who've had everything handed to them on a silver platter and who won't have any money."

Joyce smiled in astonishment. "Of course they'll have money. Lots of money."

"No. They've spent it and haven't saved," he said, then added with a smirk, his voice taking on a more personal tone, "They won't be able to afford a pot to piss in, let alone an expensive RV to vacation in."

"Then they'll buy the damn thing to *live* in!" she snapped. "Boomers are still the only market that counts, because there are seventy-six million of us! *We* set the trends. And if we have no money, and have to live in an RV, then *that* will become the trend. We'll be *Easy Riders,* only with RVs. And it'll be cool, because whatever we do defines cool."

He had arched an eyebrow, and said, "You really think going down the tubes will be 'cool'? Well, you're right on one account, Joyce—it will be a trend, only we'll have difficulty making any money off it."

Joyce moved her suitcase off the desk and set it on the floor. She looked around the room, feeling a sense of loss unlike any since her parents died. It brought tears to her eyes and made her stomach churn.

"Hi!" Julie, one of the secretaries from the floor below, a twenty-something with curly brown hair and a round, innocent face, stood in the doorway. She was wearing a baggy blue sweatshirt and jeans; this was "casual Friday," an idea Joyce had opposed, believing sloppy attire promoted sloppy work. That was why she, Joyce, always wore a suit, like this navy and gold knit she would be wearing when she left this job.

"Just wanted to say goodbye and good luck before you left," the woman said chirpily.

Joyce, from behind the desk, said, "Thanks."

The woman, still standing awkwardly in the doorway, blurted, "Everyone's going to miss you terribly."

Joyce smiled, but said nothing.

Julie entered the room, stood before the desk, and said, "I wasn't around, of course, but I know you practically single-handedly made this company what it is today."

Which was true. It was Joyce's genius that had brought the struggling ad agency to the forefront of the industry in the early 1980s with the "I'm worth it" campaign. Then, in the nineties, sensing that people were feeling guilty about their excessive spending, she coined the phrase "provisional hedonism," understanding the need for a rationale now to keep on spending—don't buy it for yourself, buy it as an investment.

"The company's not going to be the same," Julie was saying.

"The company will be fine," Joyce replied. To be honest, she wasn't so sure; to be brutally honest, she hoped the agency would go down in flames, taking everyone with it, including perky Julie.

"What will you do now?" Julie asked. "Travel, I suppose?"

"Yes. Travel."

"I've always wanted to see Paris," the woman said, her eyes as big and brown and bright as a chipmunk's, and every bit as intelligent. "You'll send me a postcard?"

"Yes. From Paris."

The woman sighed dreamily. "Oh, how I envy you!"

Later, in the parking garage, Joyce got into her silver BMW and started the engine. The radio came on, her favorite oldies station, playing "Live For Today," and she shut it off with a *click*. The stereo system in the BMW was so far superior to anything she'd had in the sixties, none of the classic songs sounded quite right.

She'd have to downsize the car; maybe it had enough equity in it for a down payment on a Geo.

In her condo up the Gold Coast, she threw her keys on the ornate wrought-iron-and-glass entry table, and went back to the kitchen and poured herself a glass of Chateau Latour, which she downed in a few gulps.

Her mind beginning to numb from the drink, which was precisely the effect she desired, she wandered the spacious apartment that had been her home for the past ten years, then entered the master bedroom, which had recently been redecorated with King Louis XV furniture that she'd bought as an investment. There she sat at a small writing desk, opened a drawer, and pulled out her financial statements.

Her savings account had enough for two, maybe three months' rent. Her investment portfolio, once healthy, was now nonexistent: the mutual funds went for the down payment on the car; the annuities, for a younger man she'd met in a bar on Rush Street and thought loved her—they took a world cruise, and when the money ran out, so did he.

Now she wished she had contributed more toward her company's pension fund, but, then, she'd thought there would be plenty of time for that.

She sat and stared, trying to imagine what it would be like to live in an RV.

Through the tears welling up in her eyes, she saw the new dress she'd bought a month ago, hanging in the open closet. The tags were still on it! The garment could be returned for cash, if she could only find the receipt.

A tear slid down one cheek and splashed on the expensive watch on her wrist. She wondered what a pawnshop would give her for it—assuming it was waterproof.

"Mr. Bogen will see you now," the receptionist said, a young, attractive woman, with porcelain skin and blond hair pulled back from her face. Like her makeup, her dress was simple, which was quite a contrast to Joyce's elegant suit and splashy jewelry.

Joyce stood up from the comfortable chair where

she'd been sitting in the reception area and gave the woman her friendliest smile. "Thank you." After all, the woman might one day be *her* secretary.

The office Joyce entered was masculine in decor, and rather untidy. On the walls were pictures of ducks and geese mixing oddly with autographed photos of baseball players, and here and there a plaque or two, awards won by the advertising company, which had been a competitor of her former employer.

Sitting behind the desk, its top littered with papers and files, was Frank Bogen, owner of the company. Approaching sixty, his thick hair a steel gray, he wore black-framed glasses behind which was a chiseled, character-lined face that (unlike hers) only got better with age. He was wearing a navy sports coat and white shirt punctuated by a red polka-dot tie. As Joyce entered the room, he stood up, smiling broadly, and extended one hand.

"Joyce," he said. "What a pleasure."

"Frank," she responded warmly. "It's so good to see you again." And she shook his hand, which was warm and firm.

"Please, have a seat." He gestured to the chair in front of the desk, which Joyce took, and he returned to his seat.

He leaned back, the chair making a creak. "I read in the *Trib* you'd retired. I couldn't believe it. I was sure I'd beat you to pasture. But then, you were always smarter than me."

Joyce smiled. "And *you* still know how to make a woman feel better," she said. Years ago, they had met at a business function, became close friends, then lovers; but he hadn't wanted to leave his family.

"So what brings you out to the suburbs?"

She took a deep breath, her gaze dropping from his eyes to the papers on the desk. "Well . . ." Suddenly, despite the deodorant, her underarms felt wet. "I heard through the same grapevine that you're looking for an associate."

"And you have a candidate in mind?"

"Yes."

He was smiling. "I guess we all have a nephew or niece who wants to get into the advertising business, right?"

"No." She paused. "The person I had in mind was . . . me."

The smile faded a little. "You're kidding, of course."

"No."

He leaned forward, the chair making the same creak. "But . . . Joyce," he said, smile completely gone. "It's an entry-level job. You're *beyond* overqualified."

"That doesn't matter."

"And the pay is pitiful . . . not anywhere near what you were making."

"I don't care."

His face took on a tortured look and he said haltingly, "Joyce, I . . . I just don't think you'd be happy. With your reputation, you should open your *own* agency." Then he added with a little laugh, "Though I wouldn't welcome the competition."

Her laughter sounded brittle. "Yes, well, that takes capital."

"Oh. I see."

She sat forward in her chair. "Frank, I was forced to retire," she admitted, "despite what the papers said.

And I'm miserable not working, and I need the money." The words had come tumbling out. She sat back in the chair, looking at her hands in her lap, and added slowly, "I just thought that *you* might be able to help."

Frank stood up and turned his back to her and looked at the wall where an autographed photo of Ernie Banks stared back; perhaps he was hoping the legendary Cubs ballplayer would tell him what to say.

When Frank turned around his voice was soft. "Joyce, the company needs young blood."

"But I *have* young blood. I just had a complete physical. The clinic says I'm as fit as a thirty-year-old woman."

"What I meant was . . . young ideas."

Joyce studied his face. "I see," she said testily. "Of which I have none?"

"I didn't mean that," he said, and stood and came around the desk, putting one hand on her shoulder. "Look, Joyce, I'll see what I can do."

Hope blossomed, and she rose from the chair and patted his hand, still on her shoulder. "Thanks, Frank, I knew I could count on you."

He smiled weakly. "Sure. I'll call you by the end of the week."

She exited the office into the hall. Frank would come through for her, she thought, pausing at a drinking fountain. She hated calling in that marker, but she was desperate—no other jobs had come through. Should she have let him know she was available in other ways as well? Or would that only have made him uncomfortable? She still had a nice body. And everybody in the ad game was a whore. . . .

Dreading the commute back into the city in slow,

rush-hour traffic, she wandered down the hallway to find a rest room.

She was in the last stall, straightening her skirt, and about to flush the toilet, when female voices trailed in.

"So who was the rhinestone cowgirl?" one woman said. Joyce could see her through the crack of the stall door, at the mirror, applying lipstick, a slender girl, with shoulder-length brown hair. "Couldn't she get *one* more bracelet on that wrist?"

From another stall the other woman laughed. "I think she was an 'old friend' of Frank's."

Joyce froze in the stall, recognizing the secretary's voice.

"Old is right," said the woman at the mirror. "Hasn't she heard, less is more? So what did she want?"

A toilet flushed. The secretary joined her friend at the mirror. "What makes you think I listened?"

"Ha! Spill." Water ran in the sink.

"She was asking about the new position."

"But I thought that had already been decided . . . that cute black guy from Northwestern. Nice butt!"

"I guess poor Frank just didn't know how to tell her."

The voices trailed out, as the bathroom door whooshed open and shut.

After a few moments, Joyce came out of the stall and stared at the mirror, where a tired, middle-aged woman wearing overdone makeup, an outdated suit, and too much jewelry stared back. Middle-aged? *For me to be "middle-aged,"* she thought, *I'll have to live to be a hundred and ten.*

She didn't remember leaving the building, or

whether or not Frank's secretary even saw her, nor did she remember driving back into the city, parking and returning to her apartment.

But she did remember standing in the dining room with its beautiful parquet floor, where she had, over the years, entertained VIPs, from publicists to politicians, royalty to rock stars, at her elegant dining-room table, which she'd had to sell to an auction house. (The Louis XV furniture had gone earlier, at a loss.)

And she remembered going into the kitchen and pouring herself a large glass of chablis, and entering the bathroom, getting a bottle of sleeping pills, and taking them all with the booze, then reclining on her bed, arms folded upon her chest, as if preparing herself for the coffin.

A phone rang by the bed—very far in the distance, it seemed—and the answering machine picked up.

A once cheerful, vibrant Joyce told the caller to leave a message. So he did.

"This is Jason Laroma with X-Gen Incorporated. I'd like to meet with you as soon as possible about a job I think you'd be interested in. We're excited about the prospect of working with you, and hope you'll feel the same about our company."

Joyce's eyes flew open, and she jumped out of bed, ran into the bathroom, stuck her finger down her throat, and threw up.

The man who appeared at Joyce's apartment door the following afternoon was tall and thin, with a pasty complexion and hawkish countenance. His eyes were dark and dead. Conservatively dressed in a black suit, black tie, and white shirt, and carrying a black briefcase, he looked more like a religious zealot going door to door handing out tracts than a corporate headhunter.

She immediately, and instinctively, disliked him, but tried not to betray her feelings as she invited him inside.

Earlier, when she had returned his phone call, he had insisted on coming to her apartment rather than receiving her at his place of business. She had found this strange, even inappropriate; but perhaps he just wanted her to feel comfortable, and, not wanting to seem difficult, eagerness and desperation clouding her better judgment, she had consented.

She ushered him through the empty entryway and into the sparse living room, the only furniture left being a couch, coffee table, and floor lamp, arranged in front of the ornate fireplace.

"Please have a seat, Mr. Laroma," she said, gesturing to the couch. "And please excuse the apartment. . . . I'm redecorating, and my new furniture hasn't arrived yet." She hoped the lie wasn't transparent. She then asked, "Can I get you something to drink? Coffee? Tea?"

"No thank you," he said, sitting down.

Joyce, dressed modestly in a beige silk blouse, brown skirt and flats, and no jewelry, joined him on the couch. Nervously, she clasped her hands in her lap to keep from fidgeting; she wanted this job so bad. Whatever it was.

Several things bothered her, however. Though she'd made half a dozen calls, she could find out very little regarding X-Gen Corporation, other than that the company did exist. The Better Business Bureau confirmed it was a job-placement service. But since she had never contacted them, why were they contacting her?

Mr. Laroma cleared his throat. "If you don't mind, Joyce—if I may call you Joyce—I'll get right down to business."

"Please do."

"Before we discuss your future," Laroma said, "I'm afraid you'll have to sign this confidentiality agreement."

He removed a single folded sheet from his briefcase, handed the paper to her, and a pen; it was simple—merely a pledge to keep the terms of X-Gen's offer to herself, whether she took it or not.

"I really should run this past my attorney," she said.

With a meaningless smile, Laroma rose, snapping shut his briefcase. "Then I'm afraid we've misjudged you."

"No—uh, legal advice isn't necessary for something this rudimentary."

And she signed the paper.

Laroma's dead eyes came momentarily alive as he sat again. "I'm here to offer you a job on the West Coast. Los Angeles, to be exact."

She adored L.A.! She had frequently done business there and loved the sun, the glitz, the sophistication. And there was certainly nothing to keep her here.

"You'll be working for C. W. Kafer Advertising, in the capacity of vice-president in charge of new accounts."

Her jaw dropped open. C. W. Kafer was one of the largest, most prestigious agencies in the country, primarily handling motion-picture-industry accounts. She couldn't believe her luck!

"Your starting salary will be thirty thousand *above* what you were being paid at your former job."

Joyce damn near fell off the couch. She stared at him speechless, not knowing whether to laugh or cry. She felt like doing both.

"Of, course," he went on, "our company will be taking its fee from your earnings, which amounts to half of your annual salary for as long as you hold the job."

That brought her down to earth. "You're kidding," she said.

"I'm quite serious."

"Isn't that a bit excessive? Excuse me, but how can you charge such a high finder's fee? And an open-ended one, at that . . . ?"

"Because we can."

Her laugh was harsh. "No one would agree to those terms."

"They frequently do. And I believe you will, too."

Joyce got up from the couch and stood before the fireplace, one hand on the mantel, staring into the hearth, at a fire that wasn't there. Even with a fifty-percent cut she would be making a nice salary. Still, L.A. was expensive; her lifestyle couldn't be what it had been.

But, then, what was it now?

She turned to face Laroma.

"All right," she sighed. Then, in a last-ditch grasp at self-respect, she added, "But only if you can guarantee the salary you indicated as a minimum."

"I can. Fall below it, we'll take no commission whatsoever."

"Done."

Laroma shrugged. "Done."

His small, satisfied smile made her feel a little queasy.

She returned to the couch. "When do I start?"

"In six months."

"Six months!" The words struck her like a blow. "But . . . I was hoping . . ." She looked helplessly around.

"Don't worry," he interjected. "My company will advance you some cash, to get you by." He patted her hand with his; his touch felt cold. "The time will fly by. . . . You're going to be a very busy young woman."

She recoiled from his touch, eyes narrowing, thinking his word choice peculiar; she was hardly "young." "Doing what?"

"Receiving a new identity. . . . Face-lift, nose job, breast implants, various nips and tucks. . . . Whatever it takes to turn you into the thirty-five-year-old woman that Kafer thinks they're getting."

Joyce recoiled further. "What? Are you insane?"

He smiled broadly for the first time, showing white teeth that looked too perfect to be real. "Some people might think so. But most of our clients have come to see me as their savior. A savior who rescued them from a society that deemed them worthless and put them out to pasture long before they needed to be. A society that punishes *women* for growing older and less attractive. A youth-obsessed society that denies itself the benefit of so much talent, experience, and, yes, wisdom!"

He again opened his black briefcase and drew out a binder and plopped it in her lap.

"Open it," he ordered.

She eyed him cautiously, then lifted the notebook's cover.

It contained photos of women, both before their new makeover, looking worn and haggard, and after, looking fresh and sexy—and happy.

"These women, age fifty to fifty-eight, have all been successfully transplanted into new jobs across the country. Once destitute, they are now living successful, productive, *younger* lives. It's a win-win-*win* situation. You win, we win, society wins."

Joyce turned another page. "Oh, my God . . . it's . . . it's Heather. The woman who got *my* job."

"She was a fifty-seven-year-old systems analyst in Des Moines, Iowa," he explained, "who got laid off and couldn't find a job. We gave her a new name, new body, new credentials . . . a new life."

Joyce shut the book, and looked at him hard. "Can I keep the same initials?" This absurdity was all she could think to say. "I have a lot of things monogrammed."

"How about Joy Lerner?" he suggested.

"Who pays for this overhaul? I suppose you 'advance' me the expense of the surgery . . . ?"

"No. The expense is ours. It's our investment in you."

"I've already had a complete physical," she told him. "Even without cosmetic surgery, I have a much younger woman's body."

"I know. We own that health clinic. Where do you think we got the referral?"

She felt giddy, dazed; it was all so much to absorb. "What happens when I can't work anymore?"

"Ten percent of our commission goes into an accelerated retirement plan. Should your health fail, and Kafer's own bennies fail to cover you, we pledge to take care of you. It's all in writing . . ." He reached into the briefcase again. "But no attorney, Joy."

She looked toward the fireplace for a moment, then back at Laroma.

"Where do I sign?" she asked.

The woman who exited the Kafer Building on Wilshire Boulevard in Beverly Hills, with her trim yet lushly top-heavy figure, *Baywatch* blond hair, pert nose, full lips, and dewy skin, might have been thirty, even a gloriously well-preserved thirty-five years of age—but certainly not fifty-six.

Even in a town full of beauties—where waitresses who looked like the Playmate of the Year moonlighted as porn kittens, where the streets were littered with Midwestern beauty queens with C− high-school averages, B-movie futures, and A-list aspirations—this was a striking beauty, the perfect Hollywood combination of class and ass. Joy Lerner's subtly hip-swinging gait caused men with younger women and more expensive cars to crane their necks as she strolled down the sidewalk and into the parking garage, where her Geo awaited. There she got into the compact car, to head home after another productive day in a fulfilling, fascinating job.

Life was good.

She'd been at the agency just over six months, and had loved every minute of it; just today she had had lunch with a Warner Brothers vice-president of development, and tomorrow a honcho from Fox TV was on her menu.

And her performance excelled; her new and improved body made her feel more aggressive and powerful, yet at the same time more feminine. (She knew there were medical risks, due to the implants, but at her age—her real age—it seemed a minimal threat, and besides, she had the X-Gen clinic's support for any health problems.)

Best of all, her peers at the office seemed to marvel at such insight and maturity coming from one so relatively young.

It was only after work that she felt something missing, as she made the drive each day in bumper-to-bumper traffic over Laurel Canyon and down into Studio City, where she lived in a minuscule bungalow. She had fixed up the ramshackle Hobbit house as best she could, and told herself it was charming. Even so, she could barely afford the rent.

After a typically spartan dinner of fresh fruit and/or salad (to keep down the cost and her weight), she would relax for a while, sometimes vegging in front of her portable TV, other times heading back into Hollywood to browse the used-books stores or secondhand boutiques, looking for castoffs from the wealthy. Appearances must be maintained, after all. On the weekends, she would drive to Santa Monica and spend the day at the beach, using the highest sunblock known to man, or would engage in other activities that were free—a play or concert was out of the question, unless it was an outdoor concert or college theatrical production. She splurged on a movie now and then, sans popcorn and beverage.

Actually, Joy didn't mind not having much money; it reminded her of when she was first on her own after college. She found herself surprisingly good at adjusting to this new life; with this new face and body, she was, after all, a new person—on the outside, anyway. But when her old eyes, the eyes of the old her, Joyce Lackey's eyes, looked back at her in the mirror, she was reminded of the one thing she could never adjust to: growing old.

Once a month she paid a visit to X-Gen's health clinic near the Beverly Center, where a nurse drew her blood and gave her another month's supply of "vitamins." The clear capsules, one of which she had to take every day, kept her skin moist and wrinkle-free. The nameless drug was obviously experimental—this was no prescription, rather a small silver-capped plastic medicine bottle refilled at the clinic itself— but she didn't let it worry her. The pills worked. That was all she cared about. They were the Fountain of Youth. Life in a capsule.

Not that the wonder drug was without its drawback.

Dr. Green—a physician with a round face echoed by round-framed glasses, his face as unwrinkled as a bisque baby's—had warned her that if she stopped taking the drug, her skin would react with a vengeance, quickly drying up.

"That's the only side effect of this medication," Green said with a bland, inappropriate smile.

"You mean, I'd be left looking more wrinkled than I did before?" she asked. Movie images of vampires hit by sunlight flickered through her mind's eye.

"Yes."

She would have liked a more in-depth explanation, and had joked, "Then how did you get this past the FDA?"

"We didn't."

She knew Dr. Green wasn't exaggerating about the risks of ending the medication. Once, she had forgotten to take a capsule in the morning and went off to work. By the time she got home in the evening she could see a marked difference in the texture of her skin. After that, she carried the pills in her purse.

Dr. Green's bedside manner might have been clipped, but he did show interest in, and even concern about, her welfare. When, on the regular visits, the nurse would finish Joy's blood test, Dr. Green— looking too young to be out of medical school— would come in and ask Joy if she was having any problems. Because of his age, she felt skeptical about discussing anything with him, but the third time she saw him she blurted, "Yes."

His eyes narrowed to slits behind the glasses and he leaned toward her, stethoscope dangling from his neck, and said, "Tell me."

"I'm lonely."

A smile appeared in the bland balloon of his face, not making a single dimple or crease. "Is that all?"

She nodded.

He shrugged. "So date. You're an attractive woman. We've seen to that."

". . . I'm afraid."

"Of what?"

"That, you know . . . that they'll find out how old I really am."

He placed a hand on her shoulder, gently; something like compassion appeared in the doctor's eyes. "Just be careful. . . . And don't get too attached to any one man. . . . Remember the terms of your contract."

And he left the examining room. Left her to wonder what terms he was referring to—terms of the only contract this businesswoman had ever signed before reading it.

For the next few months, Joy dated—men in their twenties and thirties she'd met through work, or friends or in some of the more upscale bars. They were all decent enough guys, and with her looks she was able to land the most handsome among them, and perhaps this was why they were so self-centered and cold; she hated that in people. But it was useful, in a way, because it made becoming attached to any of them no problem.

All they seemed to want was sex. Which was all right with her. She enjoyed making love, especially with her new body. And these younger men, who were much more uninhibited and experimental than those of her generation, took her to new heights . . . though some of them wanted her to do things that she didn't feel comfortable doing. But she supposed if a man was going to bring her to multiple orgasm with his tongue, the least she could do was learn to swallow his indignities.

Still, where was the romance of her youth? Even one-night stands used to have a pretense of love— fleeting love perhaps, but love. After the sex she felt lonelier than before.

Then she met someone in the elevator at work. Tall, sandy-haired, with a smoothly handsome face grooved with just enough character, and eyes Pacific-ocean blue, he was wearing a sensible Brooks Brothers suit and smiled shyly at her when she got on at the fourteenth floor. He might have been thirty-five, even forty. The only ones in the elevator, they stood silent on the ride down to the lobby. When the loud elevator

Muzak began to play an absurdly awful rendition of "Purple Haze," they looked at each other.

"Jimi Hendrix is probably rolling over in his grave," she laughed.

"Could just be the drugs kicking in," he said wryly. "But this isn't so bad—not compared to what I heard earlier."

"What's that?"

"Strings and flutes having at 'In-A-Gadda-Da-Vida.'"

They both laughed, as the elevator doors opened onto the lobby, where they walked along together. He introduced himself as Eric Meyers, a vice-president with the L.A. insurance company that handled the Kafer agency's coverage. And she told him who she was, and they paused in the lobby, talking a while longer before going their separate ways.

A few days later, Eric called her at work and asked her out for dinner. He seemed nice enough, and she was definitely attracted to him; he was a real man, and since she was hungry for a real meal, she accepted.

They went to Le Perroquet on Sunset, an expensive French restaurant that didn't take reservations. It was crowded and noisy and after an hour of nursing drinks at the bar, she decided that no meal was worth that, and turned to him and said, "Do you know what I'd like?"

"What?" he smiled.

"A hot dog down at the pier. With ketchup and relish. And onion rings. The greasier the better."

"You can't be serious."

A little hurt, she stuttered, "Well, if . . . I mean, we can stay. . . ."

"Mustard, not ketchup! Have you no refinement, woman?"

And his infectious smile turned into a grin. And they left, laughing, hand in hand, exchanging the raucous restaurant for the beautiful beach, and a wonderfully romantic evening. Later, on her doorstep, with a full moon watching high in the sky and a balmy California breeze running its fingers through her hair, they kissed, tentatively like teenagers, as if it were the first kiss either had experienced.

"Goodnight, sweetheart," he said, and now it was his hand running fingers through her hair.

Then he disappeared from her porch into the night.

She wasn't offended, or even puzzled, as to why he hadn't wanted to sleep with her. In fact, she was touched by the courtliness of a man who could call her "sweetheart" with neither embarrassment nor irony. She sensed, as he must have, that this relationship was special, more than a one-night stand, and neither wanted to compromise it by being in too much of a hurry. She felt a youthful glow that, for a change, did not come from the clear capsules in the silver-capped plastic tube.

For the next few weeks they saw each other often— for walks on the beach, evenings at coffeehouses, and matinees at neighborhood second-run theaters and classic-movie houses.

"You know, a client of mine gave me a couple of tickets to the Smashing Pumpkins concert," he said over coffee at a vintage diner. "It's sold out . . . it's a hot ticket, everyone says they're great. . . ."

She stirred creamer into her coffee. "Can I share a secret, Eric?"

"Well, of course."

"I think their music sounds like their name."

"Oh. Well, so do I, actually . . . I just thought . . ."

"I saw in the paper something about an outdoor concert, up the coast . . ."

"I read about that," he said. Almost to himself, he said, "I think I know somebody I can sell these tickets to. . . ."

That seemed a slightly peculiar comment, from someone as well off as Eric; but maybe Eric wasn't so well off. After the concert—at which the Turtles, the Grass Roots, and Bobby Vee performed—he brought her back to his house in West Hollywood.

The white stucco bungalow was even smaller than hers, but inside it was tidy and clean, though the furnishings were of the anonymous, rent-to-own variety; this was definitely a man's decorational touch. And it would appear Eric didn't make as much money in the insurance business as she'd thought, or possibly he was dinged by alimony and child support—she hadn't pried about his past.

They sat on a brown sofa in front of a small fake fireplace and they began to pet. There was no other word for it: it was as if they were in the backseat of a Chevy at a drive-in movie, as he caressed her breasts through her blouse, taking forever to slip his hand under and around to undo her bra strap. Her new breasts had never been too responsive before; under rougher hands, they had seemed lifeless lumps, but Eric's sensitive touch brought them alive, and when his lips found their erect tips, he nuzzled them with such loving tenderness that she shimmered with delight, wept with bittersweet happiness. He seemed surprised when she got down before him, on her knees, and unzipped him and took him into her mouth, and he liked it all right, but he wanted more to be inside her, and soon he was, the two of them half-dressed, fumbling on the couch like kids, washed in the artificial glow of the fake fireplace as, masterfully atop her, he brought her to a slow, endless climax that sent youth radiating through her.

Afterward, Joy gathered her things and rose to use the bathroom. She was looking for something to freshen her breath, toothpaste or mouthwash, and opened the metal medicine cabinet above the sink. Her eyes fell on a silver-capped plastic bottle. She picked up the bottle and opened it; the familiar clear capsules within confirmed a suspicion she had never allowed her mind to form.

She returned the plastic bottle to the shelf and shut the cabinet. Her face stared back in the mirror, the young face with the old eyes. The face had no expression at first; but then, slowly, a smile formed.

"What the hell," she said to the two women in the mirror.

Then she returned to the living room, dressed and freshened, and sat next to Eric on the couch. He was dressed, also, looking pleasantly rumpled.

"You look like the cat that ate the canary," he said.

"Not a canary exactly," she smiled, then leaned closer to him, a hand on his thigh, and whispered, "I'm one, too."

He frowned. "One what?"

"One of *us,* silly."

She reached for her purse on the floor by the couch and rummaged inside and pulled out her own silver-capped bottle, which she displayed on an open palm.

At first his face was a blank mask; then half a smile

began to form. "No wonder. No wonder we hit it off. . . . I should have known."

"You should have?"

"I haven't been able to connect with these shallow young bitches. . . . Funny, it was one of the things I wanted, younger women. One of the things I thought I wanted."

"What did you really want?"

"Someone I could relate to. Someone who'd lived through some of what I'd lived through. Someone with the same . . . values. Someone . . . someone I could fall in love with."

This time she was on top, and as she rode him, they were ageless, not young, not old, two passionate people in love, fucking their brains out.

For the next hour they huddled on the couch, in their underwear, speaking in low voices, like co-conspirators, as she told him all about her past, and he told her about his.

In his former life, he'd been a private investigator with an agency whose major client was a large insurance company in Omaha, Nebraska; finally he'd gone to work for the insurance company itself, with the promise of an executive position—only time and time again he'd been passed over for promotion by younger men. His first wife had died of breast cancer at age fifty-five and medical bills had eaten their retirement funds; their only son had died in a motorcycle accident. At age sixty, a man alone, a man with nothing, he was forced into retirement. He'd been in Los Angeles, working at his new job, for about two years.

"I'm so glad I stepped onto that elevator," Joy finally said, kissing him. But when she pulled back, there was a sadness in his eyes.

"What's the matter?" she asked.

"I'm afraid," he said softly.

"Why? Whatever for?"

"For . . . us."

She tousled his hair like he was a boy. "What's to be afraid of? This couldn't be more perfect. We look great, we feel great, and we aren't alone, anymore."

"*They* won't think it's so great. They'll put a stop to it."

She shook her head, unwilling to accept that. "But . . . why? What do they care as long as they're getting their damn money?"

"Our contract says not to fraternize with others in the program, remember? Our identities are to be kept a complete secret."

That must have been another part of the agreement she hadn't bothered to read. "So we'll be careful," she said with a shrug. "They won't know. . . . We'll sneak around on 'em, we'll have an affair, that's what lovers do."

He shook his head. "I bet they already know," he said morosely.

"You act like X-Gen Corporation is big brother."

"*Little* brother is more like it. And you know what creeps little brothers can be."

She turned on the couch to face him better. "So they struck a hard bargain. I'm satisfied with what I got out of the deal."

But his expression was grave. "They struck a harder bargain than you think, Joy."

"What are you talking about?"

He glanced around nervously. "Not here. Let's take a drive. Walk on the beach."

They did.

"I told you I used to be in the investigating business," he said as they strolled along barefoot, the full moon a silent observer, its reflection silvery on the black waters.

"Right," she said, kicking at the sand like a child.

"So I did a little investigating of my own into X-Gen Corporation. It's run by a bunch of young punks who've found an ingenious way to exploit our generation."

"*Exploited,* are you kidding?" she countered, laughing a little. "I feel like I got a new lease on life."

He stopped and put both hands on her shoulders. "Well, your new lease on life won't mean diddly squat the minute you aren't able to work."

"Eric . . ."

Bitterness edged his voice. "Don't you get it? We're workhorses, fattening their pockets until we drop in the field. . . . Then they shoot us in the head."

She pulled away from his touch. "That's ludicrous. I was told that when I can no longer work, the company will take care of me."

"Yeah." He laughed hollowly. "Like the mob takes care of people."

She stared at him, then said, "You're imagining things."

He raised his eyebrows. "Am I?"

He walked her back to his five-year-old Buick LeSabre and from somewhere he produced a manila envelope, which he handed to her. They were seated within the car.

"Open it," he said. "Take a look inside."

She did, and found a pile of newspaper clippings and looked at them. They were obituary notices. She gave him a confused look. "What's this about?"

"Each of those people is . . . was . . . one of us. Patients of Dr. Green's, clients of Mr. Laroma." He let out some air. "They all died of heart attacks."

"So what?" she shrugged. "What's so odd about that? Their bodies looked young, but their hearts were old. This new shell they've put on us doesn't change life-expectancy statistics. Eric, I'd think an insurance man would know all about that."

"I ran the stats," he said. "It's all wrong—this group of people dies almost ten years too soon, according to the computer. . . . But they do have something in common: every one of them was unemployed at the time of their death."

She blinked. "Why were they unemployed?"

"Why does anyone lose a job? Their productivity slipped. Perhaps their health was failing in other ways . . . other old-age-related diseases, some of which affect memory, for example. The bottom line is, they were no longer employable. So they were bounced out of the program . . . the hard way."

She looked at him closely. "I just can't believe what you're saying," she said, shaking her head. "This just has to be a coincidence."

"Maybe," he said, stuffing the clippings back into the envelope. "But as soon as I gather a little more evidence, I'm going to reintroduce myself to some old friends in the FBI. Some friends who will be very surprised, and interested, to find out I'm still alive."

She felt numb. "If this is true, we'll lose our jobs. . . ."

"Probably. But with the government's help, we'll go into a witness-relocation plan. We can stipulate that our cooperation is contingent on getting new jobs. Of course, at our age, we may get lower-level positions than X-Gen could arrange, but hell—we'll get to keep all of what we make, and won't that be a nice change of pace."

"We won't get the pills, anymore. We'll start looking old."

"I know." They could see the beach from the car; the moon shimmered its silver design on the rippling tide. Eric tipped her chin up with the fingers of one hand. "Is that so bad?" he asked softly. "Two people in love—growing old together? Isn't that what God had planned for us?"

She sighed. She'd made her decision, and her face blossomed into a glowing smile. "Oh, Eric . . . I love you so. I'll grow old with you. Gladly. . . ."

"We're young when we're making love, aren't we?"

"Oh, yes . . ."

"Then let's get into the backseat where we belong."

And they did. They humped frantically like the overgrown kids they were, and they didn't even use protection.

Eric told her he wouldn't see her for a few days, while he gathered more evidence. It would be safer if she stayed away.

But after the third day, she drove over to his house in the evening and used the key he'd given her to let herself in. She waited awhile, then wrote him a note that she'd been there, and left.

Two days later, while eating a breakfast of fresh fruit, she opened the newspaper and read his name in the obituary column. Another young person struck down in the prime of life from a premature heart attack. Tragically.

"No," she said. "No."

And she wept for a very long time.

She had hated to tell Dr. Green what Eric had shared with her. But her job, her medicine, her new life, were at stake.

The doctor had convinced her it would be in her best interest to drive over to Eric's house and replace his capsules with another bottle. And she had agreed. After all, finding a new man would be much easier than finding a new job.

This reminded her that she needed to take her own capsule, and she rose from the breakfast table, going to her purse for the plastic bottle. She went into the bathroom and ran a glass of water.

With the capsule in one hand, glass of water in the other, she had a sudden thought. This was a fresh refill, that the nurse had given her, at the same time Dr. Green had given her the replacement pills for Eric.

Could these pills be . . .

No. No, she'd shown them that she could be trusted.

But could *they* be trusted?

She stood by the sink, the clear capsule in her palm, an inch from her mouth, as she looked at her young face, staring into the old eyes, wondering whether or not to swallow it, wondering whether life was in the capsule or something else.

Barbara and Max Collins: *"As aging Baby Boomers, we began kicking 'Regeneration' around as a response to our generation's failure to plan for the future and the Boomer* *inability to handle the notion of growing older. In addition, we became aware of the growing resentment of Generation X toward the Boomers, whose sheer numbers (and overriding, overbearing self-absorption) maintained a hold on the worlds of business and popular culture. Finally, articles in various magazines on cosmetic surgery and various anti-aging drugs provided a vehicle for describing one encounter on the collision course these two generations are traveling down."*

STRANGE THINGS

O'Neil De Noux

A former homicide detective, De Noux has penned several mystery novels, including Grim Reaper, The Big Kiss, Blue Orleans, *and* Crescent City Kills. *His short stories have appeared in dozens of magazines and anthologies throughout the world. He also teaches mystery writing at Tulane University.*

> For indeed strange things shall happen,
> and secret things be known—
>
> Edgar Allan Poe, "Shadow—A Parable"

As I stand here, my bare ass pressed against the trunk of a magnolia tree, I hold my breath and wonder if those men in the pickup can see me in the moonlight. The pickup slows as it turns down Johnston Road and passes next to the meadow where I stand. It doesn't stop, so I let out my breath. I'm disappointed, I guess, and a little frightened.

A breeze moves in from Vermilion Bay and flows over my naked body as I step away from the tree. I feel the cool, night grass on my toes, through my sandals. My heart stammering, I walk across Frenchman's Meadow to a stand of oaks and move beneath the strands of long Spanish moss. It smells musty here, like dead leaves.

I run my hands through my long light brown hair, lifting it up. The sweat at the base of my neck feels cool with the breeze. I look at my body as I move, at my white skin. In the moonlight, I seem to glow. At thirty I still have my figure, for all the good it's done me over the years. It bored my ex-husband and didn't light much of a fire in the eyes of the two boyfriends I had before I married. Average. I have an average build. At five-five, even my height is average for a woman.

The call of cicadas echoes like an ebb-time, back and forth, in the south Louisiana night. And I wonder, as I walk, if this little cat-and-mouse exhibitionism game I'm playing is more dangerous than exciting. I know, I must be crazy, slipping out of my safe home outside the little village of Cannes Bruleé to take naked midnight strolls.

But the exhilaration, the sheer naughty feeling of standing naked in a meadow, of feeling the evening breeze on my skin, knowing I could be seen any second, is so stimulating, so daring, so unlike me I can't believe I'm doing it. My ex-husband called me chopped liver, said I was boring when he left. All my life I've felt like a plain Jane. Until now.

Only two men have spotted me so far. Old Mr. Sayers, who lives across the road from my house, peeked at me from his upstairs window as I crept home last night. I stopped beneath the yellow streetlight to give him a good look. And tonight, earlier, as I walked next to Vermilion Bay, I surprised a midnight fisherman who nearly fell into the bay.

I can see the bay again, as I come out of the oaks. It glimmers in the moonlight, stars reflecting off the still surface of its wide expanse. I move behind a willow tree, stop, and look to my left at a long wooden fence. Beyond the fence, a stand of pecan trees, lined in neat rows, leads straight to the oldest and most frightful house in Vermilion Parish.

Chula House was once a plantation home, before the Civil War. Half-burned, it's been abandoned for over a hundred years, except for the ghosts that are said to haunt it.

When I was a teenager, a boy brought me out here once to park. We heard noises, like drums beating, and saw a dim light in Chula House. I never came back again at night, until tonight—if I'm brave enough to slip through the fence.

I close my eyes and listen to the night. An owl hoots some distance away, and the tree leaves rustle in the saltwater breeze. It's as if civilization is a thousand miles away.

Should I?

I take in a deep breath, smelling the chlorophyll scent of grass now, and take a hesitant step toward the fence. I hear something off to my right, the sound of a small animal scurrying through the underbrush. I wait a second, then another, then remember how my ex used to tease me—"You never take chances. You're the most careful person I've ever known."

I swallow hard and walk straight to the fence. It's a low fence, so I step over it easily with my long legs and move through the pecan trees. Darker here; I watch where I step. Stopping every few steps to listen, I continue until the trees fall away, and I see Chula House directly in front of me.

In the moonlight, it's a gray hulk, part of its roof

missing, its vacant windows like black eyes leering at me. I continue forward slowly to the three large oaks in front of the plantation house.

It's so dark under the trees, I can barely see my feet as I move up to one of the trees and press my hands against the rough bark. Closer to the house now, I watch it carefully. A gust of wind blows through the leaves, then dies away, and I hear something else.

Faint at first, it rises and I'm sure I hear it. Drums. Or is it my heartbeat? I try to swallow, but my throat is too tight. I take in a deep breath and back away from the house.

Something grabs my left arm and I jump! A dark hand has a hold of my arm. Another hand grabs my right arm, a hand even darker, and another hand covers my eyes.

I cry out as I'm lifted and carried away. Quickly. I bounce in their arms as they race with me. I cry out again as the coolness fades away and I feel warmth now and their footsteps echo, as if in a chamber. I smell cooking, rich scents, like spices.

They slow down and turn me around and stand me up. They tilt my head back and pull their hands from my eyes. I blink up at a high ceiling. Part of the roof is missing. Chula House!

Still holding me by the arms, the men walk me forward to a table where a dark-haired woman lies on her back. Naked, the woman rises and looks at me. Her light brown skin shimmers wet in the flickering light. She climbs off the table, which looks more like an altar now. She waves me to it and the men pick me up and lay me on the table.

I look at the men for the first time. On my right

stands a heavyset man. Cajun, his reddish skin glows in a flickering firelight. On my left stands a black man, tall and thin. Both are shirtless.

I raise my head carefully and look past my feet at the fire that flickers beneath a large black cauldron. And slowly, as my eyes adjust to the dimness, far dimmer than the moonlit night, I see faces leering at me, eyes glistening in the firelight.

A low drumbeat rises and then falls away and I see movement beyond the cauldron, something rising and falling with the beat of the drum. It is the drum-beater's arm.

I start to push myself up and the Cajun-looking man reaches over and shoves my shoulder down. He glares at my body. I try to cover myself with my hands and he pulls them away. The black man grabs one arm and the men shove my arms down against my sides. They look at my body, their gaze moving down my body; and I'm too frightened to move. My heart thunders in my ears.

Slowly, both men back away.

I'm so frightened I can barely breathe.

The drumbeat rises and voices start a low, guttural chant. There are a lot of people here. I want to close my eyes, but I can't.

The Cajun man moves toward the firelight. The black man moves away, too. Carrying a black bowl in both hands, the Cajun returns to my table. He places the bowl on the wooden table next to my feet. The other man places a red bowl next to it. Both men reach into the bowls with both hands. When they raise their hands, I see they are wet.

They rub their hands as they move up either side of

my table. The black man stops at my knees; the Cajun moves up to my neck, reaches over, and rubs his hands across my throat and over my shoulders. The other man begins with my feet, rubbing his oily hands against them.

The Cajun leans his mouth close to my ear and says, "Just enjoy, little lady."

The oil smells sweet, like peppermint. Their hands are so warm and my oiled skin feels cool. I close my eyes as the Cajun works his big hands around my breasts. I feel the other man's hands on my thighs now.

I bite my lower lip.

Both men stop and when I look, I see them dipping their hands into the bowls and coming back up to where they left off. I close my eyes again.

The Cajun runs his hands across my breasts and then kneads them as he rolls his fingers around my nipples. The other man runs his hands along my hips and then his fingers move through my pubic hair, softly and gently.

I hear myself let out a little cry as the Cajun squeezes my breasts before moving to my stomach. And their hands move past one another until the Cajun's fingers are in my pubic bush and the black man is kneading my breasts, touching my pointy nipples.

The men back away and the chanting voices rise. I hear words, but can't make them out. A woman appears at my feet. It's the woman who was on the table. Dressed now in a long black gown, she wears a red bandanna around her head.

She kneels on the earthen floor and drops something. She chants, reaches down, and picks up the objects she dropped. Raising both hands, she shakes them, then tosses the objects back on the floor. They are bones.

And I know now.

The VooDoo ritual—the tossing of chicken bones, the active laying of hands, the smoldering cauldron, the chants and drums. I'm lying naked on a table in the middle of a VooDoo ritual.

My God! What have I gotten myself into?

I feel tears welling in my eyes. I choke back a sob and quickly wipe the tears away. I dare to look around again and can almost make out the faces now. Men and women, mostly dark-skinned, but some faces as white as mine, all eyes leering at me. I feel their gaze on my oil-slicked body, like hundreds of tiny fingers; and I can't help myself. I'm so turned on, I simmer as I lie here.

The woman throws her head back, lets out a howl, then looks at me and smiles. She picks up her chicken bones and disappears back into the crowd.

The drums rise. The chanting increases. Words are distinct now, but I still cannot understand any of it. The drums beat even louder.

And I see a movement at my feet.

A huge black man is there, skin so dark it looks blue-black. His chiseled face is clean-shaven, a classic African face. Stoic, the face has no expression. He stares at my eyes and I feel his gaze pulling at me. His hairless chest is slick with sweat. He moves to my right and I see he is naked.

I look away and he moves around my head to the other side of the table. I watch him and his face remains without expression, yet his eyes are luminous and I feel them.

The chanting voices and drums are so loud, my ears hurt. I cover them with my hands and the two men are there immediately to pull my hands away. They hold my wrists as the huge man moves to stand at my feet again.

His flat belly presses against the end of the table. He looks at my body and I feel even hotter than before. And slowly, he reaches under the table with both hands. I hear a metallic click sound and suddenly the table moves.

The men on either side reach over and grab my legs as the bottom half of the table opens and my legs spread. I feel an immediate coolness as the air flows over the wetness between my legs.

The men lean over and dip their hands back into the bowls and start rubbing me down again. The naked man moves forward, reaches under the table again, and rolls his shoulder. I hear the crank as he cranks the table down.

I look down between my legs and see the tip of his swollen dick now as the table descends. Sticking straight up like a flagpole, it is the largest male organ I've ever seen.

Hands caress my breasts, hands move between my legs and softly brush across the folds of my pussy. The men look down at my body parts as they fondle me and I can't stop my hips from gyrating to their touch. Fingers slip inside me and I shudder at the penetration. Hands squeeze my breasts. Fingers softly rub against my clit and I'm so hot I'm panting.

The Cajun stops kneading my breasts and reaches for something. He pulls his hand back and there's a silver goblet in it. He reaches under my neck and pulls my head up and presses the goblet to my lips.

It's cool and sweet and my throat contracts at the sudden coldness. I greedily drink it all and it's so nice. I can breathe. I can swallow.

The two men back away.

I look down at the big man standing between my open legs. He stares at my pussy, reaches down and touches his dick, then strokes it up and down. And the drums continue their rhythmic beating and the voices rise and fall and I feel my body respond, feel such an intense pleasure, I almost come as I lie there.

He reaches under the table and cranks it again and my hips descend until it's in the perfect position. He looks at my face for a moment, then at my pussy. Leaning forward, he presses the tip of his dick against my pussy and slowly, ever so slowly he works his huge dick into the wet folds of my pussy. I'm getting screwed by this big African right here in Chula House in the middle of all these people.

I moan loudly.

His dick fills me immediately and he works it even deeper. A fire engulfs me. He reaches for my breasts, squeezes them as he works his dick in me. And I shudder with pleasure.

He humps me, screws me, fucks me, and it is so delicious. I cry out with pleasure. I feel myself come as his hips drive against me in a long rhythm. His balls gently slap my ass, his dick fills me so completely, I can't breathe again.

And yet I breathe. I gasp. I moan and cry.

It is wild and hot and dizzying.

And he continues fucking me, working his dick in me.

I come again and jerk against him, fucking him back.

And it goes on and on and I rise and fall like the rhythm of the chants.

Again and again the dick works back and forth in me and again and again I pant in response. Until—in a cataclysmic spurt, he comes in me and his spurting makes me come in the deepest, most convulsing climax I've ever felt.

It takes a while to catch my breath.

The big man slips out of me and I'm so wet now, my ass lies in a puddle of our juices. He moves around to my head, runs his finger through my hair, and leans forward to kiss me gently on the mouth. Then he steps away.

I lie there, spread-eagled on the table, and the faces pass around me.

The Cajun brings another goblet and I drink it all.

And I feel their gaze, each of them staring at my body parts as they circle me. Hands reach out to caress my breasts and brush past my pussy. They feel me up and my body responds and I'm so hot again, I can't believe it.

It's too late now to realize the drink has made me dizzy.

It's all a blur now, the faces and the hands and the fingers rubbing my clit.

I feel my legs give way into another climax.

Another dick slips into me and I look but can't see who's fucking me now. My hips respond and we fuck and it's such a wonderful pleasure. I come again and feel myself falling and everything going dark. . . .

My eyes!

It takes a minute to get them open. I blink up at my bedroom ceiling and for a moment I think it was a dream; but as soon as I move, I feel it, feel the sweet, sore pleasure between my legs.

I sit up and open my legs. My pubic hair is crusty and still damp. I swing my feet off the bed and sit there wondering how they knew where I live. I look around, but I'm alone. And I smell of semen.

Holding my head in my hands, I think, What have I done? What have they done to me? Am I all right?

And the word strikes me immediately—AIDS!

What if? No. It can't be.

My stomach feels funny, so I lie back down. I rub my belly and the queasiness goes away. I think about AIDS again. But as I wonder, I feel I know something deep inside, something that tells me not to worry. Weird. I'm not worried and I don't know why.

I sit up, suck in a deep breath, and look around my bedroom. I feel good, very good actually. Rested and satisfied.

Rising on wobbly legs, I move to the doorway. It's gummy between my legs and the good screwing has left me weak. I look around my living room to make sure I'm alone. The front door is closed tight.

Moving slowly, I go into the bathroom, avoiding the mirror. I turn on the shower, check the water, and step inside. Hot. I like my showers hot; the warmth relaxes my muscles. Reaching up, I adjust the shower head to the massage mode and turn my back to it.

The gentle beating of the water on my shoulders echoes with the memory of the chanting voices in a nearly perfect rhythm. What language was that? It was the language of the body. Pure venereal pleasure. It was a sexual rush to top all sexual rushes.

It was exhilarating.

Liberating.

I'm not boring anymore, am I?

I feel the power of my sex as I've never felt it before. They pleasured *me* and it felt good, so damn good.

I reach for the soap and start to lather up. My body aches with such a sweet, well-used pleasure. I rub myself and wash away the sweat and semen. And I feel different, stronger, better than I've felt in a long time.

I shampoo my hair and take a long time showering. After, I climb out and towel off, then finally look at myself in the mirror. I'm pink from the hot water and my eyes look tired, but I feel nice and used and sexy.

I wrap my hair in a towel and prance naked out of my bathroom. I move to my front windows and open the blinds. If anyone's out there, let them look. I peek out, but don't see anyone.

Maybe tomorrow I'll go to New Orleans. Buy some new shoes. It should be fun trying on shoes while wearing a miniskirt and no panties.

It should be a lot of fun.

I walk back into my bedroom where the big black man who fucked me is standing there with the Cajun man.

The black man gives my body a long look up and down. I feel my heartbeat.

The Cajun grins at me and says, "Hey, little lady. Did you think we were finished with you yet?"

O'Neil De Noux: *"I was inspired to write this story because of an incident that happened when I was a police officer. One quiet summer night, as I patrolled near Jean Lafitte National*

Park in a very rural area of southeast Louisiana, I spotted a naked woman walking through a stand of oak trees. At first I thought I was hallucinating, until I saw her a second time a few minutes later, running away from me. I never saw her again. That image remained in my mind, however, and I always wondered what happened to her."

BODY PIERCING, BY NED

Marthayn Pelegrimas
and Robert J. Randisi

Author of numerous short stories in the horror and dark fantasy genres, Marthayn Pelegrimas's work has appeared in Borderlands 3, Love Kills, *and* Hot Blood: Crimes of Passion, *among others. As Christine Matthews, she has penned mysteries for several anthologies. Her first novel,* Murder Is the Deal of the Day, *written with Robert J. Randisi, is due in 1998. Randisi has had 26 books published under his name, as well as some 275 others written under fourteen different pseudonyms. He has written in the mystery, western, men's adventure, horror, fantasy, historical, and espionage genres. He is the author of the "Nick Delvecchio" and "Miles Jacoby" private eye series. Randisi is the founder, executive director, and current vice president of the Private Eye Writers of America, the creator of the Shamus Award, and the cofounder of* Mystery Scene *magazine. He has edited sixteen anthologies. His novel* In the Shadow of the Arch *will appear in 1998, as will* Murder Is the Deal of the Day *and its prequel,* Alone with the Dead.

I make holes in people for a living.

You'd think they'd be just a little intimidated. I mean, I'm standing over them with a needle, and they're usually sprawled out in the chair beneath me. Sometimes naked. Lots of times naked. You'd think they'd be shaky and quiet. Well, you'd be thinking about this all wrong.

They come determined. Seeking enhancement, ready to invest in a forbidden extension of themselves. Some come direct from a screamfest with a significant other. Running their mouth on fast forward, they vow they'll prove to so-and-so their body is their own—to mar, cut, or even drill holes through. Waving an invisible flag of courage, they're gonna show just who's in charge of what.

Not like tattoos. They're a whole different thing. They show the world a philosophy. Like a bumper sticker slapped on the back of a Chevy tells what's going on inside the driver's head. And with a tattoo you've got lots of other details to consider: size, color, placement.

This biker I know has a wreath of roses on his upper right arm. Roses are real popular. But sticking out from between each rose is a thorn, little drops of blood on each tip. Very artistic. The word "Mother" is scrawled across the middle in a lovely shade of blue.

I've got this theory that all men have a fearful respect for their Mother. This love/hate thing goes on even after the old lady croaks. Then he's got the guilt. It never ends. Know what I mean?

And while most tattoos are meant to be seen by the general public, piercing is more personal, private. Holes punctured into certain areas of the anatomy, filled with jewelry, making the designated area three-dimensional.

Lots of the customers like to talk. Sometimes they tell me stories. Maybe it takes their minds off what I'm doing.

Had a guy in here last week, sporting a three-piece suit. Looked like he was on his way home from some uptown job, except he needed a shave and looked like he'd slept in that suit. It was Tuesday. Things were slow.

"How much for the tongue?" he asked, slapping his Mastercard down on the counter.

"Forty-five. Everything's forty-five."

Now, I know my clientele are the kind that strive for a reaction, a raised eyebrow. But I've always wondered why someone would want a tongue job. This time I decided to ask, and he just started talkin' and didn't stop.

"I work down at International Life and Casualty." He shook his head and stared down at the credit card, rubbing his index finger over the embossed numbers. "Boring . . .

"Every morning I take the eight-oh-five downtown and every night I catch the five-oh-eight back to Chesterfield. I pay my taxes . . . early, usually in February . . . never cheated on my wife and love my kids." At this point I wished I hadn't asked. This guy needed therapy, not a piercing. "On Saturdays I mow the lawn and on Sundays I go to church. I've never caused anybody one moment of trouble and have managed to go unnoticed by good luck as well as bad."

"Uh-huh," I said, just to say something.

"I went to my ten-year high-school reunion last night. I'd dieted, bought a new suit, got my hair cut, even spent an hour, three nights a week, for a month, in a stupid tanning bed. And finally it's the big night."

Jesus, I thought.

"Margie—my wife—she's great. Don't get me

wrong. I'd do anything for her and the kids. But this night was just going to be mine. Margie didn't go to the same high school and even said she'd feel out of place. But I couldn't tell her how anxious I was to see Sharon."

Uh-oh.

"We'd only dated three times, but I never forgot her. She was in the band and I went to every football game just so I could sit next to her. I've relived those autumn afternoons in my head so often that sometimes I think the memory tape will break." He laughed.

"Your choice is very limited here," I said, getting down to business. I showed him the chart. "It's best to have a stud, right down the middle. That way you won't run into any trouble chewing. Like this one." I pointed. "You don't want to get fancy. Keep it simple and sanitary."

"That's fine."

"So? What happened with what's-her-name, this Sharon chick?"

"Hey, she looked great. Ten years had only made her better. Time seemed to have defined her features, you know? I guess she must have had some baby fat back then, but now she had these big milk jugs, you know? Round and soft. She turned out to be one of those skinny girls with big tits that look so sexy?"

I didn't think that skinny girls with big tits were sexy, but I kept my opinion to myself.

"Her eyes were the most vivid blue, not that soft baby color I remembered. Her cheekbones were more pronounced and her skin . . . her skin looked like satin."

Yeah, I saw women like that every day, didn't he?

"Get in the chair," I said.

He removed his jacket, hung it on a hook, and complied.

"So? Did you make it with her, or what?" Curiosity had gotten the better of me.

"Let me tell you about it," the man said. "You mind if I get, uh, graphic?"

"Get as graphic as you want," I said. "I got time."

The man got comfortable in the chair.

"Well, let me tell you she was all over me from the time I got there, pressing those big titties up against me every chance she got, you know? I told you I never cheated on Margie, but God, I didn't have a chance. She eventually pulled me into the coatroom and that's where we did it."

"You did it, huh?" I said, because I thought it was time to say something.

"Well, sort of," the man said. "I mean, she got down on her knees and my pants fell around my ankles before I knew it. Then she had my shorts down and my dick was standing up, I mean *straight* up, you know?"

"Uh-huh."

"Well, she pulls the top of her dress down and those tits come pouring out and she got my dick between them and is rolling me. Man, they were hot, let me tell you. She's rolling my dick between her big tits and all the while she's looking up at me with those eyes, and a big sexy grin and then she's got me in her mouth and she's sucking me like I'm made of candy or something—and she's still looking up at me. Well, Jesus, this is everybody's wet dream, isn't it?"

"I guess so."

"Before I know it, I'm up on my toes," the man

said, leaning forward suddenly, "and I'm blowing a geyser and she's swallowing every drop."

The man slumped back, as if he was exhausted just from telling it.

"And then?"

"She stands up, pulls her dress back up, kisses her finger and puts it to my lips and she's gone."

"That's it?"

"No, that ain't it," the man said, sitting forward again. "This was my dream girl from high school, right?"

"Right."

"Fifteen minutes later I see her going into the coatroom with another guy."

"Uh-oh."

"She comes out in five minutes and she's adjusting her dress, you know? So I keep an eye on her and ten minutes later she's got a guy by the hand and is pulling him into the coatroom—and he's this fat guy, you know? The one everybody used to call Porky Pig?"

"Hmmm," I said. I'd been a fat kid until I got interested in sports.

"So I go over to the coatroom and sneak in, and she's down on her knees, copping this fat guy's joint, moaning like it's the best thing she ever tasted, and his eyes are rolling up in his head and then he lets loose and almost passes out. This time it was the guy who pulled up his pants and hurried out. As he went past me I could see he had a wedding ring on, and the look on his face was—well, pure shame. The poor guy had tears in his eyes. He didn't have a chance against her, either."

"Okay," I said, "keep goin'. It's gettin' interesting."

"She stands up and turns around and sees me. You know what she says? 'Back for seconds? You'll have to wait your turn.'"

"I say to her 'What's my name?' and she just shrugged."

"She didn't know your name?"

"I don't think she knew *anybody's* name. I found out later that all the guys she took into the coatroom were married, and most of them had never cheated before. This chick, she got off on it, and she didn't remember any of us."

"Power," I said.

"What?"

"It's all about power."

"Yeah, I guess you're right," the guy said. "Can we do this now?"

"Sure. Let me adjust the height of the chair here."

"What do I do?"

"Just relax and stick out your tongue. This is gonna take a while."

I try to do it quickly but the tongue usually takes about a half an hour. Can't use the gun. A receiving tube is held in place on the underside and the needle pushes through the top. From the reactions I get, this procedure is as painful as it is tedious. Fortunately, should a customer be less than satisfied, he can reverse the whole thing by removing the surgical steel intruder. The hole heals right up. Temporary commitment is all that's required to get pierced.

He jerked a little and made a surprised sound.

"You okay?"

"Shtings like a bith," he lisped.

After twenty minutes of gentle moaning we were professionally finished with each other.

"Can I talk?" he asked, thickly.

"Sure, you got to get used to it."

He moved his tongue around experimentally in his mouth for a few seconds.

"What happened to this chick?" I asked.

He touched his tongue gingerly with his fingers and said, "Se's inna cah."

"What?"

He took his fingers out of his mouth and spoke slowly.

"She's out in my car."

"Waitin' for you? You mean she left with you?"

"Well, sort of."

"Whataya mean, sort of? If she's in your car, she's with you, right?"

"Well," he said, "she's in my car, but not like you think. See . . . she's in the trunk."

"What the hell is she doin' in the trunk?"

"Well," he said, getting out of the chair and retrieving his jacket from the hook on the wall, "you see, I wasn't sure what to do with her after I killed her?"

I couldn't believe I'd heard him right. "You killed her?"

He nodded.

"Strangled her in the coatroom."

"How'd you get her out of there?"

"That's the funny part," he said. "I wrapped her in a coat and carried her out. Did I tell you she was only five-two? Nobody even noticed."

"Then what'd you do?"

"I drove around for a long time, all night actually, until I saw your sign."

"So she's dead in your trunk?"

He nodded.

"I bet nobody's gonna want to stick his dick in her mouth now," he said. "Her tongue's sticking out, and it's all black."

"Uh, what are you gonna do with her?"

"I haven't decided, yet," he said. "I came in here on a whim, you know? I wasn't even sure what I wanted—hey."

"What?"

"I don't suppose if I brought her in you'd, like, pierce a nipple?"

I wasn't sure if he was gonna go off on me or not so I tried to keep him calm.

"Well, I tell you, I usually like my clients warm and alive, ya know?"

"She'll keep still." He giggled. "Won't flinch at all. I could even bring one of her tits in here and leave the rest of her out there. Bitch wouldn't feel that. You got a sharp knife? Or a saw?"

"I deal in needles, not knives."

"So you won't do it?"

"Uh, no offense, Mister—"

"Hey," the guy said, "I'm not crazy, Ned . . . it's Ned, right?"

"That's me."

"I'm not going to hurt you. You didn't do anything to me. I'm not even sure why I killed her. Maybe because she didn't remember me. Or was I striking back for all the married, faithful guys she lured into that coatroom?"

"I wouldn't know. . . ."

"Well," the guy said, "I've got to go."

He looked out the door for a moment.

"You know," he said, finally, "if I go out the door

and turn right, I could drive straight to the river. Just throw her in and jump in after her."

"Why would you do that?"

"I can't let my family suffer over this," he said. "What are they going to think when they find out?"

"I, uh, don't know. . . ."

"On the other hand," he said, "I could turn left, head for the police station, and turn myself in."

If he wasn't going to kill me—and I was still holding the needle I'd used to pierce his tongue, just in case—it was no skin off my nose what he did.

"But maybe my family would be proud of me for doing something . . . radical, you know?"

"Radical?" How about "insane"? I wanted to ask, but didn't.

"Well." He exhaled the word and seemed calmer. "I better get going. Thanks for this." He flexed his tongue at his own reflection in the mirror. "This is just what I needed."

"How so?"

"Sometimes you just want another person to see you. Really remember the way you tell a joke, walk into a room, or make love. No matter what happens to me, every time I start believing I'm just another body taking up space, I'll wiggle my tongue. It'll remind me I'm different. Unique, huh?"

He asked, so I answered him. "I think carryin' your date around in the trunk makes you the most unique person I've met today."

"Naw, people kill each other all the time. Besides, I figured I did mankind a favor by getting rid of a whore like Sharon. But this . . ." He wiggled his pierced tongue at me. "This I did for me."

"Hey, it don't matter to me, buddy," I lied, and ran his card through the gizmo on my register for approval.

"Goodnight," I said, as he moved toward the door. "Good luck, whatever you decide."

"Thanks."

He left and I breathed a sigh of relief and put the needle down. I hurried to the door and locked it before he could change his mind. I didn't even bother to look and see if he turned left, or right.

Robert Randisi and Marthayn Pelegrimas: *"While walking through St. Louis's University City, we spotted a flyer nailed to a storefront advertising the going rate for Body Piercing by Ned. Once the title was in place, the story came out as a mainstream tale about an average kinda guy who was just trying to find some excitement . . . until Bob got through adding his part."*

THE SEX FILES

Michael Garrett

The coeditor and cocreator of Hot Blood *is an Alabama author, editor, and instructor of writing work-
shops across the nation. His first published works were
actually satirical pieces, appearing almost twenty
years ago in such diverse publications as* Dun's Review
and Pillow Talk.

*A*nother hooker was scheduled to arrive at any
moment. She was late, as hookers usually were, and in
fact would be the third to report tonight. Two candidates who had earlier failed to meet specific physical
requirements had been rejected already. Tonight's
setup called for a blonde with full, pouting lips,
average tits, and long, tanned legs. Was that too much
to ask? The escort service had apparently ignored
their threat to turn away unlikely candidates.

Johnny Lamar and Mitch Raynor reviewed the
layout of the cramped room of the Sir Rest-A-Lot
Motel for a last-minute assurance that their video
equipment was in proper working order. "I suppose
it's time for me to get my ass next door," Johnny
suggested, but Mitch shook his head.

"No hurry. Let's be sure we don't have any techni-
cal glitches." Mitch was an average-looking guy at
best, moderately overweight, and slightly balding, in
his early thirties. He sported a prominent overbite

and had never been particularly successful with women on his own. Tonight he wore a Dodgers T-shirt and ragged jeans.

Johnny couldn't shake being pissed at the service. Most outcall customers were probably too embarrassed to turn a hooker away, but not Mitch. Johnny admired him for that. The guy was brassy as a doorknob. Besides, this new service had no idea what the two of them were up to. Mitch alone had placed the order on the telephone, and for all the service knew, he was just another traveling salesman out to get laid. What the service *didn't* know was that Mitch wasn't easily pleased, and he had a hidden agenda as well.

Johnny shrugged, admitting to himself that he was somewhat jealous that Mitch got all the pussy, yet he'd agreed from the start that that was the way it should be. Mitch's camera presence was considerably more charismatic than Johnny's. On the other hand, Johnny was actually the better-looking of the two. He was only slightly overweight, with a full head of mid-thirties dark hair and a reasonably handsome face. He spoke with a slight lisp, however, about which he was self-conscious. But the objective of the amateur adult-video series *Outcalls* was to showcase an average guy having sex with beautiful women who didn't realize they were being filmed. It didn't matter that the ladies were hookers, and Mitch didn't mind his less-than-desirable image. He'd told Johnny on numerous occasions that he had the best job in the world.

Mitch checked the placement of the suitcase-concealed camera on the dresser adjacent to the bed. Hidden coaxial cable snaked through a hole drilled in the baseboard behind the dresser into the next room, where Johnny would supervise the clandestine production on a portable control panel. It'd be months, if not years, before the motel discovered the room's minor modification, and by that time the manager wouldn't have the slightest idea who had altered the place, or for what reason. Tilted lampshades spilled as much light as possible across the bed without appearing suspicious. A wireless mike behind the headboard was poised to capture even the slightest moan once the action began—*if* a show were, indeed, to occur tonight.

Johnny looked at Mitch. "You ready?" he asked.

Mitch checked his breath and underarms. Even though this was technically a job, Johnny always reminded him to present a respectable image. After all, Mitch had to look like any typical john, to keep the call girl from suspecting she was being secretly filmed. To date, the smut partners had captured over thirty-five unsuspecting hookers on film from coast to coast and had become cult heroes in the porn industry. Mitch sprayed his underarms and checked his hair in the bathroom mirror. "If this next one doesn't pan out, we should scrap it and get some sleep," he said. "We can try a different service tomorrow night."

Johnny nodded as he exited the room to check out the makeshift video control room next door.

It was almost two A.M., but still early for ladies of the night. The jarring ring of the telephone startled Johnny from a light sleep as he grabbed the receiver, spilling a can of beer on the nightstand in the process.

"We still got a clear picture?" Mitch asked from the other room.

"Everything's fine."

Johnny yawned. "You know, Mitch, I'm thinking maybe we should expand our horizons. We need a bigger audience to help us break into the big time."

"I don't know, Johnny," Mitch answered. "Seems kind of stupid to mess up a good thing. Besides, this is almost more than we can handle already. How could we take on anything else?"

Suddenly a knock sounded at Mitch's door. "Gotta run—my date's here," Mitch said. Johnny hung up the phone and settled in front of the video monitor to watch the action unfold.

Mitch's image was sharp as he crushed a cigarette into an ashtray and waited a moment before answering the door. Maybe this one would be their next star, Johnny hoped. A second knock sounded and Johnny wondered what she'd look like. He trusted Mitch's judgment, though. Mitch always seemed to keep the best ones. Then again, Johnny never saw the hookers Mitch turned away; the hidden camera was never aimed at the door.

The monitor now displayed only the stagnant image of the room's empty bed. Mitch was off-camera answering the door, sizing up their next potential victim. Johnny heard the door open, then a woman's voice with a thick Southern accent. "Mr. Williams?" she asked.

"That's me," Mitch answered.

"I hear you're a hard man to please," the woman said. "Am I what you had in mind?" Johnny was dying to know, himself.

He nodded to remind himself what a great business he was in. While it was true that Mitch got all the sex, Mitch also bore the risk of disease. Johnny could never bring himself to perform onscreen anyway. And another great thing about the business was that, unlike other porn producers, he and Mitch didn't have to pay for talent beyond the hookers' usual fee. Hell, even when the girls got wise to the hidden camera, what the hell could they do about it? The hookers were breaking the law already themselves. Who were they going to complain to—*the cops?* Mitch and Johnny had developed contingency plans to pack their equipment and check out of a motel faster than a hooker could call for some muscle. They'd only been forced to escape a couple of times since they'd begun the series, and had been impossible to track down, since they always registered under phony names. Only a P.O. box appeared on the *Outcalls* videocassette jackets. Hell, fans of the series didn't even know which city it originated from.

Johnny watched as Mitch ushered the hooker into the field of vision, guiding her to sit at the predesignated upper end of the bed, unobstructed from the camera. She leaned back against a pillow at the headboard and Johnny finally got a clear view. She had a youthful, pretty face with a creamy smooth complexion, probably no older than early twenties at most, with shoulder-length blond hair and a near-perfect shape. She wore a tight sweater and equally snug jeans. This lady was absolutely remarkable, Johnny recognized immediately. While she wouldn't be the most attractive to appear in the series, there was an aura of unmatched sensuality about her so strong it almost appeared unnatural. If that quality could be captured on film, she could be one of their most popular subjects ever.

* * *

As the hooker settled her denim-wrapped ass on the mattress, Mitch moved to a predetermined position to divert her attention from the hidden camera. This lady has more sex appeal than Marilyn Monroe, he gloated. Mitch felt mesmerized, knowing he was giving her a deer-in-the-headlights expression, but what the hell else could he do? He was completely under her spell.

She smiled and wrinkled her nose. "So, what did you have in mind?"

Mitch cleared his throat. "That depends on what you've got to offer."

She watched him in silence for several seconds, then purred, "My name is Sandra. And by the way, are you a cop?"

Mitch laughed. "Hell, no. But I find you arresting." He'd used the line time and again. Sandra laughed, then Mitch smiled at her seriously. "You're not a cop yourself, are you?" he asked.

Sandra took a deep breath and grasped her tits through her sweater. "Not at all," she said. "These would get in the way. But I need to know what you have in mind."

There were times like this when Mitch wished Johnny could zoom the camera into a close-up of her lovely face. There was something about the way she widened her eyes and flashed her eyelashes to accent certain words as she spoke. Maybe someday he and Johnny could upgrade their equipment to allow remote changes in scene composition. A static, unyielding image was a frustrating limitation of the *Outcalls* gimmick. "Do you do anal?" he asked.

Sandra rolled her eyes and wrinkled her cheeks in a look of feigned innocence. "I'm afraid not."

"How much for straight sex with a blow job?"

"No blow jobs either. But you won't be disappointed. I promise."

Mitch chuckled and cocked his head slightly. "You're the first not to do blow jobs. You gotta admit, that's a little unusual."

Sandra nodded. "As far as I'm concerned, there's only one place for a cock to go."

Mitch shook his head, still imagining what it'd be like to give her everything he had. "So, then, how much?"

"Two hundred and fifty."

It was kind of steep, considering her limitations, but Mitch wasn't about to negotiate. He was far too anxious to experience this sexpot in action, but hesitated before accepting her offer to maintain a semblance of control. "I can go for that," he finally agreed.

She winked, and Mitch swore he could shoot his load by merely gazing at her pretty face. Her eyes reminded him of those of a snake he'd seen in a nature film wherein the reptile hypnotized its prey with its stare. He felt similarly spellbound himself, and cleared his throat. "You're absolutely gorgeous," he said with a still-gravelly voice. "If you don't mind, I'd love to just sit back and watch you undress." He knew his viewers would appreciate it, too.

"That's sweet," she said as she stood beside the bed. "And your first name is—?"

"Mi—Mi—*Mark*," he finally got it out. Shit, he'd been so captivated, he'd almost given his real name.

Sandra (if that was *her* real name) watched him impatiently and finally cooed, "Well, Mark, I'll need to see some cash before we get started."

Mitch fumbled awkwardly for his wallet, happy to be standing offscreen to conceal his nervousness. He gave her $250 and smiled. "There's an extra fifty in it if it's a night to remember."

Sandra smiled back, and almost blushed. "I'll give it my best," she whispered. The bills disappeared into her purse; then she gripped the waistband of her sweater and gently tugged it up and over her head, revealing a pointed bra that reminded Mitch of Madonna's. But before removing it, Sandra sat in a chair beside the bed and kicked off her shoes, then pushed her tight jeans past her hips and down around her ankles. She wore white bikini panties surrounded by smooth, untanned skin.

It had been a while since Mitch had worried about his ability to perform on film. Fucking had become so routine that he'd developed maximum self-control. But he was so turned on by Sandra already that he wondered how much of her he could stand. Shit, if he embarrassed himself on camera, he and Johnny couldn't use this clip without heavy editing. But then, he'd always be up for a return performance, and the two couplings could be edited together to appear as one.

Sandra unfastened her bra to reveal a pair of perfect, *natural* tits. Mitch had long since grown tired of the phony silicone breasts so common in professional porn, and it wasn't unusual to meet a hooker with a fake rack. Probably dancers from strip clubs moonlighting for extra cash, he'd always presumed. But these babies were the real thing—firm, pert, pink nipples, slightly upturned. Her tits actually jiggled as she hooked her thumbs into adjacent sides of the elastic waistband of her panties. But she paused before removing her underwear and smiled sweetly at Mitch. "You're *staring*," she said in a singsong, playful voice, as if he were a bad boy peeking through a window.

"I can't help myself," he muttered in anticipation of the grand finale. "I know I'm not the first to tell you how fantastic you are." Mitch shook his head in wonder. She didn't seem at all like a hooker; more like the girl next door, or someone from a Sunday-school class.

With an innocent giggle, Sandra dropped her panties to her ankles, revealing a soft bush of light brown pubic hair. Not a natural blonde, Mitch recognized, but then, who was? She motioned for Mitch to join her on the bed and purred, "Now let's see what *you've* got," as she playfully kicked her jeans and panties into the air.

Mitch lost all awareness of time. Never had a woman exerted such control over him. Sandra licked his earlobes, then paused to focus her irresistible eyes on him. "You'll be my last trick. I want you to know that," she purred.

"Wh-wh-*what?*" Mitch was so lost in the moment that he hardly understood what she'd said. Her breath felt tantalizingly warm against his neck.

"I won't be doing this anymore after tonight. It's just not for me." She ran the tips of her fingernails lightly up and down his chest, teasing him with her touch.

Mitch swallowed hard. "Really? So what will you do next?"

Sandra sighed. "I don't care if I have to wait

tables," she said with a downcast expression. But then, just as suddenly, she cheered up again. "I want our time tonight to be special," she said sweetly. "Sort of like a rebirth for me. After all, I *will* be starting my life all over." She took a deep breath and stared deeply into his eyes. "I don't normally show this much affection to a john. But, then again, you're not my average customer." Mitch felt his erection grow harder as Sandra brushed her lips against his. "I hope you're willing to celebrate my change of life with me," she whispered.

Mitch laughed. "I thought that's what we were doing."

Sandra dipped her chin and nuzzled against his neck. "I know this sounds crazy, but I want my last trick to be special, and I'm so lucky it'll be with you." She traced circles around his ear with her nose, and the smell of her perfume wafted across Mitch's face. "But condoms take so much of the pleasure out of it for me. I promise I'm clean, Mark. I've just been tested. Will you take the risk with me?"

Mitch was shocked. Occasionally he'd asked hookers to fuck without protection. Some agreed, for extra cash, and he'd required them to show recent test results; others refused.

Sandra kissed him long and hard as he contemplated her offer. "I can show you my blood-test results from just last week," she offered as she leaned away to reach for her purse.

Mitch pulled her back, not wanting a single moment to go to waste. "I trust you," he moaned. "And I promise you've got nothing to worry about from me." For a sex goddess like Sandra, Mitch would gladly forgo the offending sheath. Sandra stared into his eyes and he absolutely couldn't resist. "Let's go for it," Mitch said.

Mitch was worried about his stamina. Somehow he'd avoided climax, but Sandra seemed intent to make him ejaculate as quickly and forcefully as possible. "Slow down," he panted, hoping to maximize the pleasure, but she grinded him like she was stomping out a fire. They'd fucked straight missionary for only a few minutes when, to avoid ejaculation and change the scene composition, Mitch had lain on his back and asked Sandra to straddle his dick, her ass to the camera. Next he'd given his usual excuse of how he enjoyed using the entire surface of the bed and repositioned himself with his head at the foot of the mattress so she'd face the camera as she sat once again on his dick. She hadn't shown the slightest hint of suspicion, and Mitch knew that, barring electronic failure, they were getting some of their best footage yet. Johnny was probably about to burst his nuts next door.

The sensation at Mitch's groin was indescribable. He couldn't believe he'd lasted this long already, and knew that the end was near. There was something about Sandra, inside, that was so different from all the others. And whatever the hell it was, it felt *great*. As Sandra rode him harder and harder, Mitch envisioned how the scene would play on the television screen, but finally lost control. "Baby," he gasped. "I just can't hold out any longer. I've got to come."

She stopped unexpectedly, rivulets of perspiration running down her breasts, and rolled over onto her back. "Come inside me," she moaned. "I want to catch every drop of you."

Mitch was happy to comply and immediately positioned himself between her outstretched legs. He clenched his buttocks tightly and lunged into her deeper than before, holding the stance as a hot eruption spewed forth inside her. Sandra squeezed his arms, digging her fingernails into his flesh. "Oh, *yes,*" she hissed between gritted teeth as the two collapsed into each other's arms.

Mitch was proud of himself. This segment would likely be described in detail in men's-magazine reviews. "Oh, baby," he huffed into her ear, still gasping for air. "I don't know how I managed to link up with you tonight, but I'm sure as hell glad I did."

She didn't answer.

"Sandra?"

She appeared to be resting, as if in a deep sleep.

"Sandra? Are you *all right?*"

When her abdomen first began to swell, Mitch thought he'd only imagined the slight movement. Had she taken a deep breath? Within moments, however, Sandra bore the expanding stomach of a pregnant female.

Mitch shook her shoulders, pulled her eyelids open to peer into her eyes. "Sandra? Are you okay?"

The bizarre transformation continued until she looked six months, seven, even eight months pregnant. Still she showed no sign of consciousness. Mitch stared at the camera. "My God, Johnny. Are you getting this?"

When the growth of Sandra's stomach stopped, her abdominal mound began to undulate with movement just below the surface of her skin. Mitch shook his head, wiping beads of perspiration from his brow. Sandra's face remained motionless; every inch of her body seemed paralyzed except for her womb. Then Mitch noted a twitching blur at her crotch. A lone slender tentacle like the leg of an octopus slithered from her vagina and snaked its way down her leg, wrapping itself around her knee. Then another tentacle followed and attached itself to the other knee, and then another. With four tentacles firmly in place, the appendages tightened and pulled to force the remainder of its body from its vaginal entrapment. With a mucky, disgusting sound and the tearing of Sandra's flesh, the trunk of whatever-it-was plopped from Sandra's vagina and coated her blood-soaked inner thighs with a greenish mucus-like substance. Mitch gasped. Was he drunk? Surely he was hallucinating! He felt both terrified and fascinated at the same time.

From the shifting jellyfish-like mass, a bulbous head emerged and two disproportionately large eyes blinked open, phlegm dripping from their newborn corners. The creature twitched in animated movement, then severed its own umbilical cord with pincer-like claws at the ends of its tentacles. The creature was small and nonthreatening until, with lightning speed, its tentacles disengaged from Sandra's knees and shot forward to attach to Mitch's legs, forcing him off balance. Mitch tumbled backward to avoid a vicious bite, but the creature managed to nip enough flesh and tissue from Mitch's throat to render him voiceless.

His legs still helplessly in the creature's grasp, Mitch's upper torso dangled over the edge of the bed and onto the floor. Mitch stared at the hidden camera, pleading with his eyes for help. The creature grew in both length and girth, and surged forward, coiling its tentacles around Mitch's shoulders and sinking its jagged fangs into his neck. Mitch grasped the slimy beast and wrestled it across the floor, but was no match for the monster's increasing strength. Mitch made hardly more than a gurgling sound as the creature tore completely through the muscle and tendons of his neck.

Mitch's consciousness waned, fading in and out like an electrical brownout, and then an eerie, silent blackness enveloped him.

Johnny Lamar was petrified. Initial shock prevented him from running to his partner's aid, and now it was too late, not that he could have done anything anyway. He paced nervously back and forth across the motel room, then stopped to watch helplessly on the video monitor as the creature continued to grow and consume every last scrap of Mitch's torso. The beast's chest cavity expanded and contracted with exaggerated breath, like the throat of a lizard; then the insatiable monster turned to its host and, starting at her feet, devoured every ounce of the hooker as well. With all flesh and bone of both corpses consumed, the creature attached its mouth to the bedsheet and emitted a fluid that soaked into the drying bloodstains. Amazingly, the creature painstakingly sucked every trace of blood from the fabric and repeated the process on the carpet, seemingly intent on extracting every molecule. When it was finished, hardly any evidence of gore remained.

Johnny shook uncontrollably. A cold sweat dampened his face. The video images appeared like a state-of-the-art horror flick, and yet he knew it was horribly all too real. He checked the monitor again. The newborn creature had grown to the size of a mature human, its movements more sluggish as it stumbled around the room like a toddler, in and out of the camera's field of view. Johnny noted subtle changes in the color and composition of the creature's skin; its maturation had begun.

For several moments the creature was offscreen, and Johnny heard the bathroom shower running. When movement returned on the monitor, Johnny found himself staring at what had almost become Sandra again. The skin tone was there, but the facial features weren't quite right, and the breasts had not yet settled into their previous form. Finally the "female" slipped into Sandra's clothing and walked offscreen, and Johnny heard the motel-room door open and close.

In the three months following Mitch's tragic death, Johnny Lamar's life had slowly become unraveled. He glared at the dimly lit video control board of his soon-to-be dismantled studio. First, he'd mourned the loss of a very dear friend. Additionally, he'd never realized what a perfect business partner Mitch had been until he'd been forced to continue on his own. Johnny had decided against recruiting a replacement partner. He simply couldn't imagine working with anyone else. And tonight he felt guilty for having attempted to capitalize on Mitch's death, even though he knew without a doubt that Mitch would approve of the mass-market release of *Alien Conception!*

Johnny had thought he'd owned a gold mine in *Alien Conception!* but the film had been branded a fake since its first day of release. Where's the physical evidence? the film's critics scoffed. How convenient that the creature itself destroyed it all. But it had perhaps been Johnny's decision to release two versions that led to certain failure. The pornographic edition had been a monumental mistake, cheapening the impact of the original. How could he have made such a costly error in judgment? As a result, he'd been virtually laughed out of business.

Johnny sat alone in the darkened room, dismantling the state-of-the-art control panel to which he'd upgraded to edit the film for release. There had been little doubt that *Alien Conception!* would generate enough profits to more than pay for the new editing deck and audio mixer, but now his creditors were calling the shots.

"Shit!" he grumbled beneath his breath. Now Johnny couldn't even enjoy a normal sex life. He alone knew what was out there—at least one man-eating beast in the guise of a beautiful woman, and there could be others. Hookers, more than likely, but who could know for sure? The beasts could simply haunt the local bars in search of men to release them for feeding. Johnny wished now that he'd married, that there was one special woman in his life with whom he knew undoubtedly he was safe. But now there was no way to know for sure. Any woman could be one of . . . *them*.

A knock at the door jarred Johnny from his unsettling thoughts. He ran his fingers through unwashed hair and stumbled across the cluttered studio floor to unlock the door. Before him stood a scowling man, mid-forties, dressed in a wrinkled business suit. Before Johnny could even speak, the man thrust a badge in his face.

"Why am I not surprised it's you?" Johnny groaned. "And put the fucking badge away. I've seen it enough already." The lawman chuckled, obviously pleased to annoy Johnny in any way possible. "Come on in," Johnny said with a sigh. "You'll barge inside anyway, whether I invite you or not." He switched on a lamp for better lighting. "Have a seat, Agent . . . Longjohn, isn't it?"

"That's Long*tree*. As if you didn't know."

Johnny hung his head and ran his fingers through his hair again. Would these guys ever leave him alone? "I thought you worked the day shift. Don't tell me you're on overtime just for me," he said sarcastically.

The agent looked him straight in the eye. "Look, it's time to cut the bullshit," he said. "We're not as stupid as you think we are. The Bureau isn't interested in the disappearance of some low-life porn hustler. That's a local matter. But when it comes to national security, we're ready to play hardball, mister."

Johnny looked up from a videotape he was labeling. "As if you haven't been already?"

The agent laughed. "Making you look like a fake is peanuts, buddy. We want the master copy of that tape for analysis, and I promise you, we'll get it—one way or another."

The agent seemed more threatening than before. Johnny felt a combination of fear and relief—fear for how far the feds might be willing to go, and relief that they were at least now attempting to communicate. He replaced the cap on his felt-tip pen and put away the videocassette labels, then looked the agent squarely in the eye. "So, what you're finally admitting is that the FBI thinks my footage is legitimate."

The agent shook his head and lit a cigarette. "I'm not saying anything. But I'll admit that we destroyed your credibility because of the *possibility* your tape could be authentic. I'll admit that the opinion of experts so far is almost evenly divided that the tape is fake. And I'll admit that I'm pissed off and fucking tired of wasting my time. You'd better start cooperating, or the shit could get a lot deeper, friend."

Johnny wove his fingers together and leaned back in his chair in a vain attempt to relax. "The original footage stays put. I don't trust you guys any farther than I can piss."

The agent laughed, fell back into his own chair, and exhaled a plume of smoke. "Then I suggest you start trying to hit the urinal from the hallway." A chunk of glowing ash fell from the cigarette's tip to the floor, but the agent made no attempt to clean up the mess. Instead he exhaled deeply and attempted to lighten the conversation. "So, listen, back when you were making those fuck films, it was always your buddy that got all the action. Did you ever get any of that pussy on the side?"

Johnny stared at the government agent for what seemed endless moments, hoping to size up the situation. Agent Longtree's attitude was definitely more menacing than before. Something was going on. "How can I be sure I'll get my tape back in its original condition?"

The agent dropped his cigarette to the floor and crushed it with his heel. "You can be assured that you *won't* get it back. I can promise you that. But you'll gladly give it up, sooner or later. You can save yourself a lot of agony if you'll just hand it over now." The flame of the agent's cigarette lighter touched the tip of another smoke and he inhaled deeply, then exhaled a thick plume through his nose. "You got any coffee around here?"

Johnny shook his head. "You've completely fucked up my life. What makes you think I should give you fucking *refreshments?*"

The agent rubbed his eyes. "Man, it's getting late," he said as he narrowed his eyes to a threatening stare. "You're not as tough or as safe as you think you are, asshole. I could run you in right now if I wanted to."

"On what grounds?"

The agent ignored the question. "How about going for a little ride with me? I got something I'd like for you to see."

Johnny broke out in a cold sweat. "No way. I want to talk to my lawyer."

The agent shook his head and rolled his eyes upward. "Come off it, will you? You're not under arrest or anything. You're not going in for *questioning.* I just want to *show* you something, that's all. You sure as hell don't need a fucking lawyer for *that.*"

Johnny forced a laugh. "Then why don't you tell me what you want to show me, and let *me* decide."

"What? And ruin the surprise?" The agent exhaled and rose to his feet, jingling the keys and loose change in his pocket. "Look, *we* want answers and *you* want answers. Wouldn't you like to know what really went on in that motel room that night?"

Johnny stared at his adversary silently, trying in vain to figure out his angle. "Forget it then," Longtree growled. "I was only trying to shed some light on the subject for you. I could get fired for showing you anyway."

"Yeah. *Right.*" But Johnny knew his rights and felt

he'd be safe. If Longtree was only bluffing, Johnny could call his attorney on his cell phone. If he was on the level, what could the agent possibly have that Johnny would want to see? Curiosity finally won out. "How long will this take?" Johnny asked.

"Oh, no more than a couple of hours, I'd guess."

Johnny reached for his coat. "Let's go."

As the two walked up the steps of the downtown federal building, Johnny felt nervous. "You lied to me. Why would you bring me here, other than to hold me for questioning?"

"Calm down, will you? I said I wanted to *show* you something. It's upstairs."

Within minutes the two passed through a security checkpoint into a top-floor detention area. A row of jail cells, most unoccupied, lined the left and right walls of a concrete-block room. As the two walked the corridor between the rows of cells, white-collar criminals peered angrily from behind bars. Agent Longtree paused. "Let me explain something before we go any further."

"That'd be a pleasant change of pace," Johnny snorted.

The agent leaned against the wall directly beneath a NO SMOKING sign and lit a cigarette. "Practically everything anybody does these days is like performing under a spotlight," he began. "With so many camcorders out there filming everything under the sun, the likelihood of someone catching an actual extraterrestrial encounter on tape increases every day."

Johnny nodded.

"We check out every tape that surfaces," the agent went on amid a plume of smoke. "The ones on *Hard*

Copy or *Inside Edition* have already been dismissed by us. Our objective is to protect the public from mass hysteria when the real thing comes along."

Johnny steadily shook his head. "Sounds like another Roswell cover-up."

Agent Longtree kicked the wall. "Shit!" he growled. "Can't you space-freaks ever get beyond that? We've got reasons that assholes like you will never understand."

Johnny groaned, refusing to debate the issue.

The agent stroked his whisker-stubbled cheeks. "Forget it. I don't owe you any fucking explanations."

Johnny waved away the agent's smoke. "But you already admitted the Bureau discredited my film to minimize attention."

"Exactly."

"So why didn't you do the same with *Alien Autopsy?*"

The agent laughed. "I've already answered that. We're only interested in films that have merit."

Johnny groaned. "That sucks! The fake films make money while the legitimate ones are laughed at."

"Hey, nobody said life is fair." Longtree started to drop his cigarette butt to the floor, then glanced at the sign above his head. He crushed it against a bar of a nearby cell, then flicked it through an opening between the bars into the cell's toilet.

Johnny weighed his options. "Suppose I give you sample cuts from the original footage?"

The agent shook his head. "Nope. Sorry."

Johnny exhaled in frustration. "Then I suppose we're at a stalemate."

Agent Longtree started to walk again, toward the end of the corridor. "No, I don't think so. We'll get what we want." The agent opened a massive door into a smaller, more secure area. "No, I didn't bring you here to question *you,*" he said. "I want *you* to question someone *else.* For *me.*"

Johnny exhaled a burst of pent-up breath in anger. "Shit!" he cursed. *"Will you please stop playing these fucking games—"* But he stopped in midsentence and swallowed hard. Just ahead was the only occupied cell in this special high-security area, and Johnny couldn't believe what he saw.

The agent pointed to the cell in question. "Go ahead. Talk to her."

Sandra stared from behind the bars. She sat on a well-worn cot, her hair mussed, and wearing what appeared to be prison garb, but she was still ravishingly beautiful. Johnny felt reasonably sure it was her, and suddenly felt more nervous. "Where did you find her?" he gasped.

"A vice cop picked her up," the agent began. "Police commissioners everywhere have been notified that our little squeeze here is wanted for questioning in a homicide. A cop was working undercover targeting outcall services when this babe showed up at his door. He brought her straight to us."

Johnny shook his head, his hands beginning to tremble. "You're crazy. Do you honestly think a cell can hold a monster like her?"

The agent laughed. "Well, I gotta admit, you're faking it to the max. But if she *is* a monster, she's still nothing but a pussycat—until she gets fucked. And she's probably getting pretty horny and hungry by now." Agent Longtree paused, and Johnny felt himself shaking. "She don't eat much of what we give her, by the way," the agent continued. "No, I think she's waiting for the right guy to come along. So it's only fair that, since you and her have crossed paths before, we put you in there with her and see for ourselves if she's the only pussy in the world that eats back."

Johnny stared at Sandra. It was his first time, live and in person, to gaze into her captivating eyes. Then the large security door behind him clanged open and two armed guards stepped inside. Johnny panicked. "Hey, there's no way!" he shouted. "You got nothing to keep me on!" He stepped around Agent Longtree and ran for the door, but the two guards refused to step aside. Without even thinking, Johnny attempted to lunge between the two.

"Oh, my dear Mr. Lamar." Longtree's shout echoed through the barren room. "Did I not just see you assault two federal officers? Well, I'll just be damned. Looks like we got something to charge you with after all."

"NO!" Johnny screamed. "You can't do this! This is against the law!" He pulled out his cellular phone, but one of the guards snatched it away.

Agent Longtree leaned directly into Johnny's face and snarled. "This ain't television, buddy. We don't always do things exactly by the book." The agent straightened and took a deep breath. "Besides," he continued, "we could've trumped up charges against you a long time ago, but we waited until the time was right. And you *are* under arrest now, by the way."

The two guards grasped Johnny's arms and dragged him toward the corner cell.

Agent Longtree stood behind two lab-coat-clad scientists whose attention was glued to a video monitor. Finally appearing on-camera and covering his face to avoid eye contact with his cellmate, Johnny Lamar screamed with all his might, "Get me *out of here!*"

"Doesn't look like he's acting," one of the lab coats said. "He looks scared shitless to me."

"We'll know soon enough," the other answered, pointing to Johnny's face on the screen. "Maybe he's more afraid of what we've got in store for him than what the hooker might do."

The woman named Sandra leaned against Johnny from behind, whispering in his ear and nuzzling against him with her now-nude body.

"Interesting," mumbled one of the scientists. "If she were just a hooker, she wouldn't be seducing him. She's up to something, all right."

Johnny's eyes were shut tight. He stood pinned against the bars, Sandra's steamy body pressed against his, her hot breath blowing against his neck. He'd given up resisting her; she seemed far too determined to get what she wanted. She ran her fingertips over his cheeks, lightly grazing her lips against his. He smelled her breath, felt her touch all over. He took a deep breath to fill his lungs for another scream, but the sound lacked its previous intensity, his willpower draining fast. Sandra wrenched his head toward hers and delivered a passionate, wet kiss. Beads of sweat covered the seduced man's face. Finally, he opened his eyes.

"No," Johnny whimpered. *"No."*

But it was obvious from the bulge in his pants when she touched him there that she had won. Johnny eyed her longingly; she appeared far less menacing now. Sandra stripped him of his clothing and within moments positioned herself beneath him on the soiled cot. Johnny lunged into her with animal intensity. She kissed him, running her fingers through his hair as she matched his lunging movement with surges of her own insatiable hips. Johnny emitted an eerie moan; he was approaching orgasm and yet, deep inside, he was simultaneously frightened to death. Within moments, he was a goner. His body tensed, but he immediately attempted to withdraw, to avoid ejaculating inside her, but Sandra clenched her hands over the cheeks of his naked ass and pulled him toward her with incredible force as he sprayed inside her.

Johnny escaped from her grasp and rolled over to collapse onto the floor, backing away on his naked hands and knees to the farthest corner of the cell. Trembling violently, he dressed himself, never allowing his eyes to stray from her as she lay in silence. "Let me out," he screamed. *"Please!"* Just as before with Mitch, Sandra lapsed into a state of mock paralysis, apparently awaiting conception.

Johnny mumbled incoherently and tried not to look, but couldn't help himself. He sobbed for what seemed endless moments until finally Sandra's eyes snapped open. The monster was not to appear.

Johnny Lamar was perfectly safe.

Johnny's head was still spinning as he leaned against the cold steel bars of the cell. He'd had the most incredible sexual experience of his life and, unlike Mitch, had lived to tell about it. He took long, deep breaths, steadying himself on his feet until he slowly began to regain his senses.

Agent Longtree ground another cigarette butt into the floor and paced outside the cell, slowly shaking his head. "I've never seen a woman play a man like that," he said with a deep expulsion of breath.

Johnny leaned against the cell's door, rattling it violently until Longtree's assistant keyed it open. "You should thank me for that," Longtree called out as the door clanged shut again behind Johnny.

Johnny struggled to speak. "I need to sit down," he finally gasped.

Longtree snapped open a couple of metal folding chairs and motioned Johnny toward one. Longtree himself straddled the other and locked stares with an assistant, nodding toward the exit to be guarded. Longtree exhaled and shook his head. "You really believed she'd attack," he said. "You really had me going." He stood and stepped quickly to the cell to gaze inside at the lovely prisoner. "And you, my friend," he said to her, "have got to be the most insatiable nymphomaniac of all time."

Sandra gazed silently, pleadingly with her eyes. Longtree's expression remained stone-cold as he slowly reached down to unlock the cell door.

"Don't open it!" Johnny screamed from the nearby metal chair, immediately bounding to his feet and heading toward the exit.

Longtree snapped his head back in Johnny's direction. "Relax and learn something," he said. The guard at the door hurried forward to restrain Johnny and force him back into the metal chair.

Longtree loosened his tie and smiled at Sandra. "Jeff!" he called out to the guard with a nod toward the cell. "I'm going to *interrogate* this prisoner." Longtree grinned wickedly, then added, "You might want to question her yourself, when I'm finished."

The guard smirked and glanced back at Johnny.

"We'll deny everything if you say one word about this," he warned. "And besides, it don't look like the little lady will have to do anything against her will."

Longtree glanced over his shoulder at Johnny. "Let me show you how to satisfy a sex-starved bitch," he boasted.

"You're crazy," Johnny gasped. "I don't know why she didn't finish me off, but she's still a monster."

Longtree laughed. "Guess you weren't man enough for her." He removed his sports coat and sat on the soiled mattress. Sandra straddled his lap immediately.

"So tell me, little lap dancer. Why are you so hot and horny?"

Sandra never spoke, but instead nibbled at his ear. Longtree was engrossed by her immediately as she slavishly catered to his needs. The agent laughed as he shed his clothes, making wisecracks that she'd finally met her match.

Johnny glanced back and forth between the guard standing at his side and the one at the door. His hands shook and his pulse soared. There was no way to escape. But, then, as long as Sandra was locked inside the cell, she should pose no danger to him anyway.

Longtree was on his back, on the cot, his prisoner grinding his cock from an upright position. He swallowed hard and gasped, "Oh, baby! Your pussy is out of this *world!*"

Johnny began to feel more at ease, contemplating why he had escaped the Sandra-monster unharmed. Mentally, he reviewed differences between himself and Mitch that might serve as a clue as to why Mitch had been murdered, while he himself had only gotten laid.

Longtree was breathing hard and heavy. "Oh, baby," he huffed. "I can't hold out much longer." The passion inside the cell was overwhelming as the weak springs of the small cot sang out and echoed against the cinder-block walls.

Johnny snapped to attention the instant the idea struck him. Suddenly, it all made sense. He watched the action closely and opened his mouth to speak, then curiously remained silent. Sandra lay in her comatose state as Longtree, fully spent, dropped to his knees on the floor and tried to catch his breath. "Hey, Jeff," he huffed. "Get me a cup of coffee, will you?"

The guard excused himself. Between the bars of the locked cell, Johnny thought he saw slight movement at Sandra's abdomen. His initial reaction was to run for the guard to come and unlock the cell, but, then again, Longtree deserved what was about to occur.

"Hey, Longjohn," Johnny called to him derisively. "Have you ever had a vasectomy?"

Longtree's expression froze. A tendril snaked forth from below Sandra's rising stomach.

Johnny laughed. "Me neither. *But Mitch did.*"

Mike Garrett: *"Amateur porn has in many ways dislodged professional productions in popularity and I wanted to create a story with an amateur-porn-production background. Simultaneously I mixed in an homage to* The X Files. *The result: 'The Sex Files.' "*

THE CELLOPHANE HEART

Dawn Dunn

Dunn has been writing professionally for six years. Her short fiction has appeared in Deathport, 100 Vicious Little Vampires, Desire Burns, *and* Demon Sex, *among others. She is featured in the 1998 Horror Writers calendar from Dark Delicacies. She also writes convention articles and takes photos for* Horror *magazine. She commutes between Colorado and Indiana.*

This place stinks," I said bitterly, thinking that all the time I had spent on my makeup and nails would be a perfect waste. "It smells like old jock straps and dirty socks."

Maggie turned and flipped her blond hair into my face. "Give it a rest, Kate. I promised you a good time, didn't I? They haven't even started yet."

"But I hate sports."

"This isn't sports. It's men. Big, beefy men. Wait till you see them. You might surprise yourself."

We were crammed shoulder-to-shoulder in the Fort Arena for the start of the NPW Championship Showdown. Our seats, which Maggie had gone to a great deal of trouble to get, were only four rows back from the ring. I couldn't resist picturing her on her knees in the men's room, between zit-faced Hanover's thighs. On weekends, zit-faced Hanover moonlighted at the Ticket Connection.

"You'd do something like that to see professional wrestling?" I had asked incredulously. "You know all that stuff's fake. It's stupid."

She'd tugged at her black thigh-high nylons and given me a dirty, indignant look. "I'm doing it for you, too. You've been a nutcase ever since you broke up with Rick," she'd said, referring to the increase in my consumption of alcohol and the self-inflicted wounds on my wrists. "Wait till you see these guys. They're the real thing. You look at those sweaty, brown muscles bulging from every inch of their glorious torsos, then tell me they're fake. Even if some of the stunts are, those bodies aren't. They have to be in great shape to do what they do."

I'd finally relented. After all, it was only going to cost me a Saturday night. It had cost Maggie a lot more. Zit-faced Hanover had torn a hole in her twelve-dollar nylons.

The crowd chanted and stomped their feet, demanding the start of the first match between such characters as the Star-Spangled Ripper and Lord Byron of the East, the Moneymaker and Bob the Gouger, famous for everyone knows what. Cardboard signs and banners danced across the smoky arena with slogans like THE RIPPER FOREVER and CHEW 'EM UP BOB. I couldn't believe I was actually sitting among that mob with a red, white, and blue Ripper button pinned to my chest.

As temperatures rose in the bleachers, several large blowers in the ceiling attempted to move the stagnant air. Then out stalked the Ripper, draped in a quasi-American flag, waving his mighty fists to egg on the audience. Next came Lord Byron, the poetic sheik in his pink and purple tights, equally well endowed and hamming it up.

"Oh, God," I groaned.

Maggie poked me in the ribs with her elbow. "Have some fun!" she cried, peeling off her blouse to reveal a Ripper T-shirt underneath.

I couldn't believe it. How could she go for this? It was all so fake, I thought again, twisting raven-black, dyed hair between air-brushed, acrylic fingernails and wondering whether my sunless tan looked too orange. Maybe everybody's a bit fake on the exterior. No one I know would walk out of their house without at least a bit of hair spray to hold their image in place, not to mention false eyelashes or a push-up bra. But what about on the inside?

Maggie's adventure with Hanover in the men's room had been completely mercenary. Neither of them had pretended it was anything else, but had she paid for the tickets with more than her body? Do the things we do on the outside cost us part of our soul, or is that sealed in plastic, too?

For nine crazy, frustrating years, I had given all that I had to a jerk who was fucking every woman he could get to spread her legs. He'd made a million promises but kept only one: that he would never fall in love with me or anyone else. Marriage is old-fashioned and boring. Commitment is thought of in only temporary terms. We have sex, then go our separate ways. There is scarcely even any community property to divide. But what do we do with the pain?

I glanced at my scarred wrists, wishing my heart were wrapped in something stronger than flesh and blood.

Maggie jabbed me in the ribs again. "Isn't he great?" Her neck was spotted and flushed with excitement. "We love you, Ripper!" she shouted.

He had flung the flag on the mats and stood beside the ring in brawny glory. There was no denying his corporeal appeal, but I was determined not to let myself be sucked in by a few rampaging biceps and pecs, however I was starting to drool.

The Ripper climbed over the ropes, his sinewy chest flexing and glistening under the lights. Lord Byron was a similarly impressive specimen of the male physique, but a little effeminate for my taste. Despite my resolve to the contrary, I whistled and shrieked for the Ripper. Maggie grinned with that I-told-you-so look. Even my jaded libido was melting in the presence of all that virile exhibitionism.

The Ripper and Lord Byron were everything Rick was not. It would've taken three of Rick to make either of them, and neither carried a laptop computer, wore a stiff white shirt, or reflected on capital gains. I wanted a real man. The kind with hair on his chest, possessed of intense animal magnetism. One who could defend me from thugs in the street but wasn't afraid to say "I love you."

My thighs ached with sudden horniness. I had done nothing since Rick's departure from my life except tear myself down and question my worth as a human being. How could I have allowed so much of myself to have become tied up with pleasing him? How could I have believed so many lies? Why had I endured all those humiliating confrontations with other women, the endless criticism of everything from my lack of muscle tone to the Midwestern twang in my voice? Something horrible had to be wrong with my psyche.

If nothing else, I had been stupid enough to fall in love with him and to keep loving him despite the obvious signs of how one-sided our relationship was. He had even given me a cancer-causing form of herpes, yet I'd gone on loving him.

As the Ripper slammed Lord Byron's face into the turnbuckle, my heart beat urgently, like the fire from an automatic weapon. I leaned forward on the edge of my seat, consumed with anger and lust. "Crush him!" I screamed. "Beat him! Kill him!"

Even death would've been too good for Rick. No one was ever going to treat me that way again, I decided, and was surprised at how fiercely I meant it. More than our relationship had changed: I was no longer the same person.

"Attagirl!" Maggie said and clapped my shoulder. We hissed as Lord Byron freed himself from the Ripper's iron clutches with an amazing, acrobatic flip. He kicked the Ripper in the groin, but our man hardly flinched. He grabbed the sheik and tossed him on the mat, then pinned him.

The match ended on a three-count. Maggie triumphantly brushed her damp bangs from her forehead. "Glad you came?"

I nodded enthusiastically. For the first time in months, I felt as though I could breathe. With each lungful of air, I cleansed myself of my self-proclaimed sins.

The Ripper's chances of claiming the Championship Showdown title were slim. He would have to beat the next thirty contestants. The crowd cheered and howled as his second challenger, the Wolf Man of London, strode into the ring wearing only a tiny brief that vaguely resembled the Union Jack.

I squeezed my legs together excitedly. I had never seen such a powerful-looking man. His thighs rippled like waves when he walked. His wild eyes were a brilliant, impossible shade of green. As he smiled and played to the audience, I saw his long, jagged teeth and imagined them biting my arms, my calves, my inner thighs. His hair flowed in a magnificent, brown mane down his tawny back, his tanned, muscular flesh covered with thick, curly hair. I was completely mesmerized. I longed to taste him from head to toe.

"Beautiful, isn't he?" Maggie gasped.

My mouth was too dry to respond. I wished the whole audience would vanish, leaving only him and me. I wanted him to tear the Ripper's heart out and eat it at my feet. I had a vision of him with the bloody, still-beating organ in his hands, his hairy knuckles and arms matted with thick, viscous crimson. I squirmed in my seat, so hot and wet I thought I would drown in my own desires.

Perspiration shone on the faces around me as we sat in the blaring glare of the camera lights that surrounded the ring. A tendril of red, like a snake or ribbon, crept from the corner of my vision and wove itself through the audience, though no one seemed to notice. I imagined them all with their throats cut and their wrists slashed, laughing, cheering, wanting more.

My hair clung to the back of my neck. My body was on fire. I rubbed my palm between my breasts to relieve the tension.

"Are you all right?" Maggie asked.

I nodded again. I had never felt better. I was in Rome, at the Coliseum, and the lions were about to roar. "Kill 'em!" I yelled.

The moment the referee turned his back, the Wolf Man pounced on the Ripper. He choked, beat, and jumped on him. The contest was brutal and unrelenting and looked so real. My mouth gaped as I watched in total fascination, loving every second of it. This was absolute ecstasy, absolute power, yet it had to be fake. If it wasn't, wouldn't the referee and all those witnesses have put a stop to it?

The audience booed as the ref finally declared the Wolf Man the winner. I, alone, stood and applauded.

Maggie yanked me down in my seat. "What are you doing?" she muttered. "Didn't you see how vicious he was?"

The Ripper appeared to limp from the ring, barely able to walk, covered with livid bruises. I was only sorry he wasn't dead. I wanted vengeance. I wanted every hour of pain, every moment of torment, I had experienced to be reconstructed and brought to life so that this time I might be victorious.

I saw the Wolf Man wrapped in the red, red ribbon that wove itself carelessly among the crowd, like a giant tongue, licking and tasting, enjoying the feeling of power and control. I felt a tremendous release. My days of rolling over and acquiescing were finished. I could quit punishing myself for being the victim I had allowed myself to become. Maggie was right: I had been crazy, but now I was free.

First the Ripper, then the Wolf Man, had liberated me. I was grateful beyond words. I wanted to belong, body and soul, to one of these burly men who understood all about pain. I ran my tongue over my lips, trying to restrain myself, wondering how long I could sit and wait. It was like being on the continual brink of orgasm.

The Wolf Man successfully crushed his opponents for the next hour. Then even I, his greatest fan, could see him weakening. When the Salesman from Seville, a wimp in black underwear, defeated him, I nearly wept. "Let's go," I said.

Maggie blanched. "But it's only half over. I thought you were having fun."

"I want to wait around outside. I want to see him when he comes out."

"You're kidding."

"No." My voice left no doubt as to my seriousness.

"You didn't believe all that garbage they said about him during the break, did you? You were the one who kept complaining about how fake it is."

"I don't care what I said. I'm going." I rose from my well-earned seat and walked toward the exit. When I looked over my shoulder, I saw Maggie following.

"I wouldn't do this for anyone else," she grumbled. "For Christsake, we're missing the best part. They haven't brought out Gorilla, King of the Jungle, yet."

"You could've stayed."

"And let you make a fool of yourself alone? You're hooked. I knew you would be. Next time, you can be the one—"

But I wasn't interested in zit-faced Hanover. "Did you see his eyes?" I asked.

"He wears contacts. It's part of the show."

"What about his hair?"

She shrugged. "Probably a wig. That hair on his arms and legs is probably glued on, too. It's a publicity stunt. Like the circus."

"You're saying he's a total fake," I said as we

walked outside and joined a small crowd near the exit.

"You said it first."

"But you said their bodies are real."

Maggie leaned against the building and took out a cigarette. "Yeah, and I think some of that stuff they say in the interviews is real, too. I think they train hard and dream big, and this is probably as real for them as winning an Olympic medal. They're actors and stuntmen rolled into one."

Away from the heat and noise, I felt deflated. There was an ache in my chest, a hole, a deep emptiness that was even worse than before. "Why did you think they'd be better for me than Rick?"

She smiled. "I wasn't saying you should fuck one of them. I just thought watching them might make you appreciate men again. Rick was a zero. He was leading you on from the start. He took major advantage of you as long as you let him. Not even his body was real. He was a pansy-ass. He was all promises, and you believed them because you wanted somebody to love you so badly. Come on, let's go home."

"You go home," I said, trying to keep the edge out of my voice. "I wish you would."

"Listen, I'm sorry if—"

"I want to be by myself. I'm going to wait around here, then get drunk."

"Kate—"

"It's my life," I said and turned my back on her, staring blindly through tears at the laughing group in front of me. I saw the red ribbon on the ground near their ankles, like a thin river of blood. It wasn't their blood but mine. I always said and did the wrong thing.

A woman tried to peer past the guard outside the exit. "The Wolf Man will be out in five minutes," he said.

I glanced over my shoulder to see if Maggie was still behind me, but she'd gone. She'd suffered the brunt of my anger for years. She was the only true friend I'd ever had, the only person who honestly loved me, and I was always hurting her. Because I was always hurting myself. Trying to put myself back together again was one of my favorite pastimes. Like Humpty-Dumpty. I was too smart to go to a shrink, too proud, too scared that I couldn't be fixed. My feelings of self-hatred had started young, when I was a kid, with my disinterested parents, and they would never end. Not until I died. They were lodged in my brain like broken glass. I wanted someone to love me so desperately—it didn't really matter who—that I would do or put up with anything.

The Wolf Man appeared in the halo of the doorway and I thrust myself forward, shoving and elbowing, trying to touch him. All the other women were seized by the same desire, and the guard had to force us back. I managed to reach around him and caress the sleeve of the husky wrestler's jacket.

Everyone shouted and waved scraps of paper in the air, demanding autographs. The Wolf Man signed a few, including mine. I trembled and blushed, though I was nothing to him but another groupie. For an instant our eyes met. I saw a glint of red, a look of hunger and need; then he turned away and I was left studying the backs of the other women. The guard followed him to his car and opened the door, keeping the fans at a distance. I watched reluctantly as he disappeared inside.

I would never see him again. He would never know how he'd changed the course of my life, the strength and courage he'd given me. You're being silly, I told myself. It was like falling in love with a movie star. But I felt a profound sense of loss. Something about him had deeply affected me. Perhaps it was the hold-nothing-back style of his wrestling, or the image of a wild beast trapped in a man's body.

I saw his headlights illuminate and his car pull out of its space. Soon I would be plunged back into the misery and despair of my ordinary life. I would be a victim again, as Maggie had said: a woman used, scorned and forgotten. Rick never mourned my loss. He always had someone else to turn to: a string of women as stupid and devoted as I had been, all hoping that someday he would fall in love with them.

I wanted to tear at my hair and scream in frustration. Instead, I sighed painfully as the Wolf Man's car rolled slowly past, taking with it the ecstasy and power I'd felt inside the arena.

How could I get him back? I wondered frantically, then thought: It doesn't have to end here. A sudden surge of determination sent an electric thrill through my veins like the charge that brought Frankenstein's monster to life. My dead, wounded heart began beating again. I ran toward my car. I'd follow him. I'd see where he went and arrange to meet him. What was the worst that could happen? He could turn me down flat, or treat me as badly as Rick had. Would I be any the worse for a little extra wear? Would my heart be any more damaged?

I started the engine, then laughed as I thought of Maggie. She'd die when I told her what I'd done. She'd never believe I could be so desperate, but this time it wasn't desperation. I was taking control of my own destiny.

My tires squealed as I swung out of the lot and nearly hit one of the pedestrians leaving the arena. Fuck you, I thought happily, and flipped him the finger. By the time I reached the light, I'd caught up with the object of my desires. I was only one car behind him. My hands shook on the wheel. My blood was aflame. I was going to win. I'd find a way to make everything right. No more doormat. No more being hurt by those I loved.

Maggie had explained to me that as part of their publicity package, each wrestler develops his own character and appeals to the audience either as a villain or hero. The Wolf Man was clearly a sympathetic villain: a man struggling with the animal inside him. She'd told me that he refused to fight on nights with a full moon and had once lost a title because of it. She said he didn't date often and was extremely reclusive. It was rumored that one of the women he'd escorted had been found decapitated in a New York alley. The woman was the love of his life, and he'd killed her. All this was supposed to make the audience believe he was actually a werewolf, an unwilling killer.

But I wasn't frightened. I had already met the real thing. Rick was the Wolf Man, Dracula, Mr. Hyde, and Jack the Ripper rolled into one. He had stolen my heart, drained my innocence, used my body and devoured my confidence. What was left to fear? To be afraid, you have to have something to lose. If anyone had anything to fear, it was the Wolf Man. Because I was so desperately empty.

Following him was easy. He made no attempt to

evade me and drove straight to his hotel. A number of other wrestlers, whom I'd seen earlier in the evening, were clustered around the lobby. He sat with them, then ordered a drink. I stood by the main entrance, as if expecting a ride, and watched them from the corner of my eye. Their talk was boisterous and happy. None of them seemed to be enemies. Fake, fake, fake, I thought, and wondered when the Wolf Man would go to his room. I could taste the sweat on my upper lip.

After several minutes, the entire group moved into the bar. I gaped in horror. But he didn't know I was waiting. He was doing what he probably did after every show. I was overly anxious to lose myself in the hairy masculinity of the stranger I had fallen in love with. We would be perfect together. Our relationship would be everything none of my previous relationships were. The bloody red ribbon I'd seen at the arena tied itself in a bow about my neck. I pulled at the ends and tried to make it look tidy.

In the darkness of the bar, I sat at the counter and ordered a whiskey sour. There wasn't enough alcohol in it, so I ordered my next whiskey straight. I laughed and flirted obnoxiously with the bartender. The red snake around my neck uncoiled itself and hung from the ceiling like a string of confetti. It draped itself in continual loops until it encircled the room. Everyone was covered with the dripping red string. It was a sign of our solidarity and made me feel better. When I slipped off my stool, the bartender suggested jokingly that maybe I'd had enough, but I talked him into a sixth.

The Wolf Man finally rose from his chair. I quickly paid my tab, spilling the change from my wallet and abandoning it as a tip for the bartender. I grinned sloppily, then bumped into another customer in my haste. The Wolf Man was getting away.

I ran and hollered ahead for him to hold the doors of the elevator, which he did. I smiled gratefully, catching my breath. I was so warm I thought I would melt. "Thanks," I muttered nervously, then toppled into him, my head reeling with passion.

"You okay?" he asked, propping me upright.

This was my moment. My heart beat so fast I could barely stand. "I saw you wrestle," I said. "You were great."

He chuckled. "I'm glad you liked the show."

Then the elevator lurched to a stop and the doors opened. I had about five seconds to forge a bond that would last a lifetime. "You lonely?" I asked.

He turned to look at me again, and I ran my tongue over my lips. I would've done anything to keep him from leaving me. I would've dropped to my knees and sucked him right there.

"You won't be sorry," I promised and moved forward to caress the bulge in his jeans. I had met Rick exactly the same way. My fingers were well trained.

"Okay," he said huskily, "but I can't stay up too late. We gotta move out early in the morning."

I wanted to shout with joy. I had won. He was mine. But I would have to be even more skillful to keep him. He was clearly ten times the man Rick had been.

As he unlocked the door, he said, "Sorry, I don't have anything to drink."

"That's okay. I've already had enough."

His room was nothing special, except for the various parts of his costume that lay scattered about. A pair of scissors and small sewing kit had been tossed on the bed. "Just shove that stuff out of the way and have a seat," he called as he headed for the bathroom.

Maggie was right about the contacts. I saw six pairs of disposables on the nightstand, but more of him was real than she had imagined. There was no fake hair to glue on his arms and legs. I took off most of my clothes, all but my bra and panties, and climbed onto his bed. He stepped out of the bathroom, naked, his cock already erect. "Sorry this has to be so quick," he said and shoved his swollen organ into my face.

I wanted him so badly. He was absolutely gorgeous. My body ached with sheer need. I wanted everything to be perfect, but as I stared down the shaft of his reddened penis I realized it wouldn't be. Sex only brought me heartache, lies, and deceit. I had made love, while Rick had sex. It was fake from beginning to end. They say that the heart is where truth resides, but mine had been wounded so many times I needed a new one. Perhaps that was all I needed . . . a new heart, then my life would be fixed. At the very least I would be good for several more one-sided affairs.

"What's the matter?" he asked, waiting expectantly as I had done in the bar.

"I can't," I said miserably, wanting him to take me in his arms and tell me how much he loved me, how nothing else mattered, but knowing he wouldn't.

"This is fucking great," he moaned and flopped back on the bed. "I thought you wanted to get laid." He waved his brawny arm toward the door. "Get out then. Go on. Hurry up." He turned his head in disgust.

I sobbed aloud as I thought of how much I could've loved him, if only he had let me. I'd waited so long.

I'd had so many plans. But I meant nothing to him. I meant nothing to anyone. Not even myself. I pulled on my jeans, wishing I could die, that God would strike me dead and save me the trouble of doing it myself. I shrugged on my blouse. I couldn't go back, not to my life, not the way it was, not after all I had learned tonight. I'd never be able to look at myself in the mirror.

I laughed brokenly as the red confetti crept in under the door like a thin tendril of fog, to comfort or condemn? I imagined I saw it weeping, tiny droplets beading up like tears and soaking into the carpet. Then it climbed the side of the table next to the bed, where I'd laid the scissors and the tiny sewing kit. I grasped the cool metal, thinking I'd plunge the blades into my heart and forever stop its useless hammering.

The red tendril wrapped itself about my hand, and I saw its pulse beat ever so lightly. This was my chance to be whole again. I turned quickly, raising my arm, clenching the scissors. He lay with one arm over his head, his face still turned away in disgust. I heard the roar of the crowd in the arena, empowering me: "Kill him! Kill him!" I aimed for his neck because it was the place where his virile body would be the most vulnerable, his Achilles' heel. I thought of Rick, of his lies and betrayals. Had he ever loved me at all?

It was like stabbing an orange, a moment of resistance, a pop of tough flesh, then victory. I was amazed at my own strength, at the surety of my actions despite all the alcohol. It was as though I were standing outside myself, watching. Did he scream? His mighty fists grabbed for my hair, then he made a soft choking sound and let go, clawing frantically at the blades protruding from his throat. He yanked the blades out, and a gurgling stream of blood leapt from the wound. I rubbed it over my face like a healing salve while his lips spewed a bubbly froth.

I found a pocketknife in his jeans. I had been hoping for something larger. I had to cut and tear, using whatever I could. I tried to imagine what he was like on nights when he became an animal and cruised the streets looking for something to kill. I finally located his heart, the one I needed to replace my own, beneath layers and layers of red confetti. To keep it from harm, I wrapped it tightly in a piece of cellophane I found on the floor beside a gift basket of fruit the hotel had given each of the wrestlers. This was my gift to myself. I cradled it in my hands, determined to take good care of this one.

Then I called Rick and told him I had something to show him.

Dawn Dunn: *"I loved writing this story. It is my favorite of my own stories to date. I like strong characters, and I like puzzles. To me, reality is a puzzle. It can look so different from different angles. The story began with its title and the mental image of a heart wrapped in cheap plastic, which grew throughout the story as a metaphor for masks and reality and seeking truth beneath the plastic wraps. The story flowed very naturally from there. I guess I was writing as most writers do about what I know or have observed. The biggest puzzle of all is why we behave the way we do. I'm still working on that one . . . and am fascinated by the experience."*

INVISIBLE

Jeff Gelb

Jeff Gelb is a lifelong fan of horror in comics, books, and films who turned his passion into a career with the publication in 1988 of his first horror novel, Specters. *That was followed by his editing of the ongoing* Hot Blood *books, plus* Shock Rock *and* Fear Itself. *He wrote last year's* Bettie Page Comics *for Dark Horse, which was authorized by Ms. Page herself. Gelb lives in California with his wife, son, two cats, and an enormous collection of comic books, hardboiled paperbacks, videos, and CDs, and often wonders why he doesn't have enough spare time to enjoy any of it.*

Avery Parker was invisible. Again.

He noticed it as he ogled the gorgeous teenage girl coming toward him on Rollerblades. He felt a familiar, erotic tingle in his groin as he stared at her openly, lasciviously. He could hardly help it: she was no more than nineteen, wearing cut-off shorts that showed the lower half of her perfect rump cheeks. Above, she wore a mini-T-shirt that barely covered the upper half of her perky, teenage breasts. A slight breeze would have revealed them, but Venice, California, was experiencing a Santa Ana condition, all heat and no wind, just heavy air that clung to sweaty bodies like a second skin. On her skin it looked especially good; her sweat made her skin glisten and sparkle like the nearby ocean. Parker swore he could see the outline not only of her nipples but of her areolas through her soaked T-shirt.

As she approached him, he smiled at her and sure enough, she looked right through him. Typical. He got that reaction more and more lately—ever since he'd turned forty, or so he'd pegged it. It just seemed that young girls didn't want to know from older men. They ignored them completely, rudely. As if they weren't even sharing the planet with men.

He'd even joked about it with one of his few male acquaintances—Parker had no real friends, feeling he had no use for them. "They say that life begins at forty," he'd commented to a fellow freelance writer, Syd Waterson, at a recent concert. "It's more like men become invisible at forty . . . at least to girls."

Waterson had countered, "Maybe you're just setting your sights too low, demographically. Get out of the diaper age and go for some women with dough. It sure beats working for a living!"

Parker had shrugged. It was true he was obsessed with younger women. Still, it was a rude surprise to have suddenly dropped off their radar screens just because he was now officially twice the age of the only girls he'd choose to fuck.

"Now, take me," Syd had said, pointing to himself. "I married Marianne for her money, not her looks. She's no Cindy Crawford, my Mary. More like Roseanne on a bad day, but with Roseanne's money. So imagine my surprise when I found out what a tigress she is in bed. The woman is outrageous. In fact . . ." Waterson had lifted his shirt off one shoulder and had showed Parker five fresh scratch marks. Parker winced. That had to hurt. He found himself wondering why Waterson would subject himself to such torture just to avoid working for a living.

"I tell you, she's the best I've ever had," Waterson had continued to brag. "You might say she's the fucking best at fucking!"

"She can't be better than a perfectly trim nineteen-year-old."

Waterson had just laughed. "Wouldn't you love to know."

Parker watched the teenager more closely as she skated straight toward him. It wasn't that she was distracted or was attempting consciously to avoid his obviously sexual leer; it was more like someone who actually didn't see anyone in front of her. At the last split second, he jumped out of her way, but still, they brushed shoulders. He watched, incredulous and pissed off, as she blinked, looking right through him, and kept skating, rubbing at her shoulder as if she thought she'd been hit by a rock or something.

Jesus, it was demoralizing. And maybe something more, he thought, breaking into a sweat that had nothing to do with the summer's brutal heat wave. This experience was the real reason he'd left his sweltering apartment in the Valley. Sure, he hoped it would be cooler at the beach. But actually he'd wanted to test his bizarre new theory, and the Venice boardwalk was the perfect place to do so. It offered him the opportunity to find young nubile girls. They were out en masse today, walking the boardwalk crowded with natives, tourists, skateboarders, bike riders, Rollerbladers, sun worshippers, merchants, and assorted freaks.

Talk about your freaks. Parker had become one virtually overnight. About six weeks ago, in fact, when he'd turned forty. There'd been no wife to throw a party for him, no girlfriend to send him gifts or cards. Not even someone to fuck. Truth to tell, though he hated to admit it even to himself, Parker was a complete washout with women—had been forever. New wardrobes, dance lessons, deodorants— nothing seemed to help. For decades he had pinned his hopes on women his age, but after years of distressing strikeouts, he'd bitterly sworn off mature women. Instead, he'd decided to set his sights lower, much lower, to an age when women might mistake his sullen behavior for self-confidence. It worked, occasionally, but only on women with very little experience with the opposite sex. And that meant young women.

Except that since turning forty, he'd become all but invisible to women—or girls—under twenty-one. On his birthday, he'd gone to a concert at one of the many faceless, smoke-drenched bars on Sunset, eyeballing the young braless girls who were watching a nondescript post-Seattle grunge band with rapt attention, as if they'd never heard of Nirvana or Pearl Jam. Parker was ignoring the faceless band and instead admiring the way the young fans' little—and sometimes not so little—boobs jiggled when they danced to the tuneless tunes. Their movements brought him to an aching erection. Finally he'd decided to try and get some action. He'd danced up to one of the prettier young girls and introduced himself. She'd ignored him totally, her attention focused entirely, Parker could tell, on the crotch of the young lead singer.

What the fuck, Parker had thought as he'd retreated to the back wall of the noisy room. *I'm too old for her, I guess.*

He'd shrugged his shoulders; girls like the one who'd ignored him were like fleas on a dog at this club. He would just keep trying till one said yes to his offer to go outside and get stoned. It was lousy pot but these youngsters hadn't smoked enough yet to know the difference. Truth was, they got stoned and he didn't, which kept him erect and in control as he fucked them back at his North Hollywood studio apartment.

Only that night he was having no luck at all. In fact, none of the half-dozen girls he'd attempted to coerce into conversation had so much as asked him to get out of their line of sight to the band. It was downright rude and even fucking weird, he thought, as he'd gone home and ended up masturbating. *Some birthday celebration.*

What was it about young girls he found so appealing? he wondered for the umpteenth time as he found a seat at the bookstore and restaurant that fronted the highest-trafficked part of the Venice boardwalk. He didn't want to admit to his own inadequacies. He preferred to think of their qualities. It certainly wasn't their minds, he thought, that got him hot. Hell, they could barely finish their sentences. It was their bodies, which were perfect in a way no older woman's body could be.

It was also in their posture, their gait when they walked, in their bearing as they thrusted out those breasts, strutting their stellar stuff on long, lean, perfectly tanned and waxed legs. *They are perfect and they fucking well know it.*

The sex wasn't perfect; they were too young to know exactly what gets a guy off. But it sure beat no sex at all. Now, however, things had come full circle: Parker wasn't getting any—even the young ones were ignoring him completely. And he had a strange feeling he knew why.

He ate flavorless carrot cake disconsolately, searching in vain for his waitress to bring him his check. He spotted a young waitress who had obviously taken over that area from the other waitress, and so he waved at her to get her attention. But the pretty waitress ignored him. *She's doing it too,* he thought. *On purpose. Ignoring me as if I was the man who wasn't there. Invisible.*

Well, fuck this, he thought as he rose. He left the bill on the table, unpaid, and actually bumped into the young waitress on his way out, in a last-ditch attempt to get her to acknowledge him. But she just gasped, dropped her tray of food, and bent down to pick up the pieces, without even glancing up or cursing him. He left the restaurant in a hurry and started walking back to his car.

What the fuck? Was this all he had to look forward to? Being invisible to the only segment of the female population he cared about? He stared at the nearby ocean and felt like walking into it until he drowned, when his focus shifted and he saw an absolutely stunning young woman laying on the beach about thirty feet away, facedown, on her stomach, bikini top removed as she allowed her back to tan. He grunted, took off his sneakers, and padded through the hot sand till he was actually creating a shadow over her back. Surely she would at least look up and ask him to move. Maybe she'd notice the bulge in his crotch and take a hint. Take matters in hand. He could hope.

He stood there for a full minute, finally clearing his throat. She didn't even move. Maybe she was sleeping? He bent over, stared into her sunglasses and saw her vacant eyes, and felt icicles crawl up his spine. It was just like the other pretty women: she was staring right through him. He bent to one knee and waved his hand in front of her face. Still no response. Finally she arched her back and turned over, adjusting her bikini top, but not before Parker got a perfect glimpse of her milky white breasts and luscious brown nipples.

He expelled hot breath in her face. She was gorgeous, all right, not a day over twenty and not even aware that he was no more than one foot away from her perfect body.

Parker was struck by a thought. *If she really can't see me at all*—he couldn't believe he was even allowing himself to think this—*can she feel me?* He reached out a tentative finger and nudged her shoulder. She blinked but refused to acknowledge him in any other way. Frowning, he poked at her breast through the thin fabric of the tiny bikini top. Still no response! Finally he felt for her nipple through the material and pinched it hard with his thumb and forefinger.

"Ouch!" She stared down at her breast as if it had pinched itself, still ignoring Parker totally. As if he were totally invisible. *Very interesting*.

He could barely believe what was happening here. He didn't know whether to jump for joy or run down the beach screaming, scared to death he'd finally gone insane after years of female neglect.

"Hey asshole, what do you think you're doing?"

Parker blinked, not even sure the voice he'd heard was real. He looked up and saw some surf-soaked, washboard-stomached dick with a boogieboard approaching from the shoreline.

"Get the fuck away from my girl," the guy ordered as he picked up his pace.

Parker got the message. He ran down the beach till he lost himself in the crowds at the water's edge. When he was certain the surfer had lost him, he slowed his pace, walking at the water's edge, considering what had just happened. If in fact he was literally invisible to the girl, he certainly wasn't to her lame-brain boyfriend. He'd have to keep that in mind as he began to gather his thoughts about his newfound gift—for that was how he was starting to think of it.

The next day he dropped off some CD reviews with the receptionist at *Punk!* magazine. Usually he faxed or E-mailed them, but he needed to test his theory further. He approached the receptionist, who was no more than nineteen, but already overweight, with pins through her lip, nose, and one eyelid. She was ugly, a total turnoff to Parker.

"Parker!" she greeted him with a grin. "What's up? You never come in!"

He smiled—she could see him. It was a most valuable piece of information. He shrugged. "In the neighborhood—thought I'd save a phone bill." He handed her a manila envelope. "Give these to Lonn, okay? They're for the next issue."

"Sure thing." She held out her hand and brushed it against his. He had to bite his lip to keep from wincing. It was obvious she was interested in him, but she had zero sexual appeal to him.

Parker walked out of the building and headed for his car, thinking about the receptionist. *I'm only invisible to the ones I respond to sexually.*

As he drove back to his apartment, he mentally played with some *X-Files*-type explanations. Maybe the L.A. smog had created some weird new hormone that kicked in whenever his dick woke up? Or mutant pheromones in his bloodstream from all the masturbating he'd done over the years? Twisted testosterone from years of smoke-and-drug-filled clubs, where he'd mixed every cocktail and drug known to man and a few he'd invented himself along the way?

Maybe he should see a doctor? He shook his head. No, not yet. Because, at least for the moment, this could be . . . fun.

Around dinnertime that night, Parker walked into his neighborhood health club and headed for the women's locker room. He knew this was the time of day the club was least used, but he still had to be careful. He made certain no men saw him as he slid through the women's locker room door and peeked inside. No one was in sight. He'd assumed it was laid out in a mirror image of the men's locker room, and he was not disappointed. The lockers were spread out in four rows, with showers and bathrooms behind them. He hid behind one empty row of lockers till he heard young female voices, and he snuck a glance. Sure enough, they were young and gorgeous—hell, every female was young and gorgeous at his health club; it was the reason he'd joined the fucking thing in the first place. He'd never seen so many already perfect female specimens spending so much time, money, and energy to maintain their perfection.

He felt his dick rise in his shorts involuntarily as he observed two girls, no more than twenty, both topless but somehow ignoring each other's beauty as they chatted away mindlessly. They both took off their skimpy panties and Parker almost creamed in his shorts as he noted that both were shaved bare, their pubic mounds proudly bulging. Parker looked around. No one else was in the locker room. His luck was holding.

He threw caution to the wind and approached one of the girls. His heart in his throat, Parker was terrified she would start screaming any second. Instead, she continued chatting to her friend as the two girls walked into the shower. They stood next to each other as they turned on the showers and started soaping themselves.

Parker stripped and started tugging at his dick as he watched the two beautiful girls bending over, their long lean legs showing perfect calves as they soaped their waxed legs. Then, one started soaping the other's back, as the willing partner trembled and sighed. She turned to face her cute friend and, after looking around to see if the shower room was truly empty, she started kissing the girl passionately. Soon the two were fingering each other's vaginas and grabbing breast flesh. Parker allowed himself to get wet by standing next to the girls, actually fondling their flesh whenever one's eyes were closed in passion. Neither girl had any idea that there was an occasional extra pair of hands pulling their nipples or inserting a finger in their anuses. When he felt one of them shudder from a sudden orgasm, it was the last straw. Parker exploded in the throes of as powerful an orgasm as he'd ever experienced, and even though he was certain he'd screamed aloud, neither girl heard him.

As they toweled off, he did the same, standing no more than four feet from them. Incredibly, even the towel he'd picked up from a nearby rack seemed invisible now that it was in his hands. He couldn't begin to figure out the twisted science involved in what had become of him, nor did he care any longer. As long as he could have sexual experiences like this, he didn't care if he was invisible for the rest of his life!

The next few weeks were a blur to Parker as he lived out all of his voyeuristic sexual fantasies, unknown to the women on whom he spied. He had to get creative sometimes, especially when he was watching guys fuck their girlfriends. But it was a cinch to break into girls' apartments when they came home from work— he simply walked in the door behind them. And there was always someplace he could hide where he'd be hidden from the guys' vision.

There was one problem, though: Parker had spent so much time playing out his sexual fantasies, he'd stopped working. So when his landlord came around threatening to evict him, Parker realized he had to get back to work—or at least get some money.

He called *Punk!* and arranged to review Chowderheads that night. When he ran into Syd Waterson in line for a beer, Parker had a sudden inspiration. As usual, Waterson was bragging about his rich if ugly wife and her prowess in bed. Parker decided to see whether Waterson was full of shit while stealing something from Waterson's house that could later be hocked for cash. Parker wasn't above casual theft; he'd broken into homes before when he couldn't cover rent checks. He hadn't been caught yet and it was a cinch he wouldn't be caught now.

"Your wife," Parker prodded. "How come she never comes with you to these concerts?"

Waterson shook his head. "She hates rock music. She'd rather spend her time at a stuffy play—right now, in fact, she's at some Noël Coward revival in Westwood. Bo-ring."

Parker nodded and excused himself, heading toward the bar. Halfway there, he changed direction and, certain Waterson couldn't see him, left the club.

He drove his complaining '86 Chevette up Laurel Canyon to a dark side street where Waterson and his wife lived in a cozy seventeen-room mansion overlooking the entire San Fernando Valley. Parker left his car parked farther up the street, doubled back, and hid in the generous shrubbery surrounding Waterson's house.

He waited patiently, and within an hour was rewarded by an unfamiliar car heading into the driveway. It had to be Waterson's butt-ugly wife. Parker watched as she left her car in the driveway and walked up to the house. She was so close to him now that he could smell her perfume, and would get his first glimpse of the infamous ugly wife.

Except that she was fucking gorgeous! Stunned, Parker took her in: about five-six, long blond hair, upturned nose, generous lips, enough of a bosom to make him wonder whether she'd already had enhancement surgery. Most surprisingly, she was young—certainly no more than twenty-five and perhaps as young as twenty-one. A multimillion-dollar heiress and she was young and gorgeous! No wonder Waterson kept her hidden to himself: he'd scored the home run of the century in nailing a young, beautiful heiress. The lucky fucking bastard.

Parker couldn't believe his own good luck: she was so gorgeous that, as she slid her key into her front-door lock, he knew he could stand up and walk right behind her. Sure enough, she was oblivious to his presence. He walked into the dark house and looked around as she relocked the door and turned on the lights.

The house was full of shit that looked valuable. As soon as she hit the sack, Parker figured he would grab a bunch of stuff in a pillowcase and get out of the house long before Waterson returned.

Marianne walked upstairs and began to take off her clothes as she approached the end of a long hallway, leaving a trail of clothing strewn along the rich carpeting. Parker grinned lasciviously as he took her in. No wonder she was such a great fuck, he thought—she was perfect! As she stood in the bath-room buck naked, brushing her teeth, Parker stood directly behind her, smelling her shampooed hair. *Even in the fucking mirror, I'm invisible to her!* It sent supernatural chills racing up his spine.

He looked at his watch—Waterson wouldn't be home for hours. Plenty of time for Parker to sample some of the little wife's carnal candy. Waterson might have been lying about his wife's looks, but Parker doubted he was lying about her prowess in bed—how could she be anything but fantastic, with that youthful body and face?

Soon she was slipping her gorgeous nude body under the silk sheets, sighing. Was she tired or horny?

Parker wondered as he stood just to her side. He watched her beautiful blue eyes close and noted the soft rise and fall of the sheets changing rhythm as her breathing slowed. In less than ten minutes she was fast asleep.

The room was nearly pitch black already, but Parker took no chances. He shut the drapes that had allowed what little breeze that existed to enter into the room, creating total darkness. Then he disrobed and slipped into bed behind the woman's sleeping form. She moaned and stirred, then fell back asleep. Grinning, Parker spooned his naked body into hers, his erection instantly growing as he felt the soft curve of her ass against his dick. He felt her twitch and awaken.

"Syd?" she asked dreamily.

Parker knew she wouldn't hear him if he did speak, so he allowed his actions to speak for him as he reached a hand over her and squeezed a perfect breast. It was heavenly!

She sighed and grabbed his hand in the darkness, holding it to her breast. "Yes," she whispered. "Pinch my nipple."

Parker couldn't believe his luck—in the darkness, she was falling for his Waterson pantomime! He guided his dick toward her pussy from the back and felt its glistening juices as he slipped inside her creamy warmth.

Just then, he heard a door open elsewhere in the house—Waterson had, for some reason, returned early!

Parker pulled out so quickly that Marianne gasped. Parker jumped out of bed and tripped on something on the floor—a high-heeled shoe?—falling heavily.

He struggled to his feet as a light switch was flicked on at the bedroom door. Waterson stood framed in light, a gun in his hand, pointed at Parker's chest. Marianne stared at her husband blankly for a moment and then at the opposite side of the bed she'd just vacated, obviously still oblivious to Parker's presence. "Who . . . what?" She stammered, staring unbelievingly at her husband, still fully dressed, across the room. Then she started screaming.

Waterson's mouth moved up and down like a marionette's until he found his voice. "Jesus! I don't believe it! You and Parker!" He turned to his still-screaming wife and shot her between the eyes. Her voice stopped midscream and she fell against Parker, who was forced to the floor by her weight. Parker pushed against her bloody body to dislodge her so he could get away.

Waterson aimed and fired again. This time the bullet went through his dead wife's back and into Parker's chest. He screamed in pain and saw his blood comingling with hers on the carpet. Not very safe in this day and age, he thought absently as he heard Waterson mumbling.

Waterson started laughing, and then crying, as he sat on the edge of the bed.

"Tell you a secret, Parker," Waterson said. "She wouldn't fuck me. At first it felt just like you said: like I was invisible to her. But then I figured out she hadda be fucking around on me. I knew if I came home early often enough, I'd find her with him. But I never guessed it would be you, Parker. Of all people."

Waterson shook his head, tears streaming from his eyes. He muttered, "Women—they'll be the death of me yet."

He heard police sirens approaching and hung his head in passive acceptance of his fate. Nudging the dying man's twitching body with the gun barrel, he asked, "How'd you do it, Parker? How'd you get her to choose you over me, you schmuck? What did she see in you, Parker, that she couldn't see in me?"

Jeff Gelb: *"What guy can't relate to the eroticism inherent in being invisible for a day? And any guy over forty should be able to relate to feeling invisible when he walks by a much younger woman. I just took things to the next horrific level."*

OLIVIA IN THE GRAVEYARD WITH PABLO

Greg Kihn

After a series of hit records in the 1980s, including "The Breakup Song" and "Jeopardy," rock musician Kihn turned to his love of horror fiction and decided to pursue his lifelong dream to become a novelist. His first novel, Horror Show, *was nominated for a Stoker Award. His second novel,* Shade of Pale, *appeared in 1997. He is currently working on the sequel to* Horror Show, *entitled* Big Rock Beat.

Osmosis: The passage of liquid through a semipermeable membrane.

I love horror writers' conventions. You meet the weirdest people, and being a novelist I specialize in weird people.

I met Olivia at the front desk of the Algonquin Hotel. I waited to check in, while she complained to the clerk that someone had stolen her makeup case from the lobby.

I couldn't help but notice.

She was dressed like Vampira, in a slinky black dress, slit down the front to reveal several breathtaking inches of milky white cleavage. She had that ultra-pale, black-haired, black-nail-polish, black-every-thing, creature-features look that I've always loved. Maila Nurmi would have been proud.

And she was pretty too, I think, though it was hard to see through the unbelievable *Cleopatra Meets the Bride of Frankenstein* eye makeup she wore.

She did have a great body; that much you couldn't help but notice.

Her dress hugged and flirted and I think it was distracting the desk clerk. He nervously kept his eyes down. I assumed she was in costume, somehow connected with the horror convention.

She spoke in low, Marlene Dietrich tones, like Nico lamenting her song, a song of lost luggage and endless torment, to the throbbing of the Velvet Underground.

"It was there. It was right there, for God's sake, didn't you see it?"

"I'm sorry, miss. I didn't see anything. Are you a registered guest at the hotel?" He was short, with graying, slicked-back hair and a pencil-thin mustache. I thought he looked almost too appropriate, like someone from central casting hired for the day to play a faceless "desk clerk" with orders to be as disagreeable and fey as possible.

"Well . . . no . . . I mean, I was, until this morning. I had a room here last night."

The clerk snorted politely. "Name?"

"Olivia Vickers."

"You want to book a new room?"

"No, not tonight . . . I've . . . made other arrangements. But forget about the room. Somebody stole my makeup case."

"Was it stolen from your room?"

"No, from the lobby, right over there. My theatrical makeup case, an old black thing about this big—" She held up her hands about two feet apart. I caught a glimpse of a thin, pale wrist and long, black fingernails. "It looks like an old-time suitcase. I left it right there with my other stuff. Somebody stole it."

The clerk pursed his lips and moved like an automaton. He had the kind of voice that carries bad news effortlessly, smooth and listless. "I didn't see anyone, but this is the lobby, and people come and go all the time. We recommend that guests check their luggage with the porter while not in their rooms."

Olivia wrung her hands. I couldn't help but stare. I was standing a few feet away, waiting for my turn with Robby the Robot.

"Don't look at me, I'm just checking in," I said when, for some reason, they both looked at me.

The desk clerk turned back to Olivia. "Hold on just a minute and I'll have the house detective come down to talk to you. In the meantime, let me check this gentleman in and get him taken care of. Why don't you stand off to the side?"

"Excuse me," I said to Olivia, "I'll just be a minute." Her face showed her displeasure, even through the thick makeup.

I whipped out my credit card and started filling out the registration form, while Olivia stalked away on shapely legs in a swirl of black lace. As she turned, I could see through the lace of her shawl, to the lithe expanse of her lower back.

Her walk was deadly.

"Wow!" I muttered.

The desk clerk looked up. "We get some good ones

here, don't we? She's pretty bizarre, but probably harmless. She's been around since Thursday."

"Is she with the horror writers' convention?" I asked.

"God, I hope so."

I checked in without a problem and, after stopping off to drop my stuff in the room, I headed for the bar to scout out for some friends, fellow horror writers I always see at these events.

Olivia was there, and she approached me straightaway.

"I saw you checking in. Are you an author?"

"Yeah, I am. I'm Kyle Gordon."

"Hey, I've read your stuff! Loved it. Good vampires."

"I think I'm vampired out. I'm giving the bloodsuckers a rest for a while. I'm working on something different now."

She pouted. "Don't. There are always more vampires."

"Who *are* you?"

Olivia smoothed her raven tresses and batted her impossibly long eyelashes. Tallulah Bankhead on Mars. The bartender watched, I watched, two other guys at the end of the bar watched. Olivia was holding court. She crossed her legs on the bar stool (no easy feat) and straightened.

"I'm Olivia," she said dramatically.

I smiled. "What the fuck are you doing, Olivia?"

"I'm just . . . You know. I'm just networking."

"Are you a writer?"

"Yes, I write poetry. And songs. Gothic rock songs. I gotta group called the Haunted, we're puttin' out a new CD soon. I wrote all the songs based on famous vampires. It's somewhat heavy-metal-ish, but with real monolithic keyboards. The melodies are sadcore."

Somehow, through all this, I'd indicated to the bartender by pointing to the tap then to a glass that I wanted a draft beer. He delivered it, icy and fresh. I sipped, and absorbed the unbroken chain of words that streamed from Olivia's mysterious red lips.

"I love the sound of dense grunge guitar with dissonant keyboards. It creates a drone, like a heavy-metal dirge. We go for the frequencies that really hurt. It's performance art."

"Sounds charming," I said.

Olivia was a piece of work, and quite the self-promoter. She had the rapt attention of nearly everyone on my side of the bar. I sipped my beer and waited to see what would happen next.

"You wanna see some of my poems?" she asked.

"Uhh . . . Here? Now?"

"Yeah, I'll wait while you read 'em."

I looked around. The bartender looked away. I was on my own now. "Okay, I guess so, but just one, okay? I really don't feel I can absorb anything right now."

She fumbled through her handbag, produced a sheaf of typewritten pages, and thrust them at me.

"Hold on, this is too many. I can't read all these. Look, I tell you what—I'll read 'em later, in my room, when I can concentrate. Is that all right?"

Olivia pouted. "Read just one or two. They're short."

"Okay," I sighed. My eyes scanned the first poem casually, and I could tell immediately that it was not very good. In fact it was bad, *Ed Wood* bad. The subject matter was all vampires. Every line praised the undead, a sophomoric litany of blood and sex, sex and blood.

Olivia, it seemed, was obsessed.

"Are all of these about vampires?"

"Yeah, I'm an expert. I've read every word ever written about them, seen every movie. In fact, I'm planning on becoming a vampire myself very soon."

I rolled my eyes and said, "Yeah, right."

"There *are* real vampires. They actually exist. I know it, I've met one."

I scoffed, smiling. "I can't believe that."

"I don't care if you believe it or not, it happened. In fact, he offered me immortality . . . and I said yes." She looked smug. "He's the real thing, I know that for a fact."

I shook my head, disappointed that this interesting creature was slightly off her rocker. What a shame.

She must have sensed this, because she immediately started to explain herself. "I know you must think I'm crazy, but I'm not. Really, I'm not. It's just that I happen to believe in vampires. There are lots of people who believe in 'em. You should know, you write about 'em."

"Purely fiction, I assure you."

"Nevertheless, there are people out there who *think* they're vampires, and other people who *want* to be vampires, and a whole lot of people who just want to *hang out* with vampires, to be that close to the evil. Ahh, and then there are the few *real vampires* out there, too.

"It's a whole subculture. They even have their own nightclubs. The whole vampire thing is happening everywhere."

"You've read all the literature, I assume."

"Of course, from Anne Rice to Bram Stoker, and everything in between. My band does a complete tribute to *Nosferatu* that's really intense."

I looked at Olivia. I had mixed feelings now. Yes, she was beautiful and provocative in a ghoulish way, but I was beginning to wonder about the overall stability of her mental condition. Still, my friends hadn't shown up, and I didn't have a thing to do until the morning, so I pressed on.

"You're interesting, but a little weird, you know?" I joked.

Olivia laughed. It was a full-throated, sexy rumble that sounded like the soul of rock and roll. "You think I'm weird? That's great!"

"Glad you think so."

We had a few drinks together and I found out that Olivia was here to try to find a publisher for her poetry, and also to publicize her rock band. They were playing at a club nearby and anyone from the convention was welcome to come. She promised real vampires. "At least two, Darius and Edward, and if we're lucky, Pablo."

"Pablo's the main dude?" I was going along with her now.

She nodded gravely. "He's a very powerful vampire who's been in these parts for a long time. He likes me, likes my band, says rock and roll makes him feel like a young man again. He might even invest some money."

"And you want him to turn you into a vampire?"

"Don't laugh." Her voice dropped to a whisper. "I want to live forever. Pablo said he'd do it, turn me into *one of them*. He says I amuse him, that I'd be an interesting companion. They don't have any female vampires. Weird, huh?"

I smirked. Olivia was getting too far out for me, and I sensed it was time to bail. "Well, I've gotta go find my friends."

"Hey, wait a minute. Could I ask you a favor?"

I didn't know what to say, so I coughed.

"Could I change my clothes in your room?"

I frowned. "Is that a safe thing to do?"

"For you or for me?" She laughed soft and low. "Yeah, I guess I trust you, you look like a nice guy. All I want to do is freshen up and change my clothes. I had a room here last night, but I'm out of money. I'll find a place to sleep later but first I need to change and stash my clothes. Look, I know you think I'm a nutcase, but give me a chance. I just want to freshen up. I've got a gig tonight. You wanna come?"

"Oh, I can't," I said.

"You don't want to see my band?"

"No, it's not that, it's just that I've only just arrived at the convention and I'm too busy right now. I've gotta meet my agent."

"Don't you like me?"

It was such an odd question and so direct that I couldn't come up with an answer right away. I looked at her again, trying to decide.

"Well, yeah, I mean . . . You're very attractive and sexy and . . ." I was stammering, making no sense now. Actually blushing, I think.

She looked into my eyes. "Would you want to fuck me?"

"What?" I was flabbergasted.

189

"If I let you, would you want to fuck me?"

"Jeez . . . I don't know."

"You don't know?"

I sighed audibly. "I don't know what to say. That's a weird question to ask somebody."

"It's just a simple yes-or-no question. Given the chance, would you or would you not want to fuck me?"

"Well . . . Yeah, I guess I would."

Olivia smiled. "All right, then. I just wanted to establish that. It's a power thing, you know. Vampires exude power. Now that I know you want to fuck me, I can control you."

I threw up my hands. "Jesus Christ, you're too much! On second thought, I'm not sure I should let you into my room, because you're starting to scare me. I mean, one minute I'm talking to you and the next minute I have to make a major sexual decision."

"I'm just fooling around with you, don't be so touchy."

I couldn't tell if she was or wasn't. The whole conversation seemed so bizarre.

She looked away and I studied her remarkable profile. Like smoke, her voice lingered. "Imagine what it must be like to be a real vampire."

"I think it would be hell," I said. "To live forever, no rest, a virtual death machine feasting on the bodies and souls of others, sucking the very life's blood out of people. Think about it. I don't see anything glamorous about it at all. It's leechlike. Besides, how lonely would you get after centuries without love?"

"Vampires can love," she said.

"Bullshit. They kill the ones they love."

"Well, I'm not a vampire . . . yet. I just want to use your room to freshen up and change. Twenty minutes, tops, okay? I won't do anything weird."

"You're scary, you know that? I'm not sure if this is such a good idea."

But I took her anyway. I was a bit apprehensive, but this interlude was so deliciously strange, and there was something so special about her. I was intrigued enough to take a tiny chance and let her into my room to change.

I *did not* intend to fuck her, though.

She spent an hour in the bathroom. I had no idea what she was doing in there, but she seemed quiet. At last she emerged, a vision in black lingerie. She adjusted the seams of her stockings and looked at me.

I gaped at her. She stood before me wearing a black leather corset, with matching gloves, black-seamed stockings with garters, and thigh-high patent-leather bondage boots. Her spiked heels drilled the rug.

"You can't fuck me," she said. "No touching."

Once again, I was astonished by her behavior. I stammered something about not wanting to fuck her, but it was a shamefaced lie, and for the first time I experienced Olivia's peculiar power. It was just as she described it—because I wanted to fuck her, she had me in her sway completely.

I was ready to grovel, a willing victim of her vampiric sexuality. And yet, as I felt the pangs of frustration, I came to realize her exquisite sense of irony. She was playing me—not the other way around, as I originally intended. Now she stood before me, the queen of denial.

The corset pinched her waist and accentuated her breasts. Her sullen pallor contrasted dramatically with the black leather. Likewise, the alabaster of her thighs was breathtaking against the sheer black nylon of her stocking tops.

"You're not saying anything," she said.

"I'm speechless. What the hell can I say?"

Olivia shifted her weight from one perfect leg to the other. "Well, you could beg to fuck me."

I felt the primal urging of a sudden, unstoppable erection. It seemed the more she denied me, even though I'd decided earlier not to have sex with her, the more I became aroused. Now I was reduced to a slavering idiot.

"I could beg . . . Hey, wait a second, are you kidding me?"

"I might be. Don't you like it?"

"Like what? Being teased?"

"No. My costume."

"Oh, that. Yeah, it's kinda . . ." Then it dawned on me: that's what this was all about. "Are you gonna wear that onstage?"

"Yeah. What do you think?"

I exhaled with relief. "Jesus Christ, I think you're definitely boner material."

"Do I look fat in this?" she asked incredibly.

She turned around, modeled the outfit for me, bent over, the whole nine yards. I was sportin' a major woody.

"No!" I shouted, beyond enthusiastic. "You look really good! Great!"

"I bet you'd like to fuck me," she purred.

"Why do you keep saying that? You know I do. I want to fuck your brains out. This is torture."

"I knew it! I just knew it." She smiled, making smoldering eye contact with me.

"Why are you doing this?" I asked. "It's gettin' kinda hard to take."

"Because I'm Olivia, she who must be obeyed."

"Oh . . ."

"You have a boner?"

"Yes," I whispered. "For God's sake, can't you tell?"

"You can't fuck me."

I howled. "How can you be so cruel? You gave me this huge boner, now the little head is thinkin' for the big head. Please, please let me fuck you."

"No. You're not worthy, I'm saving myself for Pablo."

"Pablo, the fuckin' vampire?"

"Yes . . ." she hissed.

"You're crazy. If there are such things as vampires, which I don't really believe myself, then what you're saying is that you want to become some kind of soulless living corpse, forever. And if they don't exist, which is my belief, then you're turning that voluptuous body over to God knows what kind of blood-thirsty sexual pervert. A masochist, no doubt, with vampire delusions. I can only imagine what he considers a good time. Either way, you're fucked."

Olivia smiled seductively. "You're talkin' yourself out of a fine erection, hotshot. Let's focus on me, okay? You like my tits?"

"Yeah," I stammered, "they're excellent." I realized she was scrambling for the higher ground, but I was powerless. "They look real good in that corset," I heard myself say, like a moron. "It pushes them together nice."

I started to hate myself. Olivia was hard to take, and I needed a break.

She cupped her hands beneath her breasts and fondled. "Good, I'm glad you noticed. But you'd still fuck me in second, wouldn't you?"

"Oh God, yes. I'd fuck you in a nanosecond. But . . . it's painful to be teased like this, Olivia. Really, it is."

"Yes, I know, and I must say, I'm enjoying it. But I do feel sorry for you. Here's what I'll do—" She put her gloved hand between her legs and pouted. "Hmm. I know. I'll let you masturbate on me."

"I beg your pardon?"

"I'll pose for you, and you whack off."

I was flabbergasted, but somehow it made sense. "Okay," I said, in a trance, already undoing my pants.

She began to writhe, encouraging me to play with myself, which I did, hesitantly at first, then with more enthusiasm.

She bent over and wiggled her buttocks in my face, turned around, pinched her breasts, teased me with her eyes. It was the most exquisite torture I could have ever imagined, and I quickly neared climax.

At that moment, Olivia owned me. She had me lapping at her booted feet like a dog. I moaned and crouched, slobbering and jerking—I must have looked pathetic.

At last I came, squirting my jism across the room, unmindful of where it landed. The release was deliciously primal, as I climaxed in a series of strong spurts. Then I sat back and grunted.

"Did that feel good?" she asked.

"God, yes. But . . . it was pretty weird. I don't know what to say. Did you enjoy it?"

"Yeah, I get off getting you off, pleasuring you, exercising control over you. What time is it?"

"It's nearly eight o'clock."

"I gotta go, my band is on at ten. All my vampire friends are coming. Then, at midnight, they're taking me to see Pablo."

"Where does this Pablo live?"

"In the graveyard, naturally. Tonight I'm going over to the other side. I'm so excited."

"You don't think this guy is a real vampire, do you?"

She stared out the window, then turned back to me, her exotic face as serious as death. "Yes, I think he's the real thing."

"This is insane. You could be putting yourself in real jeopardy. These people sound pretty freaky to me. If I were you, I'd stay away from them."

"But they're going to invest in the band. Pablo's got the money, and if he likes me . . ."

"What? He'll suck your blood?"

Olivia turned icy. "It's my life. If I want to become an immortal and be a big rock star, it's my decision."

"There are no such things as vampires, you know that, don't you?"

"The strength of the vampire is that people will not believe in him," she said dramatically.

I recognized the quote. "Van Helsing said that, in *Dracula.*"

"I'm leaving now. If I need a place to sleep later, can I come here?"

"Yeah, come back and tell me what happened. But don't bring any vampires with you, I'm having tons of garlic with dinner and I have a cross tattooed on my chest."

Olivia slipped into a long, black leather trench coat that completely covered her brazen stagewear. She handed me a paper flyer that advertised her gig. "Be there at ten o'clock," she said, commanding me. "Don't be late."

"Okay," I heard myself answer timidly.

She strode to the door, and without another word departed. I was left to contemplate the most bizarre episode of my life. I felt a mix of strong emotions, from shame to guilt to fear to lust. I tried to sort them out with a brain hopelessly overloaded with stimulus.

I never actually touched her, never had any physical contact whatsoever, yet I had revealed my most base and uncontrolled animal aspects to her. How did I really feel about her?

She was the most outrageous, brazen woman I'd ever met. She was overwhelming. I could definitely see her fronting a rock band—a female Jim Morrison, strutting around in a leather corset.

I entered the tiny, dark rock club alone, wearing jeans, a black T-shirt, and my leather motorcycle jacket. I didn't feel too terribly out of place at first, until I noticed the crowd.

They were dressed exclusively in black, and sported bizarre Alice Cooper–style makeup on their pale, vacuous faces. There were one hundred people in a room that probably held seventy-five.

I elbowed my way to the bar and ordered a beer.

The band came on amid a smattering of applause. They banged into their first song without introduction. The sound was deafening, and the level of play was primitive and brutal. It was part heavy metal, part punk, part droning Velvet Underground, and all noise.

Once my ears adjusted I could make out the lyrics. They were sung in a chant, ugly and moblike, by all the people in the club, led by the scantily clad Olivia. The passion with which they sang—no, shouted—was scary, and I realized suddenly that I was the only one in the room not singing.

> *We won't stop until*
> *We won't stop until*
> *We won't stop until*
> *Everybody's dead*

Then Olivia shouted the bridge: "Everybody's dead!"

And the crowd answered, "Everybody's dead!" The call and response was powerful and it swept the entire room.

Olivia chanted the last line of the song, "We won't stop until—" And the band stopped abruptly, amid the buzz of amplifiers suddenly mute. There was a pause, a great sucking of air, as if the entire club had taken a breath, and then they all shouted, "Everybody's dead!"

The next song was Black Sabbath's "Paranoid" and I thought Olivia did a decent job singing it, although the band seemed to lag. They weren't very good musically, but their stage appearance was striking. Led by the outrageous Olivia, the other guys were decked out as various famous vampires, monsters, and mass murderers. The bass player was Jack the Ripper, with a top hat and Edwardian jacket. His face was made up to resemble Lon Chaney's in *London After Midnight*. The drummer seemed to be a shaven-headed Nosferatu, complete with pointy ears and fangs. The guitarist was the mummy, his bandages semi-stripped-off and hanging in dirty ribbons that swayed as he moved. His torso showed through the loose strips of cloth, fish-belly white.

They played for fifty minutes, then departed the stage to strangely muted response. Based upon the incredible call and response she got from the people during the songs, and the fact that they seemed to know all the band's original material, it seemed odd that they didn't clap more enthusiastically. There was no encore.

I made my way to the stage door and found Olivia talking to a group of three heavily made-up, rather bizarre-looking people.

"These are my friends," she said. "This is—"

"Names are not important," the one with the pierced cheek said. "We don't really go by names."

"What do you go by?" I asked.

"Scent."

I said nothing, what could I say? These people were off-the-scale strange and I felt uncomfortable around them. Olivia, on the other hand, clearly coveted their attention.

"Olivia, darling, don't you think it's time we left? Don't want to keep the master waiting, now do we?" said one of them.

She turned to me. In her eyes I saw a flash of excitement and a twinge of fear. I thought of Natalie Wood in *Rebel Without a Cause,* and the way she looked up at James Dean while Buzz slashed his tires. Olivia had the same look in her eye.

"This is it. I've gotta go," she said.

"Are you gonna be all right?"

"She'll be fine," said one of her diabolical escorts.

They left together, flowing out into the night like liquid shadows. I got a very bad feeling.

I awakened at four in the morning to a persistent knock on my hotel room door.

When I looked through the eyehole I saw Olivia. For a moment I didn't know what to do and I considered going back to bed, but she knocked again.

I opened the door and gaped at her. She was in tatters. I pulled her into the room quickly.

"Are you okay? You look like you got raped."

"I did, but it's all right."

"You got raped? Jesus . . . what should we do?"

"Nothing, I let them. I enjoyed it."

I stared at her. "What the fuck are you saying?"

Olivia's voice was strange. "It doesn't matter, nothing matters."

Her lingerie was torn and there was dirt all over her back and knees.

Then I looked closer and saw something that really shocked me. At first I thought it was dirt, but upon closer examination I saw that it was some type of skin abrasion, like a bruise. There were others. She was covered with them. Each one was roughly the size of a golfball, purple and black.

"Look at these," she said, and peeled the last of her outfit away. The bruises covered her stomach and breasts and continued down her legs. Her neck was nearly black.

"What the fuck are they?"

"They're passion marks, you know, like hickeys?"

"Jesus, they're a little severe for hickeys, aren't they? Looks like you got tattooed."

"Pablo doesn't have fangs, none of the real vampires do. They suck the blood right through the skin."

"Oh my God."

"They suck it right through the skin with their mouths, a kind of a super-hickey. They haven't used fangs for centuries, they feed by osmosis."

"You're covered with them. . . ."

She rolled her eyes and smiled like a drug freak. "Yeah. It was incredibly sensual, I had them all feeding off me together . . . at the same time."

I shook my head, horrified.

Her slightly hoarse voice sounded like liquid sandpaper. "God, I screamed and moaned like a virgin! I couldn't stop coming, it was incredible.

"But the big moment was when I sucked Pablo's blood. He let me. I sucked a big patch of blood through his neck and it tasted like cognac. I drank it a little at a time, sucking like a baby. After a while I passed out. When I woke up, they were gone, so I came here."

"Do you feel any different?"

"Yeah, I feel weak, and a little sick to my stomach."

"Are you a vampire now?"

She looked at me quizzically, "I thought you didn't believe in vampires."

"I . . . I don't, not really. But I might believe in a guy who has some weird blood disease, who sucks blood through skin to feed some chemical imbalance in his body. You should see a doctor."

Olivia staggered over to the bed and collapsed. "I'm so tired," she sighed. "I have to rest."

A minute later she was still, sleeping so deeply as to

be almost dead. I covered her up and fell asleep in a chair.

Sometime near dawn I awoke from an incredible sexual dream to find Olivia gently sucking my neck and massaging my dick. I wanted to push her away but she held on to me until I climaxed.

I was horrified. When she pulled away, I saw her mouth red with my blood. I felt my neck. Blood!

"Shit!"

I rushed to the mirror and saw a mouth-shaped patch of wet, red skin. It throbbed now, like a burn.

"What did you do to me?" I shouted. "God damn it! You're sucking my blood!"

She grinned crimson. "Yeah, I like it. It's good. I want you to suck mine."

I rose up and took two quick steps away from her. "This whole thing is sick! I want you to get out! Now!"

She stood there for a moment. "It's too late. I coaxed you into sucking my tits while you were having your little wet dream. You've already tasted my blood."

"You're crazy! Leave me alone!"

Olivia gathered up her belongings and left without another word. She didn't look back.

When she was gone I locked the door and stood before the mirror, terrified. I took a shower and washed my neck thoroughly. I was resolved to call a doctor first thing in the morning. Then, an overwhelming fatigue overcame me and I slept.

When I awoke, I felt drugged. And I was aware of something else—an intense thirst. I felt my sanity hanging by a slender thread, ready to snap with the realization that something was terribly wrong with me.

I needed a doctor. I needed science, logic. I needed an end to the nightmare. My neck throbbed.

The phone rang, jarring me from my ghoulish fantasy.

"Hello?"

"This is Pablo," a deep voice said.

The name caused an involuntary shudder. "What do you want?"

"I want to tell you that Olivia Vickers is dead."

"Dead? How can that be? I just saw her."

"Fool! Didn't you hear me? I said she's dead. The silly harlot insisted on trying to become one of us. You should never have let her in your room."

I recoiled, wanting to shout something back into the phone, but no words came.

Pablo's voice was strange, deep and mocking. "You want to know why there are so few female vampires? Because ninety-nine percent of them can't sustain the virus, it destroys their immune system, they bleed out and die within twenty-four hours."

"Listen, you son of a bitch, I don't know what's going on here—"

"Shut up," Pablo snapped. "Your own failings got you into this, and you have no one to blame but yourself. Remember that. You are a stupid, lustful person. You fucked up."

He paused. I could hear my own heart pounding in the earpiece. I got the sense that somehow Pablo could hear it too, that he could feel my panic.

He said, "It's the same way for all of us, and you get to the point where you hate to see it in others because it's what you hate the most about yourself."

Pablo's voice turned uglier. "You thought you were so smart, you thought you had it figured out. Just a little jack-off session with Olivia, no body contact, no problem. She played you like a vintage Fender Stratocaster."

He chuckled. "You know nothing, absolutely nothing. She's a woman, you dumb shit, *women are carriers!*"

My mouth was as dry as a callus.

"Carriers?" I whispered, beginning to tremble.

"Carriers," he repeated with terrible finality. "The vampire virus is highly contagious among males, but to women, it's fatal. So, consider yourself infected. Let's see how you deal with it, you asshole."

I stared at the receiver, not wanting to believe what I was hearing, denying the fear.

"I . . . I . . ." I couldn't speak.

"Saint Lucius Cemetery, the big crypt in the southeast corner, you'll be back, I guarantee it. You're in for the shock of your life, Mr. Gordon. See ya around."

I hung up the phone and wept, the terrible weight of his words oscillating in my memory like a final, epic guitar chord. Ringing true. I had the virus now, I could already feel the weakness.

And the terrible thirst.

Greg Kihn: *"I spent the better part of my adult life on the road as a rock musician. Now, as a horror writer, I've discovered a whole nother subculture of groupie: the gothic poison ivy. You can look, but you better not touch."*

EMPATHY

Brian Hodge

*Hodge is the author of six novels. Some of his seventy
short stories and novellas have found their way into the
collections* The Convulsing Factory *and, most recently,* Falling Idols.

*I*t was the exception rather than the rule whenever
she looked up from the tabletop, actually met him eye
to eye. Hands busy at her half-empty mug, thin fingers
picking at the rim and handle as though she could
peel glazing from the ceramic. When Strauss asked
her to stop she seemed surprised, not even aware of
what her hands were up to. All that nervous energy
dissipating, wasted.

Amazing she'd mustered up enough courage to
have answered the ad at all. Strauss pictured her in a
cramped, dismal apartment with a view of Dumpsters
and walls sheer as tombstones. She agonizes for
hours, first over the newsprint, then her phone—
should she or shouldn't she? There would be a cat that
never wanted much to do with her, which she'd
periodically scoop into her arms for immoral support,
feeding on its nonchalance the way drunks feed on the
hoots of broth-brained friends.

"And what's your name again?" Strauss asked.

"Jane . . . Jane Norwood?" Inflection peaking at

the end, as if she were no more sure of her name than exchange rates for the yen.

"Pick a new one. A first name, anyway." When he saw that he'd thrown her, he added, "It's not legally binding. It's just a tool." He sighed, getting nowhere pronto by the look of her. "Think of it this way: You've got some picture of yourself in mind, how you wish you could really be. Correct?"

She nodded, compliant as a sheep.

"Then find her a name, because she's not going to answer to Jane, I guarantee you. There must be some other name that fits her. That captures her essence. Yes? No? Yes. So what is it?"

As she had to ponder this, Strauss showed mercy and didn't stare, letting his gaze wander the coffee-house instead. The arrayed subphyla of trend-clutchers were good for at least a minute's diversion. They slurped specialty brews with the smug propriety of those who'd invented them. Some chased promising careers like the hoop-jumping little doggies they were; others cultivated a sedentary disdain for ambition and punched metal through their faces, of which Strauss approved insofar as the risk of infection was possible. In his opinion there was not enough acquired deformity in the world.

"Zoe," she announced, the most declarative thing she'd said yet. "That's her name. Zoe."

Strauss tasted the name upon his lips, rolling it in place and letting it melt upon his tongue. Such a tiny name to feel so barbaric yet so elegant. It would do just peachy.

"Then the first steps on this path to Zoe lead back up to the counter," he said. "We'll need butter."

She blinked. "Butter?"

"They sell muffins, they must have butter."

Up she went, and nobody watched. She wasn't the sort who drew looks of anything. Admiration, envy, lust, disgust . . . they all passed her by in a tepid slipstream of indifference. She was a nonentity. The world would glance at her and see in the sum of her attributes a perfect zero, then forget it'd ever laid eyes on her.

Strauss, however, saw the same potential that sculptors saw in lumps of wet clay.

Her face? Oval and undistinguished. Her hair? A limp and lifeless brown. Her chest and waist were hidden inside the sail of an engulfing sweater. Her legs appeared toned, but she wore black tights and this was a colossal error, unforgiving emphasis on a dumpy ass that had no business beneath snug packaging.

Jane came back with two butter pats, and Strauss peeled the wax paper from one.

"Zoe," he said. "Solid choice. There's a lot of power in the naming of something. 'In the beginning was the word . . .'? That kind of power."

"Oh. Um. I'm afraid I was never very religious." She smiled a wobbly apology.

"Now, that's a shame. Sincerely. Much more meaningful being an ex-believer than a never-was."

Strauss laid his dagger on the table and pushed it across. It was a stubby thing; its ebony scabbard fit comfortably beneath his arm. When Jane saw it her smile flickered and snuffed.

"If those tights you're wearing have a seam in the crotch, they should be easy for you to cut straight. Panties too."

"Here?" she whispered. "Right now?"

"Split down the middle."

She balked, wide-eyed and terrified. If there was anything he had to accomplish today it was to get her past this misperception that she had anything to say about who did what, and where. He had no interest in her modesty at all, only what lay beneath it.

Jane took the dagger in a trembling hand. Beneath the table he felt her legs shift, knees splaying, and when she looked at him with her eyes on the brink of tears or epiphany, he nodded. Once. Go ahead, first cut's always the hardest. She looked down, hands between her legs, then he heard a rip, the rending of the veil.

While she worked at it, he set the anal plug on the table and used an index finger to lube it with butter. Jane's face flushed scarlet when she saw it, and for a moment Strauss thought she was ready to bolt. Two phobias squaring off across her vanilla face, a mundane war, and guess what: Fear of a dull future whipped shame's bashful ass.

He had her scoot lower in the chair, her shaky knees veering around his own. Strauss leaned forward and pushed an arm beneath the table, working by feel. The back of his hand gliding along her thigh, more slowly than needed, but oh *such* fun watching Jane gnaw her lower lip.

His fingers found the makeshift split-crotch and teased the cloth apart—the elastic tights, the soft cotton of her sensible undies. The revealed tuft of downy hair begged a more lingering touch, and by now her nail-bitten hands were clutching the edge of the table like an owl clutches its branch. South, then, along the moistened secret lips until his knuckles met the fleshy cheeks of her bottom. He found the puckered bud between and let the rubber plug track its way home, pushing it in gradually as Jane gulped down a whimper, until her sphincter naturally caught the indented ring around the base end, to hold it in place.

Strauss sat back to watch her unwind. He hadn't expected this episode to go unnoticed and wasn't disappointed; a stare here, a nudge or squelched outrage there. Nobody actually *doing* anything about it, but by God they could paper the area with flyers.

The harshest disdain came from a skanky-haired brat dressed in poverty chic and a knit hat that might've looked authentic with an actual Jamaican beneath it. He glared, an armchair Lancelot brimming with superiority. Drank his coffee black. Strauss decided to get back to him in a minute.

"I don't think I can ever show my face in here again," Jane whispered.

"Gee, there's a loss," he said. "But look on the bright side. It may not be yours much longer."

He sent her home then, to wait, and she moved funny, clearly unaccustomed to butt plugs. The walk would do her good. Meanwhile, her would-be champion had already abandoned the cause, sipping at his steaming mug and pretending to understand a volume of Anne Sexton. Strauss could tell he was deep by the way he tugged at his goatish wisp of beard.

A few slow deep breaths and Strauss was almost in his head, matching him posture for posture and move for move. It only took a few moments until the sync was perfect and he didn't have to think about it, or respond consciously, because he'd bypassed all that. Strauss mimicked him at a preconscious level, until muscle control, for at least one perfect moment, could exist as a two-way exchange.

Strauss waited until the sensitive and intellectual goat-lad hoisted his mug again, then yanked his own arm back and tipped his hand. Goat-lad did likewise. The steaming mugful of brew deluged his lap, sudden inspiration for a yodeling lunge away from the table. Laughter pealed. How long, though, before the lawsuit?

Strauss stuck around for the rest of the show—anticlimactic to be sure, but he was a completist.

Do you believe in magick?, he'd asked in the ad that Jane had responded to, and it was always a hoot to remind himself why there were much smarter answers than no.

Sailor Billy was an antique hardliner on the tattoo scene, predating the modern primitivist craze by decades, a throwback from an era when inked skin was anathema to all but the genuine weirdos, mutants, and outcasts. Strauss always got the feeling that he missed those days.

Cash on the barrelhead was the surest means of getting your way, and when you wanted the atypical Sailor Billy didn't bargain. He was a shaven-headed old cuss in his seventies, possessed of steadiness of hand and sureness of eye that age had failed to erode. While skilled with the electric needle, he was also a repository of techniques older by millennia. If you wanted a lost art, it was definitely a seller's market.

"Why put her through it?" Sailor Billy nodded his wrinkled dome toward the next room, where Jane was staring at the flash art on the studio walls, the cheap shit for impulse buyers. "Fuck me for a beggar if she's got the constitution to last this out."

Strauss wasn't biting. "You were in the navy. You must've heard somewhere that still waters run deep."

"Your money," grinned Sailor Billy. "If you can't drag her back in for tomorrow night's session, no refunds."

"Wouldn't dream of it, Billy. Don't insult me by implying I would."

It wasn't that the *subjugatum* was inherently more difficult to apply than any large design. It was, rather, purity of method that made the difference. Electric needles were too easy. Manual means would knit deeper than mere flesh, converting pain into ordeal and process into ritual.

Theater of the mind, all of it. The thing about magick was you could be an atheist and still never betray your refusal of cosmology. Strauss didn't believe in angels and devils and pacts with either any more than he believed in giant egg-toting bunnies or the doe-eyed messiah who'd muscled in on the rabbit's turf.

He believed mightily, however, in the depths of the human psyche, fathomless, uncharted, raging with turbulence and storms whose power needed only to be harnessed and directed toward a goal. That deep plunge was crucial—the conscious brains of most people were murky saucepans of confusion and tail-chasing defeat.

Any rite was valid as long as its drama dished up the raw material needed to start hammering order from chaos. He found a poetic quality in utilizing tools with sharp points.

Strauss steered Jane in, coaxed her into peeling away her clothes, and got a look at the body, finally. Her skin itself was, well, divine. Pale? Indeed. But all pales are not created equal. There are fishbellies and there are pearls, and Jane's skin was akin to the latter, a smooth, luscious hybrid of silk and cream. Sailor Billy paused in the preparation of his tools to give a lingering stare of awe and a groan of highest appreciation.

Candles were lit, incense too, while Jane lay facedown and nervous on the padded leather bench, Sailor Billy traced the *subjugatum*'s intricacies over the rich ivory canvas of her back, from the tops of her shoulders to the twin dimples flanking the base of her spine. In his rendering of line and curve and angle there was both precision and flair. He took pains to adhere to the strictures of design while incorporating them into Jane's own topography of musculature and bone: of rib and deltoid, of scapula, vertebra, and trapezius.

Strauss could never settle on what it looked like. One moment a map, the next a maze, the next a lock. And so on. And so on.

When it was complete, he handed over the bottle of blue-black ink he'd never allowed Sailor Billy to keep. Turn it so it caught the light just right, and sometimes Strauss swore he could see faces swirling in it.

"Someday you're gonna tell me where you got this," Billy said. By now it was part of the game.

Strauss's eyebrow would arch just so. "You don't want to know."

By then it was time to begin.

* * *

Process and ordeal, three nights running:

The only sounds for hours were those of wood on wood, and the soft cries Jane made, like the coo of a murdered dove, whenever the tenderest new skin was pricked. Sailor Billy used the old way, one sharp-toothed mahogany tool angled like a toothbrush against the skin, with a tapping stick to drive its inked points into the dermal layers below.

As the *subjugatum* took deeper form one slow line at a time, Strauss fell mesmerized by its progress. Trance inducement was no accident, but a crucible to alchemize everything he willed for her, everything she willed for herself. His will was the stronger, natch—practice, training—but her energies were readily gobbled up as well. All change began in the mind, where he held firm to that visualized ideal of face and body, pumped into her as sure as seed. To keep the charge going took a concoction of pleasure and pain, Strauss straddling Jane's ample haunches after removing the plug and sliding himself up that snug hot channel.

He moved no more than necessary to maintain the erection, a tortoise-slow rocking back and forth to the steady brittle tap of hardwood, a silver chain swaying around his neck as its precious locket thumped over his heart. Jane's hips rolling beneath him but her back immobile beneath that needled bite, and Sailor Billy working a rhythm of his own, breaking new skin, holding it taut and dabbing at the trickles of blood. Red, white, blue-black; the smells of ink and musk, of sandalwood smoke and the earthier aroma of animalistic union.

Together they played her and Sailor Billy gnoshed his words. Jane was a sponge, soaking up pain and ink, night after night. By the second, shyness over baring her body was shed. By the third, even the pain had been converted into something else, a commodity she seemed proud to call her own. No more whimpers, only a deeper grunt of tolerance; of challenge confronted, even.

Strauss could hardly have been more proud. His creation. It was enough to bring a tear to a jaundiced eye.

And when he looked into hers, before leaving the shop on the night the *subjugatum* was finished, he thought he saw it: the first hint of Zoe, rising from the depths of desire and time.

He, of course, would have another name for her.

"My cousin got road-rash once," she told him. "All down the side of one leg. He dumped his motorcycle over and slid about a hundred feet."

"Sounds painful." Strauss yawned. "A shame he'd never heard of leather."

"At least he was wearing a helmet. It was the law."

"Let's hear it for helmet laws, then. Government's way of thwarting nature's way of improving the breed. And your cousin has what to do with this again?"

"My back," she said. "I think I know now how his leg must've felt, is all I mean."

She was staying with him while her back healed. Strauss kept it clean, moisturized, and bandaged. Plus during this crucial time he wanted her away from the familiar turf of home, from the TV and soporific magazines and whatever other banalities she'd chewed up and regurgitated into a wit-dulling nest around her. And with a little luck, the neighbor might even forget to feed the cat.

Jane was taking vacation time off work, but even at

that she worked from home, something to do with phone orders and computer inventories for some company that catered to fools and their money, soon cleaved. Her resumé would cure insomnia and maybe the will to live. No wonder she was desperate for radical change.

A few times each day she'd ask him to hold one mirror while she held another, lying on her belly, and when properly angled she could see the *subjugatum,* fascinated that it was now such an intimate part of her anatomy. She would dip one shoulder or bow her spine and watch the design flex.

"I never thought of myself as the tattoo type," she whispered one night. "And now look how big a jump I took into it. And so beautiful. I almost hate that it's not supposed to last."

Pity, that.

He'd told her only as much as she needed to know to get her to agree to the ordeal, cognizant of the fact that she'd have to have a loose screw or two in the first place to be drawn in by his ad. *Do you believe in magick?* He'd received six replies and considered that a landslide, most of their senders so despondent over themselves that they didn't even hold out hope for plastic surgery's chances. Or maybe they just lacked the credit rating.

Jane's reply, on the other hand, had a desperate New Age reek to it. *There's a goddess inside me just waiting to get out,* she'd written. It wasn't that her faith was misplaced so much as, well, fortuitously naive. Goddess almighty. Had she been omniscient enough to know what he was really capable of, she wouldn't have wanted him within ten furlongs of her rectum.

He'd of course had to explain about the *subjuga-tum,* choosing details and omitting others with Solo-monic discretion. The design? Arabic, originally, and old as sand, although refinements had been made over the centuries, mostly in the character of letters from a pair of obscure alphabets. What obscure alphabets, she'd wanted to know. Just for yocks he'd forced himself to mention Atlantis, to see how *that* tweaked her clit, and lord how those trusting bovine eyes did light. She was his.

Historically the *subjugatum* was one of the more fabled and elusive unholy grails of those who made sport of tampering with the forces. That forerunners all the way back to Simon Magus had been said to conjure up Helen of Troy—and bed the wench—was no secret. The same for Cleopatra. One had to assume that premiums had also been placed on a bevy of lesser-knowns.

What history's dust covered up was methodology. Strauss could not accept that dead women were yanked from thin air. That greater or lesser aspects of them might be engineered from the flesh of the living held more potential, with here and there a tantalizing glimmer that the *subjugatum* was the tool. Even without that key theory verified, rumor was still on Strauss's side: Foes of Simon Magus claimed that his Helen had merely been a whore he'd bought from a brothel in Tyre. Maybe they weren't even wrong, just typical Christian busybodies in possession of half the facts.

Jane had gone weirdly gaga over the romance of it. Strauss saw no point in killing the mood with news that the "ink" used was derived from certain fetal by-products, electing only to assure her that over time it metabolized into the body of the woman so tattooed. Which he'd always neglected to mention to Sailor Billy.

"You've done it before, haven't you?" she asked one day after the fact.

"Why would you think that?" But he'd been waiting for this.

"Something Billy said right before we started. About the ink? That someday you'd have to tell him where you got it."

"No. No, no, no. I'd just showed him the bottle when I was in to block out the time on his schedule. That's all."

"Well, where *did* you get it?"

"Sumatra," he answered, off the top of his head, and that did the trick. There was no place else for her to follow the thread, so she let it drop, but then she was so ready to be lied to in the first place, as long as he was convincing about it.

They started again after the prickly discomfort had left her back, the next sequence of rites intended to keep the *subjugatum* charged. Earlier in the twentieth century another refinement had allegedly been added by Aleister Crowley, and since Strauss liked the idea they went with it: use of a leather bondage harness whose frontal design of steel rings and straps duplicated the sephiroth and pathways of the Kabbalah.

She endured all contortions and discomforts as if developing an appetite for them. Everyone suffers for beauty. It took them an entire weekend to work through the Ritual of the Ten Ecstasies but only because Strauss was at the mercy of his overworked testicles. Jane took to it with ever-mounting gusto, seeming to avail her throat and ass to him a little deeper at every stage, repeatedly coaxing him to the brink of climax, when he would pull out to anoint with his issue the area inside one of the harness's rings. All ten of them. In the proper order. In two days. Very little sleep. He hated her body then, because for now it was everything his wasn't: inexhaustible and constantly primed.

Oh. But. Look at those results.

The first changes were apparent when viewed from behind, her dumpy bum beginning to reshape itself to resemble the tightened contours of a honeydew. Then her belly, marred by a bit of slack, began to firm itself as well. Neither result was nothing that fasting and strenuous sex couldn't accomplish, but would lost weight shift up to fill out her decreasingly smallish breasts? Would it highlight her hair and thicken the strands better than Pantene? In all, Strauss thought it was going just peachy.

"How come we never once do it the normal way?" she asked one night. Candlelight turned her sweaty skin into the surface gleam on a bowl of cream.

"*Ab*normality is the general idea." If there was anything he hated it was armchair conjuring. "Let's see if we can't remember to stick with the program, okay?"

"But the other, that doesn't have to hurt anything, does it?" She took him by the hand and tried steering it to the downy patch between her legs. He clenched a fist. "Always my mouth, always my ass. It's not that I don't find that exciting—nobody's ever done these things with me, or even been much interested in it— but just once I'd like us to make love like two regular people."

"But we're *not* two regular people and we're *not* making love."

"You don't have one decent word to say to me, ever, do you?"

"I'm sure there's been one at some point. Keep thinking."

"You know what they say? That you can tell a lot about what a man will be like in a relationship by watching how he treats his mother." Jane—or was this Zoe now?—had a defiant smirk on her face that he could never have imagined her wearing before. "Based on the way you talk to me, I bet you treat her awful."

"So much pop psychology, so little time. I don't know what to rip into first," he said. "It's a moot point, anyway. I renounced my family when I was fourteen. Although if it helps your thesis, I *did* consider killing them in their sleep."

"What a liar. If you think you scare me when you say things like that, you don't. Maybe you did at first, but now I know it's just part of the act."

"Act? *Moi?*" He settled in, expectant. This should be good.

"Act! Your dyed-black hair in those fat dreadlocks. The way you trim your beard into those angles. Sunglasses at midnight. A whole closetful of black clothes. Always wearing that chain and locket. And what'd you do, jab yourself with a cattle prod until you could never smile or laugh again?"

"Keep going and I may crack up right in your face," he said.

Helping her mirror her inner goddess and this was the thanks he got? It was truly annoying when they began thinking they could talk to him like an equal. A reliable barometer of change, but annoying.

"All you need is a little cartoon caption underneath you that says 'Evil,' and then you'd be complete, wouldn't you?"

"Why, Eliza Doolittle, that'll be quite enough out of you."

Evidently she'd come to the same conclusion, now holding her tongue, but there was nothing of acquiescence in it. She was jolly well pleased with herself, maybe the first time in her nothing life she'd ever stood up to her own species and she was relishing every moment.

"They're dead," he told her, quieter now. "And no, I didn't kill them. It was an accident and it was their fault and it happened while I was at school."

"Your . . . family?" she said. "Ohhhh, I'm sorry. I didn't mean anything by it, really, I . . ."

Taken the smug wind out of her with that. Sometimes the truth was more potent than the best lie you could come up with. It was just that good lies were always more abundant and more dependable, and eventually you just forgot which was which.

Between the standard sadist and the garden-variety masochist there was a relationship of deep trust. And always a point beyond which the masochist would never let the sadist go, and the sadist wouldn't dare.

Strauss had about as much interest in that game as he had in tent revivals and high teas. He *wanted* pain, he *wanted* terror, not for their own sake but because in the right hands they were rocket fuel. Somewhere past the thorny thicket of screaming nerves was a darker realm where flesh surrendered to its master. It would bend to his will; he just had to speak its language and wipe its slate clean of the mediocrity it had always been satisfied with before.

He cuffed her by the wrists and ankles to keep her secured, with the *subjugatum* before him like a map. He heated slim golden needles in the blue tongues of a gel alcohol flame, then lanced them into strategic intersections of lines and curves. Along her body he brushed a humming wand with a soft violet glow— another latter-day refinement—and the air crackled with the pops and jolts of static electricity.

One hour, then two, and a third. He played her flesh as a conductor plays an orchestra—a hush here, a crescendo there. At first it was no more than reflexive spasms, but then it evolved into something more refined, a call and response before which her flesh and the framework below would ebb and flow like tallow.

Whereas earlier she'd shrunk from the wand, Jane now strained at the limits of her bonds to meet it. Tiny arcs leapt between the round heads of the needles, and later when he began to remove them one by one it was harder than it looked. Her flesh greedy, loath to turn loose of them. But out they came, and then he turned her over onto her back.

With a sweep of his hand he brushed her hair aside.

He always saved the face for last.

This time it had started without him.

Strauss was only trying to catch some shut-eye on his couch when he felt the hands shaking his shoulders. Dawn's early light hammered somewhere past the windows and their black curtains, and after the long night of living sculpture he was spent, nothing more to give, but they were always so demanding, these women. He did everything for them, he funneled considerable amounts of money to Sailor Billy for their betterment, he invested his time and boundless energy to elevate them to a higher plane. Yet in the end they ran away out of some screeching quirk of bourgeois morality or were spiteful enough to deny him the consideration of deserved slumber.

Saying, "Wake up, you little shit. You never cared about Zoe and you especially never cared about me."

Why he bothered when it only reaped him such grief and abuse he didn't know. He reached back to turn on a table lamp. When the light hit her it took his breath away, and he'd never been one to give it up without a fight. She was still in flux the last time he'd checked. It could've gone either way.

"You little shit. Who am I?"

While the likeness wasn't perfect, it was far more alike than not. He recognized her. He would recognize her anywhere. And he'd done it without scalpels.

"You don't like it?" he said.

"That's not it, it's beautiful, it's just not anything at all like the face I had in mind. Now *who am I?*"

Strauss reached in his shirt to draw up the chain from around his neck and the locket from over his heart. He thumbed the catch and it split like an oyster; he showed her that pictured pearl within. With those familiar eyes she stared, and she pursed those familiar lips, and as she understood—or maybe remembered—she got that same old look on her face, as if she'd never known him and never would regardless of how hard she tried. It broke his heart, and if she left again that would murder him.

"I don't like you very much," he said.

In her haste to react she cracked a stinging red handprint across his cheek, and he was so suddenly thrilled he tented his pants in front. She dropped to her knees beside the couch, full of apologies and promises to never do that again and all the rest of those soothing nothings that he craved.

"I'm sorry," she said. "But sometimes mothers aren't here to be liked."

Neither were sons, for that matter, but petty differences of opinion were hardly enough to loosen the bonds between them.

Brian Hodge: *"I'd done quite a few stories that more or less leaned toward championing various subcultures. Now I figured it was time to poke a pin into their inflated images before I got any closer to achieving self-parody."*

THE SAINT, THE SATYR, AND THE SNAKEHOLE

Stephen Gresham

To date, Alabama's Gresham has published fifteen novels and over thirty short stories. His Hot Blood story emerged from research for a Civil War novel he hopes to complete in the coming years. Gresham also publishes under the pseudonyms John Newland and J. V. Lewton.

Someone had poured oil of gladness into the snakehole.

Esther Stowers could smell it, the skunky effluvium of it, every ounce as brutal to the olfactory nerves as sudden death or rifle knock-knee or any other form of cheap whiskey.

Standing at the rim of the snakehole, she could not keep her hands from trembling. The filthy missive she held—the fourth of its kind—generated chest-tightening anger and repulsion, and perhaps to deflect some of her unease she tried to imagine one of the more supercilious owlings confiscating bottles of hard liquor while the wounded and ailing soldiers dreamed of home. She further imagined this same well-intentioned night nurse delivering the devil-inspired drink to the murky confines of the snakehole where it could never be retrieved, emptying the contents of some bottles, tossing in others unopened. Everyone knew that even fully recovered patients would not brave the snakehole, the deep, miasmic pit in which bloody bandages, amputated limbs, garbage, and nameless wastes produced by the hospital were dumped.

No bottle of fire and oblivion was worth it.

Oh, but that the snakehole could solve my *dilemma.*

Esther bit her lip and stared at the scrawly script. She considered possible explanations for the sickness her eyes could not wholly resist: drunkenness seemed a likely suspect. Yes, of course, that must be it, she reasoned, suddenly connecting the foul odors with the letter. The Reverend Thomas Everett Baldwin, his moral resolve weakened by contact with so much suffering, had bathed (nay, *drowned*) his senses in the oil of gladness. The space once occupied by those senses had been usurped by the most indecent, lewd, and revolting inclinations a man could have.

A man of God. A man who loved the Lord.

A man who could read the Scriptures so tenderly and compellingly that one heard angels singing *Agnus Dei* as he spoke, a man who could write soldier letters home that would warmly glaze the heart and bedew the eyes.

Esther gulped a lung of air and reread the first paragraph:

O sweet Virgin, heavenly Esther, how eager are my hands to explore your nipple-covered mountains of desirable flesh and how my mouth itches to suck at the same and to feast upon the honeypot hidden by the soft down of beard between your glorious thighs. And O how my lordly member, my hungry, hardened cock, my pulsing prick wishes to enter the gates of Esther's Cuntland, the Promised Land I joyfully exile myself to nightly. My lovely, delectable Esther, I must now confess something: two days ago I pilfered a pair of your virgin-white drawers trimmed with rose-tatted frills from the laundry room and in my bed I wrap that Esther-perfumed garment about my prick until my passion discharges like a cannon and . . .

Esther's entire body was quivering, a modicum from arousal, but vastly more so from disgust. Her eyes skipped down the lines; each of Baldwin's notes had concluded in much the same way:

On your rounds, my angelic Esther, I say keep thyself away from that man, Sturgis, a Sodomite and rapist as I've heard from reliable sources. He hath not my pure desires. His are the desires of a satyr. I say, "Beware the Satyr," beware this corrupt man who deserves not to live and most assuredly not to wear the proud gray as do our finest youth.

Esther grimaced.

I must tell the matron the truth about the Reverend Baldwin.

She knew she would need courage for that.

But how could she find it in watching the torn pieces of the letter float atop the slimy surface of the snakehole and then sink slowly, inexorably out of sight?

Yet, this time might be different.

This time, yes, she felt she could, for this time she
believed she could offer an explanation for the hal-
lowed man's reprehensible behavior. Yes, she could.
She straightened her shoulders and jutted out her
chin.

And thereupon she rent the foolscap eagerly, triumphantly.

Mrs. Helvestry had been the hospital's matron
since the second bombardment of Fort Sumter in the
fall of '63; she knew Esther's mother and Esther's
aunt Riselle, and as a favor to the aunt she had
winked at the regulation requiring nurses and aides to
be twenty-one (Esther was but eighteen), to be married (Esther was not), and, most important, to be
visibly wanting in handsome or fetching features
(Esther was, to anyone with eyes, strikingly beautiful
and desirable).

Broaching the matter as one essential to the salubri-
ous operation of the hospital, Esther was admitted to
Mrs. Helvestry's tiny quarters and urged to register
her complaint as succinctly as possible, for time was
precious and the men deserved every moment of care.
Quaking yet firmly resolved, Esther began. She re-
counted, occasionally employing Latin to efface the
more obscene passages, the contents of the notes as
best she could, the first dating from mid-September,
only weeks after the fall of Atlanta. She characterized
her shock and dismay at receiving them, choosing not,
of course, to mention how they had sexually aroused
her a degree or two.

"And do you, Miss Stowers, know the author of
these . . . these *writings?*"

Sedately placing one hand onto her bosom, Esther closed her eyes and nodded.

"I do, ma'am." But her voice, despite her efforts to keep it strong, weakened to a strained and barely audible whisper. "The Reverend Thomas Everett Baldwin, ma'am. And I believe, ma'am, that the spirits of demon whiskey guide his pen."

Mrs. Helvestry flinched as if she had been scored in the back by a Union saber. Indeed, it took her a few moments to regain her composure. "Young woman, do you have any idea of the *extreme* gravity of your accusation? Are you aware of the opprobrium you have heaped upon the name and person of one of the finest men I have ever known? The Reverend Baldwin is . . . he is, in the regard of *everyone* privileged by his company, considered one who transcends the most decent human kind. He is a saint. Though not officially canonized, nevertheless a *saint.*"

Esther felt more than a little woozy. Her stomach hurt furiously. Mrs. Helvestry advised her to recant. Esther would not.

"Very well, then, if you persist—show me the letters, for I *must* see them with my own eyes before I can *begin* to entertain belief."

A scalding panic surged into Esther's throat.

"I . . . I tore them up and threw them in the snakehole."

Mrs. Helvestry's anger was as visible as a brightly colored sash. And yet Esther, holding her ground, maintained that the harrassment amounted to more than the letters: "During rounds, ma'am, he has, on occasion . . . *touched* me."

Mrs. Helvestry asked for clarification.

"Well, you see, ma'am . . . he *rubs* his body against mine, against my backside . . . most obscenely."

It was as clear as a starry, Southern night that Mrs. Helvestry did not believe her. First she closed her eyes, then opened them and looked toward heaven, and then through clenched teeth she told Esther to get out or she would dismiss her summarily and inform her aunt and suggest that she be sent to Washington to join her mother, adding, "Might it be that you suffer from a fable in the blood?" The latter was an allusion to the ignoble profession of Esther's mother and the possibility that Esther would also take up that disgraceful calling.

As an addendum to the reprimand, Mrs. Helvestry assigned Esther to "owling" duty so that she could spend the long nights thinking about her misguided accusations. Esther was bearing her shame out the door when Mrs. Helvestry pitched one more indignant line at her: "Besmearing a saint . . . *how could you?*"

Sherman had begun his destructive march to the sea.

Lincoln had been reelected.

And Esther's hospital—my "house of pain," as she termed it—was filling up with wounded chiefly because the Atlanta hospitals could not handle the demand. Columbus was sent the overflow.

But on a drowned-dog, rainy night in mid-November Esther experienced something which rendered her virtually oblivious to the stream of ragged, gaunt, pale, and bloodied soldiers, to the ugly presence of pneumonia, diphtheria, diarrhea, and gan-

228

grene, and to all the evil savors and ghastliness of Death.

On the aforementioned night she met Major Robert L. Sturgis.

The Satyr.

Major Sturgis was still asleep when Esther's slumbering sexuality roared awake tooth and claw, the painful pleasure and surprise attack of it bloodlessly buckling her knees before she knew what hit her.

"O-o-o-h!" she breathed out when she saw him.

His bed had deliberately been placed in a far corner of the cotton warehouse-cum-hospital, a tactical move bespeaking the fact that Sturgis, once he had recovered from his wounds, would be returned to his home state of Virginia, where he would go on trial for his alleged offenses—among them, attacking a young girl. Moreover, a goodly lot of his fellow wounded considered him a "Jonah," a figure of bad luck best kept away from daily intercourse with anyone else.

The scene that greeted her mesmerized Esther.

An oil lamp illuminated the bed and the sheets that curtained it on three sides. The placement of the lamp was such that an impressive shadow of Sturgis, propped up with a pillow behind his head, was cast onto the background sheet. Sturgis wore no nightshirt. His midsection was modestly covered by a blanket.

And Esther had never set eyes on such a man as this.

He possessed long and wildly tousled black hair curling up in pointed wisps like small horns on either temple. His face was handsome though pocked and finished out with black eyebrows, mustache, and beard. His chest was a riot of the same black hair, horizontal lines of it reaching to his stomach, where a vertical line plunged beneath the blanket out of sight but not out of Esther's imagination.

Here indeed was a satyr. Here was Pan. Here was a living embodiment of every archetypal, satyr-like figure she had read about in the pages of Ovid's *Metamorphoses*. Only the shaggy thighs and cloven hooves were missing—for Sturgis was a double amputee, one leg removed at mid-thigh, the other at the knee.

Esther carefully approached this myth of a man, half-expecting to see his musical pipe lying nearby; instead, there was a bowie knife, quite a large one. She stared at him. And the erotic rush she felt threatened to overwhelm her. It began as a hollow yet immensely pleasant warmth in the pit of her stomach, from whence it spread throughout her body in a current of sensuousness, streaming over her breasts and cataracting from there to her genitals. Where it induced secretion. Involuntarily Esther squeezed her legs together.

"O-o-o-h," Esther whispered, for she could not help herself.

She felt that her body was on fire.

She wanted to touch this man lying before her. She wanted to be touched by him, by his large, rough hands. She wanted to touch herself. Wanted to dip her fingertips in the surge of moisture between her legs. Her cheeks flamed at the thought, for she had heard that such touching would lead to insanity and possibly suicide.

Such touching was sinful. And virtually irresistible.

Esther could feel tiny beads of sweat forming along the hairline on her forehead. She swallowed hard and reminded herself that she had come to clean the patient's stumps. Antero-posterior flap operations had been done on both legs, and while the stumps had firmly cicatrized, they needed to be washed daily.

Kneeling down by the bed with her soap and water and rag, Esther was engrossed in how to slip the blanket from the man's stumps without waking him when all of a sudden she heard a deep, rich, warm voice say, "Hello there, miss. You aren't my regular nuss, now are you?"

Their eyes met, and Esther was quite certain that she was swimming too far out to the sea of her own arousal and was in danger of drowning before she could return to the shore of her own modesty. Flustered, she pretended to look down at her pan of water.

"Oh, no, sir. Mrs. Lassiter was taken ill, and I was assigned to . . ." She glanced from the water, where she glimpsed her distorted reflection, to the soft mound of the blanket where it covered his stumps. ". . . to tend to your needs."

Embarrassment lodged in her throat as if she had swallowed a doorknob. Every molecule of her body was shouting at her to flee, but it was as if another self, an erotic self, demanded that she stay to explore this new and fascinating emotion. To Esther it did not feel "dirty"—it felt liberating.

Is this what my mother feels?

"I'm pleased you're here, Miss . . . what is your name?"

She told him, and then she mustered enough of her nurse's persona to ask, "How are you feeling, Major Sturgis?"

"Hunky, Miss Esther. Thank you for inquiring."

Taking a deep breath to compose herself, Esther folded the sheet back to reveal the stumps, and in doing so she also discerned that Sturgis was not wearing drawers. She plunged the rag in the water and wrung it hard and began to rub the soap into it, hoping the menial actions would quell her arousal. They did not, for she could feel Sturgis's eyes on her.

But she went about her duty as best she could, her hands aware of how the man's body relaxed and gave in to the pleasure of having the stumps cleaned.

"You do that most satisfyingly," he murmured.

"Thank you," she whispered, adding, "Is there . . . is there anything else I might do while I'm here?" She wanted, oh, how she wanted, to let her eyes meet his again, but she feared she would swoon. She heard him issue a slight chuckle.

"You will think this strange," he began, "but my . . . my *toes* itch powerfully."

He laughed softly, and so did Esther, and then she raised her head. "I've heard one of the doctors speak of a phantom leg," she said. His dark eyes held her, and the word "phantom" ghosted through her swirling thoughts: phantom self, vanishing self. Yes, some self, a presexual self, was vanishing. Yet, it still seemed somehow to be there—she could feel it. Incredibly so, in a matter of only a few minutes in the presence of this man that self had been severed like a mutilated or diseased limb.

Sturgis was studying her face, her beauty—Esther knew he was.

Dear God, I am dissolving, she thought, but could not understand what that meant or what else was hiding there in this man's expression.

"Are you not . . . frightened of me, miss?"

"Frightened? Why . . . why, no. Should I be?"

He smiled and shook his head. Then the smile disappeared.

"You must have heard what they say about me. But I want you to know that not a word of it is true. Not a single word."

Esther did not attempt to respond to his comments; instead she administered the man's nightly dose of morphine and smiled at his polite "thank you" and his haunting "goodnight." She excused herself, but returned minutes later to find him asleep.

Sleeping satyr.

She could not take her eyes from him. Standing there in the shadows she felt again the erasure of a former self, she felt the need to cross boundaries, the desire for union. *This is womanhood,* she told herself. She stepped closer to the man and ached to lift his hand and place it on her breast and ached to lie naked with him and to feel the weight of his broken body on hers and to experience what she imagined would be the burning pleasure of his being deep inside her.

The bowie knife was on a chair near the bed. It intrigued Esther. She picked it up and held it because it was his. Almost like a part of him. She traced her fingers along the length of it and liked the cool hardness of the sharp blade. In a sudden rise of girlish emotion she told herself that she would be like a weapon for this man, for he needed her. Yes, he was crippled—oh, how she hated that word—and not a whole and complete man, but he was immeasurably more of a man than the Reverend Baldwin.

I would give myself to this man. This beautiful satyr.

* * *

"Why do you hate this gentle, saintly man?"

A week had passed, and each night Esther had tended warmly and efficiently to Major Sturgis and they had talked of many things as their relationship took root: he spoke of his wife and two sons and how he loved them, yet having learned of the charges against him, his wife had written to him requesting that he release her from their marital bond. She promised to be a good mother to their sons, and she wished never to see him again. Esther's heart grew arms and reached out to embrace his sorrow, and she for her part told of being abandoned by her mother and how she regretted never really knowing the woman.

Esther read Ovid to him.

Sturgis recited passages of Shakespeare to her.

They laughed together when Esther pretended to scratch his phantom toes.

But the Reverend Baldwin had become aware of their nightly minutes together, and he had found opportunities to warn Esther in jealous tones that Sturgis was a dangerous man and deserved to be murdered in his sleep. Each such encounter with Baldwin caused Esther to despise the man more intensely; she loathed his long blond hair and pink complexion, the nosegays he offered to her and the cloying aroma of cinnamon from the sticks of it he chewed to freshen his breath. Most of all she was repulsed by his furtive maneuvers to pat her and caress her intimately.

She guarded her underwear assiduously.

It chanced one day that she received another note from him.

With illustrations.

And captions.

It was a crudely sketched and vile triptych, the first illustration identified as Baldwin's penis in a flaccid state. The second was his penis erect—"The state of my member whenever I glimpse or even think of my Esther," he wrote—the organ looking much like a battlefield cannon. And the third disgusting item was of the erect, and ridiculously long, penis shown entering a vagina, labeled as Esther's. The sketch was captioned as follows: "A picture of heaven on earth for your votary of pleasure."

Posthaste, Esther delivered the document to the matron only to be met with disdain: "I say again, why do you hate this gentle, saintly man?"

"I do not, ma'am. I only thought you should know his true nature."

"What stands revealed here is the true nature of *you*, Miss Stowers. *You!*"

At which point Mrs. Helvestry tore the sheet of foolscap into several dozen pieces. She then leaned back as if the action had relieved bodily tensions and accused Esther of having unfulfilled, romantic inclinations toward Baldwin. She completed her response thusly: "I am hereby giving you notice that one week from today your employ will be terminated. I recommend that you arrange for transportation and take up residence with your mother in Washington, where I assume you will be more at home."

In the days that followed, Esther would often lie down after the exhausting night duty and try to think of what would become of her, but her scrambled thoughts would give over to a lucid dream in which Major Sturgis would steal to her bed as a shadowy form and make passionate love to her, kissing her shoulders and breasts and moving methodically, knowingly lower, his lips torching her flesh with unimaginable pleasure.

She often wondered if *he* had such dreams of *her*.

One night, as the days of her final week counted down, he surprised her. She had arrived with her cleaning supplies and morphine to find him clad in a borrowed C.S.A. uniform.

Standing up.

She gasped. He smiled.

He looked so handsome that the sight of him took her breath away. He gestured for her to approach and then he sat on the edge of his bed and tugged off his trousers. With her aid, he stood again. To anyone else's eyes, the prosthetics would have been ugly, replete as they were with leather and metal and laced bindings resembling something with which a mule might be bridled.

To Esther, they were beautiful. Erotic.

She could not contain her glee: "You're a whole man again!"

"If that be," he said, "then it is *you,* Miss Esther, who has made me so."

In the flush of arousal, she helped him remove the bulky objects, and as she prepared to wash his stumps she could sense that he was lapsing into a profound melancholy.

"Whatever is it, Major Sturgis? Your new legs promise better days ahead, don't they?"

He shook his head.

"I'm gone up," he whispered. "There's no hope. I'll be sent back to Virginia in a few days now, and I'll be hanged."

"No, don't say that. I couldn't bear for that to happen."

"But, you see . . . no one believes in my innocence."

"I do."

He reached out and touched her hair and let his forefinger graze her cheek lovingly. She closed her eyes, wanting their evolving intimacy never to end.

"Lie back," she murmured, and as she washed his stumps she told him of the Reverend Baldwin's letters to her and of her dismissal and her approaching departure.

"That Baldwin is a gutless Holy Joe," said Sturgis.

"He's jealous of you," said Esther. "I suppose he thinks I'm a fast trick. But I've never been with a man in that way. I'd never even really thought such thoughts until . . ."

She gave over suddenly to the deeper, slower rhythm of her breathing. Part of her feared that she had said too much, had transgressed modesty, had invalidated any claim to being a lady. But another part of her felt animated with courage. And lust.

A fable in my blood?

Her lips parted as she stroked higher on her satyr's legs; his eyes were closed, and she heard him moan, and though a blanket covered his midsection she could easily tell that he had an erection. Mildly unnerved by the sight, she first hesitated, then slid the blanket free.

She looked up and saw that his expression was a wild mixture of apology and confusion and desire. His lips moved, and she readied herself to meet any protest that he might issue. She felt daring and bold and free from all the poisonous restraints she had been taught. On her knees she inched closer, wishing that she had been schooled in the art of pleasing a man. Her choices were instinctive; her fingers spider-walked onto his warm, smooth, hardened flesh, and she smiled as he tensed with pleasure.

It was just when she had positioned herself to lower her mouth onto him that footsteps approached. The blanket was hurriedly replaced, and she rose to meet a pale, thin, pimply-faced boy, a hospital attendant.

"Rafe, what do you want?" she snapped.

"Nuss Esther, ma'am, he's crazy—Chaplain Baldwin. Gone around the bend and ravin' about God tellin' him to kill the Satyr—pardon, I mean Major Sturgis here. And about you, ma'am, bein' a pretty rapid little case just like your mama and the Devil hisself makin' you wicked. Baldwin, he made me fetch him a lead mallet from the blacksmith and . . . and please, Nuss Esther, don't you spill to him or nobody I told you so."

"No, Rafe, I won't do any such thing. Thank you for the warning. Now go on about your business."

When the boy had departed, Esther went again to the man she loved and desired. But he only shook his head.

"No, dear Esther. This is not to be. And you must protect yourself from Baldwin. Here, keep this on your person at all times. I call it my 'toothpick.'"

He forced a grin as he handed the bowie knife to her. She clutched it to her breasts and fought back tears.

"I'll tell one of the doctors," she said. "I'll get the sheriff. I won't let—"

But he shushed her and took her face in his hands and kissed her lips ever so gently.

"If not Baldwin and his mallet, then the hangman's noose. Or some extra deep drinks from the morphine bottle you bring to me. Isn't it all the same?"

"I want to be with you always," she cried into his chest.

"I have no future to offer you," he whispered. "Go and do as you must . . . for yourself, dear Esther. Dear, sweet, beautiful Esther."

And that is what Esther did.

Though the deciding moment was not planned. As certainly as Sherman marched toward Savannah, laying waste along the way, Esther walked through a netherworld composed of horror and the erotic, and at times, yes, she believed she heard a fable being recited in her blood, an ancient tale of one being caught between a saint and a satyr. A riddle with no apparent solution.

Until the night before her scheduled departure arrived.

The usual hish and hash of supper had been served, and she wheedled with the hospital's dog-robber cook for a few choicer chunks of meat for the repast of Major Sturgis. She was leaving the kitchen when the Reverend Baldwin drew her violently aside.

"Submit to my passions, my Esther, or tonight I swear to almighty God I'll bash your satyr's brains in and I'll have my way with you by force if I must. Then the two of you can take up company in the snakehole. For all eternity."

She wrestled herself free from him, scratching at and spitting into his sweaty, pink face. Wrongly, she reasoned she had seen the last of his cowardly soul for the evening. A different sort of resolve galvanized her as she prepared for her final owling round. Having made one slight change in the usual array of supplies she carried, she began her night's work, as always leaving her attention to Sturgis for last so that she could look forward to it as the night deepened.

But the smell of cinnamon altered her course.

Terror flashed behind her eyes like vicious strokes of lightning. She dashed to the area where Major Sturgis lay and there found Baldwin kneeling, his back to her, apparently in prayer, the mallet at his side. Sturgis was awake; he was calm. It seemed clear that he was not going to make an effort to protect himself.

Never had an object felt so right in Esther's hands as did the bowie knife. Never had she felt such a surge of volition. She strode forward and gently said, "Reverend Baldwin, please, if you will, turn around."

The surprise registering on the man's face was total. And as Esther brought the knife down with all her might, she heard both Baldwin and Sturgis utter a shocked, muted protest.

Esther lost track of the number of satisfying stabs.

"No, dear God, no, my Esther," Sturgis was muttering when she had spent her fury. "My God, they'll find him," he followed. "There's nowhere to hide his body. Dear God, Esther."

Esther smiled, then leaned forward and kissed him reassuringly.

Rafe helped her.

He did not, however, stay to watch the body of the saint and the knife of the satyr disappear into the abominable reaches of the snakehole.

When Esther returned to her satyr, she felt more

emboldened than ever, felt that she had transcended all boundaries of both darkness and light. She pulled the privacy curtain so that they were fully alone and she kissed him passionately, kissed through his feeble attempts to protest. And she raised her bloodied hands and murmured, "Whatever made Lady Macbeth so upset about such spots as these?"

She could tell by his eyes that he did not fully recognize this new, dagger-minded young woman. Esther found the moment consummately erotic. And she was intent upon living, living everything, knowing more of death and desire than even the mythic creatures languoring in the pages of Ovid.

She lifted her dress and removed her underwear, and when Sturgis had released himself to meet the fire of her kisses, she lowered herself onto him and felt flames of pain and ecstasy roar throughout her body. And when she had lain for as long in her satyr's arms as she dared, she rose and held out a blue bottle of morphine for him to see.

"I have filled it for you," she said.

"Thank you," he said, "for this, and for the little death, the gift of pleasure you gave with such passion."

She hesitated, fearing that her eyes had betrayed her.

"If we can't have a life together, this is the way I want it to be."

But he looked into the secret cell of her heart and he shook his head.

"No, Esther. Hand me the other bottle."

She did not want to.

"Please," she whispered, "this is the way I . . ."

Reluctantly she handed him the other blue bottle of

morphine, also full, and he smashed it against the side of his bed.

She fought tears of anger and sadness.

"Leave me with a kiss, dear Esther . . . and with a promise, a promise that you will go to Washington and put all of the horror of this war and this place behind you and live the life you must live . . . free from phantoms of any kind."

That following morning Esther left to join her mother.

Hers was the long day that welcomes the night.

That following morning Sturgis did not wake.

His was the long night that never sees another sunrise.

Stephen Gresham: "*The Saint, the Satyr and the Snakehole' was conceived when I read about the use of 'snakeholes' in civil war hospitals as dumping spots for all manner of nasty stuff, including amputated limbs. The image stuck in my mental filter somehow as the dark side of eroticism, and from there the characters of the 'saint,' the 'satyr' and the attractive nurse came to life and the story was off and running.*"

MEMENTO MORI

Melanie Tem

Tem's novels include the Stoker Award–winning Prodigal, *plus* Blood Moon, Wilding, Revenant, Desmodus, Tides, Black River *and, in collaboration with Nancy Holder,* Making Love *and* Witch-Light. *Her upcoming short fiction includes stories in* Gargoyle, Going Postal, *and* Snapshots. *Tem was awarded the 1991 British Fantasy Award, the Icarus, for Best Newcomer. She lives in Colorado with her husband, writer/editor Steve Rasnic Tem, and their children.*

In her husband's arms, at the moment of orgasm, Ann saw the death's-head under his beloved face. She cried out, "I love you. Oh, I love you."

He moaned, as if in response, to her or to the monster. The shuddering of his climax and of her own terrified, interrupted passion dissipated the apparition and pushed it back out of sight, but not for an instant would she dare forget it was there.

"I love you," she said again after she could breathe.

Philip lay on his back, happily spent, his arm under her shoulders and his hand on the back of her head, her temple, the nape of her neck. When he played with her hair and massaged her scalp like that, the intense comfort of it could sometimes verge on hallucinogenic. But it never went on long enough. Invariably he'd stop the wonderful circular stroking well

243

before she wanted him to, claiming boredom or muscle fatigue, and her half-playful pleas for more would be to no avail. Consequently, the pleasure was always diluted by the knowledge that it would end too soon.

"What's wrong?" he asked now.

Almost every time they made love, he asked that. Ann nestled into the hollow of his shoulder, where the illusion of safety was strongest, and as usual tried, "Nothing. Nothing's wrong."

"Ann."

"Not really wrong. I—I didn't come."

That wasn't true, but he seemed at least to consider that it might be. "Oh. Sorry." He squinted down at her. "Do you want me to do something?"

Don't die, she thought fiercely. *Don't leave me.* But she knew from experience that if she said that aloud he'd protest that he had no intention of dying any time soon and she should trust by now that he'd never leave her; she and the baby were his life. Sometimes he'd become seriously annoyed; a few times he'd even left their bed. So Ann pretended to be reassured, or restrained herself from saying anything in the first place, but in truth his words helped not at all because they missed the point.

The baby made a little noise in her sleep, and both Ann and Philip were instantly alert. It wasn't a cry, not even really a whimper, but it did require parental response. Ann couldn't bear the thought of lying there waiting for Philip to return and tell her everything was okay, so she patted his shoulder, said, "I'll go," and slid out her side of the bed. On her way out of the room she was assaulted by the vivid, detailed, perfectly realized vision of coming back to find Philip dead in bed. His skin would be too cool. She'd bring her cheek lightly against his lips and there'd be no breath.

The baby was fine. For now. Ann had to touch her to be sure and even then, of course, wasn't sure: some disease could at this very moment be working inside the tiny body, hidden by the thin but opaque façade of flesh and bone.

Ostensibly this was nothing but a paranoid fantasy; certainly Philip had made clear his disapproval and disdain. But Ann kept thinking about all the parents throughout human history whose infants had, in fact, died of insidious diseases; no doubt some of those children had looked fine, too, and no doubt their parents had told themselves, or been told, that they were worrying too much. They'd been duped.

Ann rested her chin on her hands folded on the crib rail to watch her daughter. One dimpled hand was curled in the teddy-bear blanket. Dark hair silked the delicate round skull. Bright red baby's-blood oozed from the soft spot on top.

Staring, Ann clapped her hand over her mouth, but not in time to stifle her cry. The baby jerked awake, wailing before she was even fully conscious. Ann heard Philip say her name, heard his feet thump to the floor and then his rapid footsteps down the hall. Quickly she reached to lift the baby so she'd be holding her when he came in. The globe of her daughter's head fit into her cupped palm. There was no blood. Not yet.

As she turned to face Philip in the doorway, he demanded anxiously, "Ann? What is it?"

"Nothing. Everything's okay." Somewhat embarrassed, Ann met him at the door with the baby, who, not having been seriously disturbed, was already asleep again. "I—thought I saw something, but I didn't. She's okay." *This time.*

Philip took their child, examined and caressed her in one deft motion. "Shit, Ann." His head was bent over the baby, cuddled against his chest. "You're making *me* a nervous wreck."

"Sorry." She laughed a little to show she knew she'd been silly.

Philip laid the baby carefully back into the crib— on her side, to minimize the chances of SIDS—and covered her lightly with the teddy-bear blanket. The pink night-light limned his hair and beard, the line of his shoulder and arm, the tender expression on his face, and Ann was profoundly, dangerously moved by the beauty of the moment. Which would pass. Which, now, had already passed; Philip sighed and straightened. He kissed her lightly, held her briefly. "Goodnight, honey. I'll be in later. I'm going to watch that movie I taped." Ann bit back a protest and forced herself not to cling. It was entirely possible that she would never see him again.

In bed alone, she turned onto her side and flung an arm and a leg across Philip's empty place. If he were dead, she'd stretch out like this every night trying futilely to fill the endless space. Or she'd curl up like this—she brought her knees up and her arms down—in a doomed attempt to protect herself from his absence. She would miss him so much. She would be so lonely. She'd know the instant she opened her door and saw the police officers on her porch—black uniforms, glinting badges, downcast eyes and shuffling feet—that they had brought terrible news about Philip. She'd stay like this in her bed, curled up, for days, weeks. People would tell her she had to pull herself together for the sake of her daughter, and she'd say to them, "Why? What's the point? Sooner or later she'll die, too, and then it won't matter."

Ann dozed off and jerked awake several times, always with tears in her eyes and a lump in her throat and the memory or anticipation, virtually indistinguishable, of having sustained enormous loss.

Discovering Philip beside her just before dawn, not having known when he came to bed, seemed a further ambush. At first she thought he wasn't breathing, and with trepidation she held her own breath to listen; then she heard, undeniably, his faint snore, and resented the tender relief that flooded through her. Someday she would listen like that and he would, in fact, have stopped breathing, would never snore beside her again.

Up before sunrise, in a clear blue morning, she put on duster, slippers, and gardening gloves. She took up her long-nosed clippers and went into the garden with the intention of cutting a rose for the white bud vase on the breakfast table. The bush in the far back corner by the fence had just sprung into bloom, and there, at eye level, was a perfect rose, exactly the blossom she'd imagined. But now, in its actual presence, she couldn't bring herself to be so deliberate an instrument of its destruction.

The rose was like folded tissue, she thought, but it wasn't. The rose was like a fragile nest, or the inside of her baby daughter's ear. But it wasn't. It was like nothing but itself, a perfect rose, and there was no use for the glancing description provided by simile when she had direct access to the thing itself.

The flower's dominant color was pale pink. The edges of its petals were gilded peach. Its heart and the two fat buds—one on either side of the full bloom, one slightly higher on the stem than the other—were cerise. The thorned stem, the ridged leaves, the sepals like the setting of a gemstone for each bud were emerald green. A dewdrop glittered. Moist, heady fragrance brought tears—of gratitude, of terror—to Ann's eyes.

The sweet fragrance deepened into stench. The petals, now gray serrated with crackling brown, fell off over her wrist. Mesmerized, she watched as the rose disintegrated and decayed; from its center, now mushy and almost black, a pale worm reared its horned head and engorged body against her lips, which were still pursed and slightly parted in an appreciative kiss for the perfect rose.

Ann cried out, stepped back, dropped the rotted flower and wiped her mouth on her glove. The rosebush, laden with blossoms and buds and sparkling with dew, was undisturbed. The only dead flower was the one she'd broken off without meaning to. Now lying in the grass at her feet, many shades of pink and peach among many shades of green, it appeared still perfect, but she knew that was a deception for she'd been shown how it had already begun to die.

Philip was up when she went back inside. "Good morning, honey," she said, thinking how much she loved him but managing to keep the anger out of her face and voice. "You're up early."

"I'm not up. Got a headache," he said groggily, and briefly put his pajama'd arm around her on his way to the bathroom. First his body heat and then its absence enveloped her.

Brain tumor, Ann thought, and within a split second an entire scene had played itself out in her imagination: his increasing pain, finally the visit to the doctor, the moment when Philip would tell her the news.

Foolish, she reprimanded herself. But her friend's husband really was dying of a brain tumor, and in hindsight her friend realized that the first symptom had been headaches which he'd had for months before the diagnosis was made. It happened. One of these days, Ann knew, it would happen to her, or something equally awful; like now, she'd have been remonstrating with herself not to overreact, or, much worse, she'd have been caught completely unawares.

Philip shuffled out of the bathroom, muttering in an attempt at good humor, "At least it's a beautiful morning."

Ann agreed, but already it wasn't. Already the exquisite dawn cast of the air had thickened; already the sun was up and too hot; traffic noise from the highway blocks away had risen unpleasantly with rush hour. And someday she would lose everybody she loved, through their deaths or her own.

The baby was chuckling. Ann loved that sound. She and Philip stood still in the kitchen for a long moment, gazing at each other and listening to the happy sound of their daughter waking up to another day. Ann could not bear the sweetness of it. "I'll get her," she said, and Philip, holding his head and groaning, didn't argue.

As she entered the nursery again, the baby's delighted gurgling had changed to a whimper. Ann stopped in the doorway, afraid to go nearer, while a voice in her head exhorted, *This is it. It's happened. If not now, soon. If not soon, someday. There's no escape.* Desperately she studied the scene before her so that later, when she had lost her child, she could remember every detail of this last morning: sunlight shafting across the green and yellow wallpaper and the teddy-bear blanket, dust motes like lace, the odors of baby powder and wet diaper, the soft little noises her daughter was still making. Later, as she remembered these things, they would seem far more real and close to her than they did now.

By the time a half-dozen steps had carried her to the crib, her daughter had fallen silent and Ann had anticipated in excruciating detail what it would be like to find her dead or mysteriously vanished. The mattress would still hold the impression of the small body; she would lay her fists there. She would let herself be quiet for a few minutes, in order to take it in, before screaming for her husband. She would cry, "Philip! Philip! The baby's gone!" and he'd come running—

The baby was fine. Rage swept through Ann, leaving her weak and trembling.

She bent her face low, feeling the feathery baby's breath across her throat. When the breath turned rank, she flinched and coughed but didn't turn aside.

Very softly she touched a fingertip to the tiny

cheekbone. The baby laughed. The thin skin peeled away as she followed the line of the jaw, revealing the baby's skull with its hollow eye sockets and gaping toothless mouth. Ann cringed but didn't remove her hand, laid it instead flat on the small face with the heel against her child's mouth and her fingers over the nose and eyes.

The baby wiggled, tried to turn her head. Effortlessly, Ann held it. She brought her thumb and forefinger together, pinching the tiny nose so it couldn't take in air, while pressing the heel of her hand firmly over the rosebud lips to seal them shut.

It didn't take long for the baby to grow limp and still. Breath stopped, quite as Ann had imagined. Pulse stopped. Warmth began at once to fade from the soft flesh and color from the perfect skin. The bright eyes, still blue, started to glaze over.

When she was certain her daughter was dead, Ann stood back. Her heart was racing from relief and arousal. Her nerves tingled in excited anguish, and anticipation thrilled her as she visualized what would happen next:

She would ease into bed with her husband. He would say her name. Carefully she would reach to rest her fingertips on his temple, where the tumor might be lodged, and her other hand would, just as tenderly, caress his lower abdomen, the sensitive hollows of his pelvis. Her touch would put the lie to his pain, pretend to take it away, and he would turn to her as eagerly as if neither of them would ever die, as if their child were not already dead in the next room. They would make love. He would not quite reach the core of her, decaying deep inside.

Then, spent but not satisfied, she would go to check on the baby, would find her dead as she had always known someday she would, and she would scream for him, "Philip!" But, knowing, he would already be gone.

Melanie Tem: *"Somebody, maybe Socrates, once declared that the unexamined life is not worth living. Sometimes, though, the too-examined life isn't worth living, either."*

TO WHOM IT MAY CONCERN

Judith Tracy

Though this is Tracy's first published story, the Kentucky writer says, "As far back as I can remember, I've been a storyteller."

*I*f you're reading this letter, my package must have arrived safely. As a cop, you will soon see why I want this information to go public. The hurt that Tyler Harrington IV has inflicted on me is irrevocable. I am seeing to it that he will never hurt me or anyone else ever again. I apologize for the graphic nature of this message, but the raw truth must be told.

I don't know what possessed me to believe that Tyler really was in love with me. Maybe, because I wanted it so much to be true, I shielded myself from the truth. Or maybe it was because he was so convincing. Anyway, it doesn't matter. My life is meaningless now. I have no one to live for but Thomasina. Forgive me world, but a cat isn't enough.

I'm writing this to point the finger at the real culprit. Tyler Harrington IV killed me. Physically, it was the bottle of sleeping pills, but Tyler might as well have opened my mouth and poured them in. He took everything I had to offer, drained me dry, and left me here to rot by myself.

Dr. Harrington isn't what he appears to be. His friends and family see only the caricature. The real Tyler lurks beneath the guise of a human, and I'm a testimony to his dark side. One look at me will confirm my accusations.

You might be wondering, Why kill yourself? Things might have been different had I at least one good friend to confide in, someone to help me deal with this depression. Just one good friend would have made all the difference in the world. But that was the first thing Tyler took care of. He made sure I had no one but him to rely on.

For you to truly understand the circumstances, I must start at the beginning. It was at the racetrack on a crisp October day. I had put two dollars on Jumping Jack Flash in the first race and was screaming at the top of my lungs for him to finish the stretch in at least third. Someone shouted, "Jack is a flash in the pan. Anyone who puts money on him deserves to lose."

I looked back to see who was making fun of me and there he was, in the seat behind me, looking handsome and debonair. He smiled at me strangely, his front teeth biting his bottom lip. I glanced away sheepishly. Why would someone so gorgeous give someone like me a second look? So I didn't reply. But he did. When he spoke again, my heart pounded furiously against my chest.

Flash came in last. Maybe he didn't finish at all. I didn't care. It gave Tyler another chance to tease me. When I asked, he said his horse had won and I congratulated him. He had a lot more money riding than I did. Besides, what's two dollars compared to the company of this dreamboat? Later, down the road, I was to learn that Tyler was a poor loser, a true gambler with a bad temper. But that's neither here nor there and doesn't really matter now.

As I was saying, his horse won the race. He was lucky three or four other times. We ended up sitting together after the third race. Chatting, smiling, making small talk. Then dinner. I almost wish he'd lost and displayed his horrible disposition. Then at least I would have had an inkling of what a horrible man he was. But such is fate. In most probability I would have overlooked it. Just like I excused everything else he did. You see, Tyler had charisma. Everyone loved him.

I guess the hardest thing to deal with is that I'm still in love with him. He's so beautiful to look at. Tall, slender, athletic. His turquoise eyes, impish and soulful. Even his baritone voice is alluring. My mother was delighted when I told her I was dating a doctor. Mothers are like that. They think that being in a noble profession makes you respectable. I had the same thoughts in the beginning myself, so I guess she can't be blamed. A couple of times I tried to tell her of his second identity, but she wouldn't hear of it. She never believed a single bad thing I told her about him, so I quit confiding in her. Mom wanted me to be married and happy. After taking one look at this man, she made it obvious I should count my blessings and put up with his faults. She died a couple of months after meeting Tyler. I remember being grateful that I had a real boyfriend, someone who cared about me to help me through the ordeal. I'd have been better off alone.

There wasn't a day that went by I didn't wonder what he saw in me. I'm not attractive. In fact, homely would be a compliment. Why would an accomplished plastic surgeon, handsome as all get-out, want a short, big, dumpy girl? Maybe if I had questioned it more, I wouldn't be writing to you today. But if you know Tyler, then you know how devilishly charming he can be. He could con a homeless man out of his cardboard box. They say hindsight is twenty-twenty. Whoever they are, they're right.

I should have picked up on the clues. There were plenty of them, like the charitable clinic he ran in nearby Chamberstown. Although his name isn't listed on the door, Tyler is the presiding physician. To the townspeople he is a godsend, working pro bono on disfigured patients who under normal circumstances couldn't afford his high fees. I used to do some clerical work for him, but never was allowed to talk about it in public. I thought it was because he wanted to avoid the publicity. Little did I know his true purpose.

To everyone else, Tyler seemed normal. Everyone loved him. He was an only child by wealthy parents. Denied nothing. Football captain, senior-class president, voted most likely to succeed. It was no surprise he was accepted to Harvard Medical School. Now he's one of the top surgeons in the country, maybe even the world. Surrounded by beauty, he had but to ask and it was his. Who could I tell about Tyler's dark halo? Who would believe me?

From day one, people whispered behind our backs. "What does Tyler see in her? He can do better than that. She's a two-bagger if ever I saw one."

He heard. I know he did. He didn't answer them, nor did he defend us. I was much too afraid to pick a fight. I'd watch as women would come on to him. Vivacious, sexy women. Model types. Movie stars. Skinny. They'd hang all over him. None of them paid attention to the fact that he was with me. Tyler loved the attention. He was always pleasant. He'd flash them a grin and a wink, but he was always faithful. At least up until now. Now he doesn't have a reason to be. He owns me. Where can I go in a wheelchair? Nobody'd have me before. I'd have even less of a chance finding someone now.

For a while everything was perfect. A real fairy-tale romance. He showered me with flowers. Huge bouquets of red roses with a white one in the middle. "For purity, Doreen," he said, "because our love is genuine and flawless." And boxes of opera creams because they were my favorites and he told me he loved me just the way I am.

Dinner and a show, charity benefits, theatrical openings. We went to them all. First we'd hit the mall. I'd try on dress after dress till he found one he liked. It was always red or some other bright shade. Said I looked best in citrus colors. Brought out the pigmentation in my cheeks. "No black or navy for you. So what if you're overweight? Do you think dark colors hide it? No. So why not wear bright tones? Let people notice you. I'm not ashamed of you, so why should you hide behind drab dresses?"

He paid for every one of those dresses. On my salary all I could afford was discount shops. I'm a telemarketer. Only job I could find even with a college degree in fashion retailing. Department stores don't want overweight people in their showrooms. Oh, they won't come out and say it, but I know it's the truth all the same. It didn't take a lot of brains to realize why skinny people always got the job when I was more qualified. I was lucky to get a desk job doing marketing research, and I practically had to beg them for it. I think they relented because no one could see me over a telephone.

Even though they were financially hard times, they were the best times of my life. Tyler made every day special. It wasn't the parties, or the fine restaurants we went to. They were okay. It was the times we spent alone. Sex. You see, I was a virgin. Never been touched. It wasn't because of my religious or moral beliefs. No one ever asked me out for me to say no. Rosie Palm and her five friends were my previous lovers. I had many ways to get off.

Tyler loved to watch me play with myself and I didn't mind. I'd do anything he asked. Sometimes I'd turn on the shower massage. Pulse. The water would be warm. I'd station myself on my back with my ass against the tub. My legs would crawl up the tile wall till they were straight. Then I'd open myself with my hands and position myself where the water was directly beating against my clit. It felt marvelous. Now, when I think back, it must have been a sight. Obese lady, wiggling and jiggling, fucking water.

Other times he'd watch me masturbate with a dildo or my fingers. So what if it turned him on? I loved to watch him masturbate, too. His well-manicured fingers stroking his manhood. A real sight to see. He was big. Bigger than my vibrator.

The first time I saw him naked I was in awe. I was thirty years old. Imagine being thirty and having never seen a nude man. Tyler was breathtaking. His chest was hairy. Short curly hairs that matched his pubics. Broad shoulders, flat stomach, and muscular legs. Fleshy buns, too. My eyes swallowed him whole. He was proud of his body. Strutting around the bedroom with a towel dangling from his cock. "Like your new towel rack?" he'd say.

I took my time undressing. I was ashamed for him to see my body. There he was, totally unclothed, and I stood before him blubbering like an idiot. He was so gentle and loving. His soft words of love and desire dried my tears. Slowly I began to disrobe.

"You're beautiful, Doreen. I don't like skinny women. Does that seem strange to you?"

I looked at him through my moist eyes and nodded.

"Yeah, I suppose it does, but that's the truth. Call it a fetish, call it weird, but I like obese women. The bigger the better. Fat women are intelligent, better conversationalists, and more empathetic. They are better people because life is harder on them. They can't rely on their looks, so they make their way in the world on spit and spunk."

I heard the words and the hidden meaning. Big women are grateful. They don't ask much and appreciate everything. We are desperate people. Now, maybe his comments would have pissed you off. But put yourself in my place. Tyler was the first man to pay attention to me, so I chose not to read between the lines. And I yielded to his wishes.

"I care for you, Doreen. Really I do. We have a real chance to make this work. A real relationship based on love, trust, and honesty. Tonight I'm going to make love to you. Fiery, passionate love. Then maybe you'll believe me."

He played a convincing game. Our lovemaking was slow and gentle. Tyler kissed every part of my body. I shuddered at the closeness. For the first time in my life I felt beautiful and desirable. He really made me feel that way. His kisses were tender, soft, sweet.

When our lips locked I felt his tongue dart in and out and I held him tight. It took my breath away.

Then he made his way down to my breasts, gliding his tongue down my chin, my neck, and finally my breasts. He buried his head between the cleavage and nuzzled.

"Oh baby," he said. "These are the two most perfect breasts I've ever seen in my life. I don't know if I can keep from exploding."

His hands reached up and started to knead them. They bobbled. I quivered. The sensations drove me wild with a passion I had never experienced. His mouth suckled my breasts and I could feel the familiar throbbing below. A kind of empty feeling, wet and waiting. I wanted him inside me. No more substitutes. A real, hard cock was there in the room and it wanted my pussy.

"Put it inside. I want to feel you inside me," I whispered.

"What, dear? Speak louder. Don't be afraid to ask for what you want. That's what lovers do. Give and receive. Talk dirty, be aggressive. I'll do for you. You do for me. You want me to come inside you? Whatever you want. I love you, Doreen. Please, love me back."

Those words reached the very core of me. He wants *me* to love *him?*

"I do, Tyler," I shouted. "I do love you. I would do anything for you. *Anything.*"

It was as if he were waiting to hear those words, because instantly he kneeled. Like a stallion who's been primed, he mounted me. His knees nudged my legs open wide and he hovered above me, his engorged cock in his hand. I closed my eyes and waited.

"Don't hide from me, baby. Let me see those dazzling eyes. I want you to look at me. I want to know you see me and aren't fantasizing about another man. I couldn't bear it."

"How could you think that? There hasn't been anyone and never will be. Only you, Tyler."

He smiled and I relaxed, watching him as he teased my clit with the head of his shaft. Occasionally he would use his tongue. He waited patiently until I climaxed. It was an unbelievable mixture of emotions and sensations. I cried out, overwhelmed by his loving.

My pain was the ignition to his fire. He couldn't hold out any longer either. I watched as he shoved his cock inside. I was wet, but it still hurt. Both fists were clenched as I tried to keep from crying out and diminishing his pleasure. But he could sense it and I know he enjoyed it.

"Go ahead. Scream. Cry. It always hurts the first time. Pain and sex go hand in hand. I couldn't stop now if I wanted to. You feel so good, baby. Sweet Doreen. Darling Doreen. It's so good. The best. I love you. Can't stop. Going to explode."

I held on, my arms enveloping him as I felt the warm liquid invade my insides. We stayed like that for an eternity and then he rolled over.

"Tyler," I said softly. "I'm not on any birth control." I waited for his response and held my breath. Would he be angry? Instead, he was even more loving than before.

"So? If you get pregnant then you'll have to marry me. I'm not worried about it. Don't you be. We're in love. Someday we'll get married and be together for always. I love you, Doreen. I always will."

So you see, he was the perfect man. Romantic, handsome, and a delicious, carefree lover. I had more than I ever wished for. It wasn't just one night; he was like this all the time. He tended to my every need. It was as if he were the answer to my prayers. An angel. I became dependent on him. Couldn't live without him. Can you understand why I was willing to do anything for him?

But enough reminiscing. I want to get to the point. It's over. All over. He's seen to that. His little medical convention last month didn't fool me. I knew he was there with another woman. I even thought I knew her name. Jennifer Camden. Tall, blond, skinny bimbo with teensy tits. Little nothings. She doesn't have any redeeming qualities except she looks good hanging on to his arm.

Many a night I'd envision them together. I saw her batting her eyelashes and making profound statements like, "Whatever you want, dear. Ooh, I don't know. You decide, snookums." I curbed my anger, because I believed he would come back to me eventually. No way could she suck cock like I do, inhaling the whole thing and swallowing his cum. Nor could she bury his shaft between her tits. She doesn't have any. Pimples perhaps. He loved tit fucking. He would never give that up. My tongue would lick the head and he'd moan in ecstasy. I even let him slip it up my ass. I hated it, but I let him. There was nothing I didn't do for him in bed. Nothing. And so I pretended to be ignorant.

But Tyler was the sly one. I know he wanted me to find out he was cheating. He used my fear of abandonment to force me to submit to his perverted fetishes. So he played his trump card. He was a gambler when I met him. He's a gambler still. He wanted me to think he was with Jennifer so I'd give in to his last and most hellacious obsession. He played me like a maestro and won. I caved in to his pleadings and made the supreme sacrifice. I let him cut my legs off. Both of them. And all because he always wanted to make it with a woman with stumps. All because I thought it would keep him with me. I died that day. Only my body lived on. But at least I thought I still had Tyler. And I did, for a while. He fired Jennifer and I thought that was that. Boy, was I stupid.

Watch the enclosed tape, dear officer of the law. Tyler will wonder where it went. He watches it all the time. It's labeled "chainsaw," a funny, depraved joke of a title. Another testimony to his warped psyche. You see, I never had cancer. Medical files can be tampered with, and who would accuse Tyler of having another motive? Along with this statement, there should be enough evidence to expose Tyler for what he is. If you need more evidence, go to his apartment in Chamberstown. His walls are shrouded with pictures of deformed creatures, nature's jokes, multiple amputees, and accident victims. Tyler's own museum *d'art*.

Are you beginning to understand his festering obsessions? Tyler worships ugliness in a world that showers him with beauty and glamour. And I was to be his living trophy. His pygmalion. His vision of the perfect woman. Ironic, isn't it?

So, humor a corpse. Investigate. Indict and convict. Do it to save another from playing into his hands. Please show him this report. I want him to read it and know I've gotten my pound of flesh. I want revenge.

Vengeance is sweet, Tyler, and it's all I've thought

about since I received the picture you sent me of you and that other woman. I am left with nothing but hatred and despair. You are a genuine sadist. You don't just like inflicting pain, you *live* for it. When I realized I had lost you forever, I took the bottle of sleeping pills you left for me on my bedside table.

Some say those who commit suicide wander the third dimension. Believe me, if there's a shred of truth in this, I will be back to haunt you. So look for me, Tyler. I'll be in the mirror when you shave and play with your schlong. When you fall and stumble, it'll be me who pushed you. Maybe I'll even be in bed next to you when you're fucking your next victim. I hate you, Tyler, with a passion that will span eternity, for you finally found the one thing that would send me to my grave. The ultimate victory. A woman even fatter and uglier than me.

Doreen

Judy Tracy: *"The idea of 'To Whom' occurred to me when a major television station aired a report on the destructive forces society plants in the minds of young women. From a very early age, girls are taught that thin and beautiful are traits to strive for. I just wondered, What if the opposite were true? What if there was a man who worshipped ugliness? The story took off from there."*

PICNIC AT LAC DU SANG

Graham Masterton

A previous Graham Masterton story for Hot Blood, *"The Secret Shih-Tan," was nominated for a Bram Stoker Award and has been filmed for Tony Scott's TV series* The Hunger, *starring Jason Scott Lee. Masterton has just seen the publication of a new horror novel set in modern-day Warsaw,* The Chosen Child *aka* Dziccko Ciemności. *He and his Polish wife, Wiescka, are now frequent visitors to Poland, where his horror novels have regularly topped the bestseller lists. He has also published the first two in a new horror series for young adults,* Rook *and* Tooth & Claw, *and completed a third, provisionally entitled* The Hungry Houses.

The girls here are very young," said Baubay, taking a last deep drag at his cigarette and flicking it out of the Pontiac's window. "But let me tell you, they'll do *anything.*"

Vincent frowned across the street at the large Gothic-revival house. It wasn't at all what he had expected a brothel to look like. It was heavily over-shadowed by three giant dark-green elms, but he could see turrets and spires and decorated gables, and balconies where net curtains suggestively billowed in the summer breeze. The outside walls were painted a burned orange color, and there was something strange and otherworldly about the whole place, as if he had seen it in a painting, or dreamed it.

"I'm not so sure about this," he told Baubay. "I never visited a bordello before."

"Bordello!" Baubay piffed. "This is simply a very amenable place where guys like us can meet beautiful and willing young women, discuss the state of the economy, have a bottle of champagne or two, play Trivial Pursuit, and if we feel like it, get laid."

"Sounds like a bordello to me," said Vincent, trying to make a joke of it.

"You're not going to chicken out on me, are you? Don't say you're going to chicken out. Come on, Vincent, I've driven over eighty miles for this, and I'm not going back to Montreal without at least one game of hide the salami."

"It's just that I feel like—I don't know. I feel like I'm being unfaithful."

"Bullshit! How can you be unfaithful to a woman who walked out on you? How can you be unfaithful when she was screwing a *crotté* like Michael Saperstein?"

"I don't know, but it just feels that way. Come on, Baubay, I never looked at another woman for eleven years. Well, I *looked*, but I didn't do anything about it."

"So—after all those years of sainthood, you deserve to indulge yourself a little. You won't regret it, believe me. You'll be coming back for more. Hey—with your tongue dragging on the sidewalk."

"I don't know. Is there a restaurant or anything around here? Maybe I'll have some lunch and wait for you."

Baubay unfastened his seat belt and took his keys out of the ignition. "Absolutely emphatically no you are not. How do you expect me to enjoy fornicating with some ripe young teenager while all the time I know that you're sitting alone in some dreary diner eating Salisbury steak? What kind of friend would that make me? You're not backing out of this, Vincent. You're coming to meet Mme. Leduc whether you like it or not."

"Well, I'll *meet* her, okay?" Vincent agreed. "But whether I do anything else . . ."

Baubay took him by the elbow as if he were a blind man and propelled him to the opposite sidewalk. The morning was glazed and warm and there was hardly any traffic. The house stood in the older part of St. Michel-des-Monts, on a street which was still respectable but which was suffering from obvious neglect. The house next door was empty, its windows shuttered and its front door boarded up, its garden a tangle of weeds and wild poppies. Behind the houses, through a bluish haze, Vincent could see the mountains of Mont Blanc, Mont Tremblant, and beyond.

They climbed the stone steps to the front door and Baubay gave a smart, enthusiastic knock. The door was painted a sun-faded blue, and the paint had cracked like the surface of an old master. The knocker was bronze, and cast in the shape of a snarling wolf's head.

"See that?" said Baubay. "That was supposed to keep evil spirits at bay. They're quite rare, now."

They waited and waited and eventually Baubay knocked again. After a while they heard a door open and piano music, Mozart, and a woman's voice.

Vincent felt butterflies in his stomach, and he had a ridiculous childish urge to run away. Baubay winked at him and said, "This'll be Mme. Leduc now."

The front door was opened by a tall, ash-blond woman with her hair braided on top of her head. She was wearing a long silk negligee in pale aquamarine, trimmed with lace. She must have been forty-five at least, but she was extraordinarily beautiful, with a fine, slightly Nordic-looking face, and eyes that were such a pale, washed-out blue that they were scarcely any color at all. Her negligee was open almost to her waist, revealing a deep cleavage in which a large marcasite crucifix nestled. Judging by the way her breasts swung, she must have been naked underneath.

"Francois, what a pleasure," she said. Her accent was faintly Québécois, very precise and refined. "And—how exciting! You've brought your friend with you today."

"I couldn't keep you all to myself, could I?" asked Baubay. "Violette, this is Vincent Jeffries. He's a very talented man. A great musician. Like, eat your heart out, Johann Sebastian Bach."

Mme. Leduc held out her hand so that it slightly drooped, and Vincent realized that she expected him to kiss it. He did so, and when he lifted his eyes he saw that she was smiling at him in amusement. Baubay said, "Let's go inside. I could do some serious damage to a bottle of cold champagne."

They stepped into the hallway and Mme. Leduc closed the door behind them, blotting out the sunshine. "The tall one and the short one," she remarked, and then she gave a brittle, tinkling laugh. Baubay laughed too, like a dog barking, and gave her a pat on the bottom. His shortness had never given him any trouble with women, or so he said, and Vincent believed him, because he was always packed with energy and he was quite handsome in a roughly cut, unfinished way, with a square jaw and thick eyebrows and thick black curls. Apart from being taller, Vincent was much thinner and quieter, with blondish combed-back hair and a narrow, rather aquiline face, and a way of peering at people as if they were standing six or seven miles away. When she had first met him, Patricia had said that he looked like Lawrence of Arabia, trying to see through the glitter of a distant mirage. In the end, their marriage had turned out to be the mirage.

"So, you're a great musician, Mr. Jeffries?" asked Mme. Leduc. "Some of my girls are learning the piano. You will have to give them some pointers."

"Francois is exaggerating, as usual," said Vincent. "I write scores for television commercials—incidental music, links, stuff like that. Do you know the Downhome Donut music? That was mine. Right now Francois and I are working on a Labatt's beer ad together."

"You should hear what he's written!" said Baubay. "Is it dramatic? Is it sweeping? Do bears go to the woods to dress up as women?"

They entered a large, high-ceilinged living room. It probably overlooked the garden, but Vincent couldn't tell because all the windows were tightly covered by bleached white calico blinds, through which the sunlight filtered as softly as the memory of a long-lost summer day. The floor was pale polished hardwood, with antique scatter rugs, and the furniture was all antique, too, gilded and upholstered in creams and yellows. There were huge mirrors everywhere, which at first gave Vincent the impression that he had walked into a room crowded with fifteen or sixteen girls.

Madame Leduc clapped her hands and called, *"Attention, mes petites!* Mr. Baubay has arrived and he has brought a friend for us to entertain!"

Immediately, the girls came forward and clustered around them. Now Vincent could see that there were only seven of them, but he still felt overwhelmed, and more than anything else he wished that he were someplace else. He had never been simultaneously so aroused and so embarrassed in his whole life. All of the girls were pretty: two or three of them were almost as beautiful as Mme. Leduc. There was a redhead with skin as white as milk, and a long-haired brunette with dark slanting eyes that he could have drowned in. There were three blondes—two bubbly and curly, the other tall and mysterious with hair so long that she could have wrapped herself in it, like a silky curtain. There was another brunette who stood more shyly behind her friends, but she had a face so perfect that Vincent couldn't take his eyes off her.

What struck him most of all, though, was the way in which the girls were dressed. He didn't quite know what he had expected: Frederick's of Hollywood lingerie, maybe, or satin wraps like the one that Mme. Leduc was wearing. But they all wore plain white cotton nightdresses, almost ankle-length, and one of them was even wearing white socks. Vincent supposed that Mme. Leduc had wanted them to look younger than they really were, like schoolgirls; but even so none of them could have been older than eighteen or nineteen.

"Mr. Jeffries is a musician, girls," Mme. Leduc announced. "Perhaps he'll be kind enough to play for us while we bring him something to drink." She winked at Baubay, and Vincent saw her wink. She must have sensed how nervous he was, and, yes, it was a good idea, asking him to play the piano. It would help to relax him. "You like champagne, Mr. Jeffries? Or may I call you Vincent?"

"Sure you can call me Vincent. But right now I think I'd prefer a beer, if you don't mind."

"Anything you want," she said. She looked into his eyes for almost ten seconds without saying anything. Her eyes were extraordinary, like blue ink that has spilled across the surface of a mirror. He dropped his gaze and found himself looking at the cross that dangled in her cleavage. He could smell the perfume that she exuded from between her breasts. It was very summery and flowery, and for some reason it made him think of—what? He couldn't think. Something elusive. Something deeply emotional. Something that had happened a long time ago.

One of the girls came up and took his coat. Another loosened his necktie. "You like this?" said Baubay, walking up and down the room. "This is what I call pampering."

"Please, play," said the redhead, shyly, and pulled out the piano stool for him. Vincent sat down, flexed his fingers, and played one of his party pieces, a high-speed version of "Camptown Races." The girls laughed and clapped when he had finished, and one of the blondes kissed him on the cheek. The blonde with the long hair, more daring and more sensual, kissed him directly on the mouth. "Francois is right. You are a great musician. Your music is terrible—but you—you are a great musician." Bold words, he thought, almost frightening. But he had never had an erection while sitting at the piano before, as he did now. He could feel the warmth of the girl's body through her plain white nightdress. It was unbuttoned, and he could see the curve of a small swelling breast.

Mme. Leduc brought him a golden glass of beer in a frozen glass. He drank a little, and then he played something slower, more sentimental, a score he had written for a poem. The blonde with the long hair came and sat next to him, and put her arm around him, but he played this song for the brunette who stood away from the others, her eyes lowered, her fingers trailing through her hair.

"In your arms was still delight . . . quiet as a
 street at night;
And thoughts of you, I do remember,
Were green leaves in a darkened chamber,
Were dark clouds in a moonless sky."

The blond girl massaged his shoulders, and then ran her fingers all the way down his spine. The redhead stood behind him and stroked his hair. On the opposite side of the room, Baubay sat with one of the curly blondes on his knee and another kneeling on the floor beside him. He lifted his glass of champagne and gave Vincent a blissful beam. "Don't tell me this isn't the life, my friend. This is the life."

"Love, in you, went passing by," sang Vincent. He looked toward the brunette and she was lifting her hair so that it shone in the softly filtered sunlight in a

fine net of filaments. He didn't know whether she knew that he was looking at her or not. He didn't know whether she was flirting with him or not. She appeared to be indifferent, and yet—

"Love, in you, went passing by . . . penetrative,
  remote, and rare,
Like a bird in the wide air,
And, as the bird, it left no trace . . ."

He paused, and then he sang, very quietly, *"In the heaven . . . of your face."*

There was a momentary silence, and then Mme. Leduc pattered her hands together like a pigeon trapped in a chimney. "You weave quite a spell, Vincent. You must play us some more."

"Why doesn't one of your girls play? I'd like to hear them."

"Well, of course. I'm forgetting myself. You didn't come here to entertain *us*. Minette, why don't you play 'Curiose Geschichte' for Mr. Jeffries? Minette's been practicing very hard this month. And, Sophie, why don't you dance?"

Vincent left the piano and the girl with the long blond hair guided him over to the couch next to Baubay's, and sat down almost in his lap. She stroked his thigh through his chino pants and then she cupped her hand right between his legs, and squeezed it. He looked up at her but all she did was kiss him all over his face. He had drunk less than half of his beer but already he was beginning to feel that he had lost touch with reality. His cock was so hard that it ached and it just wouldn't go down.

Minette was one of the curly blondes. She sat at the piano with her eyes closed and played the slow, plaintive notes with perfect timing and inflection. Mme. Leduc was right: she had been practicing hard. She was almost concert standard. But if she could play like this, what was she doing here, in this godforsaken Canadian suburb, selling herself to any man who wanted her?

Sophie, the redhead, stood in the middle of the floor with her toes pointed like a ballerina. Then she swept her arms down, gathered the hem of her night-dress, and drew it over her head. It landed on the rug with a soft parachute rustle, leaving Sophie completely naked. She was full-breasted but she was very slim, with narrow hips and long, long legs. Her breasts were marbled with bluish veins and her nipples were a startling pink that clashed with her hair. Between her legs arose a bright red flame, although it did little to conceal the plumpness of her labia.

Sophie danced: fast, and very stylistically, Isadora Duncan on speed. She waved her arms as if she were spinning through a storm and her breasts responded with a wild, complicated dance of their own. She whirled around the room, around and around. Then she covered her face with her hands and knelt on the floor only two or three feet away from Vincent. She swayed from side to side, staring at him as she did so, until he felt hypnotized. Then she slowly arched backward until her shoulders were touching the rug, and the lips of her vulva peeled apart, revealing the glistening depths of her vagina.

As if this weren't enough, she reached down between her legs and pulled her lips even farther apart, exposing the tiny hole of her urethra, playing with her clitoris and sliding her long, manicured fingertips right inside her. The piano music. The succulent clicking of fingers and juice.

Vincent was breathless. As he watched, and he couldn't help watching, the blond girl was gripping his cock through his pants, squeezing it hard and rhythmically, and he knew that if he didn't make her stop, he was going to be finished before he had even begun.

Suddenly, Minette stood up and the music wasn't there anymore. Sophie rolled away across the rug. Mme. Leduc's hands pattered together again.

"Now, perhaps, a little something to eat, before we get down to the principal entertainment of the day?"

Vincent was trying unsuccessfully to fend off the blonde, who was licking his neck with the flat of her tongue and trying to slide her hand down the front of his pants. "You're wet," she breathed. "Your shorts are wet. I can feel it."

"Yes, food!" Baubay enthused. "I hope you made some of your crabcakes, Violette! Vincent, you should try Violette's crabcakes! And her *andouilles!*"

"I want to try your *andouille,*" the blonde breathed in Vincent's ear, and then draped her hair all over his head, so that he was tangled in it, suffocated in it.

They sat at a long table covered in an extravagantly long white linen cloth that poured over their knees and trailed across the floor. The windows of this room, too, were covered by bleached white blinds. Mme. Leduc sat at the head of the table, and the girls sat along either side. Vincent and Baubay sat side by side, each of them being cossetted and spoon-fed by the girls next to him. The food was like nothing that Vincent had ever eaten before: not all at the same meal, anyway. Cold spiced beef and fruit-flavored jellies; salads with endive and oranges; crabcakes served with fragments of honeycomb. There was a strange fried flatfish stuffed with peaches, and bowls of clear chilled soup that tasted like women's sexual juices lightly flavored with cilantro.

The shy brunette sat at the opposite end of the table, eating only a little and saying nothing at all. Vincent deliberately stared at her while he ate, but she never once raised her eyes to look at him. The blonde sitting next to him reached beneath the flowing table-cloth and started to massage him between the legs again. When he was hard, she jerkily tugged down his zipper and took out his erection, her fingers running up and down it like a piccolo player. He suddenly realized that he was beginning to enjoy himself.

"Do you think you could love me?" she asked him, in a hoarse, dirty whisper.

He kissed her on the lips. "You don't exactly make it easy to say no."

"But do you think you could *really* love me? Or any of us?"

"What? And marry you? And take you away from all this?"

She shook her head. "You could never do that, ever."

"But you're not going to do this for the rest of your life, are you? I mean, how old are you?"

"Eighteen."

"There you are, then. One day you'll meet the right guy, and you'll be able to put all of this behind you."

Again she shook her head. Vincent tried to kiss her again, but this time she raised her fingertips and pressed them against his lips.

Mme. Leduc stood up and tapped her spoon against her wineglass, so that it rang. "There!" she said. "We have fed very well . . . now for some other pleasures. Francois, have you chosen who you would like to share your afternoon?"

Baubay put his arm around Sophie's shoulders. "I can never resist a redhead, Violette, especially when she is a redtail, too."

"And perhaps Minette to accompany her?" asked Mme. Leduc.

"Wonderful! But not on the piano, this time!"

Baubay got up from the table, and took Sophie and Minette by the hand. Giggling, they led him out of the dining room, into the hallway, and up the stairs. Vincent could hear them laughing all the way along the landing.

"Vincent, how about you?" asked Mme. Leduc. "Has any one of my girls caught your eye yet?"

The blonde gave him a dreamy, creamy look, and rubbed his penis again. Vincent didn't want to hurt her feelings, but he was too fascinated by the shy brunette. He nodded down the table and said, "I don't even know her name, but if she doesn't mind—?"

The blonde immediately pushed his erection back into his pants and tugged up his zipper, almost catching him in it. "Look, I'm sorry," he said. "I think you're stunning, but—"

"But you prefer Catherine, I know. I've seen you staring at her."

"Catherine?" said Vincent, and the girl looked toward him and nodded, although she didn't smile. Vincent stood up and walked along the length of the table and held out his hand.

"This is only if you want to," he said.

"It is not her place to say if she wants to or not," said Mme. Leduc, with a slight snap in her voice.

Catherine stood up, gathering up her white nightdress in front of her so that it was raised above her knees. Vincent had never seen a girl so beautiful or so quietly alluring, and he had certainly never met a girl so subservient. She had a high, rounded forehead and huge violet eyes. Her nose was straight with just a hint of a tilt at the end. Her lips were full, as if she were pouting a little, but that suggestion of sulkiness only aroused Vincent all the more.

"One girl will be sufficient?" asked Mme. Leduc.

"Am I allowed to come back for seconds?"

Mme. Leduc came up close to him and ran her hand up the back of his head, like rubbing a cat's fur the wrong way. It was an electrifying feeling, especially since he could feel her breast swaying against him through the silk of her negligee.

"Perhaps, next time, I can amuse you myself."

God, thought Vincent. *Baubay was right. I feel like I've died and gone to heaven.*

Without a word, Catherine took his hand and led him out of the room. She walked quite quickly on her pale bare feet, as if she were in a hurry. Her hand was small and cool. She didn't lead him upstairs, but across the hallway and along a corridor with a polished parquet floor. The corridor was light, but all of the windows were covered with the same white blinds.

They reached a door at the end of the corridor and Catherine opened it. Inside, Vincent found himself in a large downstairs bedroom. In the very center stood an iron-framed four-poster bed, draped with yards and yards of white gauze curtains, and covered in giant-sized white feather pillows. The only other furniture was a chaise lounge upholstered in plain cream calico, a French-style closet painted in dragged white paint, a washbasin, and a cheval mirror at the end of the bed, tilted in such a way that whoever was lying on the bed could see themselves. On one wall hung a large, vividly colored painting of a woman in a pearl necklace, lasciviously clutching a horse's erect penis, and staring directly at the viewer as if she were challenging everything he believed in.

Catherine closed the door. She walked across to the bed and drew back the curtains. Then, without turning around, she lifted off her nightdress, so that she was naked. She had a long, flared back, and very high, rounded buttocks. Her breasts were so big that Vincent could see the half-moon curves of them on either side.

However, it was when she turned around that he had the greatest shock. He saw now why she had gathered up her nightdress when she stood up from the table. She had been concealing the fact that she was at least five or six months pregnant. Her breasts were enormously swollen and big-nippled, and her stomach was like a lunar globe. Her vulva was swollen, too. She had shaved herself so that Vincent could see the dark blush color of her lips.

Pregnant she might have been, but Vincent still thought she was achingly beautiful. In fact, her pregnancy made her look even more beautiful. That was why her hair shone. That was why her skin glowed. That was why she had the secretive, knowing, self-protective look that had attracted Vincent in the first place.

She came up to him and unfastened the top button of his shirt. He looked down at her—at her calm, perfect face; at the trees of pale blue veins in her breasts; at her stiffened, rouge-brown nipples.

"How old are you?" he asked her, with a phlegmy catch in his throat.

"Eighteen and a half," she replied, unfastening another button, and another, and running her finger-nails lightly through the hair on his chest.

"You're having a baby, and yet you're still doing *this?*"

"What else can I do?"

"You can contact your local department of welfare, for starters. You can get all kinds of financial help. You're a single mother-to-be, for Christ's sake, you're entitled. You don't have to work for Mme. Leduc."

"But I do."

"No, listen to me, you don't. This really isn't suitable work for anybody who's pregnant."

She looked up at him. "So what are you trying to tell me? That you wouldn't have picked me if you'd known that I was fat?"

"You're not fat, you're pregnant, and if you want to know the truth I find you extremely attractive. But this isn't socially responsible."

"You don't want me, then? You want Eloise instead? Or Martine?"

"I didn't say that. I simply said that in your condition you shouldn't be working in a bordello."

"I don't have any choice."

"Yes, you do. You *do* have a choice. There are plenty of people you can turn to. I mean, what about your parents?"

She looked away. "Dead, both of them."

"Brothers or sisters? Aunts or uncles?"

She shook her head.

"Then, listen, maybe *I* can help you."

She said, "I don't want you to help me. I don't want you even to try. This is what I do. This is what I am. Other men have offered to help me, too, and every time I have to tell them the same thing."

Vincent didn't know what to do. He walked over to the white-blinded window and then he walked back again.

"You came here for pleasure," said Catherine, standing exposed in front of him, making no attempt to hide her complete nakedness with her hands. "Why don't you enjoy it while you're here?"

She came up to him and stood close so that her distended stomach touched the bulge in his pants. "Pleasing men is what I do best. I got pregnant, pleasing a man. Let me please you too."

"I don't know. I—"

She kissed his chest. She unbuttoned the last of his shirt buttons and then she started to unbuckle his belt.

"What about the baby?" he said, weakening. "Isn't it dangerous or anything?"

"There's plenty of room inside me," she said, pulling down his zipper. "Once I had three men inside me all at once, and baby, too." Without any hesitation, she wrested his rising cock out of his shorts, and pushed him back toward the bed. He sat down it, and she dragged off his pants and his socks.

"Listen," he said, "maybe a blow job'll do it . . . I don't want to take any risks." But he could hear his own voice and he knew how ineffectual he sounded. He wanted her desperately, he wanted her so much that his cock was visibly pulsing with every heartbeat. She pressed him down so that he was lying among all of those white downy cushions, and then she knelt beside him and took his cock into her mouth, running her tongue around his shiny purple helmet, sucking at it, licking it, and then sliding her tongue all the way down to his walnut-crinkled balls.

From where he was lying he could see underneath her body, her big swaying breasts, her rounded stomach. He reached out and cupped her breasts, feeling her rigid nipples brushing against his palms. Then he smoothed his hands around her stomach. He was surprised how hard it was, how tight it was. He thought to himself: *Another man has fucked her, and left life inside her, and here it is, growing.* Although he couldn't understand why, he found the idea of it unbelievably erotic.

As she sucked him, he looked down the length of the bed toward the cheval mirror, and through the curtains of her hair he could see her lips enclosing his red, glistening shaft. She glanced up, and caught sight of his reflection. She smiled, and gave the head of his cock a long, lascivious lick.

In return, he lifted her right leg so that she was kneeling right over him. Right in front of him was her smooth crimson vulva, her lips thickened with pregnancy, her vagina flooded with juice. He buried his face in it like a man burying his face into a watermelon, licking as deep inside her as he could, then taking whole mouthfuls of her and sucking her until she let his cock out of her mouth and gasped, and pushed her hips even more forcefully into his face.

He lost all awareness of time. He gave her one orgasm after another, until her stomach was rock-hard and he was afraid that she was going to give birth. At the same time, she played with him, bringing him right to the edge of ejaculation and then letting him subside, until his balls ached and he was right on the edge of anger.

The bedroom was dark when she led him over to the chaise lounge and made him lie on his back. She straddled him, looking down at him, and it was so gloomy now that he couldn't see her face beneath the shadows of her hair. He could smell her, though. Her sex and her perfume and the same smell that he had detected on Mme. Leduc: the smell of memories.

"I think you should make love to me properly," she whispered. "It's what you want, isn't it, to share my body with my baby?"

He half-rose, saying, "I can't." But she pushed him back again. She took hold of his erect penis and positioned herself right over it. She rubbed the head of his penis backward and forward between her lips until it was slippery with juice. "You want to meet my baby?" she teased him. "Don't tell me that you don't want to meet my baby."

She sank down on him, until he was buried right inside the warm elastic tightness of her body. She leaned forward so that her nipples touched his chest, and then she kissed him, and made a snorting sound of satisfaction in his ear. He felt her child kick and stir against his penis and he climaxed with such violence that his whole world went black.

It was almost eight o'clock when he left her sleeping on the four-poster bed. He dressed, and crept out, taking one last look at her. She was lying on her back with her hand lying idly between her legs, her hair fanned out across one of the pillows. It unnerved him to think that he had probably started to fall in love with her. He knew for sure that he would have to see her again. You can't have an encounter like this and just forget about it, just let it go.

He had never experienced an afternoon like it in his life. The way she had eaten his balls as if they were fruit. The way she had rubbed him until he had climaxed all over her breasts, and it had dripped from her nipples like milk.

"I want to feed my baby, when it's born," she had told him, massaging his sperm around and around.

"So when will that be, exactly?"

"I looked at my horoscope and my horoscope said soon."

"What about your gynecologist?"

She had frowned at him as if she didn't understand what he meant.

He walked back along the gloomy corridor feeling both elated and deeply guilty. He loved her, he wanted her, but he knew that he had to save her, too. He had to save her from Mme. Leduc. Most of all he had to save her from men like him.

He had almost reached the hallway when he saw the shield-shaped plaque on the wall. He stopped, and peered at it, like Lawrence of Arabia peering at a mirage. It was "École St. Agathe, fondée 1923," and underneath the lettering was an emblem of a goose flying from a bloodred lake.

He was still peering at it when a voice said, "Did you have a good time, Vincent?" He turned to see Mme. Leduc standing in the hallway. He didn't know whether it was the dim evening light or maybe his own sexual satiation that made her look older, much older, and far less beautiful. She looked frigid and stern—rather like the Snow Queen, from the story that his mother used to tell him when he was young.

"I had a very good time, thank you," he told her.

"Well . . . let's put it this way, I had a very interesting time."

She reached out and stroked his cheek. Her colorless eyes were almost sad.

"Why do you—" he began, and hesitated. Then he managed to say, "Why do you *do* this? These girls, they're all so young. They have so much in front of them . . . so much life to lead."

"You disapprove," she said. "I thought, from the moment that I opened the door, that you would disapprove."

"It's not that I disapprove. It's more like I don't understand."

She gave him a smile like diluted milk. She unfolded and refolded her negligee and gave him the briefest flash of heavy white breasts, with areolas the color of rose-petals, as they turn to brown.

"It isn't necessary for you to understand, Vincent. All you have to do is to enjoy yourself, and pay."

"I mean, how did you *discover* this place?" Vincent asked Baubay, as they drove back toward Montreal along the Laurentian Autoroute. "It's great, I'll grant you that, but it's so strange."

"What's strange about it? I think it's very normal. I went to a club in San Francisco where everybody was jerking off all over the place and there were three guys trying to make out with a one-legged woman. You've been closeted, Vincent. You don't know the half of what goes on. Group sex, leather clubs, bestiality.

Compared to all of that, Mme. Leduc is respectability itself."

"So how did you find it?"

"Some guy at Dane Shearman Philips told me about it. Mme. Leduc encourages her clients to pass on her card to anybody who might appreciate what she has to offer."

"Seven young girls, not much more than eighteen years old. One of them six months pregnant."

"Don't tell me you didn't enjoy it. Don't tell me you won't be going back."

Vincent said nothing, but looked ahead at the glittering lights of downtown Montreal. It looked unreal, like a city painted on the sky.

And of course he did go back, only three days later, and on his own this time. The hot weather had broken into a thunderous electric storm, and even though he parked his rental car right outside the house he was soaked by the time he reached the porch. He was still drying his face with his handkerchief when the door opened and Mme. Leduc appeared—dressed in a robe of peach-colored silk.

"Why, Vincent. I didn't expect you so soon."

"I should have called, I know, but I didn't know your number."

"And you didn't want to ask Francois for it, because you didn't want Francois to know that you were coming here?"

Vincent gave an awkward shrug. "I just wanted to see Catherine, that's all. Well, I wanted to see you, too."

"You'd better come in, then," she said, as another

deafening burst of thunder shook the roof of the house.

Vincent followed her inside. "I'm worried about Catherine, if you must know. I haven't been able to get her off my mind."

"You're not the first."

"It's just that it isn't right, a pregnant girl having unprotected sex with strange men. Think of the infections she could pick up. Think of the baby."

"*You* had sex with her."

"Yes, I did. And I feel more guilty about it than I can possibly tell you."

"So what do you propose to do?"

"I propose to make you an offer. Let me take Catherine away from here so that she can have her baby someplace quiet and comfortable, with a decent clinic nearby. I'll make sure you're not out of pocket. If you work out her potential earnings for, say, the next six months, I'll pay you in advance."

Mme. Leduc took him through to the living room. The blinds were still drawn tight and it was so gloomy that he could barely see her. "Why don't you sit down?" she asked him. "Would you like some tea, or a glass of wine?"

"No, no thank you. I just want to hear you say that Catherine can come with me."

Mme. Leduc stood facing the mirror over the fireplace, so that Vincent could see only her dim reflection. "I'm afraid that's impossible, Vincent. None of us can leave this house, ever."

"Why the hell not? What happens when the girls get older, and lose their looks? You can't run a cathouse with a collection of senior citizens, can you?"

Mme. Leduc was silent for a long time. Then she said, "If I tell you why Catherine can't leave, will you promise me that you'll leave here, and never come back, and forget all about her?"

"How can I make a promise like that?"

"It's for her own good, that's why."

"Well, I don't know. I'll think about it, okay? That's as far as I'm prepared to go."

"Very well," said Mme. Leduc. "I suppose that'll have to do." She turned around and came toward him, standing so close that he could have lifted his hand and touched her face. "A long time ago, in the 1920s, this used to be a school, an academy for young girls."

"I saw the notice board in the corridor. St. Agathe's, right?"

"That's right. It was quite a famous school, and diplomats and wealthy businessmen used to send their daughters here during the summer to learn cookery and dressmaking and riding and all the social skills."

"I see. Kind of a finishing school."

Mme. Leduc nodded. "One July day, in 1924, some of the girls were taken by their teacher to Lac du Sang, for a picnic. Lac du Sang is a local beauty spot, and very beautiful it is, too. They call it Lac du Sang because it's surrounded by maples, and in the fall, when the leaves turn red, the lake reflects them, and looks as if it's filled with blood. They say it was a magic place, a sacred place, where even the Indians would never venture.

"Anyway, the girls set out their picnic and the day was perfect. There was never such a day in the history of days. The lake, the trees, the sky so blue that it could have been ceramic. The teacher stood up and looked around at her girls and said, 'What a perfect, perfect day. I wish we could all stay young forever. I wish the day could last for twenty-four years, instead of twenty-four hours.'"

Mme. Leduc stood looking at Vincent and Vincent waited for her to continue, but she didn't. After a while, he said, "Go on. She wished that it would last for twenty-four years. Then what?"

"Then it did."

Another long pause. "I don't understand," said Vincent.

"It's not difficult," said Mme. Leduc. "The day lasted for twenty-four years. At least, it did for them. The sun stayed high in the sky and they didn't notice the time passing by. It was all like a dream. When at last they returned to the school they found that it was closed, and that all their friends had gone. It was no longer 1924. It was 1948."

She went over to a rosewood bureau on the opposite side of the room and returned with a yellowed newspaper. "Here," she said. "This is what happened."

It was a copy of *The St. Michel-des-Monts Sentinel*. The front-page headline read SEARCH FOR ST. AGATHE GIRLS CALLED OFF—Little Hope Of Finding Missing 9 And Teacher, Say Mounties.

Vincent read the first paragraph. "Police now believe there is little or no hope of them ever finding the teacher and nine girls from St. Agathe's Academy who went missing three months ago on a picnic at Lac du Sang. The entire area has been thoroughly searched and there is no evidence to suggest that they all ran away together or that their disappearance is a practical joke. RCMP inspector René Truchaud called the

Lac du Sang incident 'the greatest single mystery in Canadian police history.'"

Mme. Leduc said, "They came looking for us on the day after we disappeared, but of course we weren't there. To them, we were still in yesterday, still lying in the grass by the lake."

"It was *you?* It was you and your girls?"

Mme. Leduc gave him a sad, elegant nod. "We had a day like no other day has ever been; or ever will be. But we came back here and found that half of our lives had passed us by. I still don't know what happened to us; or why. I still don't know whether it was supposed to be a gift or a curse. But the first part of my wish came true, too, and so long as we stay here, inside the house, we remain as we were, all those years ago. It's almost as if my wish diverted us out of the stream of time, into a backwater, and that my seven girls and I are doomed or blessed to stay here forever."

"It says here nine girls."

"Yes . . . there *were* nine. Two of them left—Sara five years ago, and Imogene just before Christmas. Sara tried to come back but she didn't look like a young girl any longer. Time had caught up with her, and aged her over forty years in a single week. I received a letter from Imogene. Only two lines. Do you want to read it?"

She passed over a sheet of paper that had been folded and refolded until it was soft. The handwriting on it was so crabbed and spidery that Vincent could barely decipher it. It said, *"Chère Mme. Leduc, I am very old and close to death. Tell all of the girls that I will wait for them in Heaven."*

Mme. Leduc said, "It appears that the further time

leaves us behind, the quicker we will age if we try to leave. So . . . the rest of us decided to stay."

"I can't believe any of this," said Vincent. "Days can't last for twenty-four years. People don't stay young forever. Who are you kidding? You're just trying to stop me from taking Catherine away from you. All you care about is how much you can make out of her. A pregnant teenager, what an attraction! Jesus, if you cared about any of these girls you wouldn't be selling their bodies to every lecherous old guy with a fat enough wallet."

"You exclude yourself from that category, I suppose," said Mme. Leduc.

"I was tempted, I admit it. She's a beautiful girl, she tempted me. But that doesn't stop me from trying to put things right."

"Vincent . . . has it occurred to you that this is the only way in which we can make a living? None of us can leave the house, so what else are we supposed to do? We may stay young forever, but we still need to eat; and we still have bills to pay."

Vincent laughed and then abruptly stopped laughing. He looked at Mme. Leduc and said, "You're seriously crazy, you know that? If you really believe that you disappeared in 1924 for twenty-four years and that you're never going to grow old . . . well, I don't know. I'd just like to know what stuff you're on."

At that moment Catherine walked into the room in her long white nightgown. Her hair was tied back and she looked especially young and vulnerable. It had only been three days since Vincent had seen her, but he had forgotten how mesmerizing she was. The way she looked up at him from underneath her long, long eyelashes. The way she pouted. The way her breasts moved underneath the fresh-pressed cotton.

Mme. Leduc took hold of her hand. "Mr. Jeffries here wanted to take you away with him, Catherine. I had to explain why he couldn't."

"And of course I believed every word," said Vincent. "That must have been some picnic, out at Lac du Sang. Don't tell me you didn't run short of sandwiches—you know, in twenty-four years?"

Mme. Leduc said, "Why don't you take Vincent to your room, Catherine? I expect that he'd like to talk to you alone."

Without a word, Catherine took his hand and led him along the corridor. She opened the door of her room and let him in. "I just came to talk," he told her.

"You mean you don't like me anymore?"

"I came to ask you to leave this place. I came to persuade you to do the best for your baby."

Catherine took a few steps away from him, and then pirouetted, and lifted her nightgown over her head, so that she was standing in front of him completely naked. *"Now* tell me that you don't like me anymore."

"Catherine, you can't go on doing this. I've found an apartment for you. It's pretty small but the landlady can take good care of you, and there's a clinic only four blocks away."

Catherine stood up close to him, smiling her dreamy smile. Her nipples were knurled and stiff, and she pressed the hard globe of her stomach up against his reluctantly rising erection. "There," she said, "you *do* still like me, after all."

"I don't just *like* you, Catherine."

"Then prove it," she challenged him. She tugged

down his zipper and pried his cock out of his shorts. He said, "No, not that," but she gave him two or three irresistible rubs with her hand and he didn't say anything else after that.

He watched her as she knelt in front of him, her eyes closed, her pouting lips encircling his reddened erection. Her cheek bulged as she took him in deeper, and her tongue swam around his glans like a warm seal. He ran his hands through her hair and fondled her ears and he felt so weak, but so transported with pleasure, that he knew he had to have her forever, for himself. He would raise her and he would raise her baby, both. He would guard her and protect her and make love to her all night.

His sperm flew into her hair and crowned her with pearls. She looked up and smiled at him, and outside the house the thunder rumbled and rattled the windows.

"Would you like to live with me?" he asked her.

She squeezed his softening penis with her hand. "Of course . . . if only it were possible."

"Then let me take you away from here. Tomorrow night, I'll come for you, yes?"

She held out her hand and he helped her onto her feet. "If only it were possible," she repeated, and kissed him, very frankly, on the lips.

"You're nuts," said Baubay. "You know what the penalty is for kidnap?"

"She wants me," Vincent told him. "She said she'd come to live with me, if I got her out of there."

"Those girls say anything you want to hear. It's what you pay them for."

"Catherine's different."

"The only thing different about Catherine is that she's got a bun in the oven."

"Francois, if you don't help me with this then I'll do it on my own."

"I still say you're nuts."

They drew up outside the house. Vincent had persuaded Baubay to bring him up here for another evening with Mme. Leduc and her girls, with the promise that he would pay, but as they approached St. Michel-des-Monts he had explained his plan to take Catherine away with him.

"Supposing Violette was telling you the truth about Lac du Sang?"

"Oh, come on, Francois. Get real. A bordello full of immortal schoolgirls?"

"I guess, when you say it like that."

They knocked at the door and Mme. Leduc answered, dressed in scarlet silk. "Well, well," she said, as she took them inside. "Like a bee to the honeypot, Vincent? Can't keep away?"

Vincent gave a self-deprecating shrug.

The girls were all in the living room, and Minette was playing Brahms on the piano. They stood up when Baubay and Vincent came in, and twittered around them, giving them little kisses of welcome and touching their hair. Only Catherine remained seated, and Vincent deliberately didn't catch her eye.

"Who takes your fancy tonight, Francois?" asked Mme. Leduc.

Baubay looked around the room. He glanced at Vincent, and then he said, "You, Violette. It's you that I want tonight."

* * *

Later, after champagne, Baubay and Violette climbed the stairs together while the girls clapped and giggled and whistled their encouragement. As soon as they had gone, Vincent went over to Catherine and took hold of her hand. "Our turn?" he suggested.

He held her hand quite tightly as they left the living room and crossed the hallway. Then—as they passed the front door—he suddenly pulled her and said, "This is it! Come on, Catherine, this is our chance!"

Catherine tried to wrench herself away from him. "No!" she cried out. "What are you doing?" But Vincent twisted open the door handle, flung the door wide open, and dragged Catherine out onto the porch.

"No!" she screamed. *"No, Vincent, I can't!"*

She deliberately sank to her knees, but Vincent bent down, and bodily picked her up. "No!" she shrieked at him. "I can't! I can't! No, Vincent, you'll kill me!"

She pulled his hair and dug her fingernails into his face, but he found the pain almost exciting. He carried her along the pathway and out into the street, where his car was parked. He opened the driver's door and managed to force her inside, pushing her across to the passenger seat. Then he climbed in, started the engine, and sped away from the house with a high-pitched squealing of tires.

"Go back!" she shouted, trying to snatch the steering wheel. *"You have to go back!"*

"Listen!" he shouted back at her. "Whatever Violette told you, it's garbage! She said it to scare you, so that you wouldn't leave! Now stop worrying about her and start thinking about yourself, and your baby."

"Go back!" Catherine howled. "Oh God, you can't do this to me! Oh God please go back! Oh God, Vincent, please take me back!"

"Will you shut up?" Vincent told her. "Shut up and put on your seat belt. Even if you don't feel protective toward your baby, I do."

"Take me back! Take me back! I can't go with you, Vincent! I can't!"

She punched him again and tried to tear at his ear, and the car swerved wildly across the highway. But in the end he managed to catch hold of both of her wrists in his right hand, and restrain her. She stopped trying to hit him, and she curled herself up in her seat, and softly sobbed.

She was asleep by the time they reached Montreal. He parked outside the apartment building and switched off the engine. He looked across at her and brushed the hair from her face. She was so beautiful that he could hardly believe she was real. He lifted her out of the passenger seat and carried her in through the entrance hall. It was stark and brightly lit, but it was late now and there was nobody else around. He went up in the elevator and by the time they reached the sixth floor she was beginning to feel heavy.

He opened the door and carried her into the apartment. It wasn't much—a plain, furnished place with two bedrooms, a bathroom, and a small kitchenette. By day it had a narrow view of the Prairies River, partly blocked out by another apartment building. He took her through to the bedroom and laid her on the bed. Over the white vinyl headboard hung an almost laughably incompetent painting of a forest in the fall.

He sat beside her and took hold of her hand. "Catherine?" he coaxed her. "Come on, Catherine. We're here now, sweetheart. We've escaped."

Her eyes flickered open. She stared at him, first in

bewilderment, and then in horror. She sat up and looked around her. "Oh God," she said. "Oh God, this can't be true."

"Come on, it's not that bad," said Vincent. "A few flowers, a couple of loose covers."

But Catherine ignored him. She climbed off the bed and went directly to the mirror over the dressing table. "Oh God," she kept repeating.

Vincent stood beside her as she peered frantically at her face. "Catherine, nothing's going to happen to you. That story that Violette tells . . . it's only a way of frightening you."

"But I was *there*. I was there at Lac du Sang in 1924."

"You couldn't have been. It simply isn't possible. I don't know what Violette did. Maybe she brainwashed you or something. But no day ever lasted longer than twenty-four hours and nobody ever stayed young forever."

"You have to take me back. I'm pleading with you, Vincent. I'm pleading on my child's life."

"You want to go back? Back to what? Back to being a whore? Back to sucking men's cocks and opening your legs to anybody who can pay the price?"

"Is that your problem? Is that why you took me away? Because you wanted me to open my legs but you didn't want to pay for it?"

"For God's sake, Catherine, I took you away because I love you."

For the first time she took her eyes away from her reflection in the mirror. There was an expression on her face that he had never seen on any girl's face before. It laid him open right to the bone, as if she had cut him with a ten-inch butcher's knife.

It was after eleven o'clock. He asked her if she wanted anything to eat or drink but she said no. He switched on the television in the living room but there was nothing on but lacrosse and an old Errol Flynn movie. Catherine stayed in the bedroom, staring at the wall. In the end he came in and sat next to her again. "Listen," he said. "Maybe I made a mistake."

She glanced up at him, and she looked very pale and very tired.

"If you want to go back, I'll take you back. I just thought I was doing the right thing, that's all. Why don't you get some sleep and we'll make an early start in the morning."

She said nothing, but closed her eyes.

"I'm sorry," he said. "I'm sorry for being in love with you. I'm sorry for being human. What else was I supposed to do?"

He watched television until just after midnight, and then he undressed and climbed into bed with her. She was breathing softly against the pillow. He reached out and touched her arm, and then her breast. Then he ran his hand over the swelling of her stomach. He could feel the baby stir and kick, like somebody kneading dough.

He slept uneasily until 3:04. He kept having fragmentary dreams about people laughing and talking in other rooms. He woke with a strong hard-on and he reached out for Catherine again. She was still quietly breathing. He caressed her breasts through her nightgown and then he drew her legs apart and climbed on top of her. Maybe it was wrong of him to fuck her while she was asleep, but he needed her so urgently. She felt dry, in the darkness, but he spat on his fingers to moisten the end of his cock. Then he pushed himself into her, and started a deep, plunging rhythm.

She woke up. He sensed her wake up. But he was too close to his climax to stop, and he kept on thrusting himself into her, harder and harder. He heard her panting, quick and harsh, and he thought, *Great, she's getting into it too*. He said, "Come on, baby, you're wonderful. Come on, sweetheart, you're fantastic."

It was then that she screamed. It was a piercing, gargling scream, and he could feel spit fly all over his face. He jerked upright, his skin freezing in fright, and then she screamed again. He scrabbled to find the bedside lamp, and managed to switch it on, but then it dropped onto the floor, so that what he saw was illuminated by an angled, upward light that made it look even more terrifying than it was.

He was kneeling between the legs of a shriveled old woman. Her sparse white hair was coming out in clumps. Her eyes were sunk into their sockets and her lips were drawn tightly back over orange, toothless gums. All that identified her as Catherine was her huge, swollen belly.

"Oh Jesus," Vincent whispered. "Oh Jesus, tell me this is a nightmare."

The old woman tried to scream again, but all she managed this time was a thick gargle. She lifted one of her bony arms, and clawed feebly at Vincent's shoulder, but Vincent pushed her away. She was collapsing in front of his eyes. Her face was tightening over her cheekbones and her breasts were shriveling. Her collarbone broke through her skin, and her chin dropped onto her chest.

"Catherine!" Vincent quivered. "Catherine!"

He lifted her head, but it dropped sideways onto the pillow and it was obvious that she was dead. Vincent climbed off the bed, wiping his hands on the sheet. He was trembling so much that he had to hold on to the wall for support.

It was then that he thought: *The baby—what about the baby? Even if Catherine's dead, maybe I can save the baby!*

He thought for one moment of calling for an ambulance—but how the hell was he going to explain an old, dead woman in his bed—an old, dead *pregnant* woman? He approached Catherine cautiously, and laid his hand on her stomach, and, yes, he could still feel the baby kicking inside her. But how long could it survive if he didn't get it out?

He went to the kitchen, opened the drawer, and took out a carving knife. He returned to the bedroom and stood beside Catherine gray-faced. He nearly decided to do nothing, to let the baby die, but then he saw Catherine's stomach shift again, and he knew that he had to give it a chance.

He inserted the point of the knife into her wrinkled skin, just above her pubic bone. Then, slowly, he pushed it in through the muscle, until he felt something more yielding. He was terrified of cutting the baby as well, but he kept on slicing her stomach open, and she was so decayed and dry and papery that it was more like cutting open a rotten old hessian sack. At last he had her stomach wide open, and he drew aside the two flaps of flesh to reveal her womb.

Shaking and dripping with sweat, he cut the baby out of her. One foot emerged, and then a hand. Miraculously, it was still alive. It was purple and slithery and it smelled strongly of amniotic fluid. He turned it over so that he could cut the umbilical cord, and then he lifted it up in both hands. It was so tiny, so frail. A baby girl. Her eyes were squeezed shut and she clasped and unclasped her fingers. She snuffled, and then she let out two or three pathetic little cries.

Vincent was overwhelmed. He started to sob out loud. Tears ran down his cheeks and dripped from his chin. He couldn't understand what had happened to Catherine, but he knew that he had saved the baby's life. He carried her through to the living room, laid her on the couch, and then went to the bathroom to find some towels.

He sped to St. Michel-des-Monts through driving, sunlit rain. At times his speedometer needle wavered over 110 kph. He managed to reach the house just after eleven o'clock. He ran to the front porch, vaulted up the steps, and banged furiously on the knocker.

Mme. Leduc appeared, with Baubay close behind her. "You came back," she said. "I'm amazed that you had the nerve."

"Well . . . I don't think I had any choice."

"Catherine?"

He lowered his head. "You were telling me the truth. Catherine's gone. But I managed to save her child. I wanted to bring her back here before it was too late."

He went back to the car, and opened the door. Very hesitantly, like somebody who has never felt rain on their skin before, or had sunlight shining in their eyes, a young girl climbed out, barefoot, but wrapped up in green bath towels. Vincent took her hand and led her toward the house. Violette and Baubay watched in silence as she came up the steps. She looked at least seventeen or eighteen years old, with long brunette hair, like Catherine's, and she was almost as pretty, although her features were a little sharper.

"There," said Vincent, as he led her into the house. "You'll be safe here."

There were tears in Mme. Leduc's eyes. "I wish that I had never wished," she told Vincent.

"Well," Vincent told her. "Sometimes we all think that."

They drove away from the house just as the rain was beginning to clear. Baubay said, "Where are you going? Montreal's back that way."

Vincent handed him a folded route map. "Lac du Sang," he said. "There's one more thing I have to do."

In the woods, he dug a shallow grave and buried Catherine's desiccated body. He filled her face with earth and leaves. "I'm sorry" was all he could think of to say. Afterward he stood by the edge of the water under a clear blue sky.

"They came here and they wished," he told Baubay. "God, they couldn't have known what they were wishing for, could they?"

"All I wish for is a new Mercedes," said Baubay.

"I just wish that I could have woken up every night and found Catherine lying next to me."

"You can go back to Violette's and try out her daughter."

"Forget it. I feel like her father. I brought her into the world, didn't I? I watched her grow up."

"In three hours? That's not fatherhood."

"All the same, it was incredible. She just grew bigger and bigger, like one of those speeded-up movies."

"Sure she did."

"She did, I swear it."

"Sure."

They climbed back into the car and drove away, leaving the waters of Lac du Sang as still as ever.

Six weeks later, Baubay phoned to tell him that he had been promoted and given a metallic gold 500SL as a company car. After that, Vincent awoke two or three times every night, and fearfully reached out to make sure that there was nobody lying on the other side of the bed.

Graham Masterton: *"This story was inspired by a recent rescreening of the classic Australian movie* Picnic at Hanging Rock—*one of those haunting stories that you never quite forget."*

PLAYING WITH FIRE

Bentley Little

*California's Bentley Little is the award-winning au-
thor of over one hundred published short stories, and
the novels* The Ignored, Dominion, University, The
Mailman, The Store, The Summoning, Death In-
stinct, *and* The Revelation. *The mysterious Little
offered this biographical information: "An expatriate
Arizonan and strict carnivore who has not spoken
voluntarily since 1990, he has been prohibited by law
from holding jobs that involve food preparation."*

*W*oman by the river. Naked. Spreading it open.
It's green not pink, I can see it from here, and I like
it better green and I stop the car, but she jumps into
the water before I can open the door and get out,
and she grins at me from the middle of the river and
waves.

Q: How old were you when your mother left?
A: Three, I think. Maybe four. No, three. I
   remember because it was only me and my
   dad at my fourth birthday.
Q: Did you miss her?
A: No, not at all.

She approaches the fire eater after the show and I
know what she is planning but I let her do it anyway. I
pretend to head for the fun house next door, but after

she goes into the tent I sneak around the back and use my pocketknife to cut a slit in the red canvas.

They are talking, she and the fire eater, and there is at first what looks like an argument, then the fire eater nods, smiles, says something, and then she is lifting up her skirt, pulling off her panties. He pours liquid into his mouth, swallows a lighted match. He lies down on the stage, and she squats over his face, and the flame emerges from his mouth, small and orange and so lithe it seems almost alive. It expands gracefully upward, touches the lips of her vagina, moves skittishly away. She moans, bites her tongue, is obviously in pain, but she remains squatting as the flame grows, flickering lightly over her spread lips, playing around the periphery of her vulva, before finally slipping sensuously inside her open hole.

When I fuck her that night, I do it hard, I make it hurt, and my cock when it comes out is coated with her juices and clinging traces of charred black ash.

I found out about her preference not long after we were married.

It was an accident. I was supposed to have gone on a one-day business trip to Chicago, but Ted was more familiar with the project and had dealt with this client before, so I had very little trouble convincing Campbell to send him instead.

She was not expecting me home that afternoon.

I called her name several times but there was no answer, and I finally found her in the backyard.

Torturing herself with fire.

The sight was so shocking and so unexpected that for almost a full minute I stood in the doorway rooted in place, unable to move.

She was completely naked and standing on the lawn, legs spread impossibly wide. She'd tied her own feet to two stakes so she could not move away, and she was bouncing up and down, over a high bright flame, swaying back and forth as she did so, passing her private parts through the fire, arms raised above her head. The flames were maintained by a tiki torch between her legs, stuck into the lawn so that only about a foot of it was aboveground, and though I could see the red heated skin on her legs and thighs, she made no effort to get away from the tiki fire but kept lowering herself onto it, mingled expressions of passionate pleasure and horrific pain battling it out on her sweating face.

"Oh my God!" I screamed, finally able to react. I ran for the hose. "Oh my God!"

"Don't worry," she said through clenched teeth.

I turned on the faucet.

"Don't!" she yelled. Her voice grew quieter. "I like to do it myself."

"Then stop it!"

"Wait." She lowered herself, let the fire dance over her burned reddened thighs and the still-bright green of her genitalia. She stiffened, arching her toes as a high flame touched her vulva.

Then she squatted, peed, put it out.

And moaned.

I call out to her, expecting her to run away, but she remains in the middle of the stream, and there is something in her face that causes me to think she is waiting for me. It is more a beckon than a wave, I see now, and I close the car door and, in spite of my slippery dress shoes, start down the embankment toward the water.

I am fully erect.

She waits until I am on the bank opposite her, then splashes over to the other side. She looks back over her shoulder, laughing, heads into the trees, and I follow her.

She makes no effort to lose me or confuse me, stops once when I fall down, slipping on pine needles, and while she stays ahead of me, she leads me directly to her camp. I see a ten-speed bike and a small pup tent. Her clothes are scattered about the remains of a campfire. Her underwear is burnt, lying in the ashes.

She's gotten there a minute or so ahead of me, and I find her crouched over the dead fire. I'm not sure what to do, so I stop in front of her, look down. I cannot see her green vagina but I can see her breasts and they are beautiful. "Hi," I say.

She leaps up suddenly, kisses me on the lips.

It is the beginning of our first date.

Is it unfaithfulness if she asks someone else to light the match?

I think it is, and I confront her with it the next day, tell her I watched her with the fire eater, and she gets mad at me for spying on her.

But it is not really the spying she is angry about, I sense. I get the feeling she knew I was spying, wanted me to spy, but I'm not in the mood to play her games, and I scream that she's my wife now and she's not supposed to be having sex with other men.

"I didn't have sex with another man," she shouts back.

"You're not supposed to be naked with other men! *That's* what I mean by unfaithful!"

"I am unfaithful to the fire when I do it with you," she says. "But I do it anyway."

"What's that supposed to mean?"

"You know what it means."

"No I don't. Tell me."

"I need my pussy burned."

We stare at each other.

"You know how I like it, and you refuse to satisfy me. That's why I have to go elsewhere."

She's right. I have resisted for the past several months, have thrown away all matches and lighters in the house, have even asked the gas company to turn off the pilot light and gas for our stove. We have been cooking by microwave.

I point a demanding finger at her. "Don't you ever let anyone else do that to you," I order.

"I need fire!"

"It doesn't matter. I don't want you to do that with anyone else."

"Well you won't do it," she angrily shoots back.

I look at her, take a deep breath. "I'll do it," I say.

Q: Are you angry at women?
A: No.
Q: Do you have any female friends?
A: No.
Q: Why do you think that is?
A: I don't need any.

I worked, when we met, in the rat factory, on the assembly line, operating the machinery that separates the healthy from the unhealthy and diverts the rats to their respective modes of death. From my post, the good rats would continue on to the skinning station and from there to the fat vats.

It is how we get soap.

Most people do not know where soap comes from or how it is made. It is one of the few products in the United States that is not required to label its ingredients. They think it is like salt, a natural element, composed only of itself.

But it comes from rats.

The foundation of our country rests on horrors people don't want to know about or are too stupid to realize exist.

I wanted her bald. It was my own fetish, and I told her that I wanted to shave her. I ran my hand through her pubic hair, imagined her crotch smooth and hairless.

She sidled next to me, whispered in my ear. "Don't shave it off," she said. "Burn it off."

We did it in the bed on the fireproof sheet. I held the match to her bush, watched the small curly black strands singe and blacken and disappear. Fire licked at her skin as well, searing it in uneven patches that resembled teardrops. By the end, she was thrusting into the air and the strong scent of her arousal mingled with the smell of the matches' sulfur and her scorched hair and skin.

I took her bald and burned.

Two years, eight months, and four days.
It's all we had together.

* * *

Timothy Leary was a pussy at the end. He died in the conventional way, surrounded by family and friends, afraid at the last to follow through with his plan of Web-documented suicide. It was his final statement, this fallback on convention, and it invalidated everything else he had done before, everything that he had worked toward, everything his life had meant. It exposed the lie that lay at the heart of his existence.

Final statements are the ones that matter.

Cancer, the doctor said.

Color is the only difference. Otherwise, it is the same as any other woman's. It feels the same, smells the same, tastes the same. It is structurally identical, and it is only the hue of the skin that varies from the norm.

She pours lighter fluid on my cock, and she tells me it won't hurt a bit. I don't believe her, but I'm willing to do it anyway, and I get her started by waving the candle beneath her vagina until both she and the wax are dripping.

She lights my cock with a Bic, and she's right, the fluid burns but I don't feel it, and I quickly shove it in, and her pussy is hot and tight and it instantly puts out the flame, and we both climax at the same time.

She is asleep when I set the house ablaze, knocked out by some painkilling drug her doctors have given her for the cancer.

* * *

If I'm in an accident, I tell her, if I'm in a coma, if I'm paralyzed, if I'm one of those guys who can't move a muscle but can only blink "yes" and "no," pull the plug.

"How can you say that?" she asks me.

"It's quality of life I care about," I say. "Not the length of life."

"Who's to say that the quality of life is any worse for someone who's paralyzed? Is it better to be able to walk and run—or to be able to think? Physical movement is not all that important, you know, physical life is not all there is, and I refuse to buy into society's rap that some illiterate basketball player's life is worth more than mine because he has the use of his limbs and I do not. That's a value judgment only God can make."

"Do you believe in God?" I ask her.

"I don't know. But I believe in life. And I don't think the sole criterion for living a fulfilling happy life is limb movement. As long as I can think, I can live a good life."

"So I take it you don't want me to pull the plug?"

"No. Never pull the plug," she says. She pauses, thinks. "Unless . . ."

She says I can do anything I want as long as it involves fire, and I tie her up and break out the box of matches.

She smiles, and I strike the first match on her teeth, and then I place it on her right nipple. She cries out and she is already arching her back and I shove my hand between her legs and she is wet. I light another match, place it there, follow it up with four more.

There are tears in her eyes, but she's moaning with pleasure, and I poke a burning match in her belly button, light her little toe on fire. Soon there are black spots of burnt flesh all over her torso and abdomen, up and down her arms and legs.

I singe her earlobe, touch a flame to her neck.

The bed is covered with matches by the time we are through.

I kiss her burns, I lick her burns.

Did she want to go that way?

I don't know.

I think so.

But I don't know.

I never asked her.

She bends over, picks up her clothes around the campfire, puts them on, letting me watch.

"My name," she says, "is Elise. What's yours?"

I hear her screams over the flames.

And no matter what anyone else may think or may later say, they are screams of ecstasy.

Bentley Little: *"I spent several years working for various carnivals throughout the rural Southwest, and at one of these, I was lucky enough to encounter an honest-to-God freak show. I was there for the show's last year, before its owner went bankrupt and abandoned his 'people' in Benson, Arizona, setting off for parts unknown in the middle of the night. Needless to say, I saw the show many times, and I was always astounded by a South American fire eater who could do* *amazing things—like make flames come out of his mouth straight or curved or forked, and sustain a flame from his mouth long enough to cook an egg on an aluminum skillet. I thought he'd make a great character in a story.*

"After hours, there was also an unbilled sex show in the freak house, featuring an absolutely gorgeous female masochist. I started wondering what would happen if those two— the fire eater and the masochist—ever got together.

"The seeds of this story were planted there."

313

FULFILLMENT

Graham Watkins

Watkins' credits include the novels Dark Winds, The Fire Within, *and* Kaleidoscopic Eyes, *as well as the script for his* Hot Blood *story "Hillbettys," and numerous appearances in anthologies. His most current works are* Virus *and* Interception. *He lives in North Carolina.*

With wide eyes, Leah Quinlan stared fixedly at the man who was sharing her bed. Her mouth was dry, her heart pounding. She was lying on her back, nude, her body already glistening with a fine film of perspiration. The man was kneeling between her widespread legs; her hips were up on his thighs, his erection deep inside her. With his left hand he held one of her thighs, pulling her hard against him. Her own right hand was resting on his thigh in turn; in her left she held a long slender dagger, the blade gleaming brightly in the soft bedroom light. The moment of truth, the ultimate moment for her, was just minutes away now.

It wasn't easy to decide when, exactly, she'd made the decisions that had brought her to this point. She understood, all too clearly, that the fantasies she'd long toyed with—the ones she'd always felt were unique to her and were more than a little "sick"—had been with her for a very long time, but she'd succeeded, she'd thought, in suppressing them completely.

Until she'd discovered the Internet.

She'd been on the Net for quite a long time; actually, she'd been surfing the Web long before she'd gotten the news that was to change her life completely. That news had changed her attitudes, however; as the reality of it sank in, she began to spend more of her time in front of her computer, and she found herself spending much more time in the virtual chatrooms than on the Web—although the men she met there for the most part seemed boring to her. She'd begun looking at Usenet too, at the newsgroups, and she'd subscribed to a few that seemed interesting to her.

Then came the evening she'd decided to update the newsgroups, to see if any new ones had been added. To her surprise, there were several hundred. Only moderately interested, she quickly scanned down the list of names; nothing was very exciting.

Until, flashing by, she saw one called "alt.sex.fatal."

That stopped her; she ran the list back up, stopped there. No, she hadn't been mistaken. "Alt.sex.fatal." She laughed at the screen; it couldn't, she was sure, be what the title seemed to suggest it might be. Even so, she clicked on the button that would update the "articles" in the group, and took a look at them.

For the most part, the content was disappointing; most of the articles were advertisements for pay-per-view Web sites and 900 phone-sex numbers. A few—very few—actually seemed to address the presumed content of the group, and the majority of those were either short stories—the one she chose to read, a story about an execution by hanging, wasn't at all well written—or pictures taken from various movies.

Others were more enigmatic. One, she noticed, had a title of "Scared yourself, Darklady?" She opened it, read it:

> You've scared yourself, Darklady. You should come back, we should talk some more. You know where to find me: on IRC, on Undernet, on #lovedeath, most any Friday or Saturday night.
> I'll be looking for you.
> All my best,
> Simon

She read the posting over several times; some of the terms—IRC, Undernet—weren't familiar to her. But, her curiosity piqued, she decided to find out. A quick Web search using Netscape gave her more information than she really wanted, but, after a few hours, she'd figured out that "IRC" stood for "Internet Relay Chat," that Undernet was one of the three major IRC networks, and that #lovedeath was a virtual chatroom on that network. Needing an IRC "client" program, she downloaded one; once it was up and running she skimmed through the help files until she was familiar enough with it to feel she could use it.

It took a while to find a server that would accept her, but, at last, using the nickname "Annabel" from Edgar Allan Poe's famous work, she managed to connect. As the "help" manual had instructed, she first did a list command; to her surprise, a very large number of virtual "rooms" came up, taking several minutes to load. Once that was done she scanned down through the list—but discovered that there was no group called #lovedeath listed. A dead end, she told herself with a little laugh. That it didn't really exist didn't surprise her.

But then she remembered something else she'd read in the help files—a room could be hidden so that it did not list. Figuring she had nothing to lose, she typed the command "/join#lovedeath"; and a window came up informing her that she was "now talking in #lovedeath." There were at least a dozen people here already—and one of them was using the nickname "Simon." She examined some of the others; Crazydog, Wildun, Santa, Swerve, Justine, Enemymine. Simon, in fact, was one of the few—besides herself—using anything resembling an actual name.

She'd hardly had time to digest this when her computer made a dinging sound and a window popped up informing her that Simon, of all people, wanted to chat with her. Though unsure of herself, she accepted his offer, and a new window, a private chat window, appeared.

"Hello, Annabel," he said. "New here, aren't you?"

"Yes," she answered. "First time."

"I see. Could I ask, who told you about this room? Most of the time, people do not come here without an introduction."

She smiled at the screen. "You did," she answered.

"I?"

"Yes. You posted something on Usenet, 'alt.sex.fatal.' You mentioned the room."

"Ah, yes, I remember. And you decided to come by. Tell me, are you a top or a bottom?"

The terms weren't really familiar to her. "I'm a curious."

"I see. A mere curious. It's good you're here, I think."

"You do?"

"Don't you? It interested you. You tell yourself you're merely curious, but there's more . . ."

How could he know? she asked herself. She'd said almost nothing to him yet. "No," she told him. "No, just curious."

"Curious about what frightened Darklady."

Yes, she said silently. Yes. "Just curious about what this place is all about."

"This place," he answered, "is about your fantasies, and the ways they might get fulfilled. Your most extreme fantasies."

She laughed. "Judging by the name of the group," she told him, "I don't think I have fantasies that extreme."

"Oh? Well, then; let's just talk then for a moment. Tell me about yourself. Do you think of yourself as a violent person, Annabel? Do you have fantasies of doing violent things?"

Her answer came immediately. "Not at all, no."

"I see. Then perhaps you have had thoughts about being the object of violence . . ."

This time, she hesitated—but then, doggedly, she started typing. "No, of course not, anyone in her right mind would have a fantasy like that—" She stopped, sighed, started a new line. "*No* one in her right mind, I meant," she corrected, using the asterisks to emphasize the "no."

He didn't buy it, that was obvious. "I see," he came back. "Let's talk, then, Annabel. Let's talk."

"I don't know . . ."

"Are you so unsure of yourself you're afraid to talk?"

"No! I'm not!"

"Then tell me about yourself."

"I'd rather hear about you first. And Darklady, and what scared her—though I think I have a pretty good idea!"

"I'm sure you do. I will tell you this—Darklady did come back. Earlier tonight. She's past her fear now. She's on her road."

"She was afraid of—what? Her fantasies? If the fantasies you people play with here are what I think they are, I can see why some people might be frightened by them!"

"No," he answered. "She wasn't afraid of her fantasies. She's become quite comfortable with her fantasies, in fact."

"What, then?"

"What do you think this room is about, Annabel?" he asked, ignoring her question.

"Well, from the title—'lovedeath'—and from the fact that you posted on 'alt.sex.fatal'—I'd assume it has to do with fantasies of dying while you're having sex."

"Ah. You should have answered my original question, then."

"I did."

"No. I asked if you were a top or a bottom. You're not a top, Annabel."

She laughed at the screen. "And how could you tell that? We've only been talking for a very few minutes!"

"From what you said. 'Fantasies about dying while having sex.' For many of us—about half of us, I should say—the fantasy is about killing while having sex. But that isn't what you said, is it?"

Smart guy, she told herself. "I haven't even said I have any fantasies like those, Simon."

"No. But you're here. And you're still here. If you have no interest, why don't you log off?"

"Maybe I will."

"Do so, then. Choose to never understand what might've been."

Feeling challenged, she moved her mouse pointer to the square that would close the chat window, but she couldn't quite bring herself to click it, not just yet. What good, she asked herself, would that do? She'd get no real satisfaction from it; and besides, she was totally anonymous to this person.

"I think I'll stay awhile," she responded at last. "If you want to waste your time talking to me, I might satisfy that curiosity. I might get you to tell me about Darklady."

"What did you want to know, Annabel?"

"Well, I asked you already! I wanted to know what scared her so badly."

"Understanding frightened her, Annabel. A true understanding of what a fantasy is. She came to understand, and she tried to run. But she couldn't."

"I don't know what you mean."

"A fantasy," he replied, "is a reality yet to be. Nothing more. Darklady has been talking about her fantasies here for years. Playing games, having cybersex here. With me, with Santa, with Enemymine. And now, she understands that's what her fantasy was."

"You make it sound like she means to live it out in the real world."

"That's exactly what I mean, Annabel."

"Oh, you aren't serious!"

"I am. This is Friday night; by Sunday, my sweet Darklady will have made her fantasy reality."

She laughed again. This was good, she told herself, very good; she did not believe a word of it, but Simon was convincing, he was spinning a good story.

"And I take it you are going to be the one to make it a reality for her?"

"Yes I am, Annabel. As I have done for many before her."

"So you're a serial killer, then."

"The law would call me that, yes."

"I see. I'm sitting here chatting with a real live Ted Bundy."

"You can believe me or not, Annabel. And yet, if you read the newspapers, you know that these things have happened before."

"Oh . . . yes . . . I did hear something, some case . . . a woman went to meet a man in another state, in the South, I think, and he . . ."

"Yes. In real life. No fantasy."

"But that wasn't you. Not unless you're connected in jail!"

"No. It wasn't me. Nor will it be, Annabel."

"So, Mr. Simon Serial Killer. How many have you killed?"

"Let me see . . . eight now. Darklady will be my ninth."

"And you're going to do this tomorrow."

"No. Sunday."

"How are you going to do it? And how can you be sure you won't get caught?"

His lines started coming at a steady, even pace then. Darklady, he told her, had long been fascinated with hanging, and that's what he was planning to do, hang her. In intricate and seemingly loving detail he described how he'd strip her naked and tie her hands, how he'd tie one end of a rope around her neck and lash the other off to a doorknob, how he'd have her standing on a stool or a chair, how he'd pull the rope up to the point where she could barely stand, how he'd support her weight with his hands, kick the stool away, and slowly lower her into the noose. Leah, watching the words appear, one after another, kept touching her lips with her fingertip; he surely, she told herself, painted a very vivid picture. Darklady, he explained, lived in Boston; he was going to have to fly there.

At this she laughed, noting that air travel leaves the police a very clear picture of a person's whereabouts; but he then explained that there was nothing to connect him with her, and more, he'd long ago set up a false identity, complete with driver's license and always-paid-up credit cards, that he used for this sort of thing—an identity that could simply vanish if he ever came under suspicion.

She could not, after listening to him for several minutes, find any flaws in his plan. "And she's invited you to come to her place and do this."

"Yes, Annabel, she has."

"Come on, Simon, let's be real here for a moment. Fantasy may be fun and all that, but nobody'd do this in real life!"

"You did read that newspaper article. Didn't you?"

That stopped her; this had, evidently, happened at least once before. A little less sure of herself, she steered the conversation away from Darklady, asking Simon about himself, where he was from, how old he was, all the usual questions one asked on the Internet chats. He didn't object, he followed her smoothly, telling her that he was forty, a little over six feet tall, two hundred pounds, dark-haired, dark-eyed.

And he told her he lived in Charleston, South Carolina. He opened his questioning about her by asking where she lived, and she, without thinking, answered that she was in Savannah—not very far away at all. Somewhat mesmerized by him, she answered his other questions truthfully too; that she was twenty-nine, unmarried, five-two, auburn-haired, dark-eyed. She told him she weighed a slight ninety-five pounds without mentioning that she'd not been that slender in ten years. He seemed pleased, and he pressed her for ever more personal details, and for a while she answered his every question.

Then, abruptly—just when he'd asked for her E-mail address—it dawned on her that she was revealing quite a lot about herself to him. She almost panicked. "Look," she said, "I have to go now. It's been nice talking to you, Simon. Maybe I'll drop back by."

"Do," he replied. "Just remember, I won't be here Sunday!"

"(grin) Yes, I know. You tell a nice tall tale, Simon."

"If you wish it so, Annabel. I will see you again."

"Maybe."

"No. Not maybe. You'll come back." He didn't give her time to frame an answer to this; he clicked off, and when she looked back at the nicknames list in #love-death, his wasn't there anymore. She closed the program too, turned off the computer, got herself ready for bed, put the whole encounter out of her mind.

But that the images she saw as she was falling asleep were those of a nude woman hanging did not really surprise her at all.

That next day—Saturday—she tried not to think about the Internet at all. Instead, she went to Savannah's waterfront, thinking to relax in the warm spring sunshine. At first, all she could think of was the days she'd spent here the previous spring with her boyfriend Larry—Larry who'd shown a side of his personality she'd never expected he might have when she'd told him her news several months before. He'd suddenly found their relationship confining and oppressive, and by then he was no longer a part of her life. Trying not to think about that—such thoughts could still bring her to tears—she found herself standing near the water's edge, looking northward. Not for quite a while did it occur to her why she might be looking north, rather than south or out across the Atlantic.

The outing took a toll on her energy, and, well before evening, she found herself obligated to go back to her apartment. After a nap, she wandered back to the computer. At first, she refused to go on-line at all; once she'd surrendered that point, she firmly promised herself she'd limit herself to the Web, that she wouldn't even surf the Usenet, much less go out on IRC. That lasted an hour; it was another thirty minutes before she gave in to the insistent voice in her head and updated the articles in alt.sex.fatal.

Two hours had passed before she surrendered completely, before she returned to Undernet and the room called #lovedeath.

To her simultaneous relief and disappointment, Simon's nickname did not appear in the list of nicknames. She chatted with some of the others and finally consented to a cybersex session with Enemymine. It was fun, it was even arousing—but it lacked the impact of her purely platonic conversation with Simon. When they were finished, she asked Enemymine if he knew the man.

"Of course," he told her. "Simon's been a regular here for a long time. Don't believe what he tells you, though."

"No?"

"No! Simon just likes to make people believe he does this stuff in the real world! Every time some female drops off this group he spins a yarn about having snuffed her. Everyone knows it's just his own little fantasy." In answer to her further questions, he said he had known Darklady, but he assured her that Darklady was simply "playing along" with Simon's scenario. He theorized that she was either dropping off IRC for some personal reason or perhaps planning to reappear under another nickname—he even teasingly asked Leah if "Annabel" and Darklady might be one and the same, since she'd appeared just as Darklady was disappearing. "He does," he concluded finally, "sometimes freak the newbies, though."

"I have to admit, he freaked me a little," she answered. "So it's not real?"

"No. None of it. This is all just fantasy, Annabel."

"I read about a couple that did it for real . . ."

He didn't respond for a second. "Well, yes. We all know about that. No one understands it all very well, Annabel. But it's an—aberration. It's not what we're all about here." There was quite a long hesitation before he sent another line: "I surely don't want to do this r/t . . ."

She acknowledged this without argument and spent another few minutes just chatting with Enemymine; once he'd moved on she talked to Justine for a while, who confirmed Enemymine's opinion that Simon merely tried to make his fantasies realistic. Justine discussed her own fantasies—fantasies of being killed with a knife while having sex—for a long while, in very lucid terms. When the discussion finally ended, Leah wasn't altogether convinced that Justine did in fact consider it a mere fantasy, never to be enacted in real life.

"Bunch of crazy people," she muttered. "Completely crazy." And yet, even as she spoke the words, she understood that what Justine had been saying, especially, had struck a chord within her. . . .

As time passed, Leah found herself on the computer, chatting on IRC, more and more frequently. Both Enemymine and Justine became on-line friends, she talked with them frequently—and, slowly, began to circle around the possibility of admitting to her own dark fantasies, those she thought she'd gotten rid of years ago.

To her disappointment, though, Simon did not reappear. She hadn't expected him Sunday; it would have ruined the illusion if he'd appeared, she understood that. More days passed, another weekend was approaching, and still he'd not returned. Almost whimsically she did a Web search for weekend news in the Boston area, and was taken aback when she did find an article about a woman found murdered, hanged. The article gave few details; she decided, in the end, that it really didn't prove anything. Boston's a big city, she told herself. People get murdered there all the time.

Finally, on Saturday, he did come back—and he told her, once they were alone in private chat, that the "scene," as he called it, had gone exactly as he'd expected it to, as he'd told her it would. He'd also suggested that the article she'd seen had referred to this same event. But, by then, her discussions with Justine and Enemymine had bolstered her own original opinion that Simon was simply spinning elaborate fantasies. Even so, he spun them very well, very well indeed. She was, she had to admit, fascinated with him; that night, she confessed it to him.

"Maybe you'd be interested in one of my visits someday," he suggested seductively.

"You mean like your visit to Darklady?"

"Of course, Annabel . . . of course . . ."

"Well, I don't know, Simon. Besides," she teased, "how can you be so sure, if you've done nine of these, that I'm not a policewoman trying to trap you?"

"You didn't come on like one," he told her bluntly. "Besides, I'm not a suspect in any of these deaths. I keep track. I have my ways of keeping track."

She asked about those ways, and here he ducked her questions, making her even more sure he wasn't doing these things in reality. She spent a long time chatting with him that night; Sunday he was there again, and so was she. Days merged into weeks, weeks into months; more and more, what was important in her life was what appeared on the computer screen. No longer fearful, she cooperated with Simon as he wove complex tales starring the two of them, tales in which he, unerringly sensing her tastes in things, romanced her, made love with her, and then, in a variety of ways, executed her.

Encircling all this, she found herself building, more by E-mails than on IRC, something resembling a real relationship with Simon. She hadn't yet told him about the matter that was so central to her life now, and he'd been reticent about his daytime existence, but they shared many things. They exchanged pictures by E-mail; he was very complimentary about hers, and she spent quite a long time, on more than one occasion, gazing at his rugged face, at his off-center smile. He was, it seemed to her, terribly sensitive; often he picked up on her true feelings about things just from a few words, as he'd done from the very beginning.

They'd known each other for about four months when he began to suggest, obliquely at first but then much more directly, that he'd like to bring some of the fantasies they'd been sharing into the real world.

"You mean you want to kill me now, Simon?" she asked teasingly.

"Of course, Annabel. I have for some time now. Isn't that what you want too?"

"Well, of course," she told him, giving him the answer he expected. "I just don't know if it's time yet."

"It is, I'm quite certain," he said firmly. "I can sense these things, Annabel."

"I do believe you can, Simon," she replied. She found herself wondering what he'd do if she were to start agreeing with him, and she decided to push the envelope just a little more. She paused for a moment, focused herself on her other, her real-world, problems for a few seconds—she'd learned quite early that if she did that she could be very convincing when she spoke of a desire to die.

"Maybe you're right, Simon," she shot back suddenly. "Maybe it is time."

"You can't back out once I'm there, Annabel, once I'm in the room with you."

"(smile) I can say no, Simon. No means no. It has to be consensual for you, doesn't it? That's what Enemymine says, it has to be consensual . . ."

"Enemymine has his own opinions. For me, it doesn't matter."

She blinked. "It doesn't matter? It doesn't matter if the woman is willing or not?"

"Not to me. Though it is better this way, there's less risk, fewer problems. I never said, Annabel, that all the women I've done were willing."

"They weren't?"

"Not all, no. Only three were."

She blinked again. "You aren't serious . . ."

"Of course I am, Annabel. One such as I takes opportunities wherever he finds them. At times one runs across women who are, let us say, vulnerable. A hitchhiker. A schoolgirl perhaps, waiting at a bus stop alone at night. Vulnerable."

She closed her eyes for a moment and shook herself. The mere fact that he could say this, that this was a part of the fantasy for him—or that he could think it would be part of it for her—told her starkly that he wasn't the man she thought he was. But that couldn't be so, she told herself wildly, it just couldn't be, she couldn't've been that wrong! Fighting the pain in her lower body and feeling suddenly reckless, she made a decision.

"All right, Simon. This Saturday, this Saturday you come to me. I'm serious and I'll prove it. My real name is Leah Quinlan." She went on, giving him her real address, her real phone number, everything. When she'd finished she sat back to wait for his reply.

"Good, Annabel . . . I'll be there, then, Saturday—three days from now. We'll be together Saturday, Saturday night, Sunday afternoon. On Sunday night we'll take the ultimate step, we'll do it together."

She grinned at the screen. Okay, Simon, she said silently. Okay. Maybe this weekend we'll finally see what you're actually all about. And, she promised herself, we'll make some preparations, too—just in case I'm wrong about you.

That Saturday—the time seemed to pass very quickly, and that surprised her—she rose and breakfasted as usual, behaved much as if it were an average day—but she left her front door unlocked. By noon nothing at all had happened, and she was beginning to wonder if the whole thing was a fake, if he wasn't even going to show up at all. Frowning, looking outside at the street and seeing nothing unusual, she finally drifted into the room where her computer was kept, planning to go on-line to see if he was waiting on IRC with some excuse.

She stopped short when she saw a large man sitting in the swivel chair in front of it, his arms folded, smiling at her. The face was familiar to her, though she'd only seen it before on her screen.

"Simon, I presume?" she asked with an uncertain grin.

He nodded. "Hello, Leah . . ."

He didn't even give her a chance to nod in return. He was up quickly, sweeping her up into his arms, pulling her now almost frail body against his massive one, kissing her deeply. She melted into his arms; this part, she told herself as her thoughts spun, wasn't a fantasy at all.

Whatever she'd expected, he did not disappoint. A perfect romantic, he'd brought her flowers, he'd planned an evening out. Acting as if they'd been dating for quite a while, he was almost courtly in his behavior toward her; only after they'd returned from dinner and a stop by a nightclub—a stop cut short when she began to admit she was becoming exhausted—did he begin to approach her in a more overtly sexual way. It wasn't long, however, until they were both in her bed. Exhausted or no, he managed to make this perfect, too.

The next day was the same. Several times she tried to bring up and discuss his plans for Sunday night, but he postponed those discussions every time, telling her to enjoy the moment, not to anticipate.

In the early evening he offered her dinner, telling her he'd find a way to provide whatever she wanted. She didn't misunderstand; but, too nervous about the evening, she was unable to eat at all.

Finally, a little after eight o'clock, he took her in his arms and kissed her deeply. "It's time," he said softly.

"Time we talked," she told him.

"The time for talk is over," he told her as he began steering her toward the bedroom.

"Simon," she said quietly, "I don't know what you're really planning. I don't think I know very much about you. But there's something you should know about me, Simon. Something that might affect whatever future we might have . . ."

He steered her inexorably toward the bed. "It

doesn't matter much now, Leah." Turning her around, he started removing her clothing, slowly and methodically. "You don't," he went on, "really have a future beyond the next hour or so . . ."

Her eyes were wide. "So it is real . . . you really were serious . . ."

"Yes, Leah, Annabel. I was, I am."

"You're going to kill me . . ."

"Yes."

"Maybe you shouldn't. Maybe I called the cops. Maybe this place is being watched."

He laughed. "No, it isn't. I know." He reached into his pocket, drew out a wallet, flipped it open; she stared at the badge, suddenly understanding many things. Putting the wallet away, he continued to undress her until she was nude; then he laid her gently back on the bed. Reaching into another pocket, he withdrew a slender six-inch dagger and put it on the bed beside her.

"Your fantasy," he said as he laid it down. Watching her, he began undressing.

"You really did kill Darklady . . . you did . . ."

"Yes. As I told you."

She looked at the knife. "May I . . . see it?"

He handed it to her without hesitation; she rolled it over in her fingers, testing the very sharp edge, the needle-like point. "Simon," she said slowly, "before we begin . . . I want to know, I really do . . . what you told me, about hitchhikers, girls at bus stops—was that true too?" She held the knife by its handle, the blade pointing upward.

"Yes," he said quietly. "It is." Letting her hold the knife, seemingly unconcerned about it, he climbed onto the bed with her. After caressing her body for a long time, he knelt between her legs, lifted her hips onto his thighs, and slipped his erection inside her. She sighed and moved her hips against him while he toyed with her rigid nipples.

Finally, he reached for the knife. She gave him a wide-eyed look, but she offered no resistance as he took it from her. Giving her a smile of a sort she'd never seen before, he propped it on her belly, just above her navel. Looking down at it, she grabbed the bedposts with both hands. He seemed to hesitate, as if waiting for something.

Leah glanced up at his face. "Do it," she hissed.

Immediately, he pushed hard on it; Leah arched her back and moaned as the sharp steel breached her skin and sank deeply into her body. It's begun, she told herself, it's real, he's killing me . . . she looked down at the blade, watching and fighting back her cries as he pushed it deeper, as her blood welled up and began spilling over her side, soaking into the sheet. She felt an odd sort of triumph; not only was he killing her but he was also killing the cancer that she'd tried to tell him about, the untreatable cancer that meant she had very little future left in any event. The pain, severe at first but hardly worse than the pain her malignancy had been causing her, quickly began to abate as endorphins began to flow and shock began to set in. Still holding onto the bedposts, her fingers bright white with the strain, she offered no resistance as he drew the blade out and put it in again, slowly and sensually, through her breast and between her ribs this time.

Leah's world became hazy; she could taste something hot and salty, she was aware he was stabbing her again, but it didn't matter much anymore, one way or another. Her thoughts drifted, to her computer; she knew he'd remove or erase her hard drive, eliminating the evidence of the connections between them.

He could not know that she'd betrayed him, that she'd made copies of all those files on backup tapes, that she'd sent those copies, complete with his picture, to her ex-boyfriend, to her parents, to several other friends, and even back to herself. All had been asked to merely hold the tapes for her unless something unexpected happened to her—as was happening to her right now.

Amazingly, she even managed to smile a little. She was fulfilling a very old fantasy, she was cheating her cancer of the suffering it had in store for her—and she was taking a dangerous predator off the streets, all at the same time.

All in all, she told herself, not a bad way to die. Not a bad way at all.

Graham Watkins: *"Almost all of the background of this story is real, taken from current events. There are, on the Internet, a number of chatrooms devoted to what the patrons call 'snuffsex.' In them, any night of the week, you will find people (mostly men) whose fantasy is to kill, and other people (mostly women) whose fantasy is to be killed. There is as of right now more than a score of sites on the World Wide Web devoted to these fantasies. The once-obscure artist Dolcett, whose drawings depict women being hanged and impaled, now enjoys a large cult following.*

"For the most part, these people are indulging pure fanta-

sy. If you talk with them, you find that almost every one felt that he or she was alone in this until the magic of the Internet brought them together. Their numbers are higher than practically anyone would suspect; one site, which requires payment for entry and keeps a member log, numbers more than eight hundred paying members."